WELL OF VENGEANCE

SYDNEY RAIN

CONTENT NOTES

This note serves as a way for readers to inform themselves about potential triggers this book includes.

Potential triggers include:
- Implied rape
- Graphic violence
- Heavy mental health themes

This is by no means an extensive list. Please visit my website at sydneyrain.com/well-of-vengeance to find a more exhaustive list.

For my sister, Bailey. Remember you can do anything

For my parents. Thank you for allowing me to chase my dreams

For my loving husband, Adam. I could never have done this without you

SYDNEY RAIN

WELL OF VENGEANCE

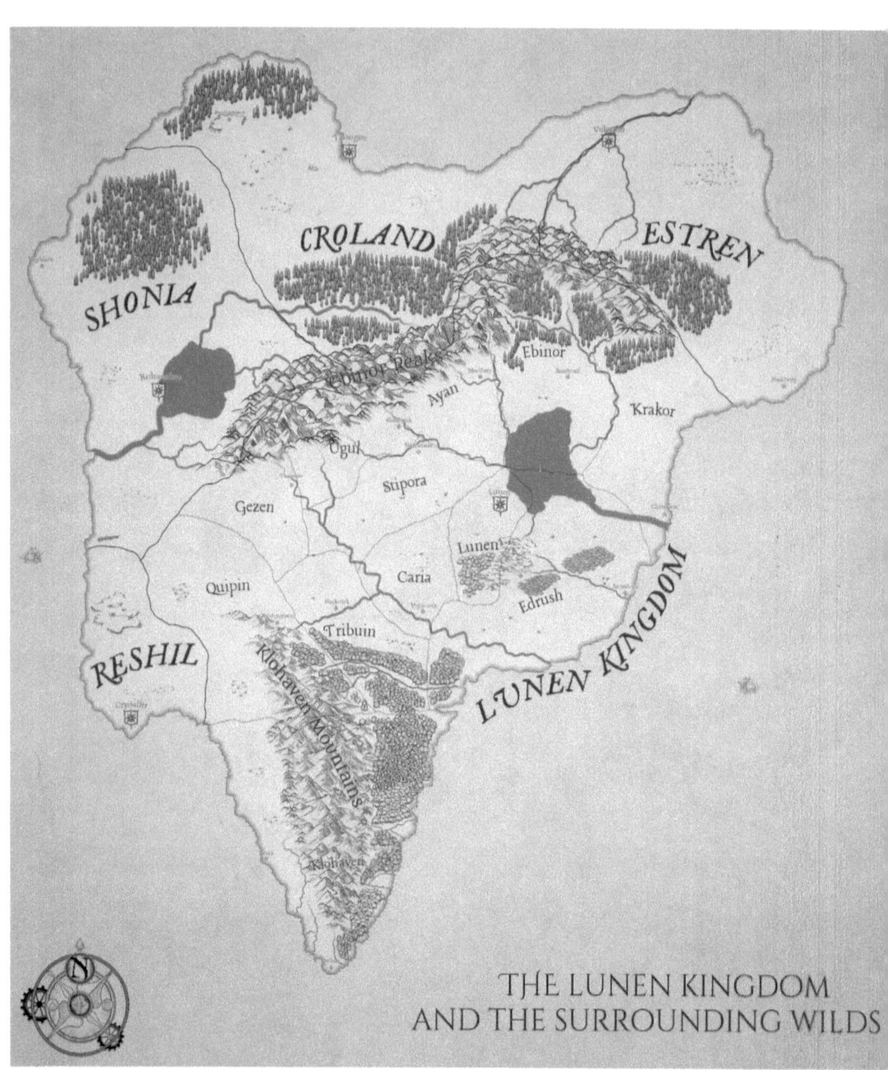

SHONIA
CROLAND
ESTREN
Edinor Realm
Ebinor
Ayan
Krakor
Ugul
Stipora
Gezen
Lunen
Caria
Edrush
Quipin
LUNEN KINGDOM
Tribuin
RESHIL
Klohaven Mountains
Klohaven
N
THE LUNEN KINGDOM
AND THE SURROUNDING WILDS

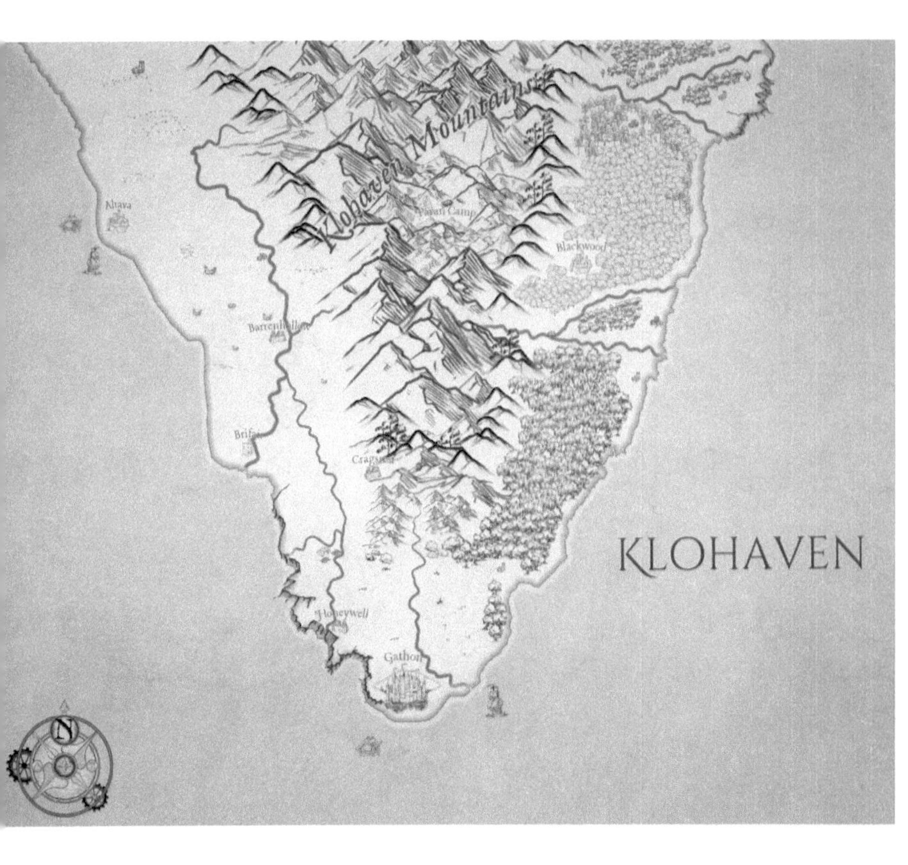

Klohaven Mountains
Altava
Pavati Camp
Blackwood
Bartenhollow
Brisa
Cragsen
Honeywell
Gathor
N
KLOHAVEN

CHAPTER ONE
EMOLIN

The bells in the distance signaled quarter till seven as I ran out the door. I was late, again.

"Lady Emolin, your scarf!" a maid called after me.

Cursing, I turned back, creating a cloud of rust-colored dust as my sandals skidded on the hard-packed dirt. The Klohaven sun burned even the richest skin tones in mere moments, and I already suffered more burns than I cared to count. I ran up the steps to my family's estate, taking the pale, golden strip of fabric from the maid and giving her a nod of thanks before running off.

I tucked my wavy, scarlet hair under the scarf, wrapping the silk around my head while dashing through the streets. As grateful as I was that my Light Aura allowed me to take a more passive stance in potential battles, I hated that the Magistrate required all female Mages to wear headscarves to match their affinity. Many wore crimson, blue, or even brown scarves, and the men wore bands around their upper arms. The color system was supposed to allow for ease of organizing forces if a war was on the horizon. Instead, I found my peers and the Altavians only shunned me for having a more "impractical" type of Aura on display.

Even though the air rippled with heat, shoppers, children heading to school, slaves, servants, and Mages packed the roads. It was difficult to navigate the bazaars of Altava on a normal day, but with the approaching Bonfire Festival, more merchants and stalls were crowding the already narrow streets. Dozens of colorful stalls hid the drab sandstone buildings. Tents in a variety of colors shaded the streets, tapestries and banners fluttering in the breeze from people walking by.

I entertained the idea of scaling the nearest building and making my way to the Sitori Training House, leaping from roof to roof. While traveling above the shops made getting through crowds much easier, Magistrate Magdra made it clear that he didn't appreciate his Mages behaving in such an unfavorable manner after the last time. Though I was risking being even later by choosing to navigate the crowds, the beating from Sojourn would be far better than the punishment I would get from the Magistrate for taking the elevated route.

The smells from the vendors made my mouth water and reminded me I missed breakfast. The many skewered meats tempted me to stop and purchase them, but Sojourn despised tardiness above all else, and walking in with food would only make my beating worse. There were several times I was late when I started training and Sojourn liked to say even the most stubborn beasts could be beaten into submission, though I seemed to prove him wrong so far. My stomach growled in protest as I continued, and I promised I would feed it later.

My sword beat against my thigh in a steady rhythm, tugging comfortingly on my sash. I made the sword under Sojourn's guidance once my training began when I was ten, and I was rarely without it. The blade, along with my robes, made it easier to weave through the throngs of people, no one wanting a Mage to accuse them of being in the way.

The crowds became a solid mass as I neared the center of the city. Servants and slaves wove past people, slaves keeping their heads down to avoid being punished for impeding aristocrats and scholars. It was common to hear slaves being shouted at and punished in numerous languages, but my anger against slavery rose every time.

The crash of breaking pottery rang through the streets over the droning of people haggling prices and advertising their wares. Hajana sat in front of the potter's shop, eyes wide, glaring at a group of boys running off, and broken pieces of a hand-painted vase in front of her. Seeing the fear in my friend's face, I shoved my way toward her. It was well known her master, Minister Aldous, commissioned a vase for his wife several months before, and I could only imagine what he would do once he discovered what happened.

Many on the street ignored Hajana and walked around her, some stopping to collect pieces of the vase with gold leaf on them as they passed. I reached down to help her up, her attention focused on the potter's shop. She tucked her raven hair behind her ear, and I couldn't help but glance at the tattoo on the side of her neck. A small lock. The mark of a slave.

"Are you okay, Ra?" I asked, choosing to struggle with rolling the *r* at the beginning of her Paran nickname instead of mispronouncing her full name, Ra-Hana.

"I'm fine, but you know you shouldn't be talking to me in public," she hissed, cutting off the consonant at the end of each word.

Before I could respond, the gruff voice of a portly man cut me off as he stormed out of the shop. "I thought I told you to be careful, you wench. Now, who is going to tell the Minister his commissioned vase will take another four months? I'm not going to take the blame, that's for sure." He paused, turning to me when he realized I was standing there. "She didn't harm you, did she, m'lady?" He gave a deep bow of respect.

The potter didn't wait for me to respond. He reached out, grabbing Ra's hair, and spun her to face him. Smacking her across the face, he threw her to the ground. Despair rose in Ra's eyes as she let out a cry of pain. She looked so small on the ground, even though she was a handbreadth taller than me, her childlike innocence hiding behind the rough exterior her five years of slavery created.

Raising my hands, I shook my head. "No, nothing like that. I heard the crash and came over to make sure no one hurt themselves on the broken pottery until it could be taken care of."

The shopkeeper's face softened, and he nodded. "You Mages are a gift from the gods."

Ra climbed to her feet, and the shopkeeper turned to her.

"Go get a broom, you insolent girl," the shopkeeper snapped before turning back to me. "Thank you for caring so much about the citizens. I will stay here and oversee the girl in cleaning. I'm sure you've got more important things to do than to supervise a slave."

As if agreeing with the shopkeeper, the bells in the square signaled the top of the hour. I fought back the dread and smiled at the potter.

"There's no need to thank me, but I must be off."

I gave the man a small nod, which he returned with another deep bow, and risked a glance at Ra. Her cheek was already swelling and she wrapped her arms around herself, a slight tremble only visible to those who paid her any mind. Hajana glanced toward me, her gray eyes glistening as she gave me a half-smile. I turned and slipped back into the crowd, pushing past people as fast as I dared, not wanting to cause any fear or commotion.

The dread in Ra's eyes fueled my anger at slavery. Forcing someone to work from the moment they woke until they fell asleep on their feet because of crimes they committed was one thing. Making a fifteen-year-old girl do the same because of her parents' religion was appalling. My father and I spent many evenings arguing about his desire to keep slaves and fire as many of our servants as he could. His reasoning was always the same: Slaves were cheap and easy labor and, if they didn't do what you wanted, you could either beat or kill them. The number of times my father punished me for disagreeing with him never made my desire for freedom for the slaves waver.

The streets cleared some as I headed toward the south-east gate. The numbers were far sparser than before because of the lack of shops and stalls. Though I was still dodging throngs of people, several bowed and stepped aside when they noticed my robes.

The bells chimed quarter past seven. I was always amazed by how long it took to get through Altava's center, especially with the crowds being thicker than normal from festival preparations. I took off at a sprint again, pushing past people as I ran. There's only so polite one can be as they shove someone out of the way. I responded to the hurried apologies of the crowds with a mumbled apology of my own as the Sitori came into view, the statues of the gods peaking over the tops of the apartments lining the streets.

I was still quite a distance away and more than fifteen minutes late. It wasn't a new occurrence, too many nights spent struggling to sleep or reading by candlelight. Many of my peers argued I should be expelled from training. I tried to ignore their comments and ridicule. There was nothing they could do to me. That was Sojourn's choice, and while he'd threatened in the past, he would expel no one without the permission of the Magistrate. The only good thing that came out of his friendship with my father. None of that stopped the worrying though.

I contemplated telling Sojourn about the vase, but explaining that would not only cause the other Mages to call me soft, but it could also raise suspicion of my allegiance to the Lunen Kingdom, or worse, put Ra in danger. Sojourn would come up with a reason why it was wrong for me to stop and help anyway, and I didn't need to give him yet another excuse to beat me. The first lesson Sojourn taught us was to respect him. If we didn't, he would make sure we would fear him.

The number of people on the streets was almost nonexistent as I approached the training house, the only ones I passed being fully trained Mages who shook their heads and stepped out of the way as I ran by.

The clang of metal against metal rang as Sojourn trained the others in swordsmanship. Now and then, Sojourn's powerful voice traveled above the noise, reminding me of his many years in service to Altava, Klohaven, and the entire Lunen Kingdom. I caught my breath as I walked into the shadow of the building. I was already late, so the few seconds I took to slow my heart and calm the Aura within my Well wouldn't make it much worse.

I contemplated trying to sneak into training; Sojourn liked to walk around, watching as we trained, critiquing our stance or the way we connected with our Wells. It would give me plenty of time to slip in next to Natalia and feign innocence about being late. Everyone was still working through sword sequences, though, meaning I would risk injury trying to weave through the swords to get to my spot. I had no choice but to accept my fate and admit to my tardiness without giving a reason.

I tugged open the large stone door of the training house and slipped into the cool shade of the building. I unwrapped my scarf and placed it in my crate stacked along the wall with dozens of others. Slipping out of my sandals and switching into the soundless slippers allowing for better grip, I took a deep breath and walked out of the antechamber.

Sojourn noticed me walking toward the front of the room, continuing to call out drills to the others until they finished their sequence of scales. Glancing up at Natalia, she shook her head, giving me a look I was all too familiar with, lips pursed, eyebrow arched, eyes fierce. I refused to look at the others and instead kept my focus on the loose sand floor or high stone walls sparsely decorated with the Mage's Crest along with the flags for

Altava, Klohaven, and the Lunen Kingdom. I usually found strength in the two golden tiger hawks with their crossed wings on the Crest, but that morning it felt like they, too, were shunning me.

"Once again, Emolin is late," Sojourn said, moving to stand next to me once the scales were done.

His voice echoed against the stone ceiling, daring any of my peers to make a sound, his gold eyes scanning for any sort of movement. I stood with my head raised and jaw set, waiting for whatever punishment he deemed worthy of my transgression.

"Tell me, Aaron," Sojourn continued, "how many times has Emolin been late now?"

Aaron smirked, swiping his bronze curls out of his brown eyes before speaking. "If you're asking for this month, seven times. If you're asking in total, I lost count years ago."

The other Apprentices snickered, and I fought down the rising heat in my neck and cheeks.

Sojourn raised his hand to silence the group before turning to me. "Tell me, Emolin, what do you have to say about such a poor record?"

I had no regret for being late, but I couldn't share my reasoning so I hung my head in mock shame as I responded. "I have no excuse for my tardiness. I was up late and overslept."

"Oversleeping is no excuse; you are right. As you are well aware by now, I must punish you for your continued tardiness. The hope is that punishment will become an obsolete occurrence, preventing you from bringing shame to our city and the Magistrate alike. With you, however, this seems to have failed in the past. Let's see if this time is any different."

I never cared about shaming the Magistrate because I was late, but I didn't dare say so. Instead, I nodded and raised my head.

"I will accept whatever punishment I am given and I will do so without enmity in my heart," I said, reciting the *Oath of Penance*.

"You will receive twenty-five canes for the number of minutes you were late and the number of days you have wasted not only my time but the time of your peers. Bare your back."

I refused to let the dread show on my face as I pulled my arms out of my sleeves and let the top part of my robe fall, turning to face the wall. The bandages binding my breasts would help lessen some pain, but twenty-five strokes of the cane would leave my back a bloody mess. I tried not to think about the mesh of healing wounds I would have to suffer through training with.

I squeezed my eyes shut, determined not to make a sound. I didn't need to give the others another reason to mock me. I kept my arms at my sides and my nails bit into my palms. Sojourn grabbed one of the training staffs from the collection in the large clay pot and gave it a few test swings. The wood cut through the air with a *swish* and I squeezed my eyes shut, grateful my back was facing the rest of my class.

The first stroke of the staff stung, and I let out a small grunt of pain through gritted teeth.

"Count them, Emolin."

"One," I said, my voice steady.

Swish.

"Two." The second swing hurt more than the first, but I stayed unmoving.

Swish.

"Three."

Swish.

As the caning continued, my thoughts wandered to Hajana and the punishment she would receive for breaking the vase. I thanked the gods caning was a rare occurrence for me compared to what Ra dealt with and asked the gods to spare Ra at least some of her master's and the potter's violence.

My back stinging with the last swing, I thanked Sojourn for my punishment and waited for him to dismiss me.

"Natalia, help Emolin treat her wounds. I expect to see both of you back here in half an hour."

"Yes, Sojourn."

Natalia jogged over and walked on my right, her left arm draped around my shoulders, keeping my modesty as she led me to the small infirmary within the training house, shutting the door behind us.

As soon as Natalia and I were alone, she turned to me, placing her hands on my shoulders. "You were hanging out with that slave again, weren't you?"

My eyes searched hers, the blue a stark contrast from my green and the varying shades of brown of other Mages. I hoped to find a hint of pity, or at least understanding. Instead, she gave me the same look she had when I walked in.

Natalia grabbed a container of salve from a cupboard, not waiting for an answer as I climbed onto the bed and turned so my back was facing her.

"We weren't hanging out. She dropped the vase her master ordered. I didn't know it was her, and the responsibility to stay and make sure no one cut themselves on the broken shards was too strong to ignore. Otherwise, I would've been on time."

Natalia said nothing, letting me continue.

"When I discovered it was her, I had to stop and help."

"No, you didn't. You were more than able to continue on your merry way without a care in the world for that slave. Being late because you're up late reading is one thing, but helping slaves is another digression entirely."

I hissed as Natalia rubbed the salve into my back, my skin sealing enough to prevent the wounds from ruining my robes and developing infections.

"I've told you before, I would stop to help anyone, any slave, not just her. You've seen me do it yourself."

"No, what I've seen is you trying to get yourself killed. Why must you insist on helping the slaves? They're heathens! They worship false a god, pillage towns, rape women, and kill children. We need to eradicate them before they attack us. Why would you want to help someone who cares so little for anyone else?"

I had no answer to Natalia's question, at least not one I could explain. The Parans I knew weren't malevolent. They weren't behind the attacks everyone blamed on them. One of the newest slaves my father bought, a young girl about eight, told me about the Royal Enforcement Division, REDs, attacking their village and murdering her family. It wasn't the Parans who were doing the killing. I wanted to speak up, but I didn't need Natalia more frustrated with me, so I pushed back the thoughts and focused on Sojourn's muffled voice through the door as he led our group through another set of scales.

"That should do it," Natalia said as she rubbed the last bit of salve into my back.

My muscles were sore and my skin pulled every time I moved, but I was in good enough shape to continue training.

"Thank you, Nat. I don't know what I would do without you."

"Well, your back would look far worse than it does." She gave me a small, quick smile. "Just remember what I said when you get into a predicament you can't get yourself out of. I won't always be there to pull you out when that happens."

Natalia left without another word, her long, silvery braid whipping behind her, leaving me to sit and contemplate everything she said.

CHAPTER TWO
HAJANA

I took a moment in the shop to gather myself. Though I was glad Emolin tried to help, her intervening possibly angered the potter more, or worse, gave him a reason to believe Emolin and I were friends. I shuddered at the thought of what would happen to me and her if that happened and pushed the images of guillotines and gallows out of my mind.

A wave of nausea passed over me and I braced myself on a nearby counter as the intense cramping followed. The bleeding had already stopped, but the pain would continue to haunt me for another few days at least. I took a deep breath and pushed the pain aside, focusing on each step as I grabbed the boom in the corner of the room. The cramps faded away and I leaned back to stretch.

Not wanting to risk getting in even more trouble, I headed out the back door of the shop through the alley, reaching the front with the broom and a pan to sweep up the mess.

"It's about bloody time, Ha-Jana."

I cringed at the horrible pronunciation of my name, the unknown curse against Para they were speaking. Regardless of how many times I heard it pronounced the Klohavian way, the fear that climbed up my spine never went away, the worry that Para would direct his anger at me instead of them. When I was first captured, I tried to correct them on the pronunciation, *It's Ra-Hana*, I tried, emphasizing the rolling of the *r*. Now, I knew better and waited until I was in my room at night to pray to Para that I be spared his wrath when he came to exact his revenge.

"You were gone for a long time. I'm going to have to check and make sure you didn't steal anything once you're done," he said, licking his lips.

"There were other customers in the shop and I am required to respect their space," I lied, making sure to keep my head down and tone of voice as neutral as possible.

"Quit making excuses, girl. Clean up this mess you made, then I'll decide on your punishment. I know Minister Aldous won't mind me helping to teach you a lesson."

Without a word, I swept up the bits of broken pottery into the pan. It wasn't my fault the vase shattered. It was too large and heavy for a single slave to carry, though I couldn't explain that to my master without risking not only a beating but having what little rations I was given taken away. I made sure I got every last piece, not wanting to give the potter another reason to be angry with me.

"What would you like me to do with the pieces of pottery?" I asked, keeping my head down.

"Take them inside and place them on a table in the back. You are to wait there for me."

I turned and headed for the shop, using the back alley again so I didn't inadvertently get in the way of someone. I placed the pan of pottery pieces on the table and put the broom back in the corner. With nothing else to do but wait, I glanced around at the pottery in different stages of the creation process.

Many of the pieces were either ready to be glazed or waiting to be displayed on shelves. There were a few items still sitting as lumps of clay, but most had been baked at least once. The smells of the shop reminded me of my friend, Dalila's, parents' shop back home in our village. The many hours the two of us would spend making small dishes for our dolls or helping to recycle pottery that cracked in the fire. I forced myself to move past those thoughts before my emotions took over.

"There seem to be two rather expensive pendants missing and I'm willing to bet an entire month's sales you stole them. Strip," the potter said as he walked into the back of his shop.

As much as I wanted to protest, I knew from experience doing so would only make the whole process worse. I slipped my arms out of the feed sack dress I'd been wearing for over a week and let it fall to the floor around my ankles.

"When I say strip, I mean everything."

I ignored the potter's hungry eyes and focused on keeping my face expressionless as I moved to unbind my breasts, grateful my tattered shift still covered the lower half of my body.

"Good sir, I apologize for interrupting, but I am in great need of your help."

I froze at the sound of the new man's voice and looked up at him through my eyelashes, praying he wasn't someone who would be more than willing to help the potter in "punishing" me.

Instead of another shopkeeper or one of the REDs, a young man in an unfamiliar grey uniform stood in the doorway. He wore a long saber and quiver off his belt and a bow strapped to his back, the quiver and hilt of the sword the same deep blue as the stripes on his cuffs. My eyes landed on the large scar that started on the left side of his face, near his chin, and extended across his face, over his right eye, and stopping just below his dark hair. His brown eyes rested on me and I realized he could tell I was staring at him. I dropped my eyes and hoped my hair was able to hide my blush, failing to ignore the fact I was nearly naked.

"Ah, Lord Mycroft, how may I be of service?" The potter gave a deep bow and turned all his attention to the lord.

"It's my mother. Today is her birthday, and I have been the most wretched son and forgot. I was hoping you could show me your finest jewelry or perhaps make me something?"

"I can most certainly do that," the potter said before turning to me. "It seems it will be left to Minister Aldous for your punishment for the vase. Don't think this means I've forgotten about the punishment I owe you for the missing pendants."

The potter turned and asked the lord to follow him. The lord tossed a gold coin to me and winked before heading into the main shop.

Catching the coin, I hastily pulled up my dress and ran out of the shop into the alley before my luck ran out. I didn't need a random lord accusing me of stealing from his purse.

I gripped the coin tightly, keeping my head down as I made my way through the streets. There was only one stall on my way that sold food to slaves. The merchant was familiar with me and said nothing as we exchanged coin for bread before I headed off again, not having much time before my master expected me back. I didn't want him to find out what happened before I had the chance to explain. That would only make things worse. Walking as fast as I dared, not wanting to have any REDs stop and accuse me of stealing. I stuck to back alleys, places where only slaves, street urchins, and the occasional wench traversed to avoid the crowds.

Stopping in front of an ordinary, weathered, grey door under a bridge and knocked three times, paused, and followed with two more knocks. There was some shuffling on the other side and several locks clunking. An elderly man peered out, his unwashed grey hair falling in front of his wrinkled face, making sure no one was around before ushering me inside and shutting the door.

"I didn't think I would see you for another week," he said, staring me up and down.

"Normally you would be right, but Para blessed me, and I was not only spared a punishment but also given a coin by a lord I have never seen before."

Flinders stared at me and the loaf for a few seconds before reaching out for the bread. I handed it to him and he muttered a small blessing before placing it on the table next to an unusual assortment of overripe produce, rotting meat, stale bread, and many other things most wouldn't dare eat.

"Hajana, you are far too kind for this world. I pray you're granted the freedom you deserve."

"Thank you, Flinders. I am grateful I can help. There are far more who are struggling more than me and the least I can do is give what I can."

He reached out and clasped both of my hands, his callused skin rough against my own.

"You must go now. Take the path along the river, the REDs aren't patrolling there at this hour."

I thanked him one last time and looked out the small hole in the door before slipping back into the sun. The locks clunked again behind me and I turned north. I focused on my surroundings, knowing there would be many who would take advantage of a slave on her own. However, my thoughts drifted back to the man with the scar, Lord Mycroft, now and then. I wanted to know who his family was and why he helped me. I hadn't heard of a new lord in town cordial with slaves, and Flinders didn't seem to know anything either.

It didn't take long to make my way back to my master's estate, the wandering hands of lonely men thankfully absent. I forced myself to walk up the path to the back entrance to the estate, through the kitchen, and into the back parlor where my master said to meet him. I was expected to be back by half-past ten, so I didn't have too long to wait until he discovered what happened.

"...she is going to be so excited to see it."

My heart sank as my master's words floated down the hall, the dread bringing another bout of cramping. I hadn't expected him to be with someone, and if he was, it could result in a punishment far worse than usual.

"...when you see it—" My master cut himself off when he walked in and saw only me standing there with head bowed and eyes lowered.

"Ha-Jana, where is the vase I asked you to fetch?"

"I apol—"

"Look at me when you're speaking," he snapped.

I looked up and swallowed a gasp, seeing the same lord from the pottery shop standing in the doorway.

"Were your parents too savage to teach you not to stare? Tell me what happened before I have your daily rations cut in half for a week."

I collected myself and swallowed. "I apologize, Master. The vase was quite large and the crowds were thick with people preparing for the festival. I tried to navigate through carefully, but I was too clumsy. I tripped and the vase broke not too far from the shop. Please forgive me," I said, giving a deep bow and not daring to rise.

"You mean to tell me you broke a vase costing 3,000 gold? Look at me!"

I stood and was met with a smack across the face. My already swollen cheek stung and the familiar taste of iron filled my mouth. I refused to cower and stood tall, hands behind my back and fingers locked to distract me from the throbbing pain in my face.

"You dare smirk at me?"

My master raised his hand again to strike me, but the lord grabbed his wrist.

"I can attest to what the girl is saying. I was there this morning to get a present for my mother. The girl was struggling greatly under the weight of the vase. If anything, I think it is you who was foolish to send a single, malnourished slave to retrieve something so lavish. If you cared about the vase, you would've sent a carriage for it."

My master snatched his hand back and glared at me before looking back at the man.

"I forgive you, Lord Mycroft, for not knowing the way of things in Altava, but no one would waste their resources on errands they could send slaves for. All my other slaves were busy or I would've sent them. I know they would've been more than capable of completing such a simple task. But Ha-Jana was free and I figured even she could handle such a simple task."

The lord shook his head. "If the vase meant that much to you, you should've made sure you were advising its safety. And you said it was for your wife? It's one of the most hideous things I've seen, and it's a blessing from the gods the vase broke before your wife saw it."

My master's face grew red and I curled my toes into the plush blue and green rug, bracing for the screaming that followed. However, my master took a deep breath and calmed down, causing me to suck in a breath.

"You're right, Geoffraie, I guess the gods are looking out for me. I still can't leave this one without punishment, though. She mustn't think she can get away with things." He moved to strike again, but the lord stopped him once more.

"You still have to come up with a replacement gift, do you not? Why not let me teach her a lesson while you go take care of your errands? I've always heard rumors about slave girls and I want to see if they're true."

My master's eyes lit up and he gave a wry smile. "Ah, I see now. At first, I thought you were soft. Let me give you a hint, she likes it rough, no matter what she says."

My master glared at me one last time before leaving me alone with the lord, a slight limp to my master's gait as he shut the door. I forced myself to stand my ground and look at the lord square in the eyes as he approached. I didn't have the power to do anything, but I could make it known I wasn't going to enjoy it.

"Please, relax. I'm not going to hurt you, Hajana. Come, join me on the sofa," the lord said, turning to sit on the sofa and patting the cushion next to him as he looked at me.

"I'm not going to fall for some trap. I will remain standing, thank you," I said, trying not to let the surprise of his correct pronunciation of my name show in my voice.

The lord sighed and stared at me wistfully. "If that is what you wish. I want you to know you're not alone in any of this, though that may be what it seems. Para forgives you."

I stared at the lord, not sure how to respond. Hearing someone who wasn't Paran speak Para's name with the reverence he deserved was something only Emolin had ever done. Yet, here was a lord I had never met, who wasn't Paran, giving my god the same respect he would give his own gods. Realizing he was waiting for me to respond, I said the first thing that came to mind.

"Why would Para care about a fifteen-year-old girl who has been forced into slavery and committing sins since she was first captured years ago? I have been made to do so many things Para forbids, my only hope is that he has mercy on my parents and siblings for what I've done. There's no way Para would accept and embrace such a horrid child."

I hadn't meant to reveal that much, but the words all tumbled out and I bit the inside of my cheek to stop the sob in my throat from escaping.

"Any of the acts forced upon you or you were forced to do have been forgiven, absolved by Para himself for the horrors you have faced. I know you're not going to believe me, but I promise I can show you things, in due time, as long as you promise not to tell anyone what I have said."

I considered his proposal and was about to agree when an idea came to me, one a slave should never ask, but something I felt the lord would listen to. "I will listen to you and, in time, consider trusting in you if you can bring me food whenever possible."

"I can most certainly do that, but may I ask why and how much?"

I hesitated, not wanting to put Flinders' cause in jeopardy. "I can't tell you much until I know you're trustworthy. I would be putting far too many people in danger by doing so. Just know the more food I can get, the better. You would be helping a lot of people."

The lord smiled, his front teeth slightly crooked where the scar crossed over his mouth. "That is something I can most definitely help you with. Just tell me when and where to meet you and I will have more food than you'll know what to do with."

"Don't worry, I'll know exactly what to do with it."

CHAPTER THREE
EMOLIN

After spending the morning practicing swordsmanship, a break for a lunch of kebabs and pitas generously provided by a merchant, and gathering Aura from the world to attack with instead of the Aura within our Wells in the afternoon, Sojourn finally dismissed us near supper time. I worried Sojourn would have me stay back. He had asked me to in the past to continue lecturing me, but he said nothing and I slipped into the antechamber with my peers.

My back burned as I bent over to change out of my training slippers and into my sandals. I bit my lip until it bled to ignore the pain and adjusted my sash so my sword hung securely around my waist. Draping the strip of silk over my head, I slipped between other Apprentices and out into the hot late afternoon sun.

I tucked my hair into my scarf as I walked, making sure I covered my face and used the edge of the silk to wipe away the sweat so sand wouldn't stick to my skin. The scarf allowed me to hide my face as I headed home, making it so I didn't have to worry as much about keeping up a facade. My peers knew it was me as I passed, my scarf standing out among the others, but that didn't stop them from talking about me.

"One would think she would learn not to be late by now."

"Maybe she should just sleep at Sitori; at least she wouldn't have to worry about being late."

"Maybe she's a masochist and is purposely being late?"

"She does always head back with Natalia after each caning."

The conversations were the same every day, even if I hadn't been late for training, and I learned to ignore them, mostly. However, their words seemed to pierce me more than usual, and I took a different route home to avoid their goading.

I wandered over to the streets where merchants sold trinkets and jewelry, wanting to look at different baubles and maybe get a gift for Mamma. While there was still a sizable amount of people shopping, there would be until the festival—the crowds were significantly less than the streets with vendors selling food.

I enjoyed looking at the jewelry and decorative combs displayed at the different booths. Many of the merchants were engaged with customers or advertising their wares. Nothing caught my attention, so I turned to leave. I wanted to get home to wash off the sweat and dust from the day's training when a snippet of conversation caught my attention.

"… attacked by bandits."

I stopped in the middle of the street, causing a few shoppers to bump into me and apologize before hurrying off. I moved closer to a stall where the merchant was with another customer and pretended to be interested in the combs on the table.

"… the guard who came back from Cragsrest mentioned it when he was looking at something for his beloved."

"How much were you able to get him to tell you?"

"I offered him a deal and he told me everything. He said the Magistrate sent them out to the Craggy Dunes because of rumors about an alleged attack from the Parans. They never came across any Parans, but on their way back they came across a small caravan of performers who were slaughtered. Dead were strewn everywhere, most of the bodies of women and even children were left with little clothes on…"

"Can I help you, m'lady?"

The merchant startled me and I nearly dropped the comb I was holding. I took a second to collect my thoughts before responding.

"Yes, I'm looking for a gift for my mother. I believe she would like this comb, but I left my purse at home. Can you hold this until tomorrow?"

The man assured me he would and I promised I would try to make it back the following day. I turned to leave, hiding my bag of coins, and was upset to discover the men moved on in their conversation. I needed to know what happened.

The bandit attacks were getting worse and I feared they would soon reach Altava. They hadn't tried to outright attack a city, but they seemed to be getting more daring, and if they reached the walls, I would be required to help defend Altava since I was in my last two years of training as I had turned sixteen a few months before. Had I still been with the younger group of Mages, I would be required to protect the children instead.

If someone stormed the city, I would be forced to shed blood or become a slave for betraying the Altavians and have my Well locked for disobeying orders.

My hand wandered up to the spot on my neck where the tattoo would be placed, and I tried to imagine what my life would be like without my Well. I had been born with my Well, like most of the Mages I knew, and the idea of living without it caused my Well to fold in on itself. *I need to hope it doesn't come to that, then.*

The crowds grew thicker and the people closed in around me as I made my way toward home, the crowds of shoppers turning into crowds of merchants and sailors heading to the port. It had been a while since I struggled with crowds, but I needed space before I would no longer be able to control my breathing. I turned down the nearest alley and welcomed the shade from the sweltering sun.

The alley was surprisingly empty. Normally, several urchins would surround me as soon as I entered their domain, but there was only one hiding in the deep shadows behind some crates. I tossed him a few coins and continued, the voices from the bazaars fading away.

As I moved deeper into the shadows of the shops, the smell of sewage and rotting garbage weren't the only things that seemed off. I considered pulling out my sword for protection, but the alley was too small for me to properly use it. Instead, I drew Aura from my Well even though I was already exhausted from training. I would have to make sure I relaxed before going to bed.

I summoned a small orb of Light Aura in my hand, gathering Aura from the sparse bits of light streaming into the small space, grateful to the gods again for giving me an affinity to Light Aura. I hoped I was only being hyper-aware after training, but my Well pulsed, letting me know danger was near.

Shadows moved ahead of me and I continued as if I hadn't seen them. A figure stepped out, but I was prepared. I stepped back and kicked their weapon, a long wooden staff, out of their hand.

"I won't harm you if you cooperate. Keep your hands where I can see them and walk toward me."

The figure didn't move and I took a step closer, letting the orb of light grow until I could almost see their face.

"You are quite bold for someone who is in the *dark.*"

The figure's staff flew toward them and they thumped it against the hard-packed dirt street, the whole alley going dark. The orb of light in my hand dimmed to a flicker. No matter how much Aura I poured into it, the light wouldn't grow brighter.

When I looked up again, the figure was inches from my face. Their soot-black eyes glowed and I flinched as the figure leaned even closer, hot breath on my cheek and a shiver running up my spine. I had never seen anyone with eyes so black before, but the figure still seemed familiar.

"I've been watching you."

"You've been watching me?" I asked, struggling not to let my voice tremble while straining my Well to pour more Aura into my orb so I could see the man before me.

His deep chuckle seemed to surround me, bouncing off the walls. "There are things in your world you don't agree with, yet you do nothing. You stand by injustices and wait for others to act. You know people are being degraded and killed for the wrong reasons, but you stay silent. If you want change, then make it."

I wanted to argue against what the figure was saying, but before I could, the light returned to the alley and slaves were apologizing as they darted past. I leaned against a wall, too weak to stand, and tried to make sense of what happened. I hadn't heard of any visiting Mages in the city, certainly none with the power to remove all light from an area. There weren't any parables or prophesies I was aware of describing anyone like the figure either. Not wanting to worry about it anymore at that moment, I told myself I was hallucinating from a fever brought on from the caning.

It took several minutes before I was strong enough to stumble out of the alley and back onto the main streets, not realizing how cold I was until the warmth of the sunlight became a welcoming thing. I couldn't remember the last time was so chilled when it wasn't winter. I held back shivers as I pushed my way through the crowds of people. I didn't want to cause any commotion by seeming sick and hurried home as quick as my body would let me.

Surprisingly, I made it back to my parents' house without passing out, but struggled up the steep walk to the door. Our butler must've been looking out the window because he came rushing out to help me.

"Lady Emolin, are you alright? What happened?"

I raised my hand to wave him off, about to tell him I was alright when my knees buckled and he caught me before I hit the ground. He told me he was going to help me into the house and, once I nodded, scooped me into his arms, calling for the nearest servants to send for the healer. He carried me up the steps and through the door. I tried to explain that I was only overworked from training, but opening my mouth made me nauseous and bile forced its way up my throat and onto the rug.

"What is it?" my mother asked, rushing in and seeing me lying pale and weak in the butler's arms.

"We're not sure, m'lady."

"Healer coming?"

Even in my delusional state, I couldn't help but smile at my mother's broken Lunian.

"It's okay, Mamma, I'm alright."

I fought back another wave of nausea so as not to worry her more and smiled as the butler carried me into the parlor.

"Please, place me on my side, not my back," I whispered as he laid me on the sofa.

The butler arched an eyebrow at my request but said nothing as he positioned me on my side and removed my sword from my belt. My mother covered me with a blanket and placed a cool cloth on my forehead, yelling at some of the slaves in Reshilian to bring her some broth.

"Really, Mamma, I'm okay. I'm just a little tired after training today," I tried reassuring her, responding in Reshilian.

I hated that Father forbade me from learning Mamma's language or anything about her culture. She still taught me once I was old enough to not tell my father. She and I would speak to each other in Reshilian when he wasn't around, and there were a few times Mamma muttered something under her breath in Reshilian about my father when he was home and I struggled to keep a straight face.

"You are not well. This is something more than being tired

from training. I have seen you tired before and this is not it," Mamma said, stroking my hair

One of the servants came in with a bowl of broth and informed us the healer was on her way. My mother accepted the bowl and held the spoon to my lips.

"You must drink. You need to regain your strength. Your father will be home soon and you will need to be strong for it."

The healer came rushing in and knelt beside my mother before I could respond to the news of my father.

"What happened?" the healer asked, checking my pulse.

The butler recounted what he knew, and the healer's brow creased.

"Emolin, what happened today?" the healer asked again, aiming the question directly at me.

I didn't want to worry my mother, but I explained what happened with the broken pottery, the caning, and finished with a slight lie about feeling overwhelmed with the extra vendors for the festival.

The healer furrowed her brow and made it clear she didn't believe me.

"If I could have a moment alone with Emolin, I would like to do a thorough examination. Please send for the Head Sage and tell her to make haste."

My mother squeezed my hand, oblivious to my lie, and stood to go.

"Help, please."

The healer assured my mother she would, and soon it was just the healer and me in the room.

"Why are you calling for the Head Sage?" I asked, trying to keep the fear out of my voice, but failing to hide the crack.

"You and I both know there are things you're not telling me. The Head Sage will know more. Now, let me look at your back."

Calling for the Head Sage meant something was troubling the healer. The Sages spent decades serving the king as Mages before being appointed the role of Sage. The Sages saw many things no one else had and knew where to look if they came across something they weren't familiar with.

Not wanting to anger the woman who could cause me a great deal of pain with the touch of her hand, I allowed the healer to roll me over so my back was facing her. She slipped off the top of my robe, cut the bindings around my breasts, and stared at the wounds for a long moment.

"I have told them time and time again this form of punishment does more harm than good, but they still don't listen." She sighed and laid her hands on my back.

I sucked in a breath through my teeth as the healer's Aura seeped into my back, knitting the wounds together. It wasn't the first time healing Aura graced my body, but it seemed to hurt more each time. It was like lying on a bed of hot coals as my skin stitched itself together and the healer's aura smoothed the welts.

"We're almost done, Emolin. Take a deep breath."

I sucked in a breath and pressed a cushion against my face, screaming as my vision blackened around the edges. I asked before why the last part of healing hurt the most, and the healer explained it was because she was forcing her Aura into my Well to heal any damage caused by my weakened state.

The pain subsided, and I took in a full breath as I pulled the cushion away from my face and let the healer help me roll onto my back, covering me with a blanket for modesty.

"Miss Emolin," the butler said as he bowed, "the Head Sage is here to speak with you."

I nodded and pushed myself up, leaning against extra cushions for support. I still struggled with the fog from the healing and had to remind myself why the Head Sage was visiting.

The Head Sage bowed her head to me and I did my best to give her a deep bow in return from my seated position. The healer collected her things and excused herself, closing the parlor door so the Head Sage and I had some privacy.

"Hello, my dear. I heard there was something you wanted to discuss?"

"It's not that I want to discuss it, but even I am a little worried after nearly fainting in the front drive."

The Head Sage nodded and sat in a chair near the sofa, waiting for me to continue. I looked down at the blanket in my lap and played with the colorful fringe on its edge. I wasn't sure where to begin, but something was tugging at my Well, coaxing me to explain and causing the words to tumble out.

"I met a figure, shrouded in dark robes with eyes darker than any I've seen. They rapped a staff of sorts along the street of the alley and all the light was sucked out of it. I couldn't make my Aura brighter than a flicker. I kicked their staff out of their hand when they approached, but they were able to pull it back to them as if it were attached to an invisible thread."

"Did they say anything?"

I nodded. With little energy left for speaking, the tug on my Well coaxing me to talk drifted away. The Head Sage held out her hand for mine and looked me in the eyes.

"May I?"

I placed my hand in hers and focused on the ceiling as her Aura slipped into my own. It wasn't that it hurt like the healer's Aura; it was more uncomfortable than anything else. I knew better than to ask questions during a Well Reading, but I hoped she learned what she wanted to quickly. The last time she read my Well was when my father insisted it was a mistake I was to be a Light Mage, refusing to believe I didn't have a more offensive Aura.

The Head Sage's Well unwrapped itself from mine and she released my hand. She gave me a warm smile and placed her hand on my shoulder.

"What did you discover, Head Sage?" I didn't want to know,

my heart racing and my Well pulling itself into my core as if to protect me from danger, but my curiosity was too strong to ignore.

"I need to confer with the other Sages about these findings, but there is no need for you to worry. Your Well is strong and the figure you met will not harm you."

Her words, while meant to reassure me, caused my palms to sweat.

"Thank you, Head Sage." I bowed again as best I could from the sofa, not wanting to show any disrespect. "I eagerly await discovering what you learned."

The Head Sage gave me another smile as she stood and showed herself out, my mother curtsying in the parlor doorway before heading to my side. The healer came in to check on me one last time and informed us she would be back to check on me in the morning.

My mother held my hands and my heart broke at seeing her puffy eyes. I hated how much she worried about me, but there was nothing I could do to help her.

"What did she say, Kitten?" she asked, her eyes searching my face.

"She said it was nothing to worry about, Mamma." I gave her what I hoped was a smile of reassurance.

"Well, if she says it's nothing to worry about, then I guess we should heed her advice."

I wanted to forget the day's events and decided to ask my mother for something I knew she wouldn't turn down, something to lift both of our spirits.

"Mamma, can we have tarts for supper?"

She smiled at me. "Of course, Kitten."

CHAPTER FOUR
EMOLIN

I spent the rest of the evening resting, trying not to think about the Well Reading or what the Head Sage discovered. Mamma and I had a wonderful supper of fruit-and-cream-filled tarts and spent the evening reading one of the few Reshilian books Father let in the house.

My night was fitful, filled with nightmares and worries about what the Head Sage was going to tell me. The healer informed the butler when she left I was to take the day off from training. I was excited to wake up on my own without having to rush around so as not to be late for the first time in months.

I had little issues getting out of bed and getting ready for the day. My maid came in to help me not too long after I woke.

"Are you sure you don't want to wear a dress on your day off? Maybe this one Master Stokton brought from his last trip?" She held up a long, slim, burgundy dress with golden accents scattered across the bodice and sleeves.

While I had to admit the dress was beautiful, there were two things wrong with it. One, my father chose it for me, and I didn't want to wear anything he picked out if I could help it. And two, I felt more comfortable in my robes than anything else. The freedom of movement they gave and protection from not only the sun but pickpockets as well was something I preferred not to go without.

"Thank you for the suggestion, but I will wear my robes today as usual."

The maid gave a small curtsy and helped me do my hair. I could plait it well enough, but only a single plait that went down my back, which made wearing my scarf more difficult. She, however, could plait and pin my hair into an intricate pattern on the back of my head. After she pinned the last plait in place, I thanked her and went to my wardrobe to get out a new set of clean robes.

"Is there anything else you need, miss?"

"No, that is all." I finished slipping into my robes and tied my sash while turning to her before she left. "Why don't you take the rest of the day off and go see your sister for her birthday. That is today, correct?"

My maid covered her mouth with her hand and stifled a sob as she curtsied. "Thank you, miss. Thank you!"

She rushed out of the room, and I couldn't help but smile. My father would've reprimanded me for giving any time off to "the help," but he wasn't home and there was no reason for her to stay if I wasn't planning to be back until evening.

The maids and servants my father had yet to fire never knew if they would have a job the next day, so I wanted to help them as much as I could by not only vouching for their necessity but also giving them the same respect they showed me. In return, they would share any news they could about what was happening with the servants and slaves in other households. They would also take extra food to Flinders, and they all knew about my friendship with Hajana and what to do if she needed help.

"You're leaving, Kitten?" Mamma asked as I walked past her upstairs sitting room.

"I want to go check on Hajana and maybe pick up some

candies from the market. I will be home in time for supper," I said, walking over to her and kissed her on the cheek.

Mamma was one of the few people I told about Hajana who wasn't a servant or another slave. She agreed Hajana's slavery was unjust, though she would argue for the slavery of others, of those that committed terrible crimes. Mamma admitted she felt like a slave herself, trapped in Altava with no way to return to see her family.

"Just promise you'll be safe."

"I will, Mamma."

I gave her a hug and another kiss on the cheek before heading downstairs to meet with the healer, getting the okay to head out to the bazaar. The healer warned me about not overexerting myself and made sure I took a waterskin with me so I didn't get dehydrated. I grabbed my scarf and wrapped it around my head, grabbing my sword and heading to the door.

There were more people in the bazaar than the day before. I walked by a shop with a calendar hanging by the door and realized the festivities would start in a few days. Everyone wanted to make sure they not only had the ingredients for their meals but also the supplies to make costumes for their children to take part in the parade celebrating the end of the harvest and beginning of winter.

Mamma always wanted to make delicacies from Reshil for the festival but Father hadn't let her since I turned ten and was too old to be in the parade. Every year he came up with an excuse why she couldn't. I considered buying the ingredients for Mamma myself, but it was difficult enough to find a shopkeeper who sold any Reshilian spices and no one sold Reshilian produce. It was as if Reshil was forbidden in Altava, though there was no such prejudice in place.

While there weren't any traditional harvests in or near Altava, the Bonfire Festival marked the day when the fermenting of the year's cactus wine was ready. While I preferred wine made from ashberries myself, the cactus wine was still something to celebrate.

A few of the shopkeepers who knew me gave me small sweets as thanks or to gain small bits of favor during the Magistrate's yearly appraisal. I had no input in the appraisal and wouldn't favor one business over the other even if I did. Yet another thing I didn't agree with but had no control over. *There are things in your world you don't agree with, yet you do nothing.* The figure's words replayed in my mind and I tripped mid-step, catching myself on one of the merchants' booths. I waved off comments of concern and tried not to think about the scene I made, instead focusing on making my way to Minister Aldous' to speak with Hajana.

The bells signaled midafternoon, meaning Ra was most likely outside her master's estate, tending to the gardens.

I trekked through the bazaars and made note of the tents I wanted to visit on the way back, heading to the more affluent part of the north-eastern half of the city. The only thing I hated about walking through the northern market was having to pass Magistrate Magdra's estate. He always seemed to know when I was near and would come out and chide me for not working hard enough or get far too close for my liking, yet another result of him being close to my father.

As much as I wanted to, I couldn't afford to ignore the Magistrate or make an excuse as to why I couldn't be attentive to him. The beatings from my father were already bad enough, and if he heard I was being disrespectful to one of his friends, I worried about what might happen.

I considered trying to circle back and go down one of the alleys but before I could, the deep bellow of the Magistrate calling my name rang through the street. I forced myself not to cringe as the crowds parted and the Magistrate walked out of his garden, arms wide and a big smile on his face. His silken robes the shade of blood and blond hair reminded me more of a festering wound than an exalted leader.

"Emolin, my dear, I'm glad to see you're doing well. I heard the healer excused you from training today and I feared the worst."

I walked over and held my breath as I embraced him, his cologne so strong those around us gave a wide breadth of space. Those who couldn't move farther away subtly hid their noses in their handkerchiefs. A few people lingered and whispered before moving on, not wanting the Magistrate to accuse them of disrespecting his privacy. Magistrate Magdra pulled away from me and checked over my shoulder to make sure we were alone before speaking.

"I hope for your sake you have a good reason for skipping training today. I will not have one of my Mages tarnishing the honor of this great city by being lazy. You already have a reputation of carelessness after your stunt on the roofs."

Before he could continue, I spoke up, not wanting to be stuck for hours listening to him accuse me of things that shouldn't matter.

"Yes, I was excused from training today. The healer had to see me last night after I collapsed from being overworked with a wound yesterday. Your subordinate, Sojourn, felt the need to cane me after I told him I was helping keep Altavians safe, a duty, may I remind you, specifically stated in the Mage's Creed."

Magistrate Magdra seemed like he wanted to say something else, but knew he couldn't because there were too many people around. Knowing I would be evading punishment, he placed his hands on my shoulders and squeezed to the point where I struggled not to react to the pain, certain I would have bruises for several days.

"Alright, I'm just glad you're okay. Make sure you don't let it happen again."

He let me go and his eyes blazed with Fire Aura. I bowed, making an excuse of picking something up for Mamma, and left before he could say anything else.

His eyes bore into my back as I continued down the road. I didn't want him to know where I was going so I turned down random streets until my Well no longer pulsed with unease.

I turned my focus to where I was heading and realized I was in a mostly unfamiliar area. I had been down all the streets in Altava numerous times, but many of the alleys and more residential roads weren't included in my usual routes. I had a general idea of where I was, I knew which direction to head to reach Hajana's master's estate, but nothing seemed familiar.

There were few people on the streets and none I could discreetly ask for directions without having the Magistrate hear of it. Instead, I put my hand on the hilt of my sword and walked with shoulders back in the direction I hoped would lead me to a more familiar road.

After ten minutes of walking, I reached a dead-end I was certain was new. Part of my training required me to study the maps enough to know where all the dead ends were in the city in case of a siege, and I wasn't near any of them. I went to turn back and head down another road when a thump echoed behind me and the small street became shrouded in darkness, just like the alley the day before.

I conjured an orb of light in my hand, larger than before, and kept my other hand on the hilt of my sword. I backed against the wall of a nearby building, not wanting someone to leap over the wall and attack me, focusing on the shadows for any movement. If it was anything like the last time, the figure was sure to make themselves known.

"You certainly are a unique one, kind and caring to a fault," the figure spoke as my light extinguished. "This will serve you well in the weeks to come."

The figure stepped out of the shadows and my Aura lit for a brief second, long enough for me to fully see the man before me.

The reason he seemed familiar was because his statue stood outside of the training house, guarding the right side of the entrance: Fonir, God of Cleansing. I heard stories of others being visited by the gods, but those were only things priests spoke about during service, not something that actually happened.

"Yes, dearest child," Fonir sneered, "I am here speaking to you."

"Wh—"

Fonir cut me off, his gaze boring into me. My Well jolted in pain and my knees grew weak. "I'm giving you a warning about what is coming. You seemed to want to disagree with what I said before. You will get your chance to make a change. Though, as you are right now, I doubt you'd take it."

Before I could say anything, Fonir vanished and light flooded the street. I had been unknowingly leaning against the wall blocking my path instead of a building and found myself in the dirt next to a pile of rubbish, the wind knocked out of me.

It took me a few moments to collect myself, making sure I was fully steady on my feet unlike the day before. When I was certain I was okay, I continued to Hajana's, Fonir's words pulsing in my mind like a dull ache with every step.

CHAPTER FIVE
HAJANA

I told the lord to meet me outside the center chapel before the bazaars opened. I wanted to meet in a place public enough he would hopefully be deterred from trying anything but private enough a RED soldier wouldn't arrest me for loitering.

I managed to slip out of Master Aldous' house earlier than usual as he had to leave at sunrise for a business meeting in a nearby town. That hadn't stopped him from punishing me in his favorite ways before retiring for the night, but I learned to keep seeds of Queen Anne's lace hidden under my bedroll. After chewing a few of the bitter seeds and a night of painful trips to the privy, I knew I wouldn't have to worry about a potential pregnancy.

As soon as Master Aldous left, I slipped out, eager to not only get what little freedom I could steal but also see if the lord was one to trust. Other foreign lords in the past promised to help only to show up with REDs and accuse me of stealing. I learned to be cautious and positioned myself in an alley where I could watch for the lord to arrive without putting myself in danger.

"I see you are quite cautious of people."

I jumped at the voice and turned to find the lord behind me, a wide grin on his face and brown eyes bright.

"There have been many who gave me no choice," I said, turning and walking out of the alley to give myself space to run if I needed to.

"Well, hopefully this will calm your worries some." The lord whistled and a young boy came around the corner leading a mule hauling a cart piled high with food.

I stared in complete disbelief at the sheer amount of food loaded in the cart. I scanned the shadows, certain REDs were waiting. Seeing none, I scanned the roofs of nearby buildings and the vendors opening their stalls. No one paid us any mind. Why would they? There was no way a lord would willingly give so much food to a slave, yet there were no signs of danger. I hinted at the cause, but gave no proof I wouldn't be keeping the food for myself. Yet he still brought it. *Why?*

"I'm assuming your silence means 'thank you,' " he laughed, his right eye disappearing behind the scar when his eyes crinkled.

I stood there staring at him for another few seconds before understanding what he said and gave a deep curtsy. "Thank you for your sincere generosity."

"There's no need for that. This was something I could easily do. Now, I suppose we should get this to wherever it needs to go?"

I blinked, still not sure what to think. "Right. It's a few blocks south of here."

He motioned for me to take the lead, and I led him down the street. Still cautious, I took a few random turns to make it more difficult for him to find his way back on his own. I could jeopardize the safety of many by bringing the lord. Still, Flinders and those he helped would benefit from the food, and I didn't want to turn away aid for those who needed it.

"So, tell me, Hajana, why are you risking your safety and putting trust in a stranger for food?"

I looked around the corner of a building to check for REDs before answering. "Because, even though I could argue my current life is dismal, there are still others whose lives are far worse than mine. I am blessed with a roof over my head, even if those I live with are cruel. Para has called us to help those struggling more than we are, and even if he didn't, I would feel wrong keeping the extra food and coin I had."

Realizing I was rambling to a lord I hardly knew and not looking for REDs, I turned my attention to where we were. When I realized we were only a few streets away, I stopped leading the lord in circles and hope I hadn't made a mistake bringing him there.

"It's just up ahead," I said, turning to him as we rounded a corner. "I'll need you to stay here until I call you over. This will be the first time I have brought anyone here, and I'm not sure what will happen."

The lord nodded, and I went to knock on the door. Within a few seconds, Flinders shuffled through the room and his muffled voice called out as he opened the door. "Oh, Hajana, it's you. Please, please, come in. Two days in a row, this is a treat."

Flinders started to usher me inside but I stepped back. "I'm not alone, but I promise it's for a good reason."

The old man raised an eyebrow but nodded as I called for the lord and the boy to bring the cart over. As soon as the others were close enough, the old man stepped into the street and grabbed the lord's sleeve before dragging the two of us inside and shutting the door.

"Hajana, who is this man, and why are you in the company of him?" Flinders asked, his skin glowing with the pale blue of his Wind Aura.

I walked back until I was pressed against one of the walls, trying to stop my body from trembling.

"I don't know who he is," I stuttered. "He was the one who gave me the coin to buy the bread. He asked me if there was anything he could do to help and I suggested meeting today. That's all, I promise," I said, holding up my hands in defense.

I had seen Flinders get mad before at one of the shopkeepers who tried to swindle him. By the time the REDs arrived a majority of the shopkeeper's goods had been blown away or destroyed, the shopkeeper himself cowering under his table. Flinders was able to talk himself out of punishment, how was unknown, but he still collected his supplies and searched for urchins and those in need in secret.

"Now, Flinders, is that really any way to treat a girl who just brought you enough food to feed your charges for a month?"

Flinders turned to the lord, staring at him for a moment before giving a small laugh and poking the breast of the grey suit. "Geoffraie, I barely recognized you with your new decoration. Now, I don't need you getting Hajana here into any trouble."

"All I want to do is help, Flinders, nothing more. Let me and my boy unload the food and we can discuss things after."

Flinders looked at me and back at the lord before turning and muttering to himself under his breath.

The lord turned and opened the door before speaking to the boy in a language I didn't recognize. The boy lead the mule to the open door where he started carrying in boxes and placing them on the floor.

The room was silent for several long minutes until the lord cleared his throat.

"Flinders, would you stop being so cautious and calm your Well before you frighten the poor girl to death?"

Flinders looked at me, glow fading, and the air in the room warmed again, only the fleeting shiver alerting me the room had grown cold at all.

"Pay attention, Geoffraie, you're looking at the only place in this whole bloody city that gives a damn about the health and prosperity of the street urchins or slaves like Hajana. I have seen too many young souls die in my life, and I am not willing to sit back and watch anymore. I will do whatever I have to, to protect them, regardless of who I have to cross."

The boy carried in the last crate and the lord glanced out the door, seeming lost in thought. He watched those walking over the bridge before letting the door shut with a soft click, those outside oblivious to the four of us in Flinders' front room or the countless sick and malnourished urchins in one of the back rooms.

"I can understand your feelings, trust me, I can," the lord said.

Flinders checked over the food in the crates but said nothing, letting the lord continue.

"It would certainly make things easier for you to help if you had a place with more room and access to better supplies."

Flinders eyed the lord warily but played along with the idea.

"Yes, it would be nice. The number of children I could help would rise drastically, and I wouldn't have to turn them out to the streets. They need to learn they can still overcome whatever happened in their past."

The lord was going to say something else, but the bells chiming in the distance alerted me to how late it had gotten.

"I'm sorry, but I'm going to be late." I gave a quick curtsy and ran out without waiting to be excused.

I turned down the nearest alley, staying out of the way of as many people as I could, not wanting to be punished for getting too close to others. Slaves and servants stepped to the side, knowing by my speed alone I was at risk of severe punishment.

Contrary to my original belief, many servants were treated scarcely better than slaves and we saw each other as family. There were a few servants who treated slaves as bad as the masters did, but they were pointed out to any of the new slaves and we all knew to avoid them. While I would never wish slavery upon anyone, a small part of me wanted nothing more than to see those few servants suffer the way I did.

I turned onto the road that led to my master's house and slowed my pace so as not to attract attention from the REDs. While Master Aldous wasn't home, his wife was, and she would be well aware that I was missing.

I snuck in the back door of the kitchen and was heading toward the ladder leading to the small room I shared with fourteen other slaves when the shrill voice of Mistress Aldous rang through the hall.

"Ha-Jana. Where have you been? I have been searching for you for hours and now my garden party is going to be ruined!"

I bit my tongue at the lies she was spewing at me, turning to face her as she marched over. I kept my eyes on the bare wooden floor, not wanting to anger her more as I responded.

"Master Aldous had an errand he needed me to run this morning on the other side of the city. He said it was urgent and that it needed to be done first thing."

"The other side of the city?" I cringed at the pitch of Mistress Aldous' shriek. "I bet he wanted you to go see that wench of a mistress, didn't he?"

When I didn't answer, she yanked my chin so I looked at her and slapped me across the face. The shock of being slapped was enough that I tumbled to the ground when she shoved me away from her.

"You're nothing but a worthless wench. I wish your parents were killed before they bred so they couldn't birth such a worthless creature as you."

My hands balled into fists under my short dress and it took everything I had not to leap up and attack her. There were many things I could handle being called or told, but my parents' memory being tarnished wasn't one of them.

"Get up. Scour the chamber pots before you start your garden duties."

She stepped over me and headed off to shout at one of the other servants, her voice carrying down the hall and echoing through the house. While Master Aldous gave out beatings with a heavy hand and enjoyed his female slaves far too much, his wife's words reached places Master Aldous couldn't, seeping in and nesting in one's mind until they couldn't be handled any longer; both cruel in terrible ways.

I forced myself to climb to my feet and headed to the back porch to start the revolting task of cleaning the chamber pots when I noticed the foul-smelling, yellow staining in the pot belonging to Master Aldous. Not wanting to get too close, I grabbed a pot of boiling water from the fire and drenched the pots so I could start cleaning.

CHAPTER SIX
EMOLIN

Approaching Minister Aldous' estate, I was grateful to find Hajana alone in the gardens. Making sure no one was watching, I hopped over the small stone wall and stayed near the statues and hedges in the maze as I made my way toward the beds of herbs and produce Hajana was weeding.

"Caw," I called, mimicking the cry of a Tiger Hawk and waiting for Hajana's response before moving closer.

Once given the all-clear *caw*, I moved closer, staying in the shadows and out of the direct view of the kitchen door and windows.

"How are you doing?" I asked, happy to see minimal bruising on Hajana's arms and legs.

"Better than I would've in the past." She walked closer to dump weeds in a pile near my feet. "A strange lord with a scar across his face not only prevented the punishment from the potter but also the worst of the punishment from my master. While there are many reasons I shouldn't trust him, I won't shun a gift from Para no matter how unusual it is."

I glanced at her, unsure of how to respond. Few people in

Altava were tolerant of slaves, and there were even fewer that would help them. Someone from another city preventing the punishment of a slave was practically unheard of.

"He even brought an entire cartload of food to donate to Flinders."

I stared at Hajana in complete shock. There was something off about the lord, but I didn't know what. I didn't want to get into an argument, so I changed the topic.

"The Head Sage came to visit me yesterday afternoon."

"She did?" Hajana knelt to work on a bed near me. "How come?"

I lowered my voice to a whisper and leaned out of the shadows as much as I dared. "I met a figure in an alley yesterday and again today. Somehow, they drained my Well and my butler had to carry me into the house after training because of it." I didn't mention the caning I received so she wouldn't have more to worry about. "I believe they were one of my gods."

"You saw one of your gods? What did they look like?"

I raised my eyebrow in confusion at her interest in my gods, but answered anyway. "There isn't much to say. Their eyes were as black as soot, and the complete darkness they cloaked the alley in shrouded them. I'm certain it was Fonir, God of Cleansing."

Hajana stared at me with her eyebrows raised, a weed in her hands with roots still partially buried in the soil. Her expression a mix of shock and concern, understandingly so with how Klohaven viewed the Parans. I had to focus on my breathing in order not to work myself up. It would mean death for both of us if I couldn't calm myself down.

"Ha-Jana, have you finished the weeding? I need to have the garden perfect for the party this evening and you still have to scrub the floors." Lady Aldous' voice carried across the yard.

That was my cue to leave, and I raised my hand as I shrunk back into the shadows and made my way back across the gardens to the low wall. I didn't worry about being caught after I moved away from Hajana, so I let my mind wander to the Head Sage's response to the god along with Hajana's.

I wondered if the Head Sage discovered it was Fonir. She read my Well, but at the time I hadn't known who the figure was, and I didn't know if she could glean things I wasn't aware of in a Well Reading. I hoped Hajana discovering what Fonir was the god of wouldn't upset her too much, since many used the fact of there being a God of Cleansing reason enough to destroy the Parans.

I climbed over the wall and wandered down random side streets, making sure there were plenty of other people around. Fonir only appeared whenever I was alone, and I was in no mood to deal with the weakness afterward. I considered heading toward the Hall of Sages to speak with the Head Sage, but she said she would speak with me later and I knew better than to seek an audience with her before she was ready.

Instead, I made my way back to the bazaars, wanting nothing more than to buy a few bags of sweets, sit in the gardens, and relax. I knew there would be something to prevent me from the relaxation I desired, either someone needing my attention, or my thoughts and worries about Fonir and Hajana not leaving me alone, but I still let myself look forward to it all the same.

"Would m'lady care for a necklace?"

The shopkeeper's voice startled me and I had my sword half-drawn before I realized he wasn't a threat. He took a step back, raising his hands and muttering what I assumed to be a prayer.

I gave the man a reassuring smile and sheathed my sword. "I'm sorry, you startled me. No, thank you."

I turned to walk away but something about the table tugged at my Well and I drew closer against my greater judgment.

"Please, we insist." He held out a bright yellow-orange stone hanging off a leather cord.

I reached out to examine it but pulled back when he said *we*.

"No, I really must get going."

"Here, take it. It will be of great value to you."

The man placed the stone in my palm, and a shock traveled up my arm toward my Well. I dropped the necklace on the table and stared at my hand. Not wanting anything more to do with the stone, I turned and walked away without another word, ducking into the crowds.

Once I put enough distance between the merchant and myself to feel safe, I stepped around the side of a shop and leaned against the wall to catch my breath. I didn't dare go deeper into the alley than the mouth, so I took a few moments to compose myself until I felt strong enough to blend into the crowds again.

I slipped my hand into my pocket to pull out a handkerchief when my hand grasped something cold, hard, my Well to pulsing. I pulled whatever it was out and stared at the necklace the merchant must've slipped into my pocket when I wasn't looking. I turned to head back to his stall and ran into a wall that hadn't been there the moment before. I spun back to the alley, darkness enveloping me, and once again saw the figure from before. I chose not to use my Aura and took a step toward Fonir, trying to hide my fear.

"Ah, you're learning, Emolin. There is promise in you."

I clenched my fists and kept my hand on my sword, ready to draw it if needed. "How do you know who I am?"

The figure laughed and my Well retreated from theirs as they stepped closer, closing the distance between us. "There's a plethora of things I know, dear Emolin, the real question is if you're willing to step up to the challenge or if things will stay as they are."

I pulled out my sword, pressing my back against the new wall, and pointed the blade in the direction the voice was coming from. "I am more than willing to accept a challenge, but one that's a fair fight, not a fixed one like this."

"Oh, it's not me you must fight," the figure whispered in my ear, making me jump and swing at them as the darkness faded, the wall disappearing again.

I sheathed my sword before the wall faded and closed my eyes as I tried to comprehend what happened. That was the third time Fonir appeared, each time saying little and leaving me with nothing but questions.

I needed to speak with the Head Sage to get whatever answers she could give me. I couldn't keep meeting Fonir in random alleys. Not only was he showing up more often, but whatever he was hinting at wasn't something I wanted to deal with.

I turned to head up the street toward the Hall of Sages when a servant ran up to me.

"Lady Emolin, your mother sent me. She requests you head home at once and sent me to finish your shopping."

My brows knit together and I stared at the servant for a few seconds before giving them a list of the shops I planned to visit and the things I wanted to buy. They promised to get what they could and I headed back home, not sure what Mamma wanted that could be so urgent.

<hr>

Rounding the corner, my home coming into view, my father's carriage glittered in the sun and my heart dropped. Father being home meant my hopes of relaxation that evening fell. I tried not to let the frustration get to me as I walked up to the door.

"Hello, Lady Emolin. Your father has been asking about you," our butler said, bowing as I approached.

"Of course he has." I sighed, handing the butler my headscarf, grateful for the slight breeze to wick away the sweat. "Can you tell him I will be down for dinner? I want to take a bath to wash off the day." I stepped through the door and headed for the stairs.

"I would, but the guest won't enjoy having to wait."

I stopped and turned, knowing who the butler meant, but not wanting to be right. "Who else is here?"

"The Magistrate."

I struggled not to grab the nearest vase and smash it to the floor, the rage inside bubbling like a stew. "Alright, I guess I shouldn't keep him waiting," I said through gritted teeth

The butler bowed again, failing to hide his fear, and led me into the parlor where I had been the day before. Father and Magistrate Magdra stood by the small desk near the bookshelves and sipped on glasses of brandy. Mamma sat stiff-backed on the sofa, wearing one of her nicest dresses. I walked over to her and planted a kiss on her cheek before turning to the two men whose eyes were boring into me.

"Hello, Father, I'm surprised to see you home so soon. We didn't expect you until tomorrow evening at the earliest."

"The winds were in my favor, my darling. They wished me home in time for the festival."

"I'm glad to see you've returned safely." I kissed him on the cheek, struggling to keep a neutral face as I did, and offered a small bow to the Magistrate.

I gratefully accepted the drink from the servant and took a sip far too large for a lady. I suppressed the shutter from the brandy and took a smaller sip before continuing.

"Magistrate Magdra, what brings us the pleasure of your presence this afternoon?"

"I was hoping you could answer that same question. Someone sent a messenger to my house, requiring my presence by three. I was hoping getting here early would allow me to get the answers sooner, but I discovered that is not the case."

I turned to the clock, seeing it was only half-past two. The servant sent for me was from Mamma, I could tell by her posture she sent for me when Father arrived. I gave another small bow to the men and went to sit with her, wanting to offer comfort but feeling weak myself.

"Hello, Mamma. The servant should bring back sweets soon."

"Sweets?" She stared at me blankly, her words slurring and face pale.

I didn't turn and look at my father, not wanting to know what he had done to Mamma. Instead, I placed my hand on hers and squeezed, hoping to give her some level of strength.

As much as I wanted to confront him, I knew it wasn't the right time. I would need to wait until I could get him alone.

Before I could think on it any longer, the bell rang through the hall, and the conversation between my father and the Magistrate hushed as we waited for the newest arrival. The butler led the Head Sage into the parlor and I wiped my palms on my robes, unaware of how nervous I was.

"I knew it!" my father shouted. "I'm not sure what you've done, but I knew tha—"

The Head Sage held up a hand to silence my father's tirade. "That's enough, Soteris. Emolin has not only been a great asset to the city, but the gods blessed her beyond what any of us could ever comprehend."

My father's face flushed, and I struggled to hide the smile of satisfaction from his embarrassment. The Magistrate, having more sense than to accuse me in front of the Head Sage, cleared his throat.

"Please, elaborate. How is Emolin blessed, as you mentioned?"

The Head Sage, seeming to ignore the Magistrate, turned to me and smiled. "Emolin, my dear, have you seen the thing you mentioned again since we spoke?"

"I have, twice now. Both times a wall appeared and seemed to trap me, disappearing after they left."

The Head Sage nodded and took a seat in the same chair she had the night before. "Did anything else happen?"

"The most recent time they asked if I was 'up to the challenge,' though I do not understand what that means."

She leaned forward and held my hand in hers. "It means, my dear, that the gods have chosen you as their messenger."

I sat there, not knowing how to even respond.

"Let me see if I understand this correctly," the Magistrate started. "Are you saying Emolin is the one the prophesies mention? Will we finally be able to liberate our lands from the Parans?" the Magistrate asked, standing and stroking his hair as he looked out the window.

The Head Sage turned to the Magistrate, brows furrowed. "I said no such thing. I said she is their messenger, nothing more."

"Yes, but a messenger can mean much more than someone who brings news or shares teachings, they can be someone who does much more…" The Magistrate trailed off and headed toward the door without excusing himself.

"Straven, what are you—" The Head Sage tried one last time to correct him, but the Magistrate was already gone and shouting for one of the servants to bring him his horse.

The Head Sage turned back to me and squeezed my knee. "I'll go and try to speak with him."

I gave her a grateful smile and the butler appeared to show her out.

As soon as my parents and I were alone, my father shut the parlor door before stalking over and pulling me to my feet.

"I don't care if the Head Sage says you're the next queen!" my father shouted. "I spoke with the Magistrate and found a letter waiting for me at the docks from Sojourn. I know you've been slacking on your training and costing me good coin on countless visits from the healer, not to mention the reputation of our family. No 'blessing' from the gods is going to save you from the punishment you've earned yourself."

Mamma reached for me and tried to hold me back, but I gave

her a small smile before turning back to my father. "I have done no such thing to 'earn' a punishme—"

The slap of my father's hand striking my cheek rang through the room, followed by a gasp from Mamma.

"You should know not to disrespect me. You may be a Mage, but I am still your father and you are a child. If it weren't for your Well, I would say you would never amount to anything, and even with such a gift, I wouldn't be surprised if you still managed to end up as nothing better than a wench begging for *work* on the streets."

I bit my tongue, not wanting Mamma to end up as a target in my father's tirade, his eyes flicking to her before he took another sip of his drink. An image of her beaten body flashed into my mind and I noticed faint bruising under her right eye, makeup expertly blended to almost completely hide the purple tint from her pale skin. I tried to take a step in front of Mamma, but that only seemed to anger Father more.

"Don't you try to protect that bitch; she has been nothing but a bother to me since she birthed you and was told she would never be able to have another child, leaving me without a proper successor for my trading company."

He took a breath to continue but I cut in, having heard this story far too many times. "Yes, I've heard this story at least once a month for my whole life. If you're wanting to punish me, then get on with it."

I took a step closer and glared at him, refusing to let my fear show on my face.

Before he was able to do anything, there was a soft knock on the door followed by the butler calling out. "Master, I'm sorry to disturb you, but you've received an urgent message from the docks. They said something about missing crates and wanting to charge you for the loss."

My father roared and slapped me again before turning and throwing open the parlor doors. He stomped out of the house and the panes in the windows shook as he slammed the door and marched out to his carriage.

The butler came in and asked Mamma if she would like help to her room while one of the other maids came over to check on me. We said nothing, hoping my father would be away until late in the evening and would save his rant for the morning.

CHAPTER SEVEN
HAJANA

After receiving a verbal lashing from my mistress for taking too long weeding her many flower beds, I finished up in the garden and prepared to scrub the floors. I grabbed a bucket and filled it with hot water and suds. The brush I used, if one could call it that, was barely larger than my thumb. While I had to admit it made getting between the tiles easier, the sheer amount of flooring I was told to clean with it was too vast for it to be anything other than a punishment.

I knelt and began the tedious task, letting my mind wander. Emolin didn't seem too sure about the lord. I thought the same myself, but the fact he stayed to help instead of being chased away by Flinders had to mean something. Plus, the two of them seemed to have some sort of history.

What was far more concerning was the god Emolin mentioned seeing. There were tales about people chosen by Para to be a messenger, yes, which is what it sounded like at first. I wasn't sure if Emolin's gods were the same, but if Para would visit his children, then why wouldn't Emolin's? If Emolin had seen a god or saw them in whatever capacity human eyes were capable of, then something was going to happen. The fact she said it was her

God of Cleansing, who visited worried me the most. *Was he suggesting to massacre the Parans left in Klohaven?*

My thoughts were interrupted when one of the maids hurried toward the door as the bell above it rang incessantly. The clock said it was half past three. There was still another hour before the mistress' party, so it couldn't be one of the guests. The Magistrate stormed in, calling for Master Aldous and heading up to the study, before the girl could say anything,.

Throwing the brush in the bucket of water, I climbed to my feet, letting the blood return to my legs, and stared at the mud-crusted footsteps. I was halfway done with the hall and would have to start over.

"Here, use my rag." The maid held out a cloth and gave me a small smile.

I took a deep breath and thanked her. I lugged the bucket of water over to the footprints and scrubbed at them. The runes on the bucket allowed the water to stay hot, but they also made the bucket heavier to lug around.

I continued to scrub the floor and almost finished when the door opened again and the lord strolled in followed by several more men all wearing their RED uniforms in some fashion. I kept my head down, hands pressed to the floor, hoping they would pass me by.

Thankfully none of them paid attention to me and all headed up the stairs. Once they were gone, I set about scrubbing the floor again, hoping my mistress wouldn't walk in. Of course, luck wasn't on my side and she appeared moments later.

"The party has been canceled," she wailed, throwing her decorations on the floor, the paint from the banners mixing with the water and staining the tiles. "My husband called a meeting and it's so secretive I'm not even allowed to stay. You need to finish scrubbing the floor and report to Ruta for your next chores."

My mistress stormed out of the house, slamming the door

behind her, and yelled for her carriage. I stared up the stairs for several minutes, not sure what to think. There was something serious going on and I needed to know what it was.

I scrubbed up the paint and finished the rest of the floor as fast as I could, doing a decent enough job it wouldn't be noticeable that I rushed. I dumped the bucket of water in the back garden and grabbed a small duster to have as an excuse if I were to get caught.

Heading up the back staircase, I crept down the hall and stood outside the door to the study, duster poised on the frame. I didn't think they would perceive me as a threat, seeing as I was a slave, but I didn't want to give any impression I was eavesdropping either.

"… if that is true… Emolin could… Parans…"

I strained to hear more. If they involved Emolin in the scheme they were planning, I needed to figure out what it was.

"… be rid of them once and for all."

Cheers sprung from the room and I jumped back, not wanting to believe what I heard. *Are they saying Emolin is going to destroy the Parans?* I didn't want to hear anything more and ran back down the stairs to the kitchen where Ruta was making bread.

"The mistress told me to speak with you once I finished scrubbing the floor," I said, giving a small curtsy of respect.

"Aye, she did. The problem is, I don't have any chores to give you and she didn't give me any explicit instructions on what to do if I had none." Ruta pounded the dough on the counter, flour creating a cloud as she pulled the bread into a taut ball and set it in a bowl to rest. "Since there's nothing to do, I'm going to give you your supper and warn you to stay out of Master Aldous' way."

Ruta turned and grabbed a small plate with a bit of meat and vegetables along with some bread. I thanked her, scarfing down the vegetables and tucking the meat and bread into my handkerchief, before heading for the library. I took a wandering route so no one would know where I was going, though no one paid me any mind. Unlike most of the slaves captured during wars or thrust into slavery because of their religion, I had no problems reading Lunian. There were so few of us that could read, the masters paid none of us any mind around books, believing we were all too heathenistic to understand the printed word. So, as long as we were careful, we could devour the books on our masters' shelves with no issue.

My master's library had no windows and used Alchemy lamps to light the room. There was an enormous stone fireplace using Alchemist logs to keep the hearth lit without risking harm to the books against the wall to the left of the door. For a city with potent feelings against Alchemists, they had a lot of items swung Alchemist runes.

I scoured the shelves near the fireplace first, using the footstool from one of the overstuffed armchairs to give me a little more height. The words I overheard upstairs still bothered me, and I decided I would see if I could find a book mentioning anything that would give the men reason to believe Emolin could do anything to the Parans still living in the Klohaven mountains. I wasn't sure I would find anything, but it was worth a try. My parents instilling the practice of understanding a situation before acting or judging in me.

I ended up finding a book titled *The History of The Children of the Eight Divine*. It wasn't much, but it was a start. I put the footstool back, making sure there were no prints from my feet in the velvet, and headed back to my room, the book hidden in the pocket I stitched into my dress.

I climbed the ladder into the small alcove above the kitchen where fifteen slaves were crammed into a room meant for storing grain. I crawled over the bedrolls of the other slaves and collapsed onto my small roll tucked in the corner. A lantern swung overhead, casting just enough light in the dim room for me to read by, even if it did force me to squint.

I chewed a bit of the cold meat and flipped through the first few pages of the book, admiring the illustrations and font of the drop cap. Brushing the bugs off my blanket, I read the theory of the creation of Emolin's religion, the story sounding very similar to my religion and the religions of some of the other slaves I'd met. I wasn't sure what I was looking for, but something told me I would know once I found it.

After skimming the first several chapters and finding nothing, I flopped the book open in my lap and leaned my head against the wall, eyes closed. Something was going to happen; gods didn't mingle with mortals unless it was important. What that something was, I didn't know, but there was no way to prepare without knowing what I was preparing for. If Emolin was going to be involved, I needed to know what was going to happen. She protected me several times before and it was up to me to do the same.

I stretched and rubbed my eyes before continuing with the next chapter, reports of gods interacting with humans. *The figure black as night stood before me, beckoning me closer.* I stopped and had to read the account from the priest several more times to make sure I wasn't reading it wrong. When I was certain I hadn't, I continued, trying and failing not to let my hopes rise. The chapter held something; a similarity to what Emolin described could potentially be the next clue I needed to learn more.

I flipped page after page, the paper rustling like the wings of birds, reading sentence after sentence. *The figure plunged my world into darkness… The man seemed to speak in riddles, not making sense… The deaths could've been avoided had I listened… I didn't have a choice, I had to listen to him…* Every account of meeting a god all ended the same way; a god visited then tragedy struck, often resulting in wars. It was only later discovered the god was trying to prevent it. *Is Fonir trying to prevent something?*

After reading the whole chapter through twice and focusing on particular sections, I had an idea of the reason Fonir might be visiting Emolin and I prayed I was wrong. I decided to skim the rest of the chapters and make sure there wasn't anything I missed. After finding nothing else, I forced myself to get up and return the book to the library before it was missed.

Ruta wasn't in the kitchen and I slipped down the hall without being seen. My feet padded on the plush carpet of the corridor to the east wing, the sconces throwing dancing shadows across the walls. I turned the corner and had my hand on the handle of the door to the library when voices drifted toward me. I dashed inside, quietly shutting the door and rushing to put the book back. Once the book was in its place, I paused, the voices moving closer. Spinning around, I dove under the desk on the other side of the room just as the door opened.

"If what the Magistrate was saying is true, then why would we need the armies?"

"Because it's better to have Mages and soldiers by your side instead of dying from an arrow to the head."

"You make no sense, you know that?"

"If we bring an army, then even if they're numbers are larger than we predict, we will eventually be victorious. The soldiers will be able to distract the Paran scum while our Mages take out their leaders."

The two men bickered back and forth for several more minutes before they remembered their reason for being in the library.

"Where did he say that strategy book was again?"

"I think this shelf here."

I held my breath as the men moved closer and only released it once they moved away and left the room. Waiting a few moments to make sure it was clear, I crawled out from under the desk and headed back over to the door. I found what I needed, proof Fonir showed himself to give a warning, I just needed to figure out what the warning was.

I paused to listen at the door before I snuck out of the room and headed for the study where the men were still meeting. I didn't know if I would glean anything else from eavesdropping, but it was the only idea I had. My feet padding on the stairs, I wished I had a duster for an excuse, but I didn't want to waste time. Instead, I prayed to Para I wouldn't get caught as I approached the door.

"If you were told… then why do you think… would it even work?" The voice from one of the men from the library reached me in barely audible sentences as I leaned against the wall next to the door.

"Listen," the Magistrate's voice boomed, causing me to jump, "we have been dealing with Parans in our lands since my grandfather was Magistrate. The fact that King Rupert made us take in the Parans has been haunting us for decades. The Parans have been stealing our resources and attacking our people. The ancient prophesy tells of a hero rising to purge the evil destroying the land, and clearly, this insolent Mage of ours has been chosen…"

I didn't stay to hear the rest, I didn't have to. I ran back to my room without seeing anyone else. There were a few slaves in our quarters when I climbed the ladder, but none of them said anything. I gave them a small smile if we made eye contact, but other than that, the room was quiet.

I needed to tell Emolin what I discovered and would have to wait until it was dark. I would have to stick to the shadows without getting mugged, or worse. If the REDs found me, I would be lucky to live through the night, but I couldn't let the Magistrate's plan happen, not with the things I overheard.

*M*ost nights I found myself lying awake until I had to get up, only drifting to sleep in small intervals. That night, however, I struggled to stay awake as evening turned to night and the city hushed. The meeting went on until nearly midnight and Mistress Aldous came home hours before, retiring for the evening well before her husband did.

An hour after the stable hands locked the barn for the night, I felt it was safe enough to leave. I tiptoed over the sleeping girls, climbing down the ladder and landing silently on the floor. Once in the kitchen I grabbed the shawl for slaves when using the privy at night and slipped into the gardens.

Master Aldous didn't employ any guards and sneaking through the gardens was an easy task, having done so many times before. I tried to escape several times after my parents were first killed, the hope I could run away still strong in my heart. After getting caught and punished over a dozen times, I realized the best way to survive was to pretend to be compliant and wait until Master Aldous thought I was his.

I stuck to the main roads, keeping to the shadows and slipping into alleys when footsteps approached. There weren't many people on the roads, but those that were would either want to arrest me, mug me, rape me, or a combination of the three.

The trip to Emolin's took me far longer than I thought it should. While I had never been there, she told me about it numerous times and there were very few homes in Altava that flew flags from their roofs, her father quite proud of his trading business and wanting everyone to know it was his. It didn't take me too long to find her home once near the port, but I then had to decide if I was going to try and find Emolin's room from the outside or knock on the servants' door.

My choice was made for me when a maid rounded the corner of the mansion and noticed me standing on the walk.

"Oh my, you scared me. What are you doing out here?" she whispered, grabbing my hand and pulling me into the shadows.

"I need to see Emolin, it's urgent." I showed her a small charm Emolin gave me a few years before in case I ever needed to speak with her and couldn't find her on my own.

The girl, glancing at the charm and noticing my slave garb, nodded. "It must be important if you risked getting caught by the REDs on the way here. Follow me, and remember to be quiet."

The two of us headed toward the house and she ushered me into the kitchen, the low-burning coals providing a welcome warmth from the chill outside. She led me up the back stairs, which I noted were much wider and less rickety than the ones at my master's home, and down a hallway to another set of stairs.

"When we get to the top, stay back a few steps until I let Lady Emolin know you're here." She turned to head up the stairs but turned back. "I realize I don't know your name."

"Ra-Hana," I said, stressing the pronunciation.

She turned and I followed her up the next flight of stairs, stopping when we reached a door. The maid knocked and Emolin's sleepy voice called out as she opened the door.

"Hmm? What's wrong?"

"Hajana is here. She says it's urgent."

The sleepiness disappeared from Emolin's voice, "please, come in," and she stepped into the room, lighting a small lamp as we entered.

The maid stepped to the side and Emolin rushed over and hugged me, something she had never done before because of the secrecy around our friendship, then pulled away and held me at arm's length to look me over.

"Hajana, why are you here? Are you crazy? You could've been killed if you had been spotted."

"I know, but I discovered something and I needed to let you know as soon as I could."

"And it couldn't wait until the morning?"

"No, I wouldn't know where to find you, and even if I did, there would be too many people around to overhear."

I turned and glanced at the maid, hoping I could trust her, before turning back to Emolin. "I think Fonir is trying to warn you. The Magistrate and many RED officers arrived at my master's home this afternoon. They canceled the mistress' party and sent her off to call on one of her friends."

Emolin moved to sit on her bed and motioned to the two of us to sit on the bench by the window.

"Did you hear anything they said?"

"I didn't hear much, but what I could make out was them planning on using you to remove my people from Altava. Something about you fulfilling an ancient prophesy."

"Are you sure?" the maid cut in. "Maybe you heard them wrong, especially if it was through a door. Plus, no one believes in that prophesy. A Mage having the power to destroy entire cities is nothing but stories to help children fall asleep."

"The others were difficult to hear through the door, but the Magistrate's voice boomed clear enough I could've heard him from down the hall. And the Magistrate must believe or he wouldn't have held that long of a meeting and to such secrecy."

I reiterated everything I discovered and the things I heard while hiding under the desk.

"If all this is true, then I guess the Head Sage never caught up to the Magistrate to speak with him. She was here earlier to tell me about the whole chosen messenger thing. The Magistrate heard what he wanted and took off, assumedly to your master's house where he told them what he 'discovered.' " Emolin ran a hand through her hair and looked out the window at the moons. "Thank you for letting me know all this, Hajana. I'll speak with the Head Sage in the morning to see if she can offer any more advice. Will you be able to get home okay?"

"I made it here alright. And this way I'll be heading back toward my master's if I get stopped."

Emolin didn't seem convinced, but bid me safe travels. The maid led me back down the stairs and out into the moonlight.

"The REDs patrol the bazaars at this time of night. It's safer to make your way down to the river and head home from there."

I thanked her and slipped into the darkness, heading toward the river.

That part of the city was familiar, having walked it many times to meet with Flinders. I moved through the streets faster than on my way to Emolin's, and I made it back to my master's house with plenty of moonlight left.

I used the privy so I wouldn't be lying if anyone asked me where I was and hung the shawl back on the hook before climbing up to the loft. Crawling under my blankets and wrapping them around me, the worries about Emolin and what might happen flooding my mind. Eventually, I drifted off, slipping into nightmares of the night they killed my parents.

CHAPTER EIGHT
EMOLIN

I was on the streets heading to the Hall of Sages before the sun rose, something I wasn't sure I had done before.

After Hajana visited me, I couldn't sleep and spent the night in my father's library researching. Hajana mentioned she read *The History of The Children of the Eight Divine* and not only did Father have that book on his shelves, but a few others as well. I spent the rest of the night doing research and making notes, planning on stopping to see the healer after visiting with the Head Sage to be excused from training again.

There were few people on the streets and I was able to navigate through the bazaars with little difficulty. Many of the shops were still closed and those that were open paid little attention to a Mage with no obvious interest in the baubles on the tables.

I stopped in front of the House of Elders and took a moment to collect myself. There were a few priests around, heading to the chapel for morning prayers, but I passed no one else as I climbed the stone steps and pulled the rope by the door.

Bells rang inside and I stood there for several minutes before someone finally answered.

"Oh, hello, my child. Can I help you?" The small man bowed and I returned a deep bow of my own before speaking.

"Yes, I need to speak with the Head Sage. We started speaking yesterday afternoon but got interrupted."

"Yes, please come in. She's been expecting you."

I raised my eyebrow but said nothing as I followed him inside, letting him shut the door. He led me into a small sitting room with a roaring fire and incense filling the air with the scent of cloves.

"Please, have a seat. I will let her know you're here."

The man bowed again and left, leaving me to sit and wait. There was little to look at in the room, two armchairs facing each other in front of the fire with a table between them and nothing hanging on the walls. A small rug was placed under the table to add some warmth to the wooden floors and a small statue sat in the middle of the mantel. Before I had a chance to examine the statue, the Head Sage arrived.

"Hello, my dear. I'm glad to see you're doing better today."

I bowed deep in respect before answering. "I am feeling much better, thank you."

The Head Sage sat in one of the chairs and motioned for me to do the same. "You're here because of the meeting yesterday, yes?"

I nodded. "A friend came to visit me last night. She told me of things she heard and read with her own eyes. I have no reason to believe she would lie."

The Head Sage leaned back and I told her everything Hajana told me, making sure I never actually mentioned who my friend was. I pulled out the notes I wrote and gave the Head Sage a list of people who were at Hajana's master's, emphasizing the Magistrate's appearance.

"Hm, it does sound like he has taken this out of context, hasn't he?"

She sat in silence, reading over my notes several times before speaking again. "I will visit the Magistrate after breakfast. If your friend said he left at such a late hour, there's a good chance he won't be awake yet." She grasped my hand in hers and gave it a gentle squeeze. "There's nothing for you to worry about right now. I want you to take today off from training as well; you need your rest for whatever the god has been referring to. I will send a messenger to Sojourn so he doesn't report you for the time you missed."

I thanked her and stood to leave, turning back when she continued speaking. "I'm also going to send a messenger to your father so he doesn't think you're skipping out on your training in laziness."

"No, please, there's no need for that." I smiled, hoping to negate any rudeness my refusing her offer caused.

I knew she was just trying to be helpful, but sending a messenger to my father would only make him angrier when he got home, especially since I hadn't seen him after he was called away.

"Alright dear, if you feel that is best, I won't send a messenger to your father."

I thanked her and turned again when I remembered the necklace from the merchant.

"Do you know anything about this?" I asked, pulling out the necklace.

The Head Sage held out her hand for the necklace and examined it for a few moments.

"This seems to be a replica of a mythical gem. The legend says the gem could amplify the powers of the wearer in times of great need. Of course, that is nothing but a fairytale as we know Mages can do that on their own if they gather enough Aura." The Head Sage handed me back the pendant. "Now, I recommend you go home and rest. I will speak with the Magistrate, though with the information you've given me there's a chance he won't listen."

I thanked the Head Sage one last time and showed myself out. Since I didn't have to go find the healer I headed straight home to be with Mamma so she wouldn't be alone when Father came back.

Once again, as I rounded the corner to my estate, Father's carriage was in front of the house. I ran up the stairs and marched into the parlor where I found a scene similar to the one the day before. When I saw the Magistrate sitting with my father, I struggled against the idea of trying to attack him. The Magistrate would win instantly, not only being more practiced but having more Aura in his Well than I did. Instead, I acknowledged him while purposefully ignoring the proper respect he expected.

"May I ask what this meeting is about?"

"Well," my father started, "it turns out you are good for something after all. Magistrate Magdra just gave us wonderful news. You will be leading a group of Mages to Blackwood to speak with Grandmaster Sphera, Leader of the Alchemists."

I reached for my sword out of habit and took a slow, deliberate step toward the Magistrate.

"Now, now, Emolin," the Magistrate began, "I wouldn't do anything rash if I were you, not if you don't want anything to happen to a certain Paran slave."

I tried not to show my shock and fear, but the smirk on the Magistrate's face told me I failed.

"Yes, I know all about your friend and what she is. I promise not to harm her if you agree to help me."

I wanted nothing more than to stab my sword into his gut, to watch blood sputter out of his mouth as he tried to speak.

"How do I know you're not just saying that?"

The Magistrate pulled out a paper and held it up so I could see it. "This will certify Miss Hajana would become your property to do with as you please. I will sign and date it as soon as you sign your contract with me and your mother can keep it safe for you until you come back. I've even had this printed on Alchemical paper. Once it's signed it, no one can destroy it."

I stood there seething, hating being thrown into a situation where my only choices were to save my friend and kill many or turn the other way while they murdered everyone, including Hajana.

"I'm sure this is a lot for someone like you to comprehend, so I'll give you some time to mull it over. I expect to hear from you by tomorrow evening with your answer. If you don't arrive in time, I'll let the REDs know I discovered a spy pretending to be a slave and they will need to deal with her immediately."

He stood and gave me a deep bow before showing himself out. My father stood there smirking at me, challenging me to say anything he could use against me.

"I'm going for a walk," was all I said before heading out and slamming the door.

I hoped the fresh air would make things easier, but the humidity was so thick sweat was dripping down my back before I even turned off the walk. Having devoured all the sweets the night before, I headed for the bazaars, promising myself I would consider the choice I was being forced to make once I had some cakes to munch on.

There were still few people in the market, but more were arriving as I made my way to the stalls selling small pastries filled with a sweet cream and sometimes berries. There were only two days until the festival, and the bazaar would soon be too full to move about in. I needed to get out before I felt trapped.

Memories of the time I lost sight of Mamma in the crowd weren't usually an issue when I rushed to training. This time, the crowds closed in on me and I was the little girl in the bazaars again, shoppers shoving me out of the way until I fell to the ground. I curled up and screamed as people kicked me and stepped on my hair and clothes. No one cared, no one bothered to stop and help, the crowds too thick for me to crawl away.

Someone reached down and grabbed my hand, pulling me out of the sea of legs and led me to a corner where they explained to a RED what happened. I looked up at the girl, only a few years older than me, a slave, and hugged her, sobbing into her chest. She saved me when no one else did.

"M'lady, is everything okay?"

I turned to the RED, concern in her eyes, and I smiled, grateful to have been pulled out of those memories. "Yes, thank you."

I walked away without another word, wanting nothing more than to get away from the crowds.

I didn't remember how I ended up there, but I found myself on the bank of the river, staring out at the birds circling overhead, swooping down to catch an unfortunate fish every now and then. They made it seem so simple, the idea of predator and prey. *There is no real predator and prey in humans, is there? Only killers.*

I finished munching on my sweets and climbed to my feet. There had to be a way to prevent unnecessary deaths, but I needed to figure out what it was. *You stand by injustices and wait for others to act.* I pulled the pendant out of my pouch again, staring at the brightness of the yellow stone. There didn't seem to be anything unusual about it, aside from the shock I received when I first touched it. I decided to put the pendant on and see if I could make my way back home without pushing through crowds.

I wandered back home, hoping Father was gone and I could spend the rest of the day reading in the library or thinking about everything in bed. I knew I didn't want anything to happen to Hajana, but if she knew I had a hand in the slaughtering of her people, I would lose one of the few people whom I truly felt I could talk about anything with.

My father left for the docks by the time I arrived home and praised the gods for at least one good thing happening. Having braved the crowds to stop and buy some chocolates for Mamma, I couldn't wait to share them with her. I walked into the dining room and found her sitting at the table, sipping a cup of coffee. She seemed to be still in a fog, but more aware than before.

"Hello, Mamma. I brought you some chocolates from the market."

"Hmm? Oh, thank you, Kitten, those sound lovely. Will you come and share them with me?"

I sat next to my mother while one of the maids brought in a platter and arranged the chocolates across it.

"Mamma, can I ask you a question?"

"Of course, you can always talk to me, Kitten."

"I don't know what to do about the Magistrate's ultimatum. How does he expect me to make such a large decision in such a short amount of time? I don't want Hajana killed, but I don't want her to hate me for being the reason the rest of her people are killed either."

"You need to do what feels best for you. You've always been a resourceful young woman, I'm sure you can find a way to change the options you've been given." She gave my hand a small squeeze and popped a chocolate into her mouth.

I placed a small chocolate on my tongue, a rarity in Altava, and let it melt as I considered the different options and ideas I had. Mamma spoke up again and we talked about small, random things for the better part of an hour.

"Mamma, I don't want to leave you here with Father if I do end up leaving."

"Don't worry about me, Kitten. I can take care of myself."

"But Father—"

"But Father nothing," Mamma said, raising her voice and causing me to jump. "I don't want you to end up like me, tied to a man you don't love and who doesn't love you back. Now, go, make your decision, and stick to it. You need to take this chance to discover what you want out of life. Not what others want for you, but what you truly want."

I sat there, mouth agape. I wasn't used to Mamma being so

assertive. She stood and left the room without another word, leaving me at the dining room table alone with my thoughts. Mamma wanted me to make a choice, potentially a choice I hadn't been given.

I decided the best way for me to make a decision was to distract myself. I headed out to the garden, drawing my sword and hacking away at the training dummy, occasionally shrouding the dummy with Light Aura to give me a challenge. My sword cracking against the wooden dummy echoed through the garden, and I lost myself in the motions, relieving my stress through aggression.

After a few hours of training, with too few breaks in between, I collapsed in the sand and stared up at the sky, trying to get my breath back to a normal pattern. I still didn't have a plan for what I was going to do, but I knew I had to do something. I considered going to speak with Hajana about it, especially since it was her people the predicament involved, but I didn't want to risk getting her into more trouble if the Magistrate had people watching her.

I struggled to my feet, knees stiff after spending hours with them locked, and sat at the table with my whetstone. My sword was crafted to withstand hours of continuous use, but only if I took care of it. The stone glided over my blade, producing a high-pitched squeal that used to hurt my ears but I now found to be a comfort.

As the stone honed the first edge of my sword, a small idea came to me. The Magistrate said I was going to be leading a group to Blackwood, meaning he wasn't going to be with me. If I could pick the group I traveled with, maybe I could select those known to at least be impartial to the idea of slaves. It wasn't a perfect idea, but it was a start.

Feeling like I finally the start of a plan in place, I finished polishing my sword and sheathed it, heading inside in search of pastries and perhaps a nice relaxing bath.

he following evening, I headed for the Magistrate's estate. There were few people in the streets, many decorating their houses and readying their children for the parade the next morning. Colorful banners and decorations hung between buildings, giving the city a joyful appearance, the exact opposite of how I felt. How was the rest of the world able to move forward when I found myself wanting nothing more than to pause so I could breathe and catch up?

The walk to Magistrate Magdra's was far too short and I soon found myself walking up the path to his door. Many of the flowers in the Magistrate's garden were still blooming and added color to the surrounding desert landscape, though it was late in the year and the chill of winter bit in the breeze. The bright reds and oranges with occasional spots of purple and pink scattered throughout were a favorite among many Altavians. I loved wandering through the gardens and playing in the fountains when I was younger, as did most children, but the gardens were in a state of disrepair now.

It had been many years since the last fountain was added to celebrate the tricentennial of Altava, and many of the flowerbeds needed to be rebuilt. The Magistrate didn't set aside the funds to keep the city gardens kept, let alone his own. Instead, he hired more REDs and fortified the walls, claiming he wanted to keep the city safe, even though we hadn't been directly attacked in generations.

I followed the cobblestone path and walked up the polished stone steps. The white sandstone glistening in the setting sun and the piazza providing a welcoming shade. Stone pots filled with tall trees hid the front doors of the manor, and the Magistrate's butler smiled at me from the steps as I approached.

"Good afternoon, Lady Emolin," the butler said, giving me a deep bow as he held the door open.

The sun reflected off his balding head, the few grey hairs disappearing in the sunlight. I smiled at the butler and walked into the foyer of the manor.

When the butler closed the door, the dusty hues of twilight vanished from the room and my eyes took a second to adjust. There were no windows on the first two floors to prevent attackers from breaking in. While the lack of windows provided a once needed defense for the manor, the rooms required the use of Alchemist lamps to light the space, producing a candle-like light. I used to think of the manor as a dungeon when I was younger. I still did in a way, the lack of connection with the outside world unnerving.

The butler cleared his throat and I realized I'd fallen behind. I hurried to follow him up the stairs to the third floor, a place I rarely traversed when forced to visit the Magistrate. The Magistrate and I would usually meet in his office on the second floor when discussing my training, the third floor reserved for strategic planning, and, according to rumors, the place where the Magistrate tortured his slaves.

The portraits of the former Magistrates stared at me as I followed the butler through the maze of the third floor, their stern faces making me avoid eye contact even though they were only paintings. Instead, I enjoyed looking out the occasional window at the grounds below. I got lost in the twists and turns the butler led me through—another measure of protection from attacks—soon reaching what seemed to be a dead end with a table holding a vase of flowers pushed against the wall. The butler pressed a button on the bottom of the table and the wall swung open to reveal a short flight of stairs. The orange rays streaming in from the windows of the room above hurt my eyes and I blinked several times before my eyes adjusted.

"I've been instructed to have you wait here. There are refreshments waiting for you, but if you require anything else, please don't hesitate to ring the bell."

The butler bowed and walked away before I could say anything else. I took a breath to steady myself before heading up the stairs. It amazed me that the room was still relatively cool considering I was on the third floor. A breeze mussed the strands of hair sticking out of my headscarf and I couldn't place where it was coming from. I wrapped my scarf around my neck and grabbed a few sweets from the table by the window before wandering around the room.

I had only been in there a few times before and hadn't had a chance to look around in the past. I glanced at the open door, pausing to listen for voices or footsteps. Hearing nothing, I moved about the room, letting myself examine things I never had before.

The room was slightly higher than the rest of the third floor, but I was still surprised I could see almost the entire city of Altava. The room was hidden well enough by turrets so the Magistrate could watch approaching armies while being protected from flights of arrows. Stories of the wars sweeping through Klohaven in the adolescent years of the country and the Magistrates that won battles crossed my mind. One particular war almost succeeded in concurring Altava, but the room had been essential in winning the war.

I turned away from the window and focused on the table in the center of the room, one far larger than the tables used for dinner parties. A map of Klohaven took up most of the surface, with a few smaller maps of the major cities in Klohaven on the left side. There were several miniature buildings laid out on the map, one being the manor I was standing in. A small box full of tiny soldiers stood on the right side of the table and a stack of books on the floor leaned precariously against the table leg. I stooped down to look at the books, succeeding in knocking the pile over and hurrying to pick them up. The book on the top of the stack, *Negotiations and Strategies*, had several pieces of paper sticking out at different angles, and the cover had been repaired in several places. Many of the other books were about battles as well. I considered reading a few passages of the book but wasn't sure I wanted to know what those pages held.

Footsteps coming up the stairs caught my attention and I shoved the rest of the books into a pile, standing in time to see not only the Magistrate but also a man with a scar crossing his face from the bottom left of his chin to just above his right eyebrow enter the room.

"Ah, I'm glad to see you're here, Emolin. I honestly wasn't sure if you would be or not." The Magistrate laughed at his joke and didn't seem to care I stood there with fists clenched while the stranger laughed beside him, albeit politely.

"If I were to lead this group you mentioned, what did you have in mind?"

"Come now, do you think I'm going to divulge my secrets before I know you've agreed to the deal?"

I knew he was cautious, but that was a little too much even for him.

"Alright, fine. I'll go along with your scheme."

"That's good to hear, Emolin, but there's no reason to use such language. I'm only trying to keep our country at peace and Klohavians safe. Why you're taking such a personal offense to this is beyond me. One would almost assume you had a soft spot for those animals." A wicked grin crossed his face and his roaring laugh filled the room.

"Let's just get this over with," I said, gritting my teeth.

The Magistrate motioned me over to the table and I stood next to the stranger. Something about him seemed familiar to me, but I couldn't place him.

"From the information I've been gathering, the Parans are hiding out in the Klohaven Mountains. That means the Parans have trapped themselves within our country, but I'm sure you already knew that, Geoffraie."

When I heard the stranger's name, everything made sense.

Lord Edgar Mycroft was the leading general in Klohaven, known for decimating thousands of bandits, and also destroying dozens of Paran villages. I glanced over at the lord and noticed the scar again, the same scar Ra described. The lord must be Edgar Mycroft's son.

"Are you alright, miss?" the lord asked, his brows furrowing and eyes soft.

"Yes, thank you," I said, trying to hide my anger and resentment toward him.

"As I was saying," the Magistrate cut in, nostrils flaring, "since we have them trapped, all we need to do is flush them out here," he placed a bunch of broken figurines on the map, "and we'll be able to take them out all at once."

The lord grunted in approval. "With the help of the Alchemist armies, we should be able to pluck them off within an afternoon. We will need to compensate the Alchemists for their help, but that won't be too difficult considering the honor it will grant them."

"Oh, how I like the way you think, Geoffraie." The Magistrate clapped the lord on the shoulder. "Now, Emolin, this is where you come in. You are going to travel from here to Blackwood to speak with Lisbeth Sphera, Grandmaster of the Alchemists. You must get her to agree to join our troops here," he pointed to the field where he laid the Paran troops, "and meet us for battle."

"Wait, you're expecting me to join the battle? I thought I was just going to Blackwood and coming home!"

"Why else would I send so many Mages to Blackwood? I could just send foot soldiers for that. No, I'm sending Mages because I'll need you to lead us into battle and help take out most of the Paran army. The fewer soldiers I have die, the better my reputation."

I stood there in utter shock. "But what about Haja—"

The Magistrate cut me off. "Now, you'll be leaving tomorrow morning so you should head home to pack. I have already let

Sojourn know that you and some of your peers are going to be missing from training for the next few weeks and will be bringing our city back glory. I will see you at 7:00 a.m. in the center of town. Here's the ownership paper for the slave. Now, be gone with you."

Dismissing me with the wave of his hand, I stumbled out of the room and made my way through the maze of the third floor. Once out of the manor, giving a halfhearted wave to the butler as I passed, I allowed myself to cry. Within a day I had gone from worrying about getting to training on time to having the entire outcome of a war I didn't care about on my shoulders.

CHAPTER NINE
EMOLIN

The evening was spent in a fog, not understanding what was happening around me. I remembered explaining to Mamma I was leaving and the tears running down her cheeks, but other than that, the night was nothing more than flashes of images mixed with apprehension about the coming morning.

Father had to stay late at the docks, supervising the loading of his ship for another trip, so I didn't have to worry about his opinion on the matter, but even without him there, I still heard his voice in my mind. *You'll mess everything up, you always do... Why the gods chose you, I'll never know... If you mess this up, I'll make sure it's not only you that suffers.* While I agreed it would've been nice to have the responsibility passed on to someone else, I knew from Fonir's visit there was a reason I was picked.

The morning went by much the same, flashes of things happening but not understanding any of them. My maid helped me pack a small bag of clothes after a messenger was sent to the Magistrate to collect more information about the journey and what would be provided the night before. I was told I would only need clothes for the first half of the journey and that the Leader of Gathon would provide food and supplies for the second half.

I woke early and struggled to get up, wishing I could stay in bed so I wouldn't have to face the coming dread. That, of course, wasn't the case, and I eventually climbed out from under the sheets and got ready. The pendant from the shopkeeper was laid out with my robes and I assumed my maid found it when she took my clothes down to wash. I secured it around my neck and tucked it into my robes before heading downstairs.

When it was time to leave, Mamma squeezed me tight and whispered a Reshilian prayer in my ear.

"I love you, Kitten."

"I love you too, Mamma."

Neither of us wanted to let go, but eventually, she pulled away and looked me in the eyes. "Be safe and keep your head on your shoulders."

I smiled and turned away, not wanting her to see me cry, and I left, meeting my father on the front walk.

"Don't mess this up for me, you insolent child. If everything goes well, Straven has agreed to marry you and take on the burden of the thousands of coins you've cost me."

I gasped, not wanting to believe what he said. "You're marrying me off to the Magistrate? He's more than thirty years my senior."

"And you should be honored he is willing to marry someone not only as young as you but so worthless."

I wanted to say more, but my father turned and walked over to his awaiting carriage without another word, leaving me standing there, Well flaring in anger. I considered confronting him, but the bells throughout the city chimed the top of the hour and I was once again late. I took off at a run, pack bouncing on my back and sword thumping on my thigh with every step. I meant to wake up earlier, to stop to see Hajana before I left or at least leave a note for her with my maid, but now I didn't even have a moment to let my thoughts catch up to me. *Please, Hajana, forgive me for not explaining...*

When I got to the center of Altava, I was the last one to arrive.

"Ah, Emolin, I'm glad to see you finally arrived."

Just hearing the Magistrate's voice was enough to make me want to lash out at him. I clenched my toes in my soft boots, giving my anger a distraction as I approached.

"It took her long enough. We could've been halfway to Gathon if we didn't have to wait for her."

The Magistrate gave Aaron a look but said nothing. Aaron's voice reminded me I was given no say on who would be joining me on the journey and my Well tightened. I placed my pack in a pile with the others and glanced at everyone standing nearby, sighing in relief when Natalia gave me a reassuring smile. Ziden from training was also there along with two wagons closed in with wood each pulled by two horses. I had no experience with horses and knew none of the others did either.

"I asked Galeal to help with the horses. He will keep them safe and teach you all enough horsemanship skills that by the time of the battle you will be riding in and striking fear into the Parans' hearts."

I looked at the large beasts stamping impatiently, their nostrils flaring. The idea of getting near one of those things was enough to make me queasy, let alone the idea of riding one. I subconsciously took a step back and bumped into Natalia.

"Now's not the time to lose control, those two will eat you alive," Natalia whispered, motioning toward Aaron and Ziden messing around, getting told off halfheartedly by the Magistrate.

I took a deep breath and walked over to one of the horses. He had a dark brown coat with swirling white-spotted markings around his shoulders and hind legs.

"I wouldn't get too close to him if I were you. Sampson is known to have a wild temper."

As if to prove Galeal's point, Sampson reached out and nipped at Galeal. I jumped back and let out a small yelp.

"Now, Sampson, I told you biting is not the best way to make friends. You're going to be with us for a few weeks and I suggest you learn to behave," Galeal chided Sampson, and I had to hold back a laugh because it sounded like he was speaking to a small child.

Sampson snorted in response and stamped a hoof. I glanced over at Galeal, noticing the way he handled and cared for the horses. All the boys I interacted with daily wanted to do nothing more than fight and kill. It was refreshing to meet a male who was on the calmer side. Before Galeal could say anything else, Magistrate Magdra cleared his throat and we turned our attention to him

"There are several precautions you must take. The bandits have been more desperate this year for food and flesh. There have been more attacks than usual. The path I've laid out is the one with the least amount of attacks to date, and there are also safe spots to camp marked, but only if needed. Make sure you follow the map and keep your wits about you. Horses are known for sensing danger, but you mustn't rely solely on them."

Ziden and Aaron piped up, telling stories in gruesome detail of things the REDs came across on their raids. I reached up to play with the pendant around my neck to distract me, ignoring the stories and emotions building inside me.

The Magistrate looked directly at Ziden and Aaron as he spoke, making sure they were paying attention. "If you happen upon bandits, it's best to flee. We know they are best at fighting in close combat, and with there being only five of you, they have a far greater chance of winning than if a squad of REDs ambushed them.

"If you have no choice but to fight," the Magistrate continued, "your biggest asset will be Natalia's bow. The bandits have few archers, preferring hand to hand combat instead. Natalia can take out a majority of the bandits with her arrows."

"Just be sure to stay out of my way," Natalia said. "If you're in front of my target, I'm either going to shoot you or you'll have to kill the bastard on your own."

Natalia, having shown great proficiency with the bow several years before, took special lessons with Sojourn in archery. Out of all the students in the class, Natalia showed the greatest promise, and mixing archery with her Wind Aura was a deadly combination. Having her traveling with me helped ease a bit of the worry I was facing.

"You have a lot of ground to cover today, so load the rest of your things into the wagons. Natalia and Emolin will be in this wagon," the Magistrate gestured to the wagon being pulled by a tan horse with a black mane and Sampson, "Aaron, Ziden, and Galeal will be in the other. I don't need anyone getting distracted on the journey." The Magistrate glanced at Natalia but didn't elaborate any further. I made a mental note to bring it up with her when she and I had some time alone.

"The nights in the desert are cold and you're going to want to light a fire," the Magistrate said after we loaded our gear. "Don't do this unless it is necessary. Bandits are far more likely to attack if they see a fire. Instead, wrap up in the extra cloaks and the blankets provided if you have to stop.

"After you pass through Barrenhollow, you'll have another day's journey to Brifair. From there you'll make camp for the night at one of the caravan locations before reaching Honeyshell, then Gathon."

Natalia raised her hand, and the Magistrate motioned for her to speak.

"What happens when we get to Gathon?"

"Madame Helena LeDore is aware of the prophesy and there is a plan in place. I sent a messenger ahead a few days ago. She is expecting you and will explain the next leg of your journey once you get there. I was hoping Lord Mycroft could accompany you, but he had urgent business to attend to and will only join us for the battle."

We muttered in agreement and my Well tensed in apprehension. I looked at the others and the calm facade the four of them portrayed surprised me.

The Magistrate clapped. "The sun is about to rise, time for you head out."

We climbed into the front of our appointed wagons. "Make sure you stick together and look out for one another," the Magistrate said. "May your journey be short and uneventful."

The wagons lurched forward, and I had to grab ahold of the seat to prevent myself from falling to the floor. I glanced over at Natalia as she guided the horses and noticed she was gripping the reins rather tight. While neither of us had driven a wagon, I figured holding the reins so tight wouldn't do any good. I placed a hand on Natalia's and gave her a small smile. Natalia smiled back and relaxed her grip a little.

The horses plodded down the streets, their footsteps echoing off the walls of the building. There were many people in the streets preparing for the day's festivities. Shop owners were setting up small tables outside their shops and children were running around in their costumes, ready for the parade. A little girl dressed as Kysyn, Goddess of Peace, ran by, reminding me of the parades I was in as a child. I missed the innocence of my childhood more than ever.

Children chased after the wagons when they saw us, some trying to climb aboard only to have a parent or RED pull them off and scold them. I considered pulling on a cloak and pretending to be a child myself since there were children in Altava taller than me. Natalia seemed to know what I was thinking and nudged me, shaking her head before turning her attention back to the horses.

Whenever we passed a patrolling RED, they stopped and bowed to us. By their actions, I assumed they had been informed of the journey. Ziden and Aaron called a few of the REDs colorful words as we went by and gained more than a few chuckles and names of their own.

The two of them seemed to be in good spirits, at least for that moment. While I didn't understand how anyone could be happy about the situation, I was glad they weren't blaming everything on me.

We turned down another street and I could make out the gate in the distance. REDs lined the streets there, their red coats reminding me more of blood than the principles they protected. I refused to look at them, turning my attention solely to the wagon in front of us and the gate just beyond.

A few of the shopkeepers came out of their shops to watch, one even slipping into her shop before chasing after us to hand each wagon a bag of sweets. Natalia and I thanked her and popped the candies into our mouths, savoring the sweetness of ashberries.

"We need to go on journeys more often," Natalia said as she popped another sweet into her mouth.

I knew she was joking, but I wanted to yell at her for saying such a thing all the same. Everyone seemed to be enjoying their time, not caring about the dangers ahead. I knew they'd heard the stories of bandits as I did, like the girl found shoved among the rocks, her body naked and becoming food for several desert animals.

I'd shuttered, grateful I hadn't met the girl, and said a silent prayer for her family. The bandits took what they wanted, and what they wanted most was flesh. I didn't want to end like that, to be forced to do things with someone I didn't know, let alone love, only to be killed once my body was used.

The wagons slowed to a stop as we reached the gate and one of the RED sergeants stood on the lookout above the gate so we could see him.

"On behalf of the Royal Enforcement Division, I want to personally thank you for risking your lives to rid our lands of the heretics. We are forever in your debt."

It took everything I had not to jump out of the wagon as we

rolled out of the gate. I took one last look at the city and saw Hajana standing in the crowd gathered behind us, hands clenched and face red. I wanted to yell and tell her I wasn't turning against her. But doing so would endanger us both, so I turned back and blinked away the tears forming in my eyes.

---

*B*efore we were more than a few miles from Altava, voices from the front wagon drifted toward me. Arron and Ziden were talking about girls in the city and who they hoped to court once they got back. I couldn't make out much of what they were saying, but several curses were thrown before Aaron flew from the wagon and landed with an "oof" and a cloud of dust.

"And that's what you get for talking about my cousin that way."

Natalia and I suppressed giggles as Aaron brushed himself off and climbed back into the wagon. We went back to our rudely interrupted conversation only to have more curses thrown between the two before they fell from the wagon in a tangle of limbs. The horse nearest them squealed and reared as much as the harness would let her. The wagon lurched to the side, threatening to tip over before Galeal regained control.

"Behave, both of you. If one of these horses gets hurt you best believe the horse will ride up here and you will be pulling the wagon instead."

"Yea, like we would let a commoner boss us around," Aaron huffed.

"Settle down, stable boy, you would never understand the fun between two men," Ziden added.

"Well, get your ass in the wagon and have fun with yourself."

I blushed and pretended I hadn't heard what Galeal said, the two standing there not sure how to respond. Natalia chuckled and repeated Galeal's words to herself again, laughing even harder. The two glared at us, but said nothing and climbed back into their wagon.

I ignored Natalia's humor and focused on the landscape around me. I had been out in the desert before when training with Sojourn, but we had headed east toward the mountains instead of south, steering clear of areas where bandits were known to congregate.

While, at first, the desert south of Altava was very similar to the desert to the east, several differences appeared the farther south we went. To the east, many plants made their homes among the rocks, providing plenty of food and shelter for smaller rodents. In the south, it was barren. At first, I didn't mind the absence of plants aside from a few woody thickets and small patches of tall grasses, but as we progressed, the lack of plants turned into rock outcroppings. I imagined bandits hiding behind the rocks and I took the unofficial position of watching the shadows for movement while reminding myself we would most likely be safe during the day; it was the night I needed to worry about.

We didn't travel much longer before Galeal called back to us and said we were going to stop at the oasis ahead and let the horses rest. I hadn't noticed the oasis, being too lost in worries about the bandits, and was shocked when I looked up to the lush green trees surrounding a pool of shimmering water.

The wagons hadn't even completely stopped when Aaron and Ziden jumped off and ran into the pool. Galeal climbed down and stroked the horses hitched to his wagon, whispering something to them and leading them to the pool to drink.

"Liking what you see?" Natalia asked, handing me my waterskin to fill.

My cheeks warmed and I climbed down, hiding my face as much as I could. "I don't know what you're talking about."

"Uh-huh, okay," Natalia laughed, shaking her head as she walked away.

I turned to head to the pool and smacked into Galeal, spilling what was left in my waterskin down his shirt.

"Oh, I'm sorry. Are you okay?" He stared down at me, his warm, golden eyes searching my face.

"I'm okay, just didn't expect you to be there."

He bowed and moved on to the other two horses while I went to fill my waterskin. I looked back at him checking the horses' hooves for loose shoes or stuck stones, before turning away again and going to the pool.

The water was clearer than the river in Altava, though that wasn't saying much. I could see out to the center where brightly colored stones shimmered below the surface. Small fish darted along a few feet away, the purple stripes down their backs allowing me to follow their movements.

I was about to stand when a shadow passed over me, followed by a large splash soaking my hair and most of my robes. I looked up, about to yell at Aaron or Ziden, before calling out in surprise when I realized what happened. Sampson was whinnying and splashing in the water, having a grand time and not caring he'd just leaped over me.

"Are you okay?" Galeal asked as he rushed over to me. "I tried to hold on to him but he bolted when he noticed you by the pool."

"I-I think so."

"I swear, Sampson acts more like Aaron and Ziden than the graceful Klohave he is."

I watched Sampson for a few minutes, the way he almost seemed to be watching me while nipping at the other horses when they got too close to him. His coat was something I had never seen before, white spots swirling like leaves in the wind. There were stories of horses having beautiful coats but poor health. I turned to Galeal, concern filling me.

"I've never seen a horse with a coat like his. Is there something wrong with him?"

"No. On the contrary, he is one of the healthiest horses my father and I take care of. We speculate he must be a distant descendent of the now extinct horses in the northern part of the Lunen Kingdom. His coat is noted as one of the most distinct parts of the breed, along with their high spiritedness."

I watched Sampson playing in the water a while longer while Galeal went to check on the others. There seemed to be something different about Sampson. I couldn't name it, but he wasn't like other horses. He was more aware of his surroundings, but not in the normal 'flighty' way. He turned again to look at me and took a few steps in my direction before something distracted him and he went back to splashing in the pool.

I pulled the pendant out of my robes and absentmindedly fingered it while watching the sun shimmer on the water. I wasn't sure why, but the pendant seemed to help calm me, a warmth spreading from it and momentarily giving me enough clarity to work through my thoughts. *I wonder what Hajana is doing right now. I hope she's okay.*

"We should get going," Natalia called, startling me out of my thoughts. "There's still a lot of distance we need to cover."

Galeal nodded and led the horse nearest him over to the wagons to hitch them up. I met Natalia by the wagon she and I were riding in and climbed in before Galeal hitched the horses, not wanting to get in the way. Natalia climbed up and looked over at Galeal before looking back at me.

"He's single, you know. He might be a commoner, but he would make beautiful children."

"Stop it." I shoved her playfully and pulled my headscarf over my forehead.

I considered mentioning to Natalia what my father said before I left, but I already had too much on my mind and decided I would tell her later, once the two of us were alone.

Galeal continued hitching the horses until the only one left was Sampson snapping at the water around his legs. Galeal tried whistling for him several times before sighing and wading into the water.

Sampson danced away from Galeal a few times before finally letting him jump onto his back. Sampson bucked, trying to shake Galeal off, but calmed down enough to let Galeal guide him out of the water and dry him off before strapping him to the wagon.

"We'll continue until we reach another oasis," Galeal said as he climbed into his wagon. "The horses will need to stop as often as we can to get enough water and rest while the pools are still common."

The group agreed, being able to stop, stretch our legs, and refill our waterskins fairly often, sounding wonderful. Aaron grumbled about something, but the creaking of the wagons and the horses plodding along made his voice lost to the wind. Deciding I didn't care what he said and would enjoy the journey while it was still easy. Knowing there were going to be many hardships along the way, but for the moment, I wanted to relax.

I leaned against the back of the bench and pulled out the map the Magistrate had given me, curious how far we traveled. The oasis we had just left was ten miles south of Altava, a lot shorter than I originally thought. That meant we still had another thirty to forty miles of traveling before we reached the next city.

Looking up at the sun and realizing how late it was, I worried we would get stranded in the middle of the desert before we made it to Barrenhollow. I did the math in my head a few times to be sure before bringing it up to Natalia.

"There's nothing to worry about, Em. We left a little later than we hoped, but there's still plenty of sunlight left before we'll consider camping, and I'm sure Galeal is well aware of the distance to Barrenhollow."

I looked back at the sky, not trusting what Natalia said. The stories of bandits and what they'd done flooded my mind, and I fought back the images of women running for their lives, fearful of what would happen if bandits caught them.

Before my thoughts got too bad, Natalia pointed out a small hare bounding off the rocks, stopping now and then to groom itself. The hare didn't seem to care about the hawks circling overhead, hoping to make it their lunch.

CHAPTER TEN
EMOLIN

The shrill whinny of a horse woke me. I hadn't remembered falling asleep, but I wiped away a small pile of drool on the bench.

The sun bore down hotter than the morning and the sparkling water in the oasis we stopped at called to me. I contemplated wading in to cool off, but Sampson was already prancing through the water and I didn't want to risk him leaping over me again.

Climbing out of the wagon, I wandered over to one of the trees to sit in the shade. A gentle breeze rustled the palm leaves but thankfully wasn't strong enough to kick the sand into my eyes. I took a swig from my waterskin and watched Aaron and Ziden decide to spar since we were missing training.

"Alright, if you're able to take me down, I will buy you all the spirits you want for a month once we get back," Ziden goaded Aaron.

"Buy me spirits while we're on this journey too and you got a deal," Aaron called back.

"Fine. If you lose, you'll be doing my Mage duties for the next month."

"You're going to go broke with all the spirits I'll be chugging."

The two circled each other, looking for an opening. Ziden had the advantage, being a head taller than Aaron and much broader. Aaron still had a chance, though, being known for his speed and agility. While Sojourn didn't have us sparring often, when we did, nobody wanted to be paired with either of the two.

Ziden was the first to make a move, lunging for Aaron and swinging a left hook. Aaron dodged the swing easily. He dove to the ground, tumbling before planting his foot square in the middle of Ziden's back.

Ziden stumbled forward. He kept his footing and turned to wrap his arms around Aaron. Aaron already darted to the other side. When Aaron saw his chance, he landed a palmed strike to the side of Ziden's head. Ziden swayed, barely able to stay on his feet. Aaron gave a swift kick to the back of Ziden's knees and sent him sprawling into the water.

"You should never make a bet with a member of the Prinzi family," Aaron shouted as Ziden hauled himself out of the water.

Aaron beat his fists on his chest and started hollering.

"If you don't knock that off, I'll have to knock you out myself so you sleep the rest of the way," Galeal yelled as he tried to calm one of the mares spooked from the fight.

"I'm sick of you commoners trying to tell me what to do," Aaron said, rolling up his sleeves and moving toward Galeal.

Even though Aaron was well within his rights as a Mage to discipline Galeal for disrespecting him, Galeal held his ground and didn't move to protect himself when Aaron's hand glowed a deep gold and the rocks around him trembled.

"If you're planning on attacking me, I would like to remind you the horses will still need to be taken care of properly and all the responsibility will fall on you as my property will become yours," Galeal said, only moving to block the horse he was calming from harm.

Aaron lowered his hand, grumbling and turning back to Ziden.

"You hungry?"

I looked up to Natalia holding my lunch rations, a small parcel of meats and cheeses along with a small chunk of bread.

"Yea, thanks."

I grabbed the parcel and untied it while Natalia sat next to me, untying her own.

"Did you know you talk in your sleep?"

I stopped mid-bite, nearly choking on cured beef. "What did I say?"

"Nothing much, mainly muttering about marriage and treason, but nothing about Galeal if that's what you're asking."

I tried to recall my dreams, but everything escaped me, as always. Talking in my sleep was something I did as a child, but I thought I stopped years ago. The idea of having to sleep with the others and the chance of muttering embarrassing things was yet another thing to worry about.

"Your luck you'll mention wanting to have Galeal's babies," Natalia laughed and placed her hand on my shoulder. "Don't worry, though, you were talking so soft I had to lean right next to you to hear anything. If you fall asleep last or keep yourself bundled in your cloak, I don't think the others would hear you at all."

I sighed. "I hope you're right. The last thing I need are rumors about my feelings for a commoner spreading."

Natalia gave me another smile and got up. She wandered over to the horses grazing and I leaned back to watch the few clouds drift across the sky.

"Do you want to meet the horse you'll be learning to ride?" Galeal asked, startling me.

I dusted off the sand from the bits of cheese I dropped before wrapping it all back up and bringing it with me.

"You already have one picked out for me?" I asked as we walked, wondering how closely he was watching me to already have made a decision.

"I have, though I must admit the Magistrate had a large list of requirements for the horse you would ride. Since only two horses in Altava met those requirements and were trained in pulling wagons, the choice was rather easy."

Galeal held out a hand to lead me toward the chestnut mare he'd been calming earlier, and I hid my heated cheeks as best I could. Thankfully, he didn't seem to notice

Galeal whistled to the horse. "Come here, Ashbud."

Ashbud walked over, head held high and bits of grass hanging from her lips. I took a step back, not used to being so close to large animals, and Galeal put his hand on my lower back, giving me a gentle nudge toward the horse. A surge of warmth rose through my Well and it disappointed me when he pulled his hand back, realizing his transgression.

"Ashbud is a horse we use to break others. She has the calmest temperament and soothes just about any frightened horse. She is also swift on her feet and has a high level of stamina."

Galeal reached out a hand and stroked Ashbud's nose, causing her to nicker in content. Galeal stopped scratching Ashbud, and she looked at me, letting out a small sigh. I took a small step forward and reached out a hand to stroke her.

Ashbud's coat was warm from the sun and softer than most blankets I owned. I took a step closer to Ashbud to caress her head, letting her get to know my scent and allowing me to judge her character with my Well.

"She likes you," Galeal commented.

Before I could respond, Sampson trotted over, pushing Ashbud out of the way. I laughed in surprise and couldn't help but stroke his nose pressing into my palm. Galeal shook his head and muttered something under his breath, causing Sampson to whinny.

<hr>

After trying to spend more time with Ashbud, only to have Sampson refuse to let me pet her or any other horses, Ziden called out saying we should get going.

I climbed into the wagon and waited for Natalia to join me, hoping I could talk some things out with her. I watched Sampson prance in circles around Galeal as he tried to catch the beast.

Natalia climbed into the wagon and scooted next to me. "You know, you could ride with him instead. The Magistrate isn't here to tell us what to do anymore."

I continued watching Sampson and Galeal as I responded, "Why would I want to do that? I barely know him and you know it's severely frowned upon for a Mage to spend time with a commoner outside their family."

"Because he could make a good husband. He's a hard worker and comes from a respectable family. You could try to convince your father to approve of him, Galeal knows how to calculate profits and losses."

"No, I know Father wouldn't. He—" I paused, not ready to tell Natalia yet.

"He what?"

I played with the hem of my sleeve, not wanting to respond, but knowing I could trust her with my secrets.

"He promised my hand to the Magistrate."

"He did what?" Natalia shouted, catching the attention of the others.

She waved them off and leaned in closer, squeezing my hand in encouragement to continue.

"He told me before I left. It sounded like my father wanted me out sooner rather than later, and I'm worried I'll return to Altava and walk right into my wedding."

Natalia sat in silence for a few seconds before responding. "Well, if that's your father's plan, it sounds like you need a plan of your own. Galeal might not be the most desirable of options in terms of status or wealth, but he's sweet and caring and it's better than marrying a man who could almost be your grandfather."

I looked at Galeal and felt the same warmth from when he touched my lower back. It wasn't unheard of for someone of status to marry a commoner, but as a Mage and a female, the rules were a little more difficult. Still, Natalia was right. I needed a plan or Father would see to it I would be married to the Magistrate within a fortnight of returning home.

I sighed. "I want to get to know him a bit more. I certainly don't want to marry the Magistrate, but I don't want to spend the rest of my life with someone I don't connect with."

Natalia nodded. "Don't wait too long to make your decision, though, or life will decide for you."

Galeal walked over to finish tightening the straps on the horses for our wagon, and I swore he winked at me before walking away, but I wasn't sure. Sampson snorted in annoyance when Galeal went to grab him, not wanting to be trapped again, but he behaved enough and soon we moved along again.

For the next several miles, Natalia and I talked about a few things, but we mainly rode in silence as I watched the land around pass by. There were more and more rock outcrops, some large enough for a whole cart to hide behind. No matter how many times I told myself bandits wouldn't attack our party in broad daylight, I still had to force myself to look at and think about other things. By the time we stopped at another oasis an hour later, I was relieved to have something more than an endless sea of rocks to look at. I didn't even wait for Natalia to bring us to a full stop before hopping down and heading to the pool for a cool drink.

"Is everything okay?"

I splashed my face with water one last time before wiping my face with my sleeve. I sat back on my heels and squinted against the sun to look at Galeal. "Yea, I've heard one too many stories about the bandits, and my imagination got the best of me during that stretch."

"I'm glad to hear you're taking this more seriously than the other two." Galeal motioned to Aaron and Ziden lounging in the shade. "You don't have much to worry about, though, the bandits don't attack during the day, and if they tried, the horses would let us know far in advance."

"What about making it to Barrenhollow? We still have so far to go and it's already well past lunch."

I hadn't meant to bring up my worries with Galeal, but they all tumbled out before I could stop them.

"As long as we stick to our current path and continue at the speed we have been, we'll be there with close to an hour of light to spare, plenty of time to make sure the horses are comfortable and get ourselves a nice, hot meal."

While his words were meant to calm me, only more concerns were floating around when Galeal left to go speak to Natalia. A soft nose nuzzled my hand and I was surprised to find Ashbud staring at me.

"You certainly are a sweet girl."

She nickered in response and stamped her foot a few times before looking longingly at the water and back at me.

"Are you asking me to come to play with you?"

Ashbud nodded and made her way to the pool, turning back to look at me halfway and only continuing once she was satisfied I was following. I followed her to the edge of the water, the pool calling to me as the sun caused the horizon to ripple from the heat.

Figuring my robes would dry quickly in the sun, I slipped off my boots and sighed as the cool water lapped at my toes. I took a few steps in, watching the fish dart away when drops of water landed on my face. I wiped off the water and could've sworn that Ashbud was laughing at me.

"You think this is funny?"

Ashbud nodded her head.

"Let's see how much you like it, then."

I reached down, scooped up a handful of water, and tossed it at Ashbud, dark spots appearing on her brown coat. Ashbud shook her head, spraying me with the water from her mane resulting in a much more thorough soaking of my robes. I splashed her a few more times before Sampson trotted over, having freed himself from Galeal, and waded into the water, splashing me in the process.

I splashed him back and worried only for a moment what would happen with such a temperamental horse. His eyes sparkled and he ducked his head under the surface, bringing a huge wave of water. I huffed and was about to try and splash him again when Galeal called me.

"While you're in there, could you try and lead Sampson to me? I'm sure you've seen his antics and it's clear he likes you a lot more than me. We need to get those two dry before hitching them to the wagons."

"I can try."

I had no idea what was going to happen, but I figured I would give it a shot, the worst that could happen would watching Galeal chase after Sampson. I stumbled on a pile of sand as I realized Galeal had something to him. While there was no denying he was a commoner, he didn't have the same fear or desire for power others had when it came with being related to a Mage.

Lost in thought, I didn't realize Ashbud and Sampson followed me out of the water until I noticed Galeal smiling at me and holding out two rather large towels.

"We need to make sure they're completely dry before we leave, we don't need them developing sores."

I watched Galeal dry off Sampson and mimicked his movements, the way he caressed Sampson's leg as he sopped up all the water he could. It didn't take long before the two horses were drying off the rest of the way in the sun. I glanced over at Natalia, biting my bottom lip at her smirk. I was only helping dry the horses. Why did she have to insinuate things were going to happen? Sure, he was nice looking, but that didn't mean anything.

"Alright, the horses are dry, time to move on."

We all loaded into the wagons as Galeal hitched the last horse. I found my eyes continually drifting to Galeal and I fought to look elsewhere. When we finally moved on, I relaxed and ignored Natalia's teasing.

***

*R*esting in the shade before we left another oasis, I couldn't keep my mind off Galeal. Natalia gave me the idea of courting him, if only as a way to get out of marrying the Magistrate, and, along with her continuous teasing, I couldn't help but wonder if it were an actual option. I had been so caught up with training over the years I hadn't paid attention to those around me, but courting filled my mind. *Would Galeal make a good husband? He is gentle with the horses and doesn't have the same anger in him Father does.*

To distract me, I stared at the sun glittering on the water, my fingers absently playing with the pendant around my neck. Rocks littered the area, covering the road and sheltering the oasis from the desert. I didn't like not being able to see the surrounding area, worried bandits would sneak up on us. I glanced up as Galeal led Ashbud to the wagons.

"Alright, enough of this. You either need to talk with Galeal or stop staring at him. I refuse to have you ignore me because you're too busy with your thoughts." Natalia's voice was stern, but there was a smile playing at the corners of her mouth.

I turned away, ears burning from the heat rising from my neck and face. "I didn't realize how obvious it was."

"Em, a slave would've known what was going on." I cringed at the mention of slaves, but Natalia ignored my reaction. "I'm telling you, you need to talk with Galeal if you want anything to come of this. Otherwise, your father will give you to the Magistrate and he will trap you."

Natalia was the only one who knew of my desire to be a scholar, and she was right. The last thing I wanted was a man to trap me in Altava, alone for most of my life.

"Okay, I'll make it a point to talk to him."

"Oh, bug off!"

Natalia and I looked up at the shout, finding Aaron and Ziden ganging up on Galeal.

"Hey," Natalia called, getting up and walking over. "What's going on?"

"Aaron and Ziden want to go a different way than the one the Magistrate suggested."

"Well, yea," Ziden said, "if we take the path marked on the map, we'll be going way out of our way and will never make it to the city before most of the shops close."

I got up and joined the group, looking over Natalia's shoulder at the path they were referring to on the map. As much as I didn't want to admit it, the path the Magistrate suggested was far longer than the path Aaron and Ziden wanted to take.

Natalia spoke up. "If we take the path to the left, one, if not several, groups of bandits are sure to attack—"

"Oh, so you're scared," Aaron mocked. "And after the Magistrate praised your skills as an archer. You should be ashamed."

"Ha. No, I just don't feel like wasting time and arrows fighting when we could easily circumvent any of that by going the other way."

Aaron tucked his hands in his armpits and clucked while walking in circles and bobbing his head. Natalia clenched her fists, and I braced myself as her hair danced around her shoulders. Ziden took a few steps back, knowing better than to get on Natalia's dangerous side. The horses shied and Sampson snorted in disgust. Aaron continued his dance, either not noticing or not caring. Galeal moved to climb into his wagon but stopped when he noticed the sand swirling around Natalia, her body glowing light blue with Aura.

"Do you really want to play that game?"

Aaron looked up and he stopped mid cluck, eyes bulging. He held his hands up and backed away, tripping over a rock and curling himself into a ball. "Please don't hurt me!"

"Oh, get up."

Natalia calmed and shook her head. Aaron got up and went back over to Ziden, shaking his head.

"We need to agree on which way to take because we shouldn't split up," Natalia said after she calmed her Well.

"I say we take the fork on the left, it's a more direct route to Barrenhollow. The sooner we get there, the sooner I can get my first drink of many." Aaron rubbed his hands together in anticipation.

"It's not all about the spirits. Magistrate Magdra has us going down the path on the right, toward the sea, before working our way back inland for a reason," Natalia reminded him.

"Then that's the path I think we should—"

"You don't get a say in this. There's no reason the gods should've picked you over someone more competent," Ziden said, cutting me off. "The path on the left is faster and, if we come across any bandits, we'll protect you."

Aaron pulled out his sword and swung it a few times as if

trying to prove Ziden right. He ran through a drill, showing off until Galeal yelled at him for spooking Ashbud.

"Just because you can protect us doesn't mean we should purposely put ourselves in danger," Natalia pointed out.

"You're all just a bunch of babies. Ziden and I know REDs who have killed hundreds of bandits, and I'm sure you would rather spend the evening relaxing instead of struggling to find lodgings. If we take the way the Magistrate wants us to, we won't get to Barrenhollow until late, but if we go this way, we can get there well before nightfall."

While it was tempting to think of a warm meal and a soft bed without having to push ourselves as much, I still felt it was a better idea to take the long way. Before I had the chance to say so, Ziden and Aaron hopped into their wagon and took off, leaving Natalia, Galeal, and I with the other wagon.

"We need to catch up to them," Galeal yelled, jumping onto the wagon and grabbing the reins.

Natalia pushed me forward so I could sit next to Galeal while she climbed into the back of the wagon.

I stared at the other wagon, the cloud of dust gaining in size as the horses galloped away. I scrambled onto the bench next to Galeal and before I had the chance to take a seat, he was racing off. I wanted to scream, but I tried to stay as calm as I could and grabbed hold of the bench.

Galeal urged the horses into a gallop, the landscape blurring from the speed. I prayed I wouldn't fall out and braced myself against the frame of the wagon. We were gaining on the others, but I had no idea what we were going to do once we caught up.

"Here, take the reins." Galeal didn't wait for an answer and shoved the reins in my hands. "Pull us up to the other wagon and keep us steady."

"Are you going to jump?" I asked, failing to keep the fear from my voice.

"I'll be fine. Once I leap out, I want you to pull on the reins to slow the horses to a stop. I'll get control of the other horses and lead them back here."

I tried to speak again, but Galeal had already turned away. As scared as I was, I urged the horses on and pulled up to the left of the other wagon. The road ahead was narrowing, a large cluster of rocks blocking the road on both sides.

"We're not going to make it!"

"Yes, we will, just keep it steady."

I kept the horses as close to the other wagon as I dared, watching the rocks racing toward us. I was certain we were going to crash and before I could rein the horses in to prevent our death, Galeal leaped to the other wagon. I tugged hard on the reins and Natalia cried out in pain as she and the rest of our supplies slammed into the back of the bench. We stopped less than half a wagon length from the rocks, the horses having swerved to the right and leaving one of the wheels perched precariously on a rock.

I watched Galeal as he clung to the roof of the other wagon, his feet struggling to find purchase on the side, before managing to swing out of sight. The cloud of dust grew and vanished, Ziden on the ground and Aaron following. Galeal hopped down and checked the horses as soon as they stopped and seemed satisfied they were okay as he turned the wagon around and headed back to Natalia and me.

Galeal pulled the wagon to a stop and jumped out again to stroke the horses' necks and check on the other two as well.

"When we tell the Magistrate that you—" Aaron started.

"That I was worried about the safety of the horses and did everything in my power to keep them safe? You're lucky nothing bad happened. If something happened because of your foolishness, I—" Galeal didn't continue his sentence, instead staring at the two.

Aaron opened his mouth to respond when shouts of men

filled the air. I turned and gasped at the group of men riding toward us, bringing with them the fear only bandits could.

"Yes! Time for some action!" Ziden pulled out his sword and shrouded his body in a deep golden Aura from his Well.

Aaron stepped up to Ziden, sword brandished and glowing with his light blue Aura.

"Now look at what you bastards have done," Natalia shouted, turning to Galeal. "Stay back and do what you need to keep the horses safe. Just keep the wagons within range if we need to escape."

Galeal darted to the wagons and guided the horses so the two wagons were fully shielding them. Natalia grabbed her bow and quiver before scurrying up to the top of the wagon. I turned to watch the fast approaching group, wanting nothing more than to duck behind the wagons with the horses but knowing I needed to fight.

I unsheathed my sword and connected with my Well, thankful the weakness from the interactions with Fonir was no longer an issue. Focusing on the bandits, it was easy to tell there were sixteen of them, exuding confidence palpable even from a distance. The bandits' horses were foaming at the mouth from being pushed so hard.

The twang of Natalia's bow marked our cue to charge. Her arrow took out the bandit to the right of the leader, the body tumbling off its horse and proceeding to be trampled by the others. Ziden's Aura grew brighter and a large ridge of rocks rushed toward the oncoming bandits, halting their progress at the very least. Aaron followed up with a blast of water, knocking another bandit off his horse. The bandit's foot caught in the stirrup and his screams added to the cries of battle as he was dragged off by the very beast he had been in command of.

The bandit in the lead broke away from the rest, adjusting his course so he headed straight for me. A calm I only felt during training washed over me, the horse and rider slowing in my vision. The cries of more being fatally wounded faded into the background. I let go of everything except the approaching bandit.

An orb of light grew in my palm, visible only to me under the bright sunlight, wisps of my Aura swirling into a spherical mass. The man drew closer, the hunger visible in his eyes. When he was only a few heartbeats away, I hurled my orb of Light at his face and dove out of the way. The bandit's scream filled the air confirming I, at least, permanently blinded him. Not wanting to waste time, I darted off to the others.

A quick count revealed there were still five, no four, bandits left. Ziden took out another by impaling him on a pillar of rock, his shouts causing the others to falter in their charge.

"Turn back!" a man yelled. "They're not worth it."

The other three bandits turned tail and headed for the safety of the rocks. Natalia shot two arrows in quick succession, taking out two of them. I gathered Aura from the sun and hurled an orb of Light at one of the last fleeing bandits, hitting him square in the back and sending him sprawling. Aaron blasted a torrent of water, but the bandit slipped out of sight. I turned my focus to my breath, stilling the storm inside my Well, and walked over to Aaron and Ziden.

"See, I told you guys we could handle them," Ziden laughed, sheathing his sword. He turned around and nearly walked into Natalia's blade, the tip of my sword resting in the small of Aaron's back.

"Oh, we handled them alright and lost a good deal of time because of it. If either of you ever put us in that situation again or try anything as reckless as stealing a wagon, I'll make sure two of my arrows miss their marks and end up burying themselves deep within your spines."

Ziden held his hands up in defense. "Look, I just want to get this over with and head home. I didn't ask to be out here in the middle of the desert missing the festival. You can't blame me for desiring my bed."

"No, but I can blame you for being reckless and putting us all in danger."

Aaron sheathed his sword and raised his own hands in defense. "Come on, Ziden, just admit you were in the wrong. I know I was and I'm sorry." Aaron turned to me and bowed. "I am sorry for any inconvenience I may have caused."

Aaron gave a second bow, and I almost believed he was sincere until he burst out laughing. I turned to see Galeal coming out from behind the wagons. His jaw clenched as he stared at the bodies strewn around. Fifteen bandits killed in a matter of minutes, their blood pooling on the cracked ground. I sheathed my sword and turned away from the group, my small lunch adding to the gore across the landscape.

Galeal looked anywhere he could to avoid the carnage in front of him. "Since you two are the reason for all this," Galeal spread his arms, addressing Aaron and Ziden, "I'm tasking you with rounding up any horses in the area."

"But that'll—"

Ziden elbowed Aaron in the side, cutting him off. "Let's just get this over with."

Galeal gave Aaron and Ziden a few tips while I looked back at the bandits. Even though I was right in the eyes of the law, I couldn't help but feel sick and struggled against the second wave of nausea. I closed my eyes and focused on my breathing. *They were only bandits. It's fine.*

"Galeal is going to work on calming the horses and looking over the ones the other two bring back," Natalia started, startling me from my thoughts. "Let's try to plot out a new course and potentially a camp since we definitely can't stay here."

"Alright, I guess we should know what we're doing once they round up the other horses."

I turned to watch Aaron trying to sneak up on a grazing mare, only to have her dance out of his grasp when he lunged for her. I shook my head and laughed, more in despair at the situation than anything else. I hadn't even been gone a day, and I was already taking the lives of others, guilty or not.

I climbed into the wagon, grateful for the wooden roof giving me a break from the sun, and sat next to Natalia as she spread out a map on a crate of food.

"As long as we don't run into any more bandits, we can let those two chase horses for a couple of hours before we risk having to camp out here for the night."

I stared at the map, pulling out a more detailed map of the part of the desert we were in. I threw the map off to the side and placed my head in my hands, a wave of anger rushing over me for seemingly no reason. When I couldn't calm myself, I slammed my fists on the crate and gritted my teeth.

"Why couldn't they just follow the plan?" I didn't mean to raise my voice, but Natalia flinched at the volume in the enclosed space.

Natalia glanced out the back of the wagon at Ziden and sighed. "As he said before," she nodded toward Ziden, "he just wants to get back to Altava. I mean, I don't blame him..."

Natalia trailed off and I stared at her, realizing for the first time how she looked at him. She hadn't mentioned anything to me about liking Ziden. Then again, she and I weren't as close as we once were either.

"Are you sweet on him?"

"What? No!" Her face flushed and she turned away.

"Is that why the Magistrate looked at you this morning? How does he know about you?" I paused, waiting for her to answer when I realized why he knew. "Are you two looking to get married?"

Her face grew redder and I had to cover my mouth to stop from squealing too loud.

"Shh! This is why I didn't tell you sooner."

I scooted closer to her. "Why are you two getting married? You've never shown any interest in him."

Natalia played with a loose thread on her scarf. "It was a stupid thing." Her voice was low and I leaned even closer to hear her. "Ziden and his mother were struggling on the anniversary of his father's death. My mother sent me to deliver some baklava and when I got there, only Ziden was home. He and I shared some of my mother's dessert. Twenty minutes later, he and I were lying together on his bed, our bodies coming down from the high."

We sat in silence, the sound of Aaron and Ziden chasing the horses filling the void.

"Why are you going to get married if it was only one time? The gods don't fault us for having sex. As long as we're careful..." I trailed off as Natalia placed her hand over her stomach protectively.

"Are you pregnant?" My question was only slightly above a whisper, but in the small space between us, it was like a scream.

Natalia grabbed one of the blankets in the corner and wrapped it around her shoulders. "The healer confirmed it three days before we left."

"Then why are you even here? You should be at home resting. Does Ziden know?"

"I told him as soon as I suspected it. At first, he was in denial. I mean he's the oldest in our group, and he's not even eighteen. After we talked about it and he realized when it happened, he decided to look at our child as a gift from his father. The Magistrate threatened not to bless Ziden's and my union if I didn't go, talking about how much of an honor this was and how we would be disappointing our child if we refused."

The anger from before returned and I had yet another reason to detest a man I already hated. "I promise you once all this is over you'll never have to worry about the Magistrate again."

"What are you going to do?" Natalia's eyes searched mine and her face softened.

"I'm not sure, but I have to do something and I swear to you and your baby I will."

Natalia smiled and hugged me, her warm embrace helping calm my anger still stirring. "I guess we need to finish the plan. Though I doubt those two are anywhere near close to catching even a single horse," she said.

I looked back out at Aaron and Ziden, seeing Ziden in a different light. If Natalia loved him, then I would have to learn to tolerate him at least a little.

CHAPTER ELEVEN
HAJANA

The days after speaking with Emolin were like any other. Ruta woke us up by clanging pots together. We started our chores and did our best not to anger Master or Mistress Aldous. I didn't have any errands that permitted me to leave the estate so I couldn't speak with Emolin and see if she learned anything new. I couldn't wait until it was my turn to head to the market to purchase the produce for the day's meals.

Three days later, the morning of the festival, Ruta gave me a basket and list of things for the feast. When I arrived, children darted around dressed in costumes representing their gods, screaming and laughing. I had seen four other festivals before. Each year was the same, and my master would require an elaborate meal and a deep clean of their home. While the festival was something many looked forward to, it was the most hated day of the year for servants and slaves.

I struggled to make my way toward the market, many people mingling down side streets and alleys normally frequented only by slaves. I sighed and tried not to let myself get too upset by the number of times I was elbowed and stepped on. Someone mentioned the South Gate, and I had a bit of time before Ruta expected me back, so I decided to see why everyone was crowding the alleys.

The streets were so filled with people I got stopped two blocks away and had to turn back. *Why are the streets so crowded? Even during the festival, they have never been this bad.* I doubled back and rounded a corner just as two wagons were driving under the gate. Before I turned back, one of the people in the wagon turned around and Emolin's face stared back at me.

A man's voice rang above the crowd. "Slaughter those Paran bastards!"

Those around me cheered and I did the only thing I could do. Run.

I dodged children as I ran, tears blurring my vision. I wasn't sure where I was going, but I needed to get away. Angry shouts followed me and a few people called for the REDs, but I didn't care. It didn't matter. *How could she do this to me?* I ran until I found an empty alley and ducked inside. I leaned against the wall, trying to catch my breath while choking on tears. Emolin's face as she looked back at me filled my mind and I slammed my left fist on the building behind me in rage.

I cried out as my hand crunched against the stone. I pulled it close and examined the blood running down my wrist from the roughness of the wall. I tried to move my little finger but was met with sharp pain. Hands shaking, the pain becoming more intense with each passing second, I slid down the wall until I collapsed in a pile of rotting garbage. *It's fitting that I break my hand on the day Emolin betrays me.* A dry laugh passed my lips. *There's no way I can work with my hand broken. It's only a matter of hours before the master has someone take me out back and shoot me like a lame horse.*

"What's wrong?"

I jumped, throwing my hands up in front of me for protection before crying out again in pain.

"Hajana, what happened?"

I looked up, seeing the lord, his eyes warm and mouth turned to a slight frown.

"Please, just leave me alone."

Instead of leaving like I asked, the lord stepped around me and sat down in the pile of garbage next to me, hidden in the shadows. Horns and drums sounded in the distance, playing the beginning of the Klohaven anthem, signaling the start of the parade.

"Hajana, I want to help you—"

"Why? Why would anyone want to help me? You were at my master's the other night, planning the destruction of my people."

A fresh wave of sobs wracked my body, and I covered my mouth with my good hand to mask any cries the sounds of the parade didn't hide.

"Yes, you're right. I was there, and the meeting was about attacking the Parans."

I turned to scramble away from him, putting my weight on my broken hand, only for the pain to travel up my arm.

The lord touched my shoulder, more gentle than anyone had been to me in years, and gave me a light tug to get me to stay.

"Just because I was there doesn't mean I am with them. I know everything points to me being against the Parans, and I can't explain why I'm not, but I'm asking you to trust a stranger and let me help you."

I looked back up at him, not sure how to respond, the pain clouding my brain too much for me to think. "What do you mean?"

"Let's get you some help first. I promise I'll tell you when I can." He stood up and reached out a hand to help me, not even bothering to wipe the garbage off his pants.

I accepted his help, and he pulled me to my feet, careful of my hand. He scooped up my basket and led me down the alley, away from the festival.

"Where are we going?" My hand was hurting even worse,

which I didn't think was possible, and I needed something to help take my mind off it.

"We're going to one of the few places in the city you'll be safe."

"Flinders'?"

"Do you know of a safer place?"

"No..."

"Then that's where we're going."

"Lord My—"

"Please, it's Geoffraie," he cut me off, his abruptness startling me. "I'm sorry. I may have my father's name, but I am not my father."

"Geoffraie," I said, the Klohaven name feeling weird in my mouth, "how is Flinders going to help me? I know little about Wells, but I know Wind Aura can't heal people."

"It's not his Aura that will help you," Geoffraie said, checking that it was safe for me to cross into the next alley before we continued.

After a few more minutes, we finally arrived at Flinders', my jaw set, refusing to show how much pain I was in.

"Oh, Hajana, my dear, what happened to you?" Flinders asked when he opened the door and ushered Geoffraie and me inside.

The messenger boy who had been leading the cart was sitting at the table, scribbling on a piece of paper.

"Flinders," Geoffraie said, "can you get one of the jars I dropped off yesterday? Lodal, please run to the market and pick up the items on this list?"

Flinders and the boy headed off to do what Geoffraie asked. I took a seat at the table, not able to stand any longer, while Geoffraie grabbed Flinders' jug of water and a towel.

"May I see your hand?"

I nodded, too tired to fight. Geoffraie took my wrist and turned my hand in his. "I have seen grown men show more pain for a lesser wound. You have a great deal of strength."

"It's not like I've been given a choice."

"That doesn't negate the strength you have. Just because you didn't choose this life doesn't mean your strength is lesser than anyone else's."

I stared at Geoffraie, not understanding who he was. Here was a man, a lord, in a high position of power, not yet twenty, with a smile that could charm any woman alive. *He can have anything he wants. Why is he choosing to help the slaves?*

"Here we are," Flinders said, entering the room and setting a jar on the table.

"Thank you, Flinders," Geoffraie said before turning to me. "Now, this is going to hurt, but this healing salve will help set the bones and close the wounds. It will still be quite sore, but it will allow you to use your hand."

"You're going to use a healing salve on a slave? That costs nearly 500 gold pieces per jar."

Hurt rose in Geoffraie's eyes at my words. "I'm using a healing salve on you, Hajana, if you'll let me. You may be a slave, but that doesn't define who you are."

Silence hung in the air, the music from the festival and the ticking clock on Flinders mantel the only sounds. No one moved, waiting for me to speak.

"Alright, I'll accept the salve."

Geoffraie scooped a small amount of the salve out with two of his fingers, hand hovering above mine. "This is going to hurt. A lot."

"I'm ready."

The instant the salve touched my skin it was as if someone had poured a pot of boiling sugar on my hand. I tried to jerk back my hand, but Geoffraie held my wrist tight, rubbing the salve into my skin. I couldn't remember if I screamed, all I knew was the burning in my hand that didn't fade.

Then, it was gone. A dull throbbing replaced the burning. Geoffraie let go of my wrist and I examined the side of my hand.

The broken skin was knit back together, faint red lines replacing the scratches from the wall. I flexed my hand and winced at the tightness, but had full range of motion in all my fingers.

"I'm sorry it hurt so much—"

"No, please don't apologize, I should be thanking you more than anything else."

Geoffraie smiled and wiped his hands on a towel before giving the jar of salve back to Flinders.

"As I said, your hand will still be sore for a few days, but you'll be able to complete your daily tasks—"

A knock on the door interrupted Geoffraie and Flinders rushed to see who it was.

"Ah, Lodal, thank you for running to the market."

The boy bowed, handing me the basket and saying nothing. I looked up at the clock and realized how late it had gotten.

"I need to go!" I grabbed the basket and ran to the door, realizing I should've been back to my master's twenty minutes before.

"Hajana, wait. Let me take you. The Minister will be more likely to believe what I say."

"You've already done so much for me. I don't want you to get in trouble." I reached for the door when Geoffraie scoffed.

"I may not like having my father's name, but it still holds value in this city."

Geoffraie stood and opened the door, heading out to the streets without saying another word. I still wasn't sure if I could trust him, even though he had done so much already. However, being able to avoid punishment, especially as severe as the one I would get for making festival dinner late, was not something I could ignore. I followed Geoffraie into the streets, hoping I wasn't making a mistake.

CHAPTER TWELVE
EMOLIN

It took Ziden and Aaron far longer than it should've to catch the three horses that hadn't scattered after we killed the bandits. After an hour without success, Galeal unhitched Ashbud from the wagon, and she led the three horses to him.

Ziden and Aaron spent a few minutes complaining about how much time they could've saved if Galeal unhitched Ashbud sooner before they begrudgingly went to go check the bodies for anything of value. Galeal took his time checking the bandits' horses, making sure they were okay for traveling. Once Galeal determined the horses were okay, we continued down the new route. Natalia and I talked more about her pregnancy, but she took a nap for a decent part of the afternoon, leaving me to drive the wagon.

The last rays of sunlight cast long shadows as we approached Barrenhollow. The walls were sturdy but shorter and not as thick as the ones in Altava. The gate guard stopped us and asked for our papers and the letter from Magistrate Magdra.

"How long do you plan on staying in Barrenhollow?" the guard asked, checking our papers.

"Only for the night, sir," Galeal responded.

The guard nodded. "Too bad, Galeal, you'll miss the fall pastries at the bakers."

"Pa and I will come back in a few weeks, I will get some then."

"Only if the boys and I don't eat them all first!" The guard let out a full belly laugh before returning our papers and letting us through.

Barrenhollow was like Altava, the part closest to the main gate being saloons and merchants selling goods most caravans and travelers would need for their journeys. Further in were the bazaars, closed early for the festival, and lodgings. Galeal, being the only one of us who had ever been anywhere besides Altava, guided us through the streets to the inn the guard mentioned.

"Emolin, go in and get three rooms with meals for tonight and early tomorrow. Take Natalia with you. Hopefully, there are still a few rooms left. Aaron, you take Ziden and see if you can find an open shop to replenish our supplies before heading out in the morning. I'll take care of the horses."

Ziden and Aaron, too tired to argue about taking orders from a commoner, trudged off into the twilight to see if they could find anything. Natalia led the way inside and we walked over to a barkeep to ask about rooms.

"We only have two rooms left. You're lucky there are any left at all, it being the festival and all."

I wanted nothing more than to have a meal and go to sleep, I wasn't willing to spend long bartering, something my father would have punished me for. *The only way to make money is to cheat others out of theirs.* I shuddered at the memory and turned to the barkeep. "We both know the owner would want nothing more than to make some extra coin during the festival. I'm sure there's somewhere you can stick a cot for the night."

The barkeep rubbed his chin. "Show me."

I pulled out three gold coins and laid them on the counter, followed by a small collection of silver and copper coins. I didn't want to spend a fortune on the rooms, but I couldn't afford to insult the owner of the inn and have him send us away. With the festival, there were still many people in need of a room, and it wouldn't take long to find more patrons to pay good coin. Plus, I had the Magistrate's coin, so I didn't need to be as stingy.

"Alright, let me go talk to the owner and see what can be done."

The barkeep left, taking one of the coins with him, and entered a room behind the bar. Natalia and I stifled yawns as we waited for the barkeep to come back. Natalia took a seat on one of the empty stools and I let my gaze wander.

A large fire danced in the hearth, providing a warm glow to the rest of the room and the handful of patrons talking or eating supper. The room was filled with tables and chairs, most empty and waiting for festival goers to come in for their nightly ale. A small stage was tucked in the corner and a young man in bright, silk clothes sat on a stool, tuning his lute, still wearing face paint from the festivities. Two staircases in the corners of the room I assumed led to the rooms upstairs.

"What can I help you with?"

I turned to find a small girl, maybe twelve years of age, standing behind the counter.

"We're waiting to speak with the owner—"

"Yes, I know. The barkeep came and got me."

I stared at the girl, not sure how to respond.

"We need three rooms for the night, but we were told there were only two," Natalia spoke up, covering for my shock.

"You were told correctly; we've only got two rooms." The owner stood there, arms crossed, inviting us to barter.

"I'm sure you'd like to make some extra coin. Is there a small space large enough for a cot you can part with for the evening? I'm sure you were told we would be more than happy to pay," I countered, coming out of the shock that a young girl owned an inn.

The girl squinted at me and placed the coin the barkeep gave her on the counter. "This is enough for two rooms and meals for three, but if you want a third room, it's going to cost you."

I pulled out two more gold coins, not wanting to argue about the absurd amount we were being charged.

"This should be more than enough for three rooms and two meals for five."

The girl looked like she wanted to say more, but thought better of it and swiped the coins off the counter. "Thank you for your business. You'll have two rooms in the main building here and a third over in the barn out back in the loft." She placed two keys on the counter and walked away, telling the barkeep something as she passed.

"Since there are only two of you here, I'm assuming the rest of your group hasn't arrived. Why don't you take a seat and eat while waiting? Our entertainment for the night is one of the local favorites," the barkeep explained with a smile.

Natalia and I thanked him and grabbed a table near the fire, close enough to the bard to hear him sing. The barkeep brought over two bowls of stew and mugs of ale. We thanked him and dug into our meal, not considering the idea of waiting for the other three to arrive.

The stew was rich and full of flavor, large chunks of vegetables and meat coated in a delicious broth. The barkeep brought over a basket of bread and the crustiness sopped up the broth till it was dripping and sagging under the weight.

"Welcome all. On behalf of the owner, I would like to thank you for your patronage and hope you enjoy this evening's entertainment."

Those in the room applauded the bard as he broke into a merry melody about a princess and her pig. Galeal walked in and scanned the room before finding Natalia and me.

"I took the horses to the stable my father normally uses;

they're going to care for our four for the night and hold onto the other three until Pa or I come back for them."

The room was filling fast and a barmaid came over to give Galeal his meal, advising us to have the other members of our party go up to the bar for their supper. Galeal thanked the girl profusely before digging into his meal. The bard switched to a slower song and the locals joined in, providing an off-key accompaniment.

"I'm surprised Ziden and Aaron aren't back yet. Aaron was quite keen on cashing in on his winnings," Natalia pointed out, scanning the room for the two in case she hadn't seen them walk in.

"They could be a while still," Galeal said between bites of stew. "Finding any sort of supplies this late in the evening is a challenging task on a normal day, let alone on the day of the festival. Why don't you two head up to your room? I'll stay up and wait for them."

I was grateful Galeal was offering to stay up, too tired to finish my ale. "Here's their key. Unfortunately, they only had two rooms so you're going to be staying in the barn loft for the night."

"That doesn't surprise me. Many people travel to Barrenhollow and other smaller cities for the festivities. I like the fresh air, I'll have no problems in the barn. Now go, get some rest."

Natalia and I thanked him before asking a barmaid for directions to our room and heading upstairs.

The room was small, the bed taking up most of it, with two side tables and a small wardrobe against the wall. I was surprised to find a fully equipped water closet and suggested we wash off the day's travels before turning in. Natalia agreed and we slipped out of our clothes, letting the warm water soothe our muscles and whisk away any worries from the day. We had to drain the bath twice before the water stopped turning murky from the dust we'd collected during the day. I was honestly surprised how much dirt there was from one day's worth of travel.

After Natalia and I helped each other wash our hair and scrub our backs, we wrapped ourselves in fluffy towels and crawled under the covers, not bothering to dig into our packs for nightclothes. We snuggled, resting our foreheads together as we drifted off to sleep.

The next morning was a blur of activity. We gobbled down breakfast and set off, having slept in far too late. The horses seemed well-rested, and Galeal tipped the stable hand for taking such good care of our steeds. We left within the hour and continued on our next leg of the journey, not sure how long it would take us. We knew we were heading for Brifair, but other than that, there was little to know about the actual path the Magistrate laid out for us.

Galeal warned us that oasis pools would become far less frequent, but we could follow one of the smaller rivers to Brifair and would have plenty of clean water to drink. I was eager to continue traveling, even though my rear complained about having to sit on the hard bench for another full day of travel. A few other travelers left Barrenhollow the same time we did, but they urged us on ahead, having heard our reason for the journey and saying they would only slow us down. They thanked us profusely for the sacrifices we were making, and I adjusted my headscarf to hide my anger at the travelers for thanking me for traveling to remove an entire group of people from the land just because they followed a different god.

"Hey, you okay?" Natalia asked as we pulled away from the other wagons.

"Maybe? I don't know."

"Listen, Em. I know you care for the Parans, but you have to admit the things they've done are terrible. They may not be as bad as the bandits, but they're still horrible people."

"We weren't there when it happened, though."

"Were you there when the bandits raided that caravan of supplies meant for the sick children in the mining town?"

"No—"

"Then how do we know they did it? It's the same with the Parans. We hear stories about what they've done, stories so atrocious no one could make them up. If you believe the bandit stories, you need to believe the others too."

"Just because they have different beliefs than us doesn't mean they're bad."

"I know you're fond of that one slave, but you need to see she's been playing you. She has seen your caring heart and decided you're someone who might help her get free so she can warn her people."

I turned away from Natalia and stared at the unique rock formations, wondering how they got there.

"I didn't mean to upset you, but you have to realize you're far too nice of a person and people will take advantage of that."

Not wanting to hear any more about her opinions of the Parans, I changed the subject. "So, Ziden obviously can do some things right." I motioned to Natalia's stomach, making her blush. "Have you two talked about what you're going to do when you get back?"

"What do you mean?" She tucked a piece of hair into her scarf and kept her eyes trained on the wagon in front of us.

"You know and I know the responsibilities we have as Mages. Yes, you'll be able to take some time off after the baby is born, but you'll eventually have to fulfill your quota of battles, maybe move to another city. How are you two going to handle a child and both having to work in dangerous positions protecting the country?"

"Ziden's mother offered to move with us to take care of the

baby wherever they send us. She has been lonely since her husband died and Ziden worries about her."

I remembered that day all too well. The healer had to stay with Ziden's mother for several days to care for the self-inflicted stab wound and make sure she tried nothing again. Ziden still went to training, but he was distant for several weeks until Sojourn beat some sense into him.

"I'm glad she'll have someone to take care of."

Natalia nodded and was about to say something when Aaron leaped from his wagon and ran west.

"Bandits, incoming!"

Natalia and I turned to see a small dust cloud racing toward us. Natalia thrust the reigns into my hand and reached into the back of the wagon for her bow.

"Keep the wagon at a steady pace and try to avoid as many rocks as you can!"

I kept my eyes trained on the path, keeping pace with Galeal's wagon as Natalia climbed on top the roof and Ziden jumped out to join Aaron on the ground. I risked a glance at the bandits and could just make out the group, still too far to count, but knowing there were less than the group the day before.

The wagon hit a small rock and Natalia cried out. "I said to keep it steady!"

I turned my attention back to the path, guiding the horses around any rougher spots while trying not to swerve. Natalia's bow twanged and the first cry in pain came from the enemy. The ground shook as Ziden moved the earth in large cracks toward the bandits, throwing at least two off their horses by the number of screams.

"How many are left?" I called out to Natalia

"Aaron just took out a fourth, so maybe three?" Her bow twanged again. "Make that two."

While my heart raced from the adrenaline that came from one's life being threatened, I was surprised at how easy it was for us to take out the bandits, Mages or not. The ground rumbled again and Natalia's bow twanged once more before cheers erupted from the three. Galeal and I slowed the wagons while Natalia jumped down and the two jogged over to us.

"That was too easy," Aaron said when he caught up, panting slightly but beaming all the same.

I turned to say something to Natalia but instead saw her and Ziden sharing a private moment.

I turned my attention away from the two and climbed down to check on Sampson and Ashbud. Both horses were breathing a little heavy but otherwise seemed fine. Ashbud pressed her nose into my hand and Sampson almost seemed to smile as he looked at me.

"Seems like Sampson knows he helped us win another battle," Galeal said as he approached.

"You think that's what it is? I thought he was just constipated."

Galeal laughed and Sampson nipped at me, snorting in disgust when I managed to pull my hand away in time.

I turned back to Galeal and noticed a serious look on his face.

"What's wrong?"

"Bandits are common on these paths, but it's rare for the same group of travelers to be attacked twice, especially after the news of bandits being successfully defeated by a group of traveling Mages reach the others."

"Do you think they're targeting us?" I asked, heart racing at the thought.

"I can't say for sure, but I think it would be best if we keep a constant lookout for more. If you can keep watch to the west, I'll have Ziden watch the east while Aaron watches the north from your wagon. I'll watch the south."

I nodded, not sure what else to say. Galeal called for the others to join us and they grabbed their waterskins, taking long pulls while Galeal explained his new proposition to the group.

"How far are we from the river? I need to fill my waterskin, and I would like to wash the death off me," I asked.

Galeal examined the landscape for a few moments before answering. "About another hour's ride if we don't have to stop."

"Then we should head out," I said, climbing back into the wagon.

The rest of the group agreed and Aaron grabbed his pack from the back of the first wagon before hopping into the back of ours as the wagons rolled off.

I kept my eyes focused on my right, watching the west for signs of travelers. There wasn't much to look at besides countless rocks, and I soon discovered the amount of concentration it took for me to keep my attention on the world around me. My mind wandered and I found myself wondering about the stones again.

"Nat, do you know how the stones got here?" I asked, hoping her father told her something from one of his many scholarly books.

"While I'm not certain about these stones, I know there are many others that have been deposited during great floods or sprung up during earthquakes. Why?"

I stared at the rocks more, noticing a distinct pattern to them. "These rocks just seem too uniform to have been made by nature."

"Not necessarily," Aaron piped up. "The world is full of patterns. Take flowers, for example, they all grow with their petals in the same formation unless they've been damaged."

"I guess that's true..."

"I know there's a name for it. My father is part of a group of Mages that are trying to understand the patterns of the world."

"Your father's a scholar too?" I asked in surprise, turning to Aaron.

"Yea, he convinced the Sages his talents would better serve the country and the King by learning more about the world than out fighting."

I hadn't considered being able to use my position as a Mage to gain the path of knowledge I desired. Father seemed insistent on getting rid of me, having already married me off to the Magistrate in his mind. If I could get out of the marriage, I could try to become a scholar and not have to worry about killing people, guilty or not.

"Was there anything special your father did to convince the Sages to let him become a scholar?"

"I'm not sure. Why? Don't you like being in the middle of all the action?"

"Not particularly. I don't enjoy taking the lives of others, not even spiders or snakes that find their way into my rooms."

Aaron laughed. "I knew you were different, Emolin, but I didn't realize how crazy you were."

Natalia picked up a stone that bounced in by our feet and chucked it back at Aaron, hitting him square in the head without even looking.

"Hey! What was that for?"

"For being a *lubberwort*."

Aaron opened his mouth to say something but shrugged and turned his attention back to the north. I turned back to the west and watched the clusters of rocks pass by once again, seeing the occasional lizard or hare scurrying about in search of food.

Eventually, we reached the river, the horses eager to stop to drink and cool off in the slow-moving water. Natalia and I filled our waterskins and splashed cold water on our faces, drenching our scarves in the cool water to provide a little extra relief from the heat.

"We'll be able to follow the river for the rest of the day's journey," Galeal explained as he and Aaron passed out lunch. "The sun has hit its highest point for the day, so we should be able to stay in the shade."

We let out a cheer, but Galeal held up his hands. "We now have to worry more about the bandits attacking from the east.

They not only have the trees and river to hide their approach, but the sun casting long shadows, making it that much harder to pick them out among the dense foliage."

I squinted at the other side of the river and realized Galeal was right.

"Do you want me to help watch the east, then?" Natalia asked.

Galeal nodded and went into more explanation, and I realized how much the dynamic of the group changed since we left a day ago. Sure, Aaron and Ziden still didn't enjoy being told what to do by Galeal, but they more readily listened, and I found myself not questioning his knowledge as much either.

"We'll rest here for another ten minutes before moving on. The horses deserve a nice rest."

We all agreed and enjoyed lounging in the shade. Ziden and Natalia sat under a tree together, having a conversation of their own. Aaron was showing Galeal his sword and how to use it, I assumed for protection. I wandered over to a tree by the water to watch the fish in the river, wanting to relax and not worry about the potential attacks we'd face.

Sampson wandered over and huffed at me, wisps of hair blowing about my face.

"What's wrong?" I asked as I stroked his nose.

Sampson huffed again, closing his eyes in what seemed to be content as I scratched between his eyes.

"You seem to have a way with horses," Galeal said as he approached. "May I sit?"

I scooted over some and continued to give Sampson my attention.

"He keeps following me around and I'm not sure why."

"Maybe it's because he thinks you're beautiful."

I was about to laugh when I realized what Galeal meant. I turned to look at him, his eyes searching my face. His eyelids fluttered, his long, blond eyelashes glinting in the sun. I leaned in closer to him without realizing it, my shoulder brushing against his.

"Emolin, I know we just met and I'm only a commoner, but..."

"But what?"

"I have grown to find you charming over the past day's travel. I've never really been good at showing emotions, but I was wondering if you would consider the idea of courting when we get back to Altava? I'm not sure what your father would think, but—"

"I don't care about my father," I said, cutting him off.

He smiled and we sat and talked for quite a bit, getting to know each other a little better until Aaron called out and mentioned we needed to get going. Galeal stood, holding out a hand for me, and I helped him get the horses hitched to the wagon, learning a bit about how bridals worked and making sure the straps were pulled tight.

Once everything was ready, we climbed into our wagons and continued, keeping a more vigilant eye on the east for bandits.

CHAPTER THIRTEEN
HAJANA

When Geoffraie and I arrived back at Master Aldous' estate, my mistress stormed out, ready to berate me. One of the maids who made it her goal to get as many slaves in trouble as possible smirked at me from the window.

"Ha-Jana, where have you been? Dinner is going to be late because of you and my party is now ruined—"

"Madame," Geoffraie started, cutting my mistress off, "please, let me explain."

My mistress looked up at Geoffraie, seeming to notice him for the first time and smiled. "Oh, Lord Mycroft, forgive my rudeness. How are you?"

"Minister Aldous allowed me to borrow his slave," Geoffraie continued, ignoring my mistress' pleasantries. "I had such an enjoyable time with her a few nights ago your husband was more than happy for me to borrow her to help celebrate the festival."

"I see," my mistress said, the smile disappearing from her lips. "If my husband knew you were borrowing her, then I'm sure he has a plan for entertaining our guests during the delay of dinner. Would you like to come in for some coffee?"

"That sounds wonderful, thank you."

Geoffraie and my mistress headed inside, the maid who told on me long gone. I ran around to the kitchen and greeted Ruta, placing my basket of produce on a table for her to inspect everything I brought back.

"Good, you were able to get everything. With the festival, it can be difficult to find fresh, ripe ashberries."

Ruta pulled everything out and had me put the root vegetables away in the cellar before sending me off.

I spent the rest of the day working on my chores and avoiding the master and mistress. There was still a lot of work for the slaves and other servants to do even though everyone else had the day off for the festival.

That night, Emolin's face appeared every time I closed my eyes, the way she looked as her wagon rolled away from the city. The last time I spoke with her, she hugged me and said she'd try to figure things out then she left on a journey that would end in the slaughter of my people. I thought I knew Emolin, and she ended up being like all the other Mages and aristocrats in Altava.

I pulled my rough blanket over my head and rubbed the fabric on my face, anything to get my mind to focus on something other than Emolin's betrayal. I hummed the tune my mother used to sing to me when I was upset. It used to help me forget about a scraped knee or a storm raging outside. Now, I was hoping it would help a broken heart.

This life is hard, my child,
The tiger hawk knows this well
But there are always good things
For those who choose to rebel.

The next morning, my tears crusted my eyes shut. I had fallen asleep humming my mother's song to myself, trying to rebel against the sadness in my heart. Though I got some sleep, I didn't feel any better than the day before.

I headed down to the kitchen with the other slaves, Ruta giving us our breakfast of broth and stale bread before assigning our daily chores. I wasn't sure why, but the mistress preferred having her slaves rotate some of their chores. It gave me some variety in my daily life, but I never knew when I was going to get a job I dreaded.

"Hajana, you're going to do the wash this morning before weeding the gardens this afternoon."

Laundry wasn't my favorite chore, but it was better than having to scrub chamber pots.

I headed for the butlers' pantry where the maids kept the soiled clothes. There wasn't much, but there was a foul smell coming from the pile. Scooping up the basket and trying my best not to take in breaths through my nose, I rushed outside to the washtub. I took in a deep breath of clean air, stretching and massaging my hand, and pumped the water into the tub so the runes would have time to heat the water while I grabbed the soap.

I ducked back into the butlers' pantry and opened the cupboard where the maids kept the soap.

"Ha-Jana!"

I jumped at the voice and the box slipped out of my hand, scattering grated soap all over the floor. A hand slapped me across the cheek and knocked me to the floor as I turned, my left hand reaching out to stop my fall only to send a sharp pain shooting up my wrist and arm.

"How dare you show up with that man yesterday! Not only did the mistress yell at me, but she also docked my wages for making a fool of her in front of a lord!" The maid from the day before towered over me, hands balled into fists.

I considered lashing out at the maid myself, but I didn't get the chance.

"Hajana, why are you not doing your chores? Get out there and stop slacking," Ruta said, causing the maid to jump.

I scrambled off the floor, grabbing the box of soap and scurrying out of the pantry.

"You. Clean up this mess and get back to your duties."

I smiled to myself as Ruta yelled at the maid. It wasn't often, but now and then Para would allow me a slight break from the torture of my daily life.

Back outside, the water in the tub was steaming. I scooped out some soap in my hand to dump into the water and swished it around until suds covered the surface. I dumped the basket of clothes into the tub, thankful the floral scent of the bubbles helped mask the smell.

After scrubbing several shirts, I discovered the source of the stench. Pulling out a pair of my master's pants, I found a thick, greasy, yellowish stain covering the back. I fought the urge to get sick and went back to scrubbing the pants, pulling out the plug in the tub to drain the water so the other clothes wouldn't get ruined before I finally got rid of the stain. I wrung out the pants, making sure there was no visible residue. I stood and hung them to dry with the other clean clothes, taking the moment to stretch my back.

The crunch of wheels on the walk caught my attention, and I turned to see a barred wagon pulling up. The black horses stared at me, nickering in laughter. My breath caught and memories I tried to forget screamed at me. The chaffing of the manacles and rough wood.

I tried not to look at the faces as the wagon passed, mostly young girls under sixteen but a few young men as well. There were too many slaves in the past that ended up dead at my feet. I wasn't going to let myself get attached to another person again, not after what happened with Emolin.

I turned my focus back to the tub, ignoring the occasional sobs of the girls being paraded into my master's house so he could choose which ones to buy. I had witnessed the scene many times in my years of slavery, and most of those purchased would either be sold, traded, or dead by the end of the week.

While most deaths of slaves were labeled as sickness or accident, many were either self-inflicted or caused by too severe a beating, something I had become accustomed to. Those slaves were considered lucky, gone before they were broken or too scared to do anything to bring an end to the misery of life. Most of the time, I disagreed with that idea, but once in a while, the thought of ending the misery thrust upon me was tempting. I never acted on it, but the thoughts would slip in and linger far too long.

The rest of the morning both sped by and dragged on, two more baskets of laundry brought out by maids for me to wash and hang to dry. When the bells rang, signaling lunch, I headed to the garden as we always did, not knowing whether to be relieved or upset. I told myself I wouldn't look at the new slaves Master Aldous picked unless I was forced to. If any of them made it past a week, I would get to know them then.

I stood in a row with the rest of the slaves, head bent against the sun as the mistress led in a handful of new girls.

"As you have probably heard, we acquired some new help for around the house. Seeing as we are heading into winter and have unfortunately lost several girls to the Serf Pox, I hope you will be thankful for this gift of extra help."

We gave half-hearted thanks in response, not wanting to be accused of being disrespectful. The mistress went on, explaining how much the new help cost and how we would be absorbing the cost and wouldn't be able to get new shawls for the winter.

Standing there, someone seemed to be staring at me. I ignored the feeling as long as I could before I risked a glance.

I hid my reaction behind a cough as I stared at Dalila. I hadn't seen her in three years or longer and thought she died in the destruction of our village, yet there she was. While I hadn't been paying much attention to the mistress before, everything disappeared into the background. I struggled to keep my excitement contained as the mistress finished with her speech and dismissed us to lunch, leading the new slaves into the kitchen where Ruta would assign duties and have one of the maids show everyone around.

I grabbed a small parcel from a tray on the kitchen windowsill and gnawed on a small slice of stale meat pie. Choking my lunch down, I grabbed a bucket and filled it from the hand pump to water the plants, wondering how Dalila survived the attack. I probably wouldn't get a chance to ask her for another day or two, but just the knowledge she was alive was enough to get me through the pain Emolin caused.

My mind drifted to all the things we would catch up on, and I jumped when someone came up behind me.

"The mistress sent me out here to work in the garden with you."

I turned and nearly knocked Dalila over with my hug. I knew I risked both of us getting in severe trouble by showing affection toward another slave, but I didn't care. I finally had my friend back and that's what mattered.

Once I eventually let her go, I handed her a basket. "We need to get working or the mistress will be sure this is the last time we see each other."

Dalila went to work on a bed near mine and we sat in silence for a while, making sure no one had seen us. It wasn't so much the punishment we were scared of, but how much the master would enjoy us. I didn't want to ask her how many girls she knew pushed too far. I'd watched far too many take their last breath by their own hands or the hands of their masters.

Dalila and I moved from bed to bed, staying quiet so as not to get in trouble, watching as a maid came out to show a new slave where the water pump was. Dalila kept looking over to me, seeming like she wanted to talk, but knowing better.

Eventually, Ruta called out to us. "Once you're done with the gardens, I need some help with dinner."

I told her we would be there soon and smiled at Dalila. While I was still a slave, alive by only the whim of my master, at least I had someone to walk the journey with me.

———

It didn't take long for Dalila and me to finish tidying the rest of the garden beds. The two of us working together finished the job far faster than if I had been working alone. I showed her where to put the tools and we headed into the kitchen to help Ruta.

"Go peel the potatoes. I need at least twenty large ones."

Ruta handed me two paring knives and shooed us into the small cellar where most of the vegetables were stored. I never liked being in the cellar, especially after being locked down there for nearly three days. Having Dalila with me made everything a little easier, though.

I grabbed a small lamp from the table and lit it before leading the way down the short flight of stairs to the hard-packed clay floor. Even though the sun was shining outside, the cellar was much cooler and a chill ran up my spine. I hung the lantern from a hook in the ceiling, lighting the small room and ignoring the door hidden in the shadows.

There were two stools in the corner of the room, and I dragged them over to the large bag of spuds, many vines poking their way out of the sack.

"This shouldn't take us too long. What will take the longest is finding enough good potatoes this late in the season."

I reached my hand into the sack and prayed I wouldn't grab a hold of a squishy one. "The trick is to make sure you avoid the bubbling ones, otherwise this room will reek of a smell worse than horse manure."

Dalila's eyes grew wide and she leaned back as I stopped rummaging and pulled a potato out of the bag. She let out a sigh and reached in for a potato. We sat in silence while peeling, aside from the occasional question from Dalila.

"What happened after… you know?" Dalila's sudden question pulled me out of my thoughts and I took a few seconds before responding.

"I'm sure it was the same as you. They came in and found us hiding in the house. My Pa tried to protect us, he…" I trailed off, not wanting to relive those memories again. "After I was pulled out of the house, I was thrown into a wagon with a lot of other girls. A few of them seemed vaguely familiar, but most were strangers."

Dalila nodded, the sadness in her eyes telling me the horrors I suffered were shared between us.

"The wagon stopped at many cities, girls being taken out and others returning. By the time the wagon arrived here in Altava, there was one other girl left from my original group, the other having died from some sort of sickness during the journey."

Silence hung in the air, neither Dalila nor I knowing what to say. Back in our village, the two of us were rarely seen apart, and now there was a palpable awkwardness between us.

"What about you?" I asked after several minutes. "Where were you taken?"

"I ended up in a city south of here, closer to our village. The number of times I tried to run…" She shuttered, her eyes closing as she took in a deep breath. "It was too tempting at first, the idea of there being someone there left. Something to return to. Longing for normalcy, in a way. After a few months of severe beatings, being locked in closets, and coming close to death when falling into a frozen river, I eventually gave up and was there until my master tired of me and sold me back to the slavers the next time they came to town."

The silence filled the room again, aside from the sound of peels falling into the pile.

"Ra?" Dalila piped up again.

"Hmm?" I didn't look up, not wanting the knife to slip.

"Do you think we'll ever…"

I set my peeled potato in the basket with the others and looked up at Dalila. She looked so much smaller than I remembered, her hands twisting in her lap, eyes darting around the room. Seeing her so scared, the fear in her eyes triggered memories of my first few nights after capture. When the men weren't using us for fun or handing out a pitiful amount of rations to keep us alive, we spent most of the journey in the wagon, chained and crammed in with so many other girls there was barely any room to sit.

Many of the girls cried, some quietly, others wailing into the woods until our captors dragged them out of the cage and beaten. The captors left them for dead after repetitive beatings, if the girls didn't die first. I tried to block out the sounds as best I could, but nothing could completely muffle them. One time when the captors pulled out a girl to service them, another slipped out and took off. The men chased after her, and it seemed like she might get away when the man leading the group used his Aura and struck the girl with a bolt of lightning. It was then that any idea of freedom, at least freedom I gained on my own, fled.

"I pray to the gods and hope with all my might that one day we will be," I eventually responded.

"Hoping and having it happen are two different things…"

Before we could talk anymore, footsteps crossing the kitchen above caught our attention. "Are you done with peeling the potatoes yet? I need them for supper or everything will be late and you best believe I will not be taking the brunt of the punishment."

"Just one more," I called, grabbing the potato sitting in Dalila's lap.

I quickly finished the spud and tossed it into the basket with the others. I kicked the stools into the corner and grabbed the lamp from the hook on the ceiling.

"I apologize for taking so long. There aren't many good potatoes left."

Ruta said nothing and held out her hand for the basket. She sifted through and nodded approvingly. "These will do nicely. Since you took so long I had to send another girl off to fetch the wash. That leaves preparing the guest room for you."

I hid my disgust at having to not only dust the room, but make sure the maids properly changed the mattress and beat the rug, while also looking in the corners for bugs, feces, and whatever else hiding in there. I thanked Ruta and led Dalila through the maze of halls.

"Is she always that kind?"

"Who? Ruta? She is probably the nicest person I've ever met here."

"Then why are you so timid around her?"

I stopped and turned to Dalila, not sure how to respond. "You're a slave, you know why. If I were anything but respectful to her, word would reach the master and he would be sure to take advantage of my discretion."

"If she's your friend, though, or at least someone who cares about you, why doesn't she leave the easier tasks for you?"

"Friendship doesn't mean anything when you're a slave. If she were to show a pattern of niceness toward me, it would mean we could both lose our jobs." I turned back and continued down the path, not trusting the control of my emotions.

"That's not true and you know it."

Not caring if someone could walk through the passageway and

see Dalila and I arguing, I spun on her. "It is true and I do know it because all the friends I've made since getting captured have died, a rare few being sold to another master. The other 'friends' I had turned their backs on me as soon as the opportunity introduced itself. I'm bracing myself for the moment you're taken from me too and I am once again left alone in this world."

I turned away again to continue to the guest room, partly to hide my tears and partly to avoid seeing the pain I was sure was crossing Dalila's face.

Dalila placed a hand on my shoulder and whirled me around to face her. "Do you even hear yourself, Ra? This is not the girl I knew back in our village."

"No, it's not. That girl you knew died that day along with her family."

I hurried off, not caring to look behind to see if Dalila was following me or not. She brought up far too many difficult topics, too many for me to push away, and I wouldn't have a chance to talk myself through them, to remind myself it was all in the past and the present was what mattered, for another few hours at least. I only knew how to distract myself and calm my mind when I was alone. I just had to toughen up until then.

I swallowed the lump in my throat, pushed open the door to the guest room, and proceeded to start with checking the mattress. The door to the passageway opened again and a small part of me relaxed knowing Dalila wouldn't get in trouble for wandering around instead of getting her work done.

Dalila came over to me and worked on checking the wardrobe and desk in the corner for any hidden surprises. I glanced up at her and was grateful and more than a little surprised she didn't seem hurt by my words. I didn't want to lose her friendship so soon, but it seemed she hadn't been treated the same as I had by her past masters. She still held that spark of hope. *She'll learn soon enough...*

CHAPTER FOURTEEN
EMOLIN

There were no more bandit attacks and we made it to Brifair without any issues. The guards at the gate were similar to the ones from Barrenhollow and they guided us to lodgings with a stable big enough to house our two wagons. Natalia and I were sent out to find more supplies while Aaron and Ziden were tasked with getting the rooms.

After searching the streets for the better part of ten minutes, there being thankfully few crowds, we finally found a RED and asked them for directions. We were pointed to a shop on the other side of the city, the only one open late into the evening. We found the shop, a stone building with a bright, cheerful sign, and a large assortment of things displayed in the window. The bell above the door tinkled and we were greeted by a kind, portly man.

"How may I help you fine ladies, this evening?" he asked, his accent heavy, similar to those that came from the eastern part of the Lunen Kingdom.

"We are looking to stock up on provisions for the next leg of our journey. We're heading for Honeyshell and will need to make camp for a night," I explained.

The man nodded and rattled off different things we would need, a boy pulling them from different parts of the store and placing them on the counter. Some of the things mentioned, such as the rattlesnake pipe, weren't necessarily something we needed, but the man made Natalia and I laugh and we decided to purchase it anyway to help him with his business.

"Would you like me to have one of my boys cart all this to your lodgings?" the man asked, motioning to the mountain of goods piled on his counter.

"Please, if that's possible," Natalia said. "There's no way the two of us could carry all this by ourselves."

The man got the name of the inn we were staying at and promised to have it all delivered in an hour, telling us not to pay until we got the delivery.

We thanked him profusely and bought a couple of sweets before we left, savoring the sweet and spicy mixture of cinnamon and ashberry as we walked back across town.

The sun set quite a bit while Natalia and I were in the shop. We tried to find our way back but ended up getting twisted around, walking down alley after alley in hopes of finding the main road through town again.

I glanced over my shoulder numerous times, sure I could feel someone watching me, but there would be no one there. I tried to tell myself I was imagining it until we walked down an alley much darker than the others.

"I've never seen an alley this dark," Natalia said, leading the way.

I tried to pull her back, but it was too late, and the walls of the alley closed in as what little light was left vanished.

"What's happening? Emolin, use your Aura!" Natalia cried, her voice trembling.

Knowing my Well would be drained too quickly, I pulled Natalia close. "It's okay, my Aura doesn't work when he's around."

"Who—" Natalia started, only to be cut off by a deep laugh.

"Ah, I see you're still not understanding what I meant," Fonir said as he approached.

"Whoever you are, stay back!" Natalia yelled, trying to pull away from me and move toward the voice.

"She's a feisty one, isn't she? She should be glad to have been with you this evening, she and her baby will be safe. You must make your decision about where your loyalties lie soon, otherwise, it will be too late to save the ones you care about."

Fonir laughed and his voice faded away, the light returning to the alley and the walls turning into smoke.

"What just happened?" Natalia asked, staring at me and trembling in my arms.

"That was Fonir, the reason we're on this entire journey in the first place and why I missed training."

Natalia stared at me, eyes wide. "A god just spoke to us? Are they going to come back?"

The questions tumbled out of Natalia, and I couldn't help but smile. While I found the whole thing unnerving, if not frustrating, she was completely in awe by it and all her anger and fear disappeared once she heard it was a god.

"I don't know if he's going to come back, he has in the past. He just shows up whenever he wants," I said, trying to keep the frustration from my voice.

"Emolin," Natalia hissed, "don't speak about the gods like that. The last thing we want to do is anger them." She paused, leaning against the nearest building. "What did he mean about me and my baby being safe?"

I turned to her, seeing the fear in her eyes and not knowing how to help her. "I wish I knew. Everything he says gets more and more confusing. I want to tell you more, but I'm as in the dark about him as you are."

Natalia smiled a bit at my jest, understandably unsure about the whole situation, but seeming to be okay enough to continue back to the inn.

"Let's head back before the boys wonder where we are." I turned back down the alley, hoping we would find our way soon.

"Okay," Natalia paused. "I don't think we should tell the others. I don't want Ziden to worry."

"We won't. If you want to talk about it later, we can."

Natalia agreed, and we continued trying to navigate back to the inn. We discovered we were only two streets away and found the other three sitting at a table, digging into what looked to be meat pie.

"What took you girls so long?" Aaron asked, mouth full and spewing bits of his meal all over the table.

"We had to go to the other side of the city to reach the only open shop. The shopkeeper was nice and will have his boys deliver everything shortly—"

"You haven't paid already, have you?" Galeal asked with worry in his voice, cutting Natalia off.

"No, he said we would pay when the provisions arrive," I explained, calming the others. "Though I will admit, we got a few other things we didn't need because of how nice he was."

Galeal nodded, content with our answer. A barmaid came over and dropped off food for both Natalia and me, and the two of us ate while the other three turned their attention to the bard in the corner, juggling apples while telling jokes.

I mulled over what Fonir said, not sure what to make of it. Did he mean that he saved Natalia and her baby from someone lurking in the alley? Was he referring to something about the battle in the coming weeks? *And what did he mean about my loyalties? Why is he making it sound like I will have a choice about the battle? If there's a way to save the Parans, why doesn't he just tell me?* The idea of gods being straightforward was laughable. There was more of a chance of my father hugging me. I needed to decipher Fonir's words, to come up with a plan, but I couldn't do so while surrounded by so many people.

I excused myself early, letting the other four hang out and talk. I promised Natalia I would leave the door unlocked for her, said my goodnights, and headed up the stairs. Finding the room, and once again surprised to find a large washroom, I ran hot water and let myself soak in the tub, trying to clear my mind so I could make it through the next two days.

While I didn't like the reason behind the journey, I had to admit parts of it were a rather enjoyable experience. Sure, I was sore and tired from all the traveling, but it was also my first time out of Altava and seeing the different parts of the country. *If only I could somehow discover a way to make a difference without others getting hurt in the process.*

Eyes struggling to stay open, I climbed out of the bath and slipped into a nightdress before crawling under the covers. I got up to double-check the door was unlocked, then blew out the candle on my side of the bed, letting my body drift off in pure exhaustion.

<hr>

*T*he next morning was an earlier start than the day before, and we got off on the next bit of the journey without much of a fuss. Everyone was in good spirits and Aaron and Ziden seemed to have accepted Galeal into their group. Before we left, Galeal asked a few of the locals about the bandit activity, hearing it was much calmer south of Brifair than north, and we headed off in our original groupings.

We followed the river like the day before and made frequent stops to keep our spirits up. The three in the front wagon laughed and sang songs for most of the morning, and they were losing their voices by the time we stopped for lunch.

"Maybe if you didn't scream your songs, you would still have your voice," Natalia said, laughing at Ziden's hoarse, cracking voice.

Galeal and I sat together along the river, letting our toes dip in the water as we talked.

"Emolin?"

"Hmm?"

"Why did you agree to consider courting me? Why not Aaron or one of the other Mages?"

I turned to Galeal and smiled, his honey-colored eyes shimmering in the sun. "For one thing, I would never court Aaron," I laughed, causing Galeal to smirk. "While I have many reasons, one is because I don't like how power-focused Mages can be. I'm lucky both my parents aren't Mages, but others like Aaron, his family have been Mages for several generations and I can only imagine the amount of stress he's under."

"Why would he be stressed? He's a Mage."

"Exactly, he's a Mage." I sighed and watched wisps of clouds drift across the sky. "Almost every day from the time we turn ten until we turn eighteen, we spend our days training. If we're late, or we don't act properly when we're not training, we're guaranteed a beating. Depending on how bad our transgression is, we could have our Well locked and be forced into slavery, not only ruining our lives but causing our families to be shunned and exiled as well. While many see being a Mage as a blessing, more often than not, it feels like a curse."

Galeal was silent for a moment, tossing stones into the river and watching the water ripple. "What would you do then, if you weren't a Mage?"

"I would be a scholar, traveling the world and learning about the lives of others, both in the present and the past."

"Sounds like you've thought about that a lot."

"I've had a lot of time to think," I said, finishing the last of my lunch.

Before Galeal was able to say anything else, Ziden called for us to head out. Galeal and I got up and the group agreed on the place we would stop and make camp, a small site where caravans were known to gather. We hoped to meet a caravan there to have the extra protection of larger numbers, but even if we were the only group, Galeal assured us there would be adequate protection based on the location of the camp alone, set in the fork of a large river with fast-moving waters and the bridges far enough away it would be easy enough to spot bandits trying to ambush us.

When we finally made it to the camp, the sun was setting, bathing the area in rich oranges and reds. No other caravans were staying the night there, but Galeal was right about it being a safe place to camp. The only place not guarded was the west, but the ocean cliffs would make attacking from that direction impossible.

We were tired from the day's journey and didn't bother with tents, deciding instead to sleep in the open. I helped Natalia with supper, making sure nothing we made required the use of heat. We ended up with cheese, bread, salted pork, and wine Ziden bought before leaving Brifair that morning. We tried not to make too much noise so our voices wouldn't carry and turned in early, Natalia volunteering to take first watch.

We rolled out our bedding, Aaron and Ziden making theirs farther away because they didn't want to take the time to clear away the rocks. Natalia took a position of watch close to me, sitting on a crate and resting her back against one of the wagons. I was grateful many of the bugs and other pests in the desert avoided Light Aura so I didn't have to worry about waking up with a snake in my bedding. Galeal made his bed close to mine and was also fairly safe.

"Why aren't the bugs attacking you guys?" Aaron asked, swatting away yet another desert fly from his arm.

"Because of Emolin's Light Aura. You're the ones who were too lazy to move the rocks," Natalia said, making sure her quiver of arrows were nearby and her bow was strung.

Aaron grumbled and turned over, putting his back towards us. Ziden shrugged and moved closer to Natalia. Aaron eventually followed, and the five of us huddled together, protected from the wind by the wagons. I snuggled into my blanket, sighing into the warmth, and tucking my head into my cloak.

"It's bloody cold out here, can't we light a fire?" Aaron mumbled.

"No, absolutely not. We've already had to deal with the bandits more than we were supposed to, I am not going to risk anything happening to the horses when we're nearly a day's ride from any towns except for the mining town east of here," Galeal said.

"Then why aren't we staying there for the night?" Aaron asked, propping himself on an elbow to stare at Galeal.

"I don't know about you, but I certainly don't want to spend an evening with a bunch of Paran-loving heathens who have been known to harbor fugitives in their own homes. Besides, the Magistrate had us stopping here and we know what happened last time we didn't follow his route." Galeal turned over and pulled his blanket over his head.

"Fair enough," Arron said, wrapping his blanket tighter around him.

Lying there, I struggled with my emotions, discovering the man I considered courting a few hours before was just like everyone else. I closed my eyes, squeezing them shut, and grabbed the pendant around my neck, an action that had become quite calming over the past five days. Natalia tapped my arm and inclined her head away from the others. I nodded and we both got up, grabbing our swords, Natalia taking her bow and quiver too.

"I have to relieve myself and I'm taking Emolin with me for protection," Natalia said, grabbing my hand and walking away without waiting for a response.

Aaron and Galeal shrugged and Ziden looked like he wanted to say something, but the bugs swarmed them as soon as I left and they were too busy swatting away pests to object.

We wrapped our cloaks tight around us, fighting off the chill of the night air. I wasn't sure where we were going to go or how long we were going to be gone, but I needed some time to think and calm down before returning to the group.

Ursa was high in the sky, half full and bathing the land in her purplish light, her sister, Nessa, peeking over the horizon and adding her white light to the mix. The moons covered the landscape in an eerie glow, the shadows seeming to move. The wind bit at my face and pulled my hair free of my braid. I tucked my hair into the cloak as best I could and continued, not used to the silence the desert brought.

We kept our backs to the camp, making sure we could still make it out against the night sky, and found a small rock to sit on. I focused on my breathing and let my Well gather Aura from the light of the moons, preferring that over the Aura of the sun.

"How are you feeling?" Natalia asked, breaking the silence.

"I don't know," I said, staring off at the ocean, fairly visible from the place we stopped. "Galeal and I discussed the possibility of courting when we stopped for lunch yesterday and talked more today. Courting him excited me. Now I don't know if I can finish the journey with him."

"I understand what you mean, but you have to remember most people have the same feelings Galeal has toward Parans. You're the one with the rare ideals."

"I know, but there have to be others out there like me, right?"

Natalia said nothing, and we sat there for several minutes

before eventually getting up and wandering farther. We talked about turning back, but I knew I still had a chance at lashing out at the others, so we kept going. I stifled a yawn and stretched, glad to be walking around after being stuck in the wagon all day. There was a small outcrop of rocks ahead, and we decided we would turn around when we reached it and start heading back.

A shadow covered the moon, a tiger hawk circling overhead. I thought it curious a hawk would be out after dark, but when it swooped down and caught a small creature, I realized it was hunting for a late supper.

When we reached the rocks, we found a small shrine made for travelers to give thanks to the gods for protecting them. Small lizards crawled over the rocks and the few trinkets people left behind as they passed. I had nothing to give as a token, but I hoped I could still offer my thanks all the same. I paused for a few moments, then decided I would pour out everything I worried about, giving myself relief from my fears even if the gods weren't listening, whispering them loud enough for only me to hear.

"I fear I'm not strong enough for this journey, that I won't be able to—"

A scream in the distance cut me off. I scrambled to my feet and unsheathed my sword in a single movement. Natalia drew her sword, and we stared in the direction the scream came from. The camp. We took off at a run, cursing over being gone so long, pushing ourselves to move faster. Natalia mentioned she was leaving for a bit. One of the others must've taken over her watch. *What if they didn't?*

Before I could get too far, a shadow in the corner of my eye caught my attention, Natalia running ahead. I swung around, sword ready to kill the approaching bandit. I stopped mid-swing when I noticed a desert lion, her green eyes shining in the light.

Black stripes that melted into her caramel-colored fur

surrounded her eyes, black-tipped tail flicking contentedly. My presence didn't threaten her at all.

We stared at each other for several moments, not noticing anything else. *She's beautiful, the perfect balance of danger and grace.* Two cubs came tumbling out from behind some rocks and wrestled for a moment before realizing I was there. They blinked at me before running to their mom and hiding behind her legs.

The sounds of battle pulled me out of the trance and I looked back at the camp where a fire started in one of the wagons. When I looked back at the lion and her cubs, they were gone, and I thanked the gods they hadn't attacked me.

I gathered my Aura in my left hand as I ran, my sword glistening in my right. I still couldn't make out anything in the camp since the burning wagon ruined my night vision, but I hoped I would get there in time.

A bolt of lightning crashed to the ground just in front of me, and I rolled away from two others that came in quick succession. *Do they have a Mage? Bandits don't have Mages. Are they really a Lightning Mage? That's impossible, isn't it?* There was a rock outcrop to my right, closer to the camp, and I decided to run for it. I lobbed my orb of light in the direction the bolts of lightning came from, hoping it would give me some cover, and darted for the rocks. I was almost there when a bolt hit the ground just behind me and launched me into the air. I tucked myself into a roll and landed just behind the rocks, shoulder slamming into the ground and my breath leaving my lungs.

A cry of pain filled the air, followed by the shout of anger and revenge. I wasn't able to tell whose scream it was, but it was clear someone had been fatally wounded. I muttered a quick prayer for the safety of my group and worked on gathering more Aura, thankful I focused on refilling my Well on the walk.

Sounds clashing of blades and shouts of men filled the air. I hadn't seen where Natalia ran off to, but the cries didn't sound feminine, so there was a chance she was okay.

The sharp scream of a horse pierced the air, followed by more shouts of death. I tried to run towards the battle, hoping to blind the bandits long enough to help the others get free, but I was unable to move, my Well tightening until I could barely breathe. The world around me grew dim and I didn't have the strength to fight off the darkness.

CHAPTER FIFTEEN
HAJANA

After cleaning out the chamber pots the next morning, the healer arrived for the required bi-weekly checkup for slaves. While it was touted as a way to prevent Serf Pox from ravaging households, we all knew it was really to prevent pregnancies from masters who enjoyed specific punishments. The only good thing about the healer's visits was the afternoon off.

I couldn't stand the examination, but since they were unavoidable, I tried to get it over with as soon as I could. There was only one girl ahead of me and I didn't have to wait long before the healer called me in.

"Hello, Hajana, how are you feeling?"

I still wasn't comfortable around the healer, but she swore many times that unless I told her I was going to break the law, I didn't have to hide anything from her in fear of getting punished.

"As good as a slave can, I guess."

"Please, sit down." She motioned to the low parlor table set up as a makeshift exam bed.

I climbed on the table and wished for it to be over.

"Now, is there anything you would like to talk about?"

"Honestly, I don't know anymore..." I trailed off, trying not to make eye contact.

The healer said nothing and cleansed her hands in a basin of water before feeling around my head and neck. She looked in my eyes, ears, and nose. Noting the faint bruising on my shoulders from a previous beating, she continued down my torso, having me take off my dress first. After prodding my stomach and feeling around my most private area, she moved on to my legs while I lay there and stared at the ceiling.

"You're sure I can tell you anything without you telling my master?" I wasn't exactly sure why, but the exam calmed me down to the point where I felt comfortable enough to speak.

"I promise everything here is said in complete secrecy." She stopped her exam and showed me a small glowing stone. "This stone is covered in Alchemist runes and it allows me to completely ward this room from anyone trying to listen in. Anything you tell me is kept between the two of us. Now, what's on your mind?"

Without meaning to, I told her everything that happened over the past few days, from the breaking of the vase, meeting Geoffraie, breaking my hand, Emolin leaving, the darkness I felt, and the argument with Dalila. I even mentioned the part about sneaking out, though that would've been something she could told my master since it did break curfew.

"It sounds like you've had a rough couple of days, a complete break in your routine." She helped me sit up and looked at my hand, feeling the tendons and range of motion before continuing. "I want you to understand I in no way condone slavery or what you girls suffer through. As of right now, there are many reasons why I can't do anything to change the laws, but I can make sure you are getting some reprieve from this torture until others can change things."

The healer turned away and scribbled something on a sheet of paper. "Do you know the apothecary in the West District?"

"Yes."

"The pharmacist is a good friend of mine and will be willing to help. I'm sure you're probably wary of medicine, having most likely heard stories of masters drugging their slaves, but this is a natural blend of herbs that can help regulate some of these worries and thoughts you've been having."

She reached into her bag and pulled out a few coins before depositing them and the note into my hand. "I want you to get some food in the market and ask my friend to get you a book."

I raised a brow at the suggestion to get a book.

"You're a smart girl, Hajana, I know you can read. I promise you there will be a day when your freedom will come, one sooner than you think. When that happens, I want you to be prepared for anything."

The way the healer was speaking gave me hope, but my worries grew as well. Here was someone who was helping me and going out of her way to do so, but was also saying she would wait for someone else to change the laws. *Why?* I wasn't sure what to think about it. I slipped back into my dress without being told to and tucked the coins and the note into my pocket.

"One last thing before you go, I've noticed a few peculiar symptoms in some of the other slaves here, so I will probably be by next week for another checkup. I look forward to speaking with you then."

I thanked the healer and rushed out of the room, the recent events catching up and threatening to overwhelm me if I didn't get away for a bit. I didn't care where, but I needed time alone or I felt my legs would collapse beneath me. I left the master's estate and wandered down the road, eventually ducking into a nearby alley to stop and breathe while watching the other slaves mill about looking for a place of refuge.

So many things happened in the past few days and there was never any real moment to process any of it. There were little snippets here and there I could use, but never a significant chunk of time. With the afternoon off, I had a chance to figure things out, or at least come up with a plan on how and when I could work through everything. I didn't want to let the darkness win, I couldn't. I had been given hope from the healer, though some of what she said didn't make sense, and Geoffraie helped me in the past. I needed to push through.

When I felt I could handle the crowds again, I made my way to the West District where many of the immigrant and slave ships docked. There were few shops in that part of the city, most of them selling only necessities a sailor would need to survive the next leg of their journey.

I wove through the sailors unloading cargo and spinning tales for the local urchins brave enough to come out of hiding. The mix of seawater and sweaty bodies was neither a pleasant or foul smell, but one that provided comfort in knowing there was a system and routine that would stay the same no matter the turmoil in my life.

I found the apothecary halfway down the stretch of docks, a small shop compared to the others, nestled between two large storehouses with streams of people coming and going like ants. A bell tinkled as I opened the door and it took my eyes a moment to adjust to the dimness of the room before me.

The air was pungent with spicy and floral notes of fresh herbs ground into different tinctures and salves, many shelves lined with neatly labeled bottles and jars. A voice called out from behind a curtain saying they would be right out and I braced myself for the tongue lashing they would give me when they saw a slave girl standing in the middle of their store. Fear filled me but before I thought about rushing out, a woman pushed the curtain aside and smiled at me.

"Why, hello, my dear. What can I help you with on this fine day?"

Her mannerisms caught me off guard and I stood there, mouth agape. She laughed in a chime-like way at my shock, matching the bell that announced my arrival mere moments before.

"It's okay, you're safe here. I know many would treat you differently because of what they've labeled you as," she motioned to my tattoo on my neck, "but my job isn't one of judging, but of helping. And even if I were to judge, your spirit is kind, so there would be no reason to treat you any differently."

"My spirit?" The words the woman was speaking were Klohavian, but I understand them.

The idea of someone so blatantly admitting their thoughts and REDs weren't trying to break down their door for speaking such blasphemy was confusing at best.

"Yes, my dear. Everyone has a spirit, a life force within them. The Mages and Alchemists have stronger, more developed spirits in them, but you have one just as I and the gull outside do. Your spirit guides you, tells you how to act and treat others." She clapped her hands, causing me to jump, and wiped her hands off on her apron. "Now, I'm sure there's a reason you chose my shop out of all others to visit."

I remembered the note from the healer and handed it to the woman.

"Ah, the healer sent you. That explains a lot." The woman scanned the note and ducked back behind the curtain, only to reappear a moment later with her arms full of jars and bottles.

"Now, let's see. She suggested a lavender and chamomile blend for you. Have you been feeling more stressed and worried than usual?"

I scoffed. "I'm a slave, when are we not?" My hand shot up to cover my mouth, immediately regretting the tone I used. "I am so sorry." I gave a deep curtsy. "Please, please forgive me for my rudeness. I will show myself out."

"There's no need for that, my dear, I understand your feelings of unjustly being thrown into slavery." She winked and swept her hair to one side as she poured some contents out of a jar.

In the shop's dimness, I could barely make out the faint scar of a removed tattoo, the shape very similar to the one on my neck.

"Wh—ho—were..." I stumbled over my words, not sure I could even believe what I was seeing.

Here, in front of me, was a woman who successfully escaped the bonds of slavery without the embrace of death.

"There are ways out of every situation, my dear. One just has to know where to look," she said, passing me a small container. "Can you put that on the shelf behind you, please?" She motioned to a spot with a perfect ring of dust where a container had been.

I placed the jar on the shelf and turned back to watch the woman work, glancing at the lock-shaped scar far too many times.

Now and then, the woman would glance at the note from the healer or look up at me and smile, but other than that, she focused solely on her work. There was a pattern there, a sureness that came from not only years of practicing her craft but also confidence in her movements, reaching for a container and shaking herbs into the bowl without stopping to make sure it was the correct ingredient.

"Now, the healer wants these made into pills, but if that isn't something you aren't comfortable with or couldn't take without others seeing, I can make it into whatever you feel would work best."

I blinked a few times, trying to understand what she was saying. "Pills should be fine, we don't pay each other much attention."

The woman nodded and grabbed a small tray with lots of impressions on the surface from behind the counter. I took a few steps forward and watched as she dusted the impressions with a fine powder before filling them with the mixture of herbs she created.

"These will take a while to dry, so why don't you enjoy the rest of the afternoon and come back before curfew."

"Alright." I turned to go and remembered the coins the healer had given me. "The healer mentioned you might be able to get me a book?" I held out the coins to her.

"Ah, now I fully understand why she sent you to me. Don't worry about paying me, you will need all the money you can get when the time comes. I will have the book for you as well when you return."

I thanked her and wandered onto the street, the sailors taking a break from unloading their ships by gambling. A few trinkets caught my eye, a small watch with Para's golden sun etched on it, a journal, and a scarf. I knew better than to get too close to the men, not wanting them to get any ideas, so I decided to head down to the shore where I could watch the boats coming and going.

The beach was empty aside from a few gulls and crabs. The current was known to pull people far out to sea, so no one swam there. I found a relatively clean rock and sat, staring out at the water, breathing in the salty air, and raising my face to the sun. Altava was much warmer than my village, but I was beginning to enjoy the heat, the way I could feel the energy from the sun filling me as I basked in its warmth. The burns from the sun were bad, but after a few times, my skin learned to protect itself well enough.

A small gull flew by and landed a few feet from my rock. It hopped around a bit and stared at me, head cocked to the side. It seemed to understand I was alone and needed cheering. It squawked and chased around the crabs, letting them go whenever it caught one. I found myself laughing and wished I had something to give it in return.

Remembering the coins, I leaped up and told the bird to stay. I made my way to the port bazaar and purchased a bit of bread, some cheese, and a few pieces of dried beef. The shopkeeper seemed surprised a slave was buying from him, but treated me better than most merchants in the center of the city.

I returned to my spot on the beach to find the gull still hopping about. It hopped over to me when I reached my rock. The fact the gull not only listened but seemed to understand I was coming back was fascinating. It leaned forward and pecked lightly at my toes, its beak tickling more than anything else.

"Alright, I have both bread and dried meat here, I'm saving the cheese for myself. Which do you want?" I held out both pieces.

I would be getting my rations in a few hours and there was no reason for me to be stingy with what I was offering. The gull had taken the time to cheer me up so it had the opportunity to choose. The gull looked at the two options before hopping closer to the meat, squawking at me as I tore off a bit of the dried beef for it. I tossed the beef in the air and laughed as the gull caught it and proceeded to rip off small chunks for itself, gulping each one down before tearing off another piece.

"Do you like being free?" I asked, sure it wouldn't answer.

The gull cawed at me and stared up at the sky where other gulls soared above.

"I'm glad you're free. You don't have to worry about someone beating you for scrubbing the floor counter-clockwise instead of clockwise." I grimaced at the memory and touched the base of my skull where the mistress kicked me a few weeks ago, finding the spot to still be slightly tender.

The gull and I sat together for a long time, sharing my lunch and having as much of a conversation as a girl and a gull can. The bird let me pat its head and made small cooing sounds.

"You are a rare thing, you know that?"

The gull tilted its head, confused.

"You're so trusting, letting me so close to you. You shouldn't trust humans; they can do bad things to those they deem lesser than themselves."

The gull cawed and soared into the air, flapping its wings

before catching a breeze and drifting before diving back to the ground and landing at my feet."

"Show off," I laughed, patting its head. "Just promise you'll stay out of trouble, okay?"

The gull bobbed its head and pecked at my feet again before taking off, flying toward the sun that was already dipping lower in the sky. I decided I would head back to the apothecary and see if the woman was done. There was so much I wanted to ask her but I wasn't sure how.

The bell tinkled above the door as I entered the apothecary, the spiciness of the shop hitting me again. The woman smiled as I entered, beckoning me toward her.

"I found you the perfect book," she said as she handed me a small book bound in dark green leather.

I took it and thanked her profusely, promising to take the greatest care of it.

"And here are your pills." She handed me a jar filled with lilac-colored pills. "You can take these whenever you feel overwhelmed. They won't make you sleepy or take away any of the worries, but they'll help you calm yourself down more easily."

I thanked her again and paused, not sure if I should ask her about her scar or not.

"May I ask you something?"

"Of course, I was wondering when you would."

"How did you get free?" I asked, my voice barely above a whisper.

"I had help, lots of help from friends. I knew I was meant for greater things and I needed to prove it not only to them, but to myself."

"Yes, but what did you do?"

"I survived. That is what you must do too. Never give up and always look for your chance. My way was my own, as yours must be as well."

My toes clenched in frustration, but I didn't want to anger the woman who was so kind to me.

"Oh, one last thing," the woman called after me, "I wouldn't worry too much about your master either."

"Why? What do you mean?"

"It is wrong to speak ill of a person, living or dead, but because your master has no regard for his health, let alone the health of others, he sent many consorts to me over the past few months. He didn't come to see me, though, until it was too late. There's a fair chance he won't make it through the winter, and Lady Aldous didn't care to learn the skills to manage the Aldous fortune. So, the money will be gone only a few months after her husband's death."

"When the money's gone," I started, careful not to curse myself by speaking of another's approaching death, "what will happen to the slaves?"

"Sometimes, when a master can no longer afford their slaves, that's when we can make changes."

I didn't know what she meant, so I thanked her and left, promising I would return for a new book and more pills.

The sun bathed the city in an orange glow as I made my way back to my master's, knowing I still had time before curfew, but wanting nothing more than to tuck myself into my small corner to read. I stopped at a well and tried one of my new pills before reaching the house, not sure what to expect, but hoping to feel at least a little less hopeless.

It took me a few tries, but eventually I swallowed the pill, my mouth filled with a sweet, acrid taste. I rinsed my out mouth and sat on the edge of the well, realizing I still hadn't tried to tackle any of my recent thoughts. I knew how, my parents made sure I could handle my emotions, but I doubted they thought my life would include becoming a slave. *No, don't think of them, there are too many other things to worry about.* I took a deep breath and gazed up at the sky, counting the clouds and humming my mother's song until I calmed back down.

The pill must've worked because my breathing and heart rate slowed in only a few minutes, something that could take upwards of an hour. With my mind clear, I focused on the experiences of the past week, picking apart each of them and detaching the emotion from it all. That worked for everything except for Emolin's betrayal. I placed my head in my hands and fought off the urge to cry, wanting to look at the experience without my emotions controlling my thoughts.

"Ra, what's wrong?"

I looked up to find Dalila walking toward me.

"There was a girl in the city—"

"Ooh, a girl, eh?" Dalila asked, sitting down on the side of the well next to me.

"No, it's not like that… She's a Mage and I thought she was my friend."

"What makes you think she's not your friend anymore?"

"When someone leaves to kill your people, it makes it difficult to still be friends."

"Ah."

The two of us sat in silence until Dalila spoke up again. "I have a few more things I want to do before heading back. I'll see you in our room later, okay?"

"Be careful. Stay away from the REDs, okay?"

"Okay," she said, leaning over to hug me before heading back toward the bazaars.

I sat there for a while longer before heading back, not wanting the freedom to end, but also worrying about arriving after curfew and getting locked out. When sneaking out, I could leave the door unlocked. I couldn't do that if I got back late.

Ruta welcomed me and gave me a small bowl of stew, which I

scarfed down before heading up to the slave quarters with a crusty bit of bread. No one else was up there yet, most staying out as late as they could. I slid under the covers and hid my pills in the floorboard beneath my pillow before opening the book the woman gave me.

A swirly, handwritten font greeted me and I stared in wonder. I had read many books before, but publishers printed most, making them easier to read. The ink faded in some areas but was mostly legible. Before I could get more than a few pages in, the ladder creaked as someone climbed into the loft and I hurriedly shoved the book under my pillow.

"Oh, it's you." I sighed as Dalila walked over and sat on her bedroll next to mine. "What did you do today?"

"I ended up exploring the city some, wanting to know my way around at least a bit in case I'm sent out on errands. Are you feeling any better?"

"A little, I guess."

"Did you hear about the bandit attacks?"

I shook my head. "No, what happened?"

"Bandits attacked a group of Mages heading south, maybe the one the girl you thought was your friend was in? The Mages were able to take out all but one of them. I never thought bandits would be that foolish."

A tinge of worry about Emolin's safety sat in the pit of my stomach.

"Did any of the Mages get hurt?" I asked, trying not to sound too worried.

"Not that I heard. It sounded like the bandits didn't get close, many being killed a ways off from the wagon tracks. I saw the body of one of the bandits on a cart and I have to say, they're some of the ugliest things I've ever seen."

I laughed, despite my worries. I had seen the bodies of bandits before and there was something odd about their looks, the extra ear and nose hair being one of the most obvious differences. Many of the children said bandits were part monster and that's why they looked different, but my pa said it was because of their lack of proper nourishment or stable lodgings that made them sprout more hair for warmth and safety.

We talked about the bandits until the other slaves began to return. We moved onto other topics until a slave walked over to us.

"The mistress has asked to speak with you, Hajana," the girl said, eyes full of concern for what we knew was a beating.

I thanked her and made my way down the ladder to the parlor where the mistress was waiting for me.

"You asked to see me, Mistress?" I asked, giving a deep curtsy, hoping politeness would make the beating less.

"I spoke with the healer before she left and she mentioned you and many other slaves showed potential symptoms of the Serf Pox."

I nodded, but said nothing, not sure where the conversation was going since the healer told me I was fine.

"She said she would return sometime next week for a follow-up, but in the meantime, she wanted to keep you and the others separated from the healthy girls. While this is going to cause issues, she has highly recommended we quarantine you and the other girls, otherwise, the rest of my slaves could get sick."

I wrung my hands, waiting for the mistress to make it all out to be one big cruel joke.

"You are to return to your quarters and gather your bedding and clothes. Head up to the west wing on the third floor and one of the maids will show you where you'll be staying."

The mistress' eyes were full of disgust. I was sure she was trying to figure out if I somehow faked the symptoms of the Pox, a crime punishable by death. I curtsied again and left, not wanting to make the mistress angrier. I passed a line of girls, Dalila at the end, and went to gather my belongings, managing to get my things from under the floorboards without the others seeing.

I headed up to the third floor where maids with cloths over their noses and mouths guided me to a room with the instructions I wasn't to leave unless told, wishing me good health. The door shut behind me and the soft click of the lock told me what I had been assuming, the mistress turned the quarantine into even more of a punishment.

I was surprised slaves were being put in quarters so nice and I realized they must be rooms for the maids. There were many bed frames scattered about the room and I chose one under a window. A few wardrobes were pushed against one wall and a vanity next to a washing basin on the other. A door next to the wardrobe opened to a small closet and a faded, woven rug in the center of the floor completed the room. While there wasn't much furniture, it was more than I'd had in a long time.

The door opened again and Dalila entered, tossing her things on a bed in the corner of the room next to mine. "I'm surprised they've given us quarters as nice as these. At the last home I worked in, they would lock the slaves up in an old barn that was too old for the horses."

"Oh no, that's terrible. I would rather deal with the heat than be forced to live in a barn."

"It really was terrible."

Dalila surprised me with a hug before pulling away. "We should probably get some sleep. If we do have symptoms of the Serf Pox, we don't want to push ourselves too hard."

I agreed and climbed under the covers. The rest of the girls who went to see the mistress filed in, choosing a bed for themselves and quickly falling asleep. Once their snores filled the room, I lit a candle on the table beside the bed and pulled out the book. Once I was comfortable, I read a few pages, still not knowing what the book was about, but feeling drawn to it all the same.

CHAPTER SIXTEEN
EMOLIN

The world was dim and quiet when I woke and it took a few moments to remember what happened. When I did, I frantically checked myself for wounds. I didn't find any and was glad to see my cloak unharmed as well.

I pulled myself to my feet and nearly collapsed when I tried to put weight on my right ankle. I stretched it out a few times to find it sprained, not broken, relieving my worries. I took a few steps, and the pain faded away with each one.

The smell of smoke reminded me of the stories about the bandits, and I faltered before walking toward the camp. Flames still engulfed one wagon, but the fire was dying, having burned through most of its fuel. *How long was I out?* I looked up at the sky. Vria was high in the sky, casting the landscape in her bluish glow. Ursa had already set and Nessa was light on the horizon. *It's only a couple hours until sunrise…*

As I got closer to the camp, a disturbing smell entered the mix, one of blood and feces. I knew I would find at least one body, the sounds that filled the night having been brutal, and I hoped to find bodies of the bandits. I wanted to turn away and not look beyond the wagon, but I forced myself to walk the last few steps.

I rounded the wagon and immediately turned to release the contents of my stomach. I wiped the bile from my mouth and forced myself to turn back and look at the body in front of me.

Aaron's mouth hung open in a silent scream, his eyes reflecting the smoldering fire from the wagon. His legs were bent at odd angles, a shard of bone sticking out of his left shin. The blood pooled around the leg told me it broke while he was still alive. I made myself look at the large slash across Aaron's stomach, the wound most likely causing much suffering before death. The scraps of fabric that were once his robes clung to the edges of the wound and I was grateful for not having wandered closer.

I wanted to scream; instead, all I could do was sink to the ground. My body was shaking uncontrollably and I couldn't collect my thoughts. I'd heard of battle shakes before and assumed that's what I was experiencing.

I took a few moments to process what I was seeing. Eventually, I calmed myself enough to regain control of my limbs and stand. Even though Aaron had been less than pleasant toward me at the beginning of the trip, he became a friend over the last few days. Guilt filled me, knowing he wouldn't have been out in the desert if it hadn't been for me. There was nothing I could do to help him and looking at his corpse wouldn't do anything to help me either. I forced the thoughts out of my mind and moved on.

The bandits had toppled both wagons, and the few bits of wood not consumed by fire lay strewn across the ground. Puddles glistened in the fire and I forced myself not to think about what they were, instead, looking for the others, hoping to find survivors or at least dead bandits.

A large puddle caught my attention, a silhouette just outside the light from the fire. I looked and instantly regretted it when I saw a horse lying in the center of the puddle. Her once white forehead turned red.

I didn't see any of the other horses and assumed the bandits took them. A horse could bring good money at the market.

I turned away from the horse and something lying by the other wagon caught my eye. I rushed over, hoping I could help whoever it was, but stopped mid-step when I realized the arm wasn't attached to a body.

A trail of blood led to a growing puddle around another corpse. It seemed Galeal crawled a few yards before a bandit thrust a knife into Galeal's back, the wound still fresh. Galeal's remaining arm stretched toward the darkness, desperate fear on his ashen, lifeless face.

Tears ran down my cheeks as I knelt next to him, stroking his hair out of his face. Even though he hated the Parans, it was more likely his upbringing than his spirit that caused him to hate people he never met. That wasn't an excuse. There was never an excuse to hate someone because they were different, but it meant there could've been a chance to help him learn and grow. Now, there would never be that chance. I would never get to see what might have happened between us. He was gone.

I turned and made out the shadow of another body farther away from the camp. I walked over to it and could tell by the blonde hair glistening in the moonlight it was Ziden, my heart breaking for Natalia and the life they dreamed of. I forced myself to approach him, hoping he was still alive. Instead, his body was laced with a lattice of dark lines from being struck by a Mage's Lightning.

The deep purple color to the markings meant death was instantaneous and I was glad he didn't suffer. His eyes were open and I reached down to close them when a soft moan caught my attention. I looked around, sure I was hearing things, but then it came again, louder. I rushed over to the shadows where the sound came from and knelt next to Natalia.

"Emolin, you're safe." Natalia said, her face a blank stare.

"Shh, you're going to be okay." I tried to keep my voice calm, not wanting to let Natalia know how scared I was.

I checked her over for wounds and blessedly found none. I helped her up out of the puddle she was sitting in, not wanting to think about what it was.

"Emolin, he's dead."

I turned Natalia away from the scene, hiding Ziden's corpse. She leaned on me, stumbling and tripping over her own feet like a drunkard. She mumbled, not making any sense, and caused us to fall several times until I got her a safe distance from the wagons.

"Can you stay here for a while so I can look for supplies?"

Natalia nodded and gave me a verbal promise after much prodding. I left her tucked among some rocks and dashed back to the wagons hoping to find something I could use.

The wagons were smoldering, no signs of flames. The first wagon, Galeal's, was completely charred, nothing left worth saving. The wagon Natalia and I were in was also smoldering, but less so. I poked my head inside, using a side of a broken crate as a shield in case the side of the wagon, which was now the top, decided to cave in.

Many of the crates were crushed and destroyed, a few bits and bobs sticking out, not worth saving for the bandits, but Vria gave me enough light to see the occasional apple or bit of dried meat to sustain Natalia and me for a day.

In the back corner of the wagon, I found a completely intact pack, seeming to have been looked over entirely, underneath a part of the now splintered bench. I pulled it out, careful not to disturb the structure of the wagon, and couldn't believe the blessing to discover it was my own. I also found a blanket shoved in another corner. Deciding not to test my luck any more, I backed out of the wagon and scanned the rest of the area.

I looked back over the bodies and noticed a glint on Ziden's neck. I tiptoed over to him, hoping to trick my mind into thinking he was only sleeping and found a gold chain with a small pendant. I wasn't sure the significance of it, but I hoped it would bring comfort to Natalia.

I was about to step away when I noticed the pouch of coins on Ziden's belt, untouched. It was odd for the bandits to leave something like that overlooked, but I didn't want to question fate. I grabbed the bag and wondered what else might still be hiding. I still had my sword, as did Natalia, but she didn't have her bow when I found her, and I wondered if I could find it.

I headed back to where Natalia was sitting, squinting into the shadows, and deciding to use my Light Aura. My Well burned when I tried using it, causing me to double over in pain. My leg throbbed and I pulled up my pants to discover the bolt of lightning from the bandits' Mage hit me. A faint lattice climbed my leg, spreading as I watched. I had already seen what happened to Ziden and worried what would happen if I left it unchecked. I brushed the thoughts away and continued searching; there was nothing I could do at the moment anyway.

Under the wagon was Natalia's quiver, a few arrows still inside. Her bow was a few feet away, string still intact. I decided to check the other bodies for coin before leaving, not wanting to risk the bandits coming back and finding me.

Aaron's bag of coins was gone, but Galeal's was there, his body never flipped over. Another blanket from a bedroll was also left untouched and I shoved everything into my pack. Ziden and Aaron still had their cloaks, Galeal's having been torn to pieces when the bandits killed him. I didn't want to leave the bodies in such a disrespectful state. I used Aaron's and Ziden's cloaks to cover them and found a half intact bedroll to cover Galeal. I looked up at Vria and clasped my hands over my heart. The pendant was warm against my skin and I held it as I spoke with the gods.

"Please, protect the spirits of Aaron, Galeal, and Ziden. Allow their journey to the afterlife to be swift. Let them be cleansed and reunited with their loved ones who passed before. Grant their families peace and help them heal."

I bowed my head and allowed the warmth from my prayer to dissipate into the ether. Realizing it had been half an hour since I left Natalia, I grabbed a small dagger from Aaron and found Ziden's sword and dagger.

I turned back and made my way toward the rocks where Natalia promised to stay, scanning the moonlit landscape for any signs of others roaming the desert. I saw no one and some of my worries faded when I found Natalia still in the rocks, mumbling nonsense to herself.

"Good news," I said, trying to sound cheerful, "I managed to find some things to make our journey to Cragsrest a little easier."

Natalia mumbled something in response, but it made no sense. I dug around in the pack and found my half-filled waterskin.

"Here, drink some water, and then we have to get moving."

"… I… no… Ziden…"

I ignored her mumbling and put the waterskin to her lips, making sure she had several mouthfuls before hoisting everything on my back and helping her up. She was still unsteady on her feet but didn't fight me as I led her toward the bridge.

When crossing the river hours before, the water hadn't seemed to be moving nearly as fast. The water raced below and I had to force myself not to look down as I helped Natalia navigate the planks, catching her from toppling into the water when her toe caught on a board.

Once safely across, I turned us toward the Klohaven Mountains looming in the dark, their peaks lit by the two moons and silhouetted by the third. I had no idea of the exact location of Cragsrest, having only heard Galeal mention it in passing. Having heard what he said, I hoped they would be willing to help us, or at least Natalia. I realized I didn't have a map and hadn't seen one when looking around what had once been our camp. I hoped heading in the general direction of the mountains would be enough to help us find the city once the sun rose.

The terrain was far rockier off the main road. Natalia and I stumbled more times than we didn't and our knees were bruised and bloodied by the time the sun started bathing the sky in a pale orange glow.

"Alright, Nat, we're going to find somewhere we can rest for a bit before we continue. How are you feeling?"

"… sleepy… night… bed…"

Making out enough to know she was as tired as I was, I decided to camp under the rock outcrops up ahead, hoping they would provide enough shelter from the sun and hide us from any more potential attacks.

I helped Natalia to the ground and made up a semi-comfortable bed, having moved aside as many rocks as I could and using my clothes as pillows. Lying Natalia down on the blanket, I wrapped the second one around us and pulled her to me, stroking her hair and humming in her ear, her mumbling getting more distraught.

"… he's gone…"

Her body trembled as her heart poured out every bit of anger and sadness in a torrent of tears. Her wails echoed off the rocks around us, but I let her cry despite the risk it posed to us. I didn't want her to hold it in; she needed relief.

Eventually, her sobs lessened and she drifted to sleep, still twitching and mumbling, but at least she was resting. Making sure she was okay, I finally allowed my eyes to close and sunk into a state of restlessness filled with images of bodies and the sounds of death.

I woke up to something nudging my foot and screamed, waking Natalia and causing her to scream as well. I pressed my back against the rocks and moved to pull out my sword when a set of familiar brown eyes caught my attention.

"Ashbud?" I asked, not sure if I was awake or dreaming.

I climbed to my feet and reached out to her, her warm nose pressing into my palm.

"I'm so glad to see you, girl. How did you get away?"

Ashbud huffed and nuzzled me before stepping toward Natalia and leaning down, asking for scritches.

Seeing Ashbud gave me a little more hope for the day's journey. If I could get Natalia and I onto Ashbud's back, she could carry us to Cragsrest before nightfall, if we could find it. Natalia's face was red and puffy, blotchy from all the crying over the past few hours. I pulled my waterskin out of my pack and tossed it to Natalia while I shoved everything in my bag, not worrying about folding.

"We need to get moving if we're going to make it to Cragsrest."

"Why bother?"

Natalia's question surprised me; it wasn't like her to be so pessimistic.

"Because we need to get somewhere safe so we can rest and figure out what to do next."

Natalia looked up at me, tears in her eyes. "What's the point? Why try to continue moving on if our friends are dead? Ziden is dead, his mother is all alone in the world, and things don't feel right with the baby."

"We need to keep moving for your child, for Ziden's mother. Just because things feel off doesn't mean the worst. You are what they both still have and he would want you to continue carrying on."

"No, he wouldn't. He would want me there with him. He's waiting for me and I need to be with him."

Scared of what Natalia was saying, I tried something else. "Ziden died in a brave and noble way, a way that will reward him greatly in his next life. If you want to see him again, you will need to ask the priests for guidance on what to do to assure you're reunited. Otherwise, you could be apart forever."

Natalia seemed to ponder what I was saying for a few moments before responding. "I guess I'll wait until the priests tell me what I need to do, then I'll be with Ziden again."

I mumbled, not wanting to agree with whatever she was planning, and finished packing up the rest of the things.

I placed a hand on Ashbud's neck and guided her to a small grouping of flat rocks that seemed tall enough to use as a step. Ashbud, seeming to understand what I wanted to do, stood by the rocks and waited for me to help Natalia to her feet.

Since the horses had been pulling the wagons, there were no saddles. Neither Natalia nor I had ever ridden before, but the REDs riding around Altava didn't make it seem too hard. I guided Natalia to the rocks and was about to help her onto Ashbud's back when she turned and stared at me.

"Are you crazy? This horse has no saddle, and neither of us had any experience with horses before this journey. Now you're thinking we can just ride her bareback without experience?"

I was glad to see Natalia was returning to her usual self after the shock. "Do you have a better idea? From what I can tell, it's either try this or end up having to walk there and camp out for the next two days while the little food I found runs out."

"I can't believe we're trying this."

Natalia shook her head and placed her hands on Ashbud's back. I laced my fingers together, giving Natalia an extra boost to swing her leg up onto the horse's back. After a few tries, she got up and gripped Ashbud's mane tight, pulling the mare's head back.

"Natalia, relax. You're going to hurt her if you keep tugging on her mane so tightly."

Natalia relaxed a bit, her knuckles still white as her fingers tangled deeper into Ashbud's mane. I shook my head and braced my hands on Ashbud's back, knowing it would be difficult to get up with Natalia already up there.

"Alright, I'm going to try and hop up now. All you need to do is focus on staying on her back, okay?"

Natalia said nothing and I counted to three in my head before pressing my hands onto the mare's back and jumping while trying to swing my leg over. Instead of ending up on Ashbud's back, my legs and arms got all tangled and I fell to the ground in a heap, my pack breaking my fall, but the fall still stealing my breath.

"Are you alright?" Natalia asked, turning to look at me.

"I'm okay, just a little shaken." I stood up and brushed myself off, preparing to try again.

Before I could try, gravel crunched behind me and I spun, ready for a fight. Instead, Sampson stood there, seeming to almost be grinning at me as he shook out his mane.

"You saw me fall just now, didn't you?"

Sampson nodded and snorted.

"Well, at least you're here now. Will you let me ride you?"

Natalia snorted and I ignored her, patting Ashbud lightly on the rump to get her to move. Sampson stood where Ashbud had been and looked back at me, stomping his foot impatiently.

"Well, then, someone's eager."

I climbed up on the rock and took a steadying breath. *I can do this.* I jumped, swinging my leg around and nearly falling off the other side, but managing to catch myself. It was amazing how different the world looked from atop a horse.

Before I could urge Sampson forward, shouts from behind caused my heart to race. The bandits were back.

"Follow me and hold on!" I yelled to Natalia, kicking my heels into Sampson's side and struggling to stay on as he took off across the sand. I risked a glance back and was glad to see Natalia close behind, the cloud of dust behind us growing slowly.

I scanned the horizon, looking for a place to try and gain an advantage. Seeing an outcrop that would provide us enough cover, I tried pulling on Sampson's mane like I watched other riders do with the reins to guide him toward it, but he ignored me. Instead, he continued racing on, heading directly toward the Klohaven Mountains, the rocky outcrops seeming to thin as we moved farther inland.

I looked behind me again, still seeing Natalia clinging to Ashbud, but the bandits gaining ground as well, being much closer than before.

"Sampson, we need cover!" I shouted, hoping to somehow convince him to turn.

He pushed faster, his hoofs thundering against the ground as I felt like a rattle in a babe's hand, about to be tossed to the ground.

Another glance back and could make out individual bandits, their shouts rising over the steady rhythm Sampson and Ashbud created. I contemplated throwing myself from Sampson's back, hoping I could take on the bandits with only my sword. Before I could try anything, a line of people came into view.

I screamed, thinking it was another group of bandits ambushing us when grey armor glinted in the sunlight. The soldiers stood at attention and a few stepped to the side, creating a gap. I sent up my thanks to the gods as Sampson galloped past and continued for a few more seconds before slowing. I slid off his back, amazed I hadn't fallen off.

Natalia and Ashbud appeared a moment later, Natalia falling to the ground and hugging me tightly.

"Why are these soldiers here? Did the god send them?" Natalia asked between gulps of air.

"I honestly don't know, but I'd hate to think about what would've happened if they weren't."

Before Natalia could respond, a soldier approached us.

"Are you two okay?" he asked, concern in his voice.

"I think so. A little shaken, but fine otherwise." I paused and motioned for the soldier to come closer, Natalia seeming to be preoccupied with other things. Once he was close, I whispered in his ear, "Our other traveling companions were slaughtered last night by bandits. One of those that died was my friend's love and father of their unborn child." I motioned to Natalia and the soldier nodded, folding his hands together and bowing his head in a silent prayer.

The soldier stood and whistled, a young boy running over. "Please, send for a carriage for the ladies and a stable hand for their horses. They have been through a lot and we need to get them to Lady Hyll's."

The boy gave a curt nod and ran off. I thanked the soldier for his kindness and gratefully accepted the waterskin he handed to me. The sound of generals calling the troops to battle rang in my ears and I focused on my breathing to block out the sound as much as I could. The soldier, who I discovered was a leading commander, stayed and talked with us for a bit, sitting on the ground so we didn't have to crane our necks to look up at him.

When the carriage arrived, he had one of his subordinates help Natalia while he pulled me aside to talk. "When I return to Cragsrest, I will like to speak with you about the attack. The bandits around here have been acting strangely and I need all the information I can get."

"I would be more than happy to speak with you," I said before climbing into the carriage with Natalia.

I placed my pack on the seat next to me, glad to be out of the sun for a bit. The carriage rolled away and I watched a stable hand slipping bridals over the horses' heads before they disappeared behind some rocks.

The ride to Cragsrest was short, taking less than half an hour. Natalia sat in silence the entire time, ignoring all my attempts at conversation. I left her alone after a while and watched the approaching city, the Klohaven Mountains covering everything in their shadow.

I had seen the mountains from Altava, them being impossible to miss, but they were completely different up close. I wondered what it would be like to climb them and decided one day to try.

We stopped in front of a large house, nowhere near as large as my father's estate, but much larger than the other buildings in the city. The driver opened the door and helped us down, a butler standing a few feet away, giving us a deep bow of respect.

"We heard of your arrival and Lady Hyll extends her deepest regrets to what you both faced. She knows it's not much, but she offers you lodgings and whatever else you may need during your stay here. Please, follow me."

The butler turned, leading us through the front door and into a parlor where two maids stood waiting, curtsying as we entered.

"These ladies will help you settle in," the butler explained. "Lady Hyll had some urgent business to attend to but is eagerly awaiting to meet you at dinner."

The butler gave another deep bow and left us with the maids, the two of them rushing forward and ringing a bell as they doted over Natalia. Two more maids came in and three of them led Natalia away, speaking in calming tones and gently guiding her away. The fourth maid stayed behind and gave another curtsy.

"I noted your friend needed a great deal of care. I promise you she will be safe."

The maid didn't say it, but I knew she noticed the same things in Natalia's eyes I had, the lack of will to live.

"Thank you, I worry about her a great deal, but I'm glad you'll take care of her. I should mention she's pregnant but has recently been under a great deal of stress and mentioned things not feeling right."

"I will make sure the girls know about that and have a midwife make sure everything's okay. Now, what about you?" she asked, glancing down at the ankle I was struggling not to put weight on, the pain from the Mage's attack growing worse.

Saying nothing, I bent down and rolled up my pant leg, sucking in air through my teeth as the skin sticking to my robes pulled away with the fabric, the lattice having turned a much darker shade.

"Oh, goodness! Please, sit, I will send for the healer right away."

I fell back onto the sofa, dizziness rushing over me and vision clouding. My head was in a fog and the surrounding sounds melded together to create a warped melody. I closed my eyes and hoped the dizziness would pass.

Instead, a voice whispered in my ear, "You still haven't learned yet, have you?"

My eyes flew open, finding only complete darkness. I turned my head toward the voice, tired of only getting riddles. "What do you want from me? What am I supposed to do?"

"If I were to tell you that, it would be too easy," Fonir laughed. "Now, I will give you a tip. Listen to your emotions. The world needs a heart, not a mind."

As Fonir's voice faded, a searing pain shot up my leg, and my shouts dispelled the darkness.

A glowing man sat on the floor with my foot in his hand, the room bathed in his green light. The maid stood in the corner, hands over her mouth in terror as the man gripped my ankle. He said something under his breath and another jolt of pain rushed up my leg, more screams escaping my lips as the man held my ankle still.

I clenched my teeth and took long, conscious breaths while watching the healer and my leg, the lattice seeming to have grown faster and spread throughout my body. I glanced at my hands and saw the lattice following my veins, spreading down to my fingertips. I tried to think through the fog in my brain, to make sense of what was happening. Lightning Mages were a rare occurrence, only one every hundred years. Dark purple lattice covering the skin, following the veins and boiling the blood, was a well-known symptom of a Lightning Mage-caused death, but no one knew much else. *Am I going to die?*

My entire body lit up in pain, feeling like I'd fallen into a fire. My muscles locked and my lungs burned for air I couldn't give them. My screams became so high they were inaudible, my mouth open and eyes bulging. The words of the healer rose above the pain and I latched on to them, needing something to keep me tied to the world. I couldn't understand the ancient tongue, but I made Fonir, Kysyn, and the names of a few other gods.

The pain crescendoed with the healer's final words, then vanished. Air rushed into my lungs as I gasped for breath. My hair clung to my skin, my whole body sore and tingling. Looking at my hands, the lattice still there, but fading to a pale white, a visible pattern on my tanned skin. I raised my head and looked at the healer, his chin slumped against his chest and hands trembling. While I wasn't certain, he most likely saved my life, and I had no words to thank him.

The maid rushed over, placing a wet cloth to my forehead and raising a glass of water to my lips. "Thank goodness you're okay, miss. When I came back in and found you having a seizure on the sofa, I thought for sure you were a goner. Thank goodness the healer arrived when he did."

I lifted my head again and struggled to sit up. Sweat dripped from the man's brow, body trembling, but he looked up at me with a smile, the corners of his eyes crinkling.

"I think, my dear," he said between gulps of air, "you are the first person to have ever survived the attack of a Lightning Mage. You should rest now, but I'll be back to check on you in the morning to see how you're doing."

I nodded, still not having the energy to speak, falling back into the sofa, and letting the maid change out the cloth. "If it's alright, miss, I'm going to have the butler carry you up to your room. I think you'll be more comfortable there."

I gave a slight nod and the maid scurried off, her bonnet bouncing with every step. I lay there, staring at the ceiling, and thanked the gods for my life, not sure why I was still alive, but grateful all the same.

***

After the butler carried me up to my room, the maid, along with two others, helped me out of my robes and into a light shift. They wiped my body down with cool cloths, reducing the fever and removing the dirt I'd accumulated from traveling. They kept up the conversation, unbothered by the fact I'd nearly died, and included me in the gossip of the town, talking about a Mr. so-and-so who sent flowers to a Ms. who-and-who that was courting a Mr. nose hair.

The maids' good spirits helped me feel a bit better and I gratefully accepted their offer of lunch.

"The healer was strict on what you could and couldn't have, so the cook made you some broth. He did say you could have some fruit, though, so I brought a bowl of berries if you feel up to it," the maid said when she came back with a tray.

The aroma of the broth filled the room and I had a hard time focusing on anything else. I barely managed to thank her for the food before slurping down a spoonful of broth, the richness coating my mouth. I let out a sigh in satisfaction and drank the entire serving in a matter of minutes, not caring for manners and sipping straight from the bowl.

I reached for the fruit next and the sweetness perfectly accentuated the richness of the broth, both satisfying me and making me more hungry at the same time. When I was done, the maid cleared the tray with a smile, and the other two set about detangling my hair, chatting more about the gossip of the city. I half-listened to them and let my thoughts drift back to Altava, to Mamma. *I hope she's okay. Father was leaving that next morning to trade more goods, but that left an entire day of her alone with him...* A strand of hair fell in front of my eyes, distracting me from my thoughts, and I jolted upright, staring at my hair in disbelief.

One of the maids gave me a hand mirror and I stared in shock at my once red locks now streaked with many strands of black. I didn't know what to make of it, but leaning closer, I noticed the lattice rising up my neck before fading away near my lips. The lattice covered the rest of my body, growing to an almost glowing shade of white when it reached the spot where I was hit.

"I think your hair looks lovely like that, miss, it really brings out your eyes."

I risked a glance at my eyes, fearful they'd changed too, but thankfully finding them the same green I was used too, if not brighter.

"Your hair will look even prettier once we plait it. Here, let us show you."

The maids helped plait my hair and spoke with me the entire time as if I was a good friend instead of a girl they just met. When they were done, I had to admit the streaks of black in the plaits made my hair look more flower-like when it was pinned at the nape of my neck. While I wasn't as upset with the new color, I was glad for the first time the sun in the desert was so harsh it required head coverings.

The rest of the afternoon passed without much notice, the maids leaving not too long after plaiting my hair, urging me to get some rest. I curled up under the blankets and tried to get comfortable, but between my worry for Natalia and the throbbing in my ankle, I eventually gave up on sleeping and focused inward on my Well. Not being able to use it when looking around the wagons worried me and I hoped the Lightning Mage hadn't caused permanent damage.

I started with something simple. I closed my eyes and focused on the areas of light around the room, the candle, sunlight beaming in through the window, even the light reflecting off the mirror on the vanity. I focused on the light nearest me, a candle, and imagined myself drawing the light into my Well. I wasn't trying to extinguish the light. Instead, I wanted to borrow the energy it expelled, pulling it into me so it wasn't wasted.

Drawing the Light Aura into my Well stung. Everything was strained and raw from the Lightning Mage's attack, but it was possible. I didn't want to push myself too hard, but I needed to make sure I could still emanate Aura to calm at least some of my worries.

I focused on pulling out wisps of Aura into my palm, only enough for me to verify everything was okay. The same straining sensation returned, but sharper, the Aura moving to the surface at the same speed someone would trudge through mud. I was about to give up when a wisp of pale white Aura appeared. I stared at it for a moment, not sure if I was seeing things correctly. *My Aura is usually golden, like my Father's spirit and the spirits of many other merchants. Why is mine white now?*

Before I could try and glean any more about my Aura, it dissipated, my Well flinching from overworking. I answered one question, only to bring up yet another. Not wanting to push myself anymore, I closed my eyes again and let my breathing slow, wanting to reconnect with myself and the world around me.

When the light in the room dimmed, someone knocked on the door.

Not trusting myself to walk, I called out instead. "Come in."

A woman came over and sat in a chair next to the bed, placing her hand over my own. I looked up at her, acknowledging her presence, only to gasp when I noticed her hair, the same bright red as my mother's and mine.

"I'm Lady Hyll, mayor of Cragsrest. It sounds like you had an interesting afternoon," she said, smiling at me. "If I had been through everything you had, I would be asleep for days," she laughed, sounding like bells in the distance, a light and calming sound.

"Your hair..." I paused, realizing how rude I was being. "I mean, thank you for your amazing hospitality and—" She cut me off, raising her hand.

"There's no need for such formality here, especially not after what you went through. But yes, my hair is the same as yours, the same hair everyone from Reshil has."

I wanted to ask her so many questions, thinking she may know something about my mother's arrival to Klohaven, but her lack of accent told me she probably didn't.

"Now, why don't you tell me what happened, and anything you can so I can get a better idea of your journey until now."

I launched into my story, starting with the figure and its meaning up until arriving at her home. There were a few things I left out, like the details of the bodies or the doubt I had in myself, but I told her everything else. She was quiet for a moment before speaking.

"It does sound like a lot is going on in your world right now. I want you to know you're welcome to stay here as long as you'd like, to rest and make your decision about the next leg of your journey. I promise your friend is in good hands and I will have her returned to Altava safely."

"How... how is she?"

"She and the baby are both fine. She was under a great deal of stress, but we have been able to calm her down and help her relax."

I thanked the woman and she got up to leave, turning back one last time. "If there is anything you need, please don't hesitate to ring the bell on the table next to you."

I looked at the bell and thanked her again before she shut the door behind her.

It was less than five minutes later when one of the maids

knocked and entered the room, followed by the commander from before.

"I'm glad to see you're doing better. I heard what happened and how the healer saved your life."

"I am very grateful he did."

The commander agreed and sat in the same chair Lady Hyll had. "I was hoping, as long as you are feeling alright, you could answer some questions for me."

"Of course."

"I sent out a troop of soldiers to look at your camp and they collected your companions; I can only imagine what that would've been like to come back to. You said before you could scavenge things when you returned from your walk, could you tell me what those were?"

I listed off everything I could think of, including my untouched pack, the weapons, overlooked jewelry, and the two bags of coins.

"You also said the two horses you rode in on had been missing when you arrived back at your camp?"

"Yes, they found us later. Right before the bandits appeared..." I trailed off, thinking about the odd coincidences the commander was pointing out.

"I think it would be best if you didn't bring this up to anyone else. There's something here that doesn't seem right."

He was right, something with the bandits wasn't right, but before I could think about it, the exhaustion took over and I was asleep before the commander left.

CHAPTER SEVENTEEN
HAJANA

The next morning, I awoke to the sounds of birds and sunshine pouring in from the window. There was no one to force me to get up to do chores. While it was only a slight break in what had become my life, it was a welcome one, and I planned on savoring every moment.

I sat up and looked at Dalila still snoring lightly next to me, and all the other girls in the room. None of the others were awake, and I enjoyed the blissful calm of a new day, trying to forget about the events a few hours earlier.

During the night, one girl, a younger one who slept in a separate loft than me, ended up getting sick. I learned to ignore the sounds of those surrounding me, but there was something different about it. I ended up going over to her, offering some water from the bucket. She seemed to be able to keep the water down and, after getting her a cool cloth to help with the slight fever, I went back to bed. Glancing over to where the girl made her bed the night before, I gasped, causing a few of the others to stir.

The girl must've gotten sick again after I had fallen asleep, heaping the blanket at the foot of her bed while tossing and turning, the sheets soiled with bile, blood, and other substances. The girl, maybe ten years old or so, was ashen, her face and neck covered in oozing, purple sores. She stared up at the ceiling; her face distorted in a grimace and her hands still grasping at the collar of her nightdress as the sores from Slave Pox in her throat suffocated her.

"The poor thing," a girl said, holding her hand out in front of her with two fingers raised and pressed together, the other over her heart.

"It is a terrible way to go, but at least she's no longer suffering," another responded, mirroring the first, a salute to Para.

The rest of us bowed our heads, saluting Para, while one of the older slaves led us in a plea of safe passage for the girl to the next life.

"Para, great and good, you have called your daughter back to a place of peace, to be with you. We ask that her soul is granted the grace to know the way home. Bless her, her family, friends, and anyone who knew her; give them comfort in knowing she is no longer in pain or suffering. In your name and your grace, we ask you this."

Sniffles broke the silence as we ended the prayer and one of the girls moved forward, only to be held back.

"Don't go near her. Now that the sores have burst, anything she's touched needs to be burned."

Another girl went to the door and let the servant outside know about the body. Two servants came in wearing gloves and cloths over their noses and mouths. They wrapped the girl's body in her blankets and carried her out, warning the rest of us to stay away from her belongings.

I climbed back into bed, scooting under my blanket, and stared at nothing, not sure what to do or how to feel. I had seen many slaves and even a few maids die from sickness, beatings, or by their own hand. The death of this girl was different. She was young and healthy only the night before. Then, she was gone, her body soon to be burned with the rest of her belongings.

"Are you okay?" Dalila asked, her voice booming through the silent room.

"No, I'm not…" I paused, trying to collect my thoughts.

"Why? You've seen countless deaths during your time as a slave. We all have." She motioned to the others in the room, none of them paying us any mind. "Why is this girl any different?"

"She's not, at least not really."

"Then move on. There's no use dwelling on her death."

While I knew Dalila was right, I needed to move on, I couldn't shake the girl's death. *If she hadn't been a slave, would she still be alive?* While the Serf Pox was most common among the poor and household servants, it wasn't unheard of for the children of the master of the house to get it too. The children rarely died, the cure for the Pox being discovered ages ago. The cost of the medication was the same as buying a dozen slaves, however, so for the poor, it was a death sentence.

"Here's your morning meal," a maid said as she walked in carrying a basket full of wrapped bundles.

The maid dropped a small bundle on my bed and I slowly unwrapped it, not the slightest bit hungry but knowing I needed to eat anyway. There wasn't much, a chunk of bread, some cheese, and a small piece of fruit. The fruit was a bit of a surprise, but I didn't want to question the wrinkly cactus and savored every bit of it.

One of the village doctors came in, a man well versed in healing, but not having a Well of his own. He and the two servants who removed the body grabbed the rest of the girl's belongings, including the entire bed frame. They carried it out and shut the door, leaving nothing but a puddle of cleaner on the floor, as if the girl was never there.

Deciding not to focus on the grimness of the situation, I placed the cloth with my small pile of belongings under my bed and went to pull out my book when I found the small container of pills from the apothecary. *Well, it helped last time.*

I got out of bed and headed over to the freshly refilled water bucket. I took a few sips of water, popping my pill in my mouth as inconspicuous as I could. I doubted anyone would notice or even care, but the idea of anyone knowing I struggled with controlling my thoughts was enough to make me consider not taking anything.

I took a few more swallows to make sure no one was paying attention to me before climbing back under the blankets to protect myself from the chill of death hanging over the room. Hushed conversations drifted through the air, a snippet here and there floating over to me.

"She was so young…"

"It's a tragic thing…"

"At least we were able to pray for her soul…"

I pulled out the book and rolled over so I was facing Dalila. While I was worried about the other girls using the knowledge of a book in my possession against me, my thoughts were too fast for me to tame without the help of an outside distraction.

I flipped through the pages, looking for the spot from the night before where I discovered I was reading the story of another slave and the struggles she was facing. While there were some parts of the story that angered me, the way the slave's master treated her and the awful things she was made to do, the girl gave me some hope; if she could still be positive after everything she suffered through, then so could I.

I lost myself in the story, the way the girl struggled with the near impossible list of daily chores, and the punishments she received if she failed. Her life seemed to be so much harder than mine.

I was so enthralled with the story I lost myself for hours and hadn't paid any attention to the girls around me until a scream pierced the air, followed by a dull thud. I didn't have to look out the window to know what happened. I said a quick prayer to Para and clambered out from the blankets to join the others.

On the ground, a few stories below, was the body of the girl who had been so upset over the death of the slave. Listening to those around me, I learned the two girls were sisters, the only thing either of them had left of their past life. Dalila joined me and put her hand on my shoulder. I turned to her and gave a weak smile before climbing back under the covers. Even though it was only mid-afternoon, I decided it was time to head to bed for the evening, not wanting to think about who lay just outside the window.

The day and night melded into one, only the changing light and the maids serving food allowing me to keep track of passing time. My focus on the book the woman gave me waned and I struggled to read after the deaths. I could only read a few pages at a time before having to close it.

Dalila grew more restless as the next day passed and she started pacing after lunch, running her fingers along the walls and staring out the window and at the gardens below. The two of us didn't talk much and we turned in early once again, there being nothing else to do.

After breakfast the third day, I returned to my book, only to lose interest soon after.

"I'm bored," one of the girls, Layla, said, the sudden exclamation causing me to jump.

"Me too, but you have to enjoy this break from chores and responsibilities. When was the last time you were able to enjoy your day how you wanted?" a girl with blonde hair, Daphne, asked.

"You're enjoying yourself? I'm certainly not."

Layla's words hushed the din of conversation in the room as everyone glanced at each other.

"Are any of you enjoying this?" Layla continued. "Being locked in this room for three days with literally nothing to do but twiddle our thumbs and pray we don't die. We've already seen two other girls die from the Pox and countless others outside stuck doing their work as well as ours!"

"I think this is a decent way to spend my days."

A collective gasp spread around the room and everyone turned to the young girl, Yazmeen, who spoke. She stood and walked to the center of the room to stare at us.

"They have ripped us from our homes, thrown us into slavery, and forced us to do unthinkable things. Now, we have the chance to take a break, to enjoy the life stolen from us—"

"And you think those girls out there deserve to suffer more so we can 'take a break'?" I asked Yazmeen, surprising myself by speaking up, but the rage boiling in my veins was too hot to ignore.

"We're not being told to clean chamber pots or do the wash. Are you saying you would rather be out there, standing in the scorching sun, weeding the gardens? Up here we can finally sleep and talk and relax without worrying about getting beaten for slacking."

"Hajana is right," Layla spoke up. "They're keeping us in here like the animals at a menagerie, letting us pace in our cages but nothing more."

"You're just a little bored, you're making this too big of—"

"No, we're not. You're the one that's not taking this seriously!" Layla said, throwing her hands up in frustration and pulling at her hair.

"What makes you say I'm not taking this seriously? Am I a bad person for wanting to be free?" Yazmeen asked.

"We're not free! We're being forced to follow their schedule, only able to eat when they say we can, not being able to go out and enjoy our lives!" I shouted.

"We can't go out because we could be sick. We don't want to risk the others getting sick because of us."

"The others would rather be sick!" Layla motioned to the window.

I followed her hand and looked at the gardens below, seeing a few of the slaves out weeding the garden, a chore I was grateful to take a break from.

"I don't know what you want me to see. They're out there working," Yazmeen said.

"Look closer, you'll see it."

Yazmeen sighed and peered again at the gardens below. Glancing out the window, I noticed one girl stand and nearly fall into the flowers; her face so red I could see it three floors up. She staggered over to another bed, tripping on a stone and collapsing to the ground, not moving.

"They're just dealing with heat exhaustion. It happened to me a lot when I first started weeding. They'll be fine."

"Will they?"

Yazmeen looked back again and watched the mistress march over to the girl on the ground, cane in hand. She poked at the girl a few times before calling to someone out of view. A moment later, two servants appeared and flipped the girl over, her once red face ashen and her eyes open wide. She was dead.

"Why did she die? It was just a little hot out there," Yazmeen asked, her voice cracking.

"That's the third girl in two days I've seen carted off. Who knows how many others I missed," Layla said.

"What's wrong with them?"

"They're overworked, just like the rest of us, except now they get to do our chores on top of theirs while also getting fewer rations because we're getting so much more."

"You're lying! There's no way us being up here has that much of an effect."

"The proof lies before you or did before her body was taken away. When some rise, others are going to fall, becoming the sacrifice."

The room was once again silent, no one knowing what to say. Almost everyone knew Layla was right, but Yazmeen and a few of the other younger slaves clenched their fists, some with tears rolling down their cheeks. *I know they've been through a lot, but why won't they believe what's in front of them?*

"You're speaking nothing but lies and I don't want to hear any more of it. I'm going to take a nap."

"By all means, please do. Hopefully, when you wake up, you'll realize the truth behind our words."

Yazmeen climbed into bed and turned away from us, her sobs muffled by her pillow. The rest of us returned to what we were doing, the heaviness about the room seeping into my soul. I considered trying to read more but didn't have the energy after arguing with the young girl.

The next morning I rolled over to see Yazmeen's body covered in oozing purple sores.

CHAPTER EIGHTEEN
EMOLIN

The maids came in the next morning and helped me get ready before leading me down to the dining room for breakfast. My ankle was still rather sore and one of the maids let me lean on her so most of my weight was kept off my leg. When I entered the room, Lady Hyll was already seated at the head of the table, waiting for me.

"Good morning, I trust you slept well?"

"I did, I honestly can't remember the last time I slept so soundly," I said, taking a seat at the table.

"I'm glad to hear. Your friend will be joining us in a little while. I am told she and her baby had a rough night."

The fact Lady Hyll mentioned the baby gave me hope everything was going to be okay.

"Please, sit, I had my cook prepare extra tarts after hearing how much you enjoyed the fruit last night."

My cheeks flushed and I took a seat at the table to the right of Lady Hyll. There was a vast assortment of dishes laid out before us, steaming bowls of potatoes, eggs, meats, piles of fresh berries, personal bowls of sweet cream, and several platters of pastries and sweets.

"It has been quite a while since I've had this many choices for breakfast. Is someone else joining us?"

Lady Hyll laughed. "No, it's just the three of us. Don't worry, though, none of this will go to waste. Anything we don't eat will be taken to the chapel to be distributed to those in need."

I smiled and waited for Lady Hyll to serve herself before putting a pile of potatoes and meat on my plate along with plenty of berries and a few pastries. A butler came by and poured us glasses of light wine and juice.

As we ate, Lady Hyll asked me questions about Altava and what I did before leaving. While I didn't say it outright, I tried to portray my disgust about slavery as well as I could. Lady Hyll gave me her full attention as I spoke, occasionally asking questions and giving polite reactions to my story. As I continued, something about her struck me. I couldn't tell if it was her kindness or the Aura from her Well, but I knew I could trust her.

"May I tell you a secret, one that cannot be shared outside of this conversation?"

"Of course, my dear."

"I've had Fonir speak with me several times since the first. He keeps telling me I can make changes, that 'the world needs a heart.' I'm not sure what he means, but I'm hoping I will be able to save more than I have to kill."

Lady Hyll nodded and tapped her fingers on her chin in thought. "While I'm not exactly sure what he means either, the fact he's been visiting you means there is a chance of preventing senseless deaths. What are you going to do now?"

Her question struck me and I realized I didn't know what I was going to do. If I continued on my journey as planned, I would be making it alone, or at least without those I started with. If I didn't keep going, however, I feared what Fonir would do considering how many times he came to speak with me and, in a way, it seemed like he wanted to help.

"I'm not sure..." I trailed off, my appetite gone.

"Unfortunately, I can't in good conscience give you help to complete your journey as it stands."

I raised my eyebrow in confusion and tilted my head. Before I could get any clarification, a maid entered, leading Natalia to the table.

"Hello, my dear," Lady Hyll said. "How did you sleep?"

Natalia slumped in her chair, focusing on her hands. Her skin was almost translucent and the dark circles under her eyes looked more like someone punched her instead of not resting enough. Her usually vibrant, shiny, silver hair was dull and matted against her head.

Natalia mumbled something inaudible and didn't even acknowledge the maid serving her. I had never seen Natalia in such a fragile state, and I didn't know whether or not to hug her.

Lady Hyll reached over and squeezed my hand. "Don't worry. She'll be okay. She made it through the roughest part. The first night of being fully aware of what happened is the worst. Now, she needs to focus on healing."

I nodded, not wanting to take my eyes off of Natalia and feeling a small glimmer of hope when she finally took a bite, albeit a small one.

"Now, as I was saying, I won't be able to help you if your journey continues on the path the Magistrate planned. You may not have noticed when you arrived, but there is no form of slavery here in Cragsrest. I not only detested enslaving people regardless of their crimes, but I also exile anyone who feels the need to shun anyone for their race, religion, or sexuality."

I didn't know how to react. To hear someone in a position of power speaking against the way of life everyone so dearly loved was shocking. I knew there were people against slavery, there were always deferring opinions about things, but hearing someone say it outright was something I thought I'd never witness.

"How can I change my path, though? The Magistrate was clear

about his expectations for this journey and what he'd do if I didn't go along with it."

"That's a question you must answer yourself. Fonir must believe in you, or at least think you can do things others can't. You have to make the choice, though. Are you going to do what's expected of you, or what the gods and you heart are asking of you?"

I thought of Hajana, how she was a slave only because her parents were Parans, the complete unjustness of the situation causing anger to rise within me. I didn't know how I was going to do it, but I knew I couldn't leave innocents like Hajana forced to work for the rest of their lives with nothing to show for it.

"I don't know how I'm going to do it, but I wouldn't be able to live with myself if I let something happen I had the chance to stop."

"In that case, you'll want to leave here shortly. If you leave soon, you have the chance of making it to Gathon before sundown. I wish I could send someone with you, but with increased bandit activity, I need as many people as I can to help protect the city. I'll have my maids pack your things and my stable hand will get your horse brushed and saddled.

"In the meantime, the healer is in the parlor waiting to speak with you and give you the okay to travel. While it would be best to allow you a few more days to rest, I doubt there's time for that."

I thanked her and excused myself from the table, waving to Natalia but not getting a response. A maid helped me to the parlor I was in the day before and the healer stood and bowed when I entered.

"Hello, I trust you're doing well?"

"My ankle is still a little sore, but nothing I can't handle," I said, limping toward the sofa.

"May I?" he asked, motioning toward my leg.

I nodded and he pulled a chair over. Placing my leg in his lap, he gently rolled the leg of my robes up and applied pressure to various parts of the lattice, apologizing whenever I winced.

"Your muscles are strained from the attack forcing its way into your Well and the muscles contracted from the healing." He pointed to a specific part of my ankle, "This area will probably give you the most problems over the next few weeks, but I believe it should heal just fine. I know this most likely isn't possible, but try to stay off your feet as much as you can over the next several days and elevate your leg as often as possible."

"I will stay off my feet as often as I can ride Sampson, but it's quite difficult to elevate one's foot while on a horse."

The healer chuckled. "Yes, quite so. At the very least, take it easy and make sure to see the healer in the next city you stop in."

I promised him I would and bowed my head as he left, not wanting to get up unless I needed to. Instead, I leaned back into the pillow on the sofa and sighed, enjoying the rare moment of relaxation before having to move on.

I wasn't sure how much time passed, but eventually, a butler came in to let me know my steed was ready. I thanked him and followed him out of the house to where Sampson stood tall and proud. Someone had taken great care in washing and brushing him, small plaits decorating his dark main and tail.

I walked over to stroke Sampson's nose and looked back at the house, worry filling me and tears threatening to spill.

Natalia was led out of the house by a set of maids and she rushed over to hug me, her sudden change in emotion startling me.

"Please, be safe. I can't lose you too."

Natalia's words were enough to cause the tears to run down my cheeks, and the two of us stood there hugging for several minutes before pulling away.

A maid handed me my pack and I slipped it on while preparing myself to climb into the saddle. I put my left foot in the stirrup, having watched many REDs mount before, and hoped I wouldn't make a fool of myself. I took a deep breath, grateful it was my right ankle in pain, and pulled myself up with the saddle horn while putting all my weight on my left foot. I managed to swing my leg over and get myself seated in the saddle without too much trouble.

I grabbed the reins, not entirely sure how to hold them, but Sampson seemed to know where I wanted to go and turned toward the southern part of the city. We walked through the city, and I realized how serene it all seemed compared to the others I traveled through. I wasn't sure if it was because it was smaller or the lack of slaves and more people working for themselves, but everyone seemed to be enjoying their time instead of rushing about.

A few soldiers stood at the gate and saluted Sampson and I as we headed out of the city and into the desert once more.

The desert looked much as it had, the only difference being the mountains looming overhead and the rock clusters becoming more common again. Lady Hyll had the maids pack me a map detailing the next part of my journey, pointing out the quickest route to the river and any oases I would happen upon.

Sampson seemed to enjoy the freedom of just the two of us traveling. He was able to go as fast or slow as he wanted without worrying about anyone telling him what to do. I considered trying to guide him, but not only did he seem to know where to go, I was also too busy trying not to fall out of the saddle.

I knew Sampson was more spirited than the other horses on our journey had been, but I figured it was because of how much younger he was. After spending a short amount of time with him, riding across the desert, I realized it was more than just his different temperament. He seemed to be more aware of the world.

When Sampson was walking, I was okay, but as soon as he went any faster, I felt like I was going to bounce out of the saddle. I tried to find a way to move with him, to keep myself from bouncing so much, but my ankle was too stiff and sore to allow me to try anything for too long. So, I held on as best I could and enjoyed every break I could get.

Once we reached the river, Sampson and I took a long break, enjoying the cool water and nibbling on some food. I wasn't all that hungry from eating the large breakfast at Lady Hyll's, but I still ate a bit anyway to help prevent potential heat exhaustion.

I let Sampson frolic as long as he wanted, telling him I wouldn't be able to take the saddle off so he would have to be careful. He snorted but stayed out of the water and the saddle was still tight when it was time to leave again.

As we continued, I found myself talking to Sampson, telling him stories about my life at home and the friends I had.

"Then, when Sojourn wasn't looking, Aaron and Ziden…" I trailed off, realizing they were gone.

Even Natalia was gone, not in the same way, but I knew she would never be the same. I had seen REDs come back from battles with the same expression Natalia had. Some did come out of it and were able to live their lives the same as before, but most were jumpy, always looking over their shoulders and mumbling to themselves. Natalia had been the same way the night she lost Ziden, and I would be surprised if she ever smiled again.

Tears blurring my vision, I forced myself to think of other things, anything to take my mind off that night. I started keeping track of the number of rock clusters we passed and how many rocks were in each cluster. I had no idea if that information would ever be useful, but it gave me something to focus on.

"So, groups of five stones seem to be the most common, but only if—"

Hearing what I thought were voices, I cut myself off and pulled on the reigns to slow Sampson so I could listen. We came to a stop, Sampson shifting his weight foot to foot, his ears pivoting and twitching behind us. Just when I thought it was my imagination, shouting pierced the air, and Sampson took off.

The shouts sounded like they were coming from the north, but the sound bounced off the rocks, echoing and making it difficult to tell. Sampson cantered for the good part of the next twenty minutes before I slowed him to a stop so I could listen and take a break from bouncing in the saddle. Satisfied the voices hadn't followed us, I pulled out the map to verify how far from Gathon we were.

"It looks like the main path should be close. I say we keep going and get to Gathon before dinner. Does that sound okay?" I asked, patting Sampson on the neck.

He answered by turning south, seeming to know where to go without me guiding him. I put the map away and tried not to think about how sore my rear was or the not so subtle throbbing of my ankle. There were too many other things to worry about than my comfort.

Before the thoughts of the deaths of my friends filled my mind again, the shouts filled my ears, turning into laughter and surrounding us. I urged Sampson on, fear settling in my stomach. *How do they keep finding me?* My heartbeat thundered in my ears, drowning out the sounds of the rest of the world. Images of past bandit attacks and the bodies of my friends flashed through my mind. As much as it pained my ankle, I spurred Sampson onward, not daring to look back, afraid of seeing the bandits behind me.

Sampson needed little encouragement and took off across the desert, expertly dodging rocks and thickets.

We rounded a large boulder and met with a well-traveled road. There were a few carts ahead of us and I slowed Sampson to a trot so we didn't cause any panic among the travelers. We approached the cart at the front of the small group hoping to get some help.

"Hey there, miss. What can I do ye for?"

The man in the front cart had a thick accent that distracted me for a few seconds before I could collect myself.

I kept my voice just loud enough for him to hear me over the sounds of the wagons, but not enough to scare the man's traveling companions.

"I'm being followed by bandits."

The man nodded, seeming to understand the things I wasn't saying.

"Well, ye are more than welcome to travel with us for a while. If you're heading to Gathon, we'll have to part ways at the river, but if you keep following the road after that, you should be there by nightfall."

I thanked the man and chose a spot in the center of the group. A small girl riding in one wagon turned and waved at me.

"I like your horse. What's his name?"

I smiled at the girl. "His name is Sampson."

"Sampson? That's a weird name for a horse. That's a human name."

"It might not be a normal horsey name, but I feel it fits him well. What's your name?"

"My name is Anna and my little sister is in the back with Mama."

"Do you enjoy traveling on the road, Anna?"

"I did at first, but now we have to travel a lot more and the wagon is boring. Papa says it's because of the—"

"That's enough, Anna, let the poor Mage rest," the man next to the girl said, his voice gruff and coated in the same accent as the man in the lead cart.

"Yes, Papa."

I wanted to know what Anna meant about having to travel so much, but the way her father looked at me, I knew it was a better idea not to ask. I glanced at the wagon up front, the one I assumed was in charge of how often the group traveled, and wondered what he was hiding.

I drifted over to one of the other wagons, not wanting to anger Anna's father more, but also wanting to stay in the center of the group so the bandits would be less likely to spot me. Feeling safe among the group, the exhaustion from being chased so much consumed me, and I struggled to keep my eyes open and myself upright on Sampson's back.

I was very grateful when the man called for a break when we reached another oasis, much smaller than the ones near Altava, but still plenty large for all the horses and travelers to quench their thirst. Many of the children traveling jumped out of their wagons and chased each other, playing games. Anna came over and sat next to me in the shade.

"Why are you out here traveling by yourself?"

I glanced around, making sure Anna's father wasn't looking. "Can you keep a secret?"

Anna nodded, eyes wide.

"I'm on a special quest. So special they could only send one person."

"Wow! That must mean you're really amazing."

The girl's words lit something inside me, and I was about to respond when the man in charge of the group called for us to continue. Anna ran back to her parents, and I checked Sampson's saddle before climbing up. I took a place in the center of the group as we moved on.

I listened to the surrounding families, the children laughing, and the occasional crying of an infant. While the group was loud and chaotic, it reminded me of home, of the children running to their lessons as I was running late for training. It seemed so long since I left, but in reality, it had only been five days. I didn't realize how much one could grow to miss a place in less than half a fortnight.

I was so lost in thought I nearly missed the man leading the group calling for me.

"This is where we must part. If you continue south from here, you'll see Gathon before you know it."

I thanked the man for letting me travel with them, even if it was only for a short while, and waved to the caravan as I crossed the river. Sampson, once again in charge of our speed, took off at a canter, that speed being a little easier on my ankle as we followed the road, the sun shining high overhead.

The terrain of the land changed the closer we got to Gathon. The majority of the landscape was still made up of rocks and hard-packed soil, but with far more patches of trees and shrubbery than before.

Sampson seemed to enjoy the extra plants and foliage as we continued. There was a perk to his steps and he acted like he didn't want to rest. Not wanting him to wear himself out, I made him stop every so often, even if it was just so he could nibble on some of the plants and I could get a bit of food myself.

The first thing I saw when we neared Gathon were the towers of what I assumed to be the LeDore mansion, the largest building in the capital. They looked like bits of the bright, blue sky being torn away the way they were silhouetted by the sun. My heart caught in my chest and I struggled to keep my breath steady, the full realization of how far I was from home finally becoming real. Sampson and I got in line with the others waiting to enter the city, many with carts and mules loaded with goods, but a few smaller groups of travelers most likely looking for a place to rest for the night.

A few people stared and pointed at Sampson, probably because of his Klohave markings, but many ignored us. I was glad my headscarf hid my hair as Sampson and I slowly made our way to the gate.

"Purpose of visit."

The guard at the gate, dressed in purple instead of red like the ones in Altava, phrased the question as a statement, looking bored and tired from having to stand there asking the same questions over and over again.

"I've been sent here by Magistrate Straven Magdra on my way to Blackwood to speak with Grandmaster Lisbeth Sphera."

I hoped my voice sounded more confident than I felt.

"Papers."

I reached into my saddlebag, rummaging around for the papers from Magistrate Magdra. My breath caught when I didn't feel them and I started pulling everything out before I found the papers pressed against the side of the bag.

I handed the guard my papers and he stared at me from his perch, seeming to be trying to decide whether or not to believe my story. After asking a few more questions he made a motion with his hand and many complaints rose from the crowd as a couple of guards made their way to me.

"Your papers seem all in order, but just to be safe I am going to have the commander question you."

Not wanting to cause any trouble, I agreed and let one of the guards take Sampson's reins and lead us out of the line and around the side of the wall. I wasn't sure why I was being questioned and I hoped it wouldn't take too long.

"We will need to house your horse in the stable with our mounts until we can clear you for entrance. Please dismount."

As much as I didn't want to leave Sampson and be all alone, I didn't want to anger the men by being difficult. I dismounted and stroked Sampson's nose before giving him to the guards.

"Don't worry, we'll take care of him," the guard said, giving me a reassuring smile.

I watched Samson being led off and turned to the other two guards.

"This way, please," one of the guards said, giving me a small bow and motioning down the tunnel in the wall, the doors being held open by two more guards.

My limp was far more obvious as I made my way down the corridor, not sure where I was heading. One of the guards came up to me and offered his arm which I gratefully took. A small part of my mind told me I should be warier of the men and being alone with them, but they had given me no reasons to fear them other than the fact that they were born with a saber instead of a shield.

I was shown into a small room with several plush chairs and a small table in the center. There was a tray with an assortment of biscuits and several teacups waiting for their accompanying pot.

"If you'll wait here, tea will be brought shortly. The commander will speak with you as soon as he is free."

The guards gave another bow and left, shutting the door behind them. I didn't need to test the door to know it had been locked. I sat in one of the chairs, relaxing into their softness. While I didn't enjoy the idea of being trapped in a room with hundreds of tons of stone above me, if I ignored that fact, I was able to enjoy the different biscuits and satisfy a hunger that had stayed hidden until I felt relatively safe.

The door opened after only a few moments and a maid dressed in the same colors of the guards came in and placed a large teapot on the trivet, lighting the candle beneath.

"Please enjoy the tea. There is cream and sugar next to the cups. The chamber pot is in the corner behind that curtain," the maid motioned to a beige curtain I hadn't noticed before. "If you require anything else, please don't hesitate to pull the cord by the door and one of my sisters or I will try to get you anything you require."

I thanked the girl, noticing she wasn't much older than me as she curtsied and left.

I poured myself a cup of tea while wondering what my life would be like if I hadn't been born a Mage. The mixture of cloves with the tea leaves allowed me to relax more, and I added a bit of cream and a lot of sugar before taking a sip. I enjoyed the warmth of the drink and realized how scratchy my throat was after breathing in the dust while riding across the desert. I quickly finished the first cup of tea and poured myself a second, letting the sugar coat my throat.

I ate a few biscuits and finished the second cup of tea before I realized I was getting bored. I looked around the room for something to distract myself, but found nothing other than a small desk in the corner. I hobbled over to the desk and opened the drawers, hoping to find anything to distract me. All I found were a few old quills, some dead spiders, and a few scraps of torn parchment with nothing on them.

I shut the drawer and sat back down in the chair in a huff. While I was glad I had food and drink, I couldn't help fidgeting as I sat there and decided to nibble on another biscuit. I poured myself yet another cup of tea and dipped one of the spicier biscuits into the milky sweetness.

As I finished the third cup of tea, my bladder decided to let me know I needed to visit the corner of the room. I tried to tell myself I could wait; I didn't want to be relieving myself when the commander came in.

Eventually, my bladder won out and I kept my legs clenched as I waddled over to the curtain.

I struggled with my robes, eventually pulling them off and closing the curtain just as I thought couldn't hold it any longer.

As I feared, the door opened and boots thudded on the floor as I started relieving myself.

"I don't want to alarm you, but I am Commander Flagstar. I

am here to validate your claim and help you proceed on your journey. Please, take your time."

I took longer than needed before I redressed and faced the commander. I hoped my cheeks weren't too red as I limped over to the chair and took a seat. The commander didn't mention the fact I had been behind the curtain when he entered.

"So, you claim you have the Magistrate sent you to go speak with the Alchemist Grandmaster, correct?"

"Yes."

"You also said you are traveling alone because of a bandit attack that resulted in the deaths of those you were traveling with."

I agreed and filled in the details about staying the night with Lady Hyll in Cragsrest.

"I have done some research and found verified facts within your story. How do I know you're the person you say you are, though, and not a bandit in disguise?"

The commander leaned back, folding his fingers and staring at me, anticipating my response. I knew he was waiting for me to give him some evidence that proved my identity. I remembered the note the Magistrate sent and rummaged through my pack, greatly aware of the commander staring at me. I finally pulled out a very crumpled piece of parchment that bore the Magistrate's official seal.

"This is all I have, but I can promise I am Emolin Stokton, though with this extra responsibility, I wish I wasn't."

The commander took the parchment from me and scanned the words, nodding and seeming to agree with the evidence.

"While I would usually require something more to prove who you are and allow entrance to the city, you are a unique case. Madame LeDore has also vouched for you, having seen you as you neared the city. She requested I release you into her care as soon as possible. She had her servants collect your horse, and I am told he is happily munching on alfalfa as we speak."

The commander stood and offered his arm to me. While it frustrated me having my time wasted, I was happy to have the interrogation over. I grabbed my pack and took his arm as he led me out of the room and down the hall opposite the way I entered. I was glad to be out of the room, having started feeling like the walls were closing in on me. Though, I wasn't sure about meeting Madame LeDore, especially since it seemed she had been spying on me for the last part of my journey.

The commander opened the door and I took in a deep breath of air, not realizing how much I missed feeling the breeze, no matter how slight it might be.

"Madame's carriage is waiting for you."

The commander released my arm and motioned to a carriage waiting for me at the edge of the sidewalk. I took a deep breath and tried to hide my limp as much as I could as I made my way to the street.

Before I stepped off the sidewalk, a woman who I assumed to be Madame Helena LeDore, threw open the door and rushed over to me.

"Oh no, my dear, are you hurt?" Madame LeDore was maybe ten years older than me, late twenties at the oldest, yet she held herself with such grace she seemed decades older.

"I'm fine. I got hurt when I was trying to save my traveling companions, but a healer in Cragsrest was able to repair most of the damage."

"Let me help you. I will have the healer come and see you as soon as we arrive at my home."

I let Madame LeDore help me and accepted the hand from the footman as I climbed into the carriage. While I didn't like being doted over, after spending so many days in the desert it was nice to have some help.

"I am sure you are tired and in need of a nice long soak," the woman began as she sat across from me and we started forward, "but I would like it if we could spend some time this evening getting to know one another before you retire for the night."

As much as I wanted solitude, I didn't want to disrespect my host by ignoring her small request.

"Of course, I would enjoy that."

Madame LeDore smiled and turned to look out the window. I noticed that even when she was sitting, she seemed to hold herself in a way few others did. Even her dress, made of a more simple pattern in a muted green cotton, had a look of elegance I couldn't place. She either didn't notice or didn't mind me staring, just watching the city roll by.

When we arrived at the LeDore Mansion, the Madame LeDore sent the footman running for the healer. Another man opened the door and helped her out before offering a hand to me.

"Mr. Bratton, this is Miss Emolin. She requires the healer, but once she is done we are going to have some tea in the parlor."

"Of course, madame." Mr. Bratton bowed and helped me up the stairs.

The footman came running back, followed by another man in his late forties. The older man took one glance at me and nodded to Mr. Bratton who asked if he could lift me. Once again, I found myself in the arms of a man I didn't know being carried up the stairs and into a parlor just to the right of the entrance.

"You seem to have been hit by Lightning Aura. How are you still alive? How long ago were you hit?" the healer asked, a stunned look on his face.

I explained everything I could remember as I was laid on a sofa and the healer pulled up my robes to get a better look at my ankle.

"The healer in Cragsrest was able to remove the Lightning Aura, which is good, but it looks as though they weren't able to completely heal the tissue surrounding the wound."

The healer prodded around my ankle and took note of every

time I winced or twitched when he touched a spot that was still rather sore.

"I have two options, though neither of which will be able to remove the scarring on your skin."

I nodded, having already accepted that fate. "What are my options?"

"Well, one is that I can heal your ankle in a way that gives you immediate relief from pain but will leave you with a limp for the rest of your life. The other option is for me to reform the tendons and muscles around the injury to make them stronger than they once were, though it will hurt quite a bit."

I thought about it for a few moments. I didn't like limping, though a lot of my dislike came from the pain associated with it. I also didn't like the idea of more pain, especially when I was in the presence of strangers. However, having a weak ankle would mean struggling with simple tasks for the rest of my life.

"I would rather not have the limp."

The healer nodded and placed his hands on my ankle, turning to look at Madame LeDore. "You may want to give her something to bite on or at least a hand to squeeze."

Madame LeDore placed a wooden spoon in my mouth one of the maids had given her and took my hand in hers. I nodded to the healer and was met with immediate pain. The healer's Aura surged through his hands and invaded my body, searching for any impurities and fixing the ones it could. The tendons in my ankle pulled and shifted as the healer's Aura guided them in place and strengthened them. I bit down on the spoon and screamed, the pain similar to when the healer in Cragsrest saved my life. I didn't notice myself squeezing Madame LeDore's hand and only released it once the pain began to subside.

The healer removed his hands from my ankle and wiped the sweat from his brow. Madame LeDore took the spoon from my mouth and rubbed her hands together to bring feeling back to the one I had been squeezing.

"It will take a day or so for the ankle to fully heal, but it will be stronger and shouldn't give her any more issues. I forbid her from using her ankle until tomorrow evening at least."

Madame thanked the healer and led him out of the room, leaving me alone for a few precious moments. I looked down at my ankle and saw the fading imprint of a hand from where the healer's Aura entered my body. I gently traced my fingers over the area and was surprised to find it was cool to the touch.

"Mr. Bratton will be here with the tea shortly," Madame LeDore said as she sat in a chair across from me.

"I know your healer said that I needed to stay off my foot, bu—"

"I am not going to hear of it. He said you are to stay off your ankle, and that's what you're going to do. Now, let's have some tea and a chat."

CHAPTER NINETEEN
EMOLIN

After Mr. Bratton brought in the tea, Madame LeDore and I sat in silence for several moments before she spoke up.

"I'm not sure what your thoughts of me are, but I can promise you I am not stuck up."

Her comment made me laugh, and I had to set down my tea before I spilled it all over. Still laughing, I glanced up at Madame LeDore, hoping I hadn't offended her, the smile on her lips helping me relax more.

"That's not what I thought of you at all," I said once I caught catch my breath.

Madame LeDore arched an eyebrow and smirked, telling me she knew I wasn't telling the full truth but said nothing else on the subject. Instead, she started asking about me.

"The Magistrate sent word several days ago that a group of Mages would arrive to refill their supplies before the next part of their journey. I heard about the tragedy you faced, and I'm glad you and Natalia could reach Cragsrest safely."

I nodded, not sure how she knew so much about me or had watched as I approached the city when I had never met her. *How does she know all that?* I became more skeptical of the woman in front of me and contemplated trying to dash to the window despite the healer's caution.

"You don't seem like someone who would desire to go on such a trip, especially not for the reasoning behind it."

I tried to hide my surprise, wondering if the only reason she vouched for me was to throw me in the dungeon.

"I can also say I have never met someone whose Aura has changed, I've read many accounts on the phenomenon, but have never seen it in person."

I dropped the biscuit I'd reached for in shock, remembering the experiments the day before. I conjured an orb of Aura in my hand and hoped to see my once pale yellow Aura. Instead, there was now pure white Aura, not a trace of yellow. My Aura also seemed to glow far brighter than before. I felt like Madame LeDore was staring into my very Well, something only the gods could do.

"How did this happen?"

"From what you've told me and what the healer said, the only thing that would make sense would be something that happened when the Lightning Mage struck you. As I'm sure you know, you're the only documented survivor of Lighting Aura, and there is very little we know about any of this."

"Why do you know all this?" Madame LeDore knew too much to be an average Mage placed in a position of power, not to mention how young she was.

"I am a scholar for the king and am the lady of Gathon."

"That explains how you know so much about the Lightning Mage and my Aura changing color, but how do you know so much about me?"

"Lady Hyll sent a messenger as soon as you arrived at her home and knew of your reason for the journey. She wanted me to keep an eye out for you since you were injured. As for everything else, you told me a lot about yourself with how you scanned the room and made note of all the exits. The healer was also able to see the last bits of your golden Aura hiding amongst the pure white."

I wanted to shrink away from the woman. I didn't like her seeming to know everything about me, and I didn't want to stay with her if she was able to read me that clearly. I tried to come up with an excuse or a reason that would allow me to stay at an inn, considering creating a lie about needing to leave early the next morning and not wanting to inconvenience her. However, she spoke before I could voice any objections.

"I'm sure you're wary of the idea of staying here with someone who knows so much about you after only knowing you less than an hour. I can assure you I mean you no harm and you will not be kept here if you decide to stay somewhere else. Would allowing you to read my Well calm any of your worries?"

"Read your Well?" I thought only Sages could do a Well Reading and now the lady of Gathon was asking me if I wanted to read hers. "I-I don't know how."

"I can show you if you'd like."

I had no idea what would happen if I said yes, but my curiosity was too strong and eventually, I agreed.

"Alright, I'm assuming you've had your Well read before. The concept is similar. I will guide you through how to read my Well, but it is up to you to determine the meaning of what you discover."

"I'm not entirely sure what you mean, but I'll try."

Madame LeDore smiled and held out her hand for mine. "Now, like how you move your Aura from your Well into your hand when calling forward an orb of light, you'll need to move your Aura through your hand into mine."

"I don't know how I feel about this anymore..." I clasped my hands in my lap and focused on the lattice of scars disappearing under my sleeves.

"If you don't want to do this, Emolin, you don't have to."

I looked up at Madame LeDore, the warm smile and crinkles

around her eyes reassuring me.

"I guess I'll try."

Madame LeDore held out her hand again and I took it in mine.

Her palm was already tingling with Aura and I had to stop myself from pulling my hand away. Taking a deep breath, I reminded myself Wells could only be read one way and she wouldn't be able to read mine without my permission. With a final breath, I moved my Aura from my Well into Madame LeDore's, my whole body tingling as I did, and the room vanishing.

I found myself in a blank, white expanse, no walls or ceiling, only whiteness. I had no idea where I was or what I was supposed to be doing, but something pulled me forward, so I walked.

My footsteps echoed, the only sound accompanying my breathing and heartbeat. There was nothing to see and no real indicator that I was moving at all. I could still vaguely feel myself sitting on the sofa in Madame LeDore's parlor and knew I could get back from wherever I was. I considered giving up when something in the distance, a small brown blur against the white, caught my attention.

After a few minutes of walking toward the spot, I could almost make out what it was. The creature was still quite a distance away, but from her proud stance and swish of her tail, the desert lioness let me know she was the one now in charge of our interaction.

She stalked forward, her shoulders prominent with every step. Her green eyes stared at me and held me in place. Though the lioness would be more than capable of tearing me to shreds, I had no fear. It was the same as the night of the attack when I met the lioness and her cubs. I held nothing but respect for the creature and let her do as she pleased.

I held my breath as the lioness stopped mere inches from me and sniffed at my hands. Never before had I been so close to such a beautiful creature, and now the lioness held my life in her claws.

I let out a small gasp when the lioness butted her head against my hand, similar to the cats near the docks in Altava. She looked up at me expectantly and a deep rumble sounded from her throat as she yawned, her sharp teeth glinting in the light; she was purring. She bumped her head into my hand a second time and I reached out to stroke her.

Her fur was warm, like she was lying in the sun, and slightly coarse. I scratched the top of her head and rubbed her ears, eliciting a small sigh almost lost to her purr.

Before I could move my hand to scratch her neck, a commotion sounded in the distance. The lioness leaped a few feet in front of me and roared, the sound causing me to jump.

Then, I was back in the parlor, the same cream floral wallpaper and shelves lined with books greeting me.

"Before you speak, I should tell you that it is a widely believed superstition that the gods will smite you if you share exactly what you saw with the person whose Well you read. That being said, what did you discover?"

I thought back to the lioness, how gentle she was, and how she put herself between myself and the commotion before I was startled back into the parlor. "I believe I will be safe here, at least for the night.

"In that case, let us eat."

Madame LeDore clapped her hands and several servants walked in carrying trays laden with food. The smell wafted toward me and made my stomach growl before the meal was even placed in front of us. Mr. Bratton came in and helped me turn so I was able to eat at a table brought in and a plate was placed in front of me.

I helped myself to several scoops of potatoes and vegetables, along with a few large pieces of beef and a roll. I waited for Madame LeDore to start eating and then dug in, savoring the flavors mingling together. I ignored everything around me and focused on the food.

"I know we are still eating, but do you have any questions for me?"

I swallowed the bite I had just taken and asked the first thing that came to mind.

"How are you the lady of Gathon and ambassador of Klohaven, while only being a few years older than me?"

"The same as anyone else who comes into a position of power. I proved myself worthy."

I wanted to press more but decided to save that question for later and move onto something a little easier.

"If you're a scholar for the king, then why are you in Klohaven instead of the palace?"

Madame LeDore smiled, seeming amused.

"I had enough of my time in the palace and wanted time away from all the chaos being near the king inevitably brings."

"But why would the king allow you to be an ambassador if you're one of his scholars?"

"The king has no say over what his scholars do or don't do. He gets the findings of our research and nothing more."

Madame LeDore slammed her fork down, shattering her plate. Mr. Bratton came in almost immediately, the maid in tow. He placed a new plate in front of Madame LeDore while the maid swept up bits of food and broken porcelain before taking away the plate.

"I apologize, I didn't mean to scare you," Madame LeDore said, serving herself another roll and some potatoes. "I hope my actions haven't made you change your mind about staying here. I spent many years being recognized only as one of the king's scholars. I still struggle to move past that label."

Not sure how to respond, I moved onto my next question. "What sort of things did you enjoy researching?"

I was sure I already knew the answer, but I wanted to ask

something that didn't upset her again.

"While I did a lot of research on mundane things such as the best soil for different crops, my favorite topics were the gods and Wells of Aura."

The last bit of information she gave me piqued my interest, but I tried my best not to show it. Instead, I focused on cutting my beef and chewing, not having to pretend I was savoring the flavor. Before I could ask any more questions, the servants came in to clear away the food and replace it with a pie and several other sweets. Mr. Bratton cut me a slice of ashberry and dessert cactus pie.

"While I'm sure you have many more questions, I have other things to attend to. Please stay and eat as much as you'd like. If you're okay with it, I would like to have Mr. Bratton carry you to your room so you can stay off your foot."

"While I feel more than capable to walk to my room, I understand your concern and will allow Mr. Bratton to help me."

Madame LeDore gave me a small nod of respect and left the room. I took a few bites of pie before I struggled to stay awake. I glanced out the window to see two of the moons high in the sky and leaned back against the cushions to rest my eyes, letting myself sink further into the plush pillows.

Mr. Bratton lifted me from the sofa and I caught a few glimpses here and there of the mansion as the butler carries me to my room. Among the more usual paintings and tapestries on the walls, there were also many sculptures and statues scattered throughout. I forced myself to stay awake until I reached my room and the butler laid me in bed so I would know my way out if need be.

A maid came into view and gently removed my clothes, replacing them with a soft, cotton shift. She pulled the blankets over me and I drifted off before she blew the candles out.

woke with the sun shining in, feeling much better than the night before. A maid came in not too long after I woke and helped me get dressed for breakfast. Though my ankle was feeling much better than it had the day before, it was still too tender for me to put any weight on it. The maid gave me a crutch I was able to get around with fairly well after a little practice.

"Madame LeDore is waiting for you in the dining room for breakfast, please follow me."

The maid led me out of the room and through a confusing amount of turns before she helped me down a flight of stairs and into the dining room.

"Good morning, my dear. I trust you slept well?" Madame LeDore asked, taking a sip of her tea and motioning for me to take a seat.

I sat down at the table to the left of madame and served myself some potatoes and a slice of egg tart. Madame LeDore served herself and I ate much quicker than one should if they wanted to be polite.

As with the night before, the food was wonderfully seasoned and the flavors danced around my tongue, even the wine had a much deeper flavor than any I'd had. I was so lost in the food I barely heard Madame LeDore address me.

"Now, the healer said you weren't to put any weight on your ankle until this evening, but I was wondering if you would like to go out to some of the shops?"

I swallowed my bite of food and nodded. "I would greatly enjoy that."

Madame LeDore rang a bell and Mr. Bratton appeared at her side. She asked him to bring the carriage and he bowed before turning and walking off. I grabbed a pastry and took a bite, enjoying the sweet, buttery flavor before Madame LeDore cleared her throat.

"The carriage should be pulling up just now."

Madame LeDore stood and grabbed my crutch for me, helping me out of my chair and making sure I was balanced. I followed her out of the dining room and headed out to the front walk.

Mr. Bratton held open the door to the carriage and helped me climb inside before helping Madame LeDore. The door shut tight behind us, and the carriage lurched forward. I looked out the window and watched the city go by.

The buildings of Gathon were much different from the ones in Altava and the other desert cities. Many of the homes and stores we passed were made out of a combination of stone and wood, wood being something usually reserved for carts and carriages in Altava. The buildings were painted muted colors but bright curtains could be seen fluttering through the open windows, adding small pops of color throughout the city like banners for a festival.

The streets were paved with cobblestones and the sidewalks wide enough for pairs of couples to pass without having to unlink arms. Some women wore headscarves, but since there wasn't a need to protect oneself from the sun, many of the women let their hair flow free, a sight that made me conscious of my new hair color.

The carriage pulled up in front of a line of shops and Mr. Bratton opened the door for us. I stared up at the buildings, surprised at how tall they were, and how much space was between them. Madame LeDore took my arm and led me down the street, going slow enough that I didn't have to struggle to keep up and allowed me to wonder at the city.

Like in Altava, there were many shops with displays of their wares except these were in store windows instead of open-air bazaars. What was vastly different was the stark contrast of clothing displayed, some being dresses I was used to seeing in Altava, the kind that would protect one's skin from the sun, while others had very little to them and left your arms and legs bare, small shawls used for warmth when needed.

Other shops displayed things like weapons, dried goods, sweets, furniture, anything one would need to not only live in the city but take care of themself as well. Madame LeDore would let me stop and gaze at the displays as long as I desired, never making me feel I was wasting her time.

A deep voice floated above the crowds of people and I searched to see where it was coming from, finding a man standing on a crate in front of a very colorful building.

"Come see Mr. Giuseppe's Menagerie. See the wonders of the Lunen Kingdom as well as exotic creatures from the far reaches of the world."

The man made eye contact with me, and it felt as though he was staring into my soul. Madame LeDore tugged me along, breaking the trance the man seemed to have me under. She pulled me farther down the street and only stopped once we turned a corner.

"Who was that?"

"No one to worry about. Now, we should continue with the task at hand. Let's get you some more appropriate clothes for the next part of your journey."

Before I could say anything, I was pulled into a tailor's shop and greeted by a surge of Aura.

"Oh, hello, madame."

A portly old man met us at the door and bowed, the tape measure hanging from his neck sliding off and almost hitting the floor before he caught it. "And this must be the beautiful young Mage one of your maids told me about last night."

I ignored the comment from the old man and instead studied the shop around me. There were bolts of fabric strewn across many tables and several Aura lamps hanging from the ceiling making up for the absence of sunlight. Half-made dresses hung on dress forms and scraps of fabric littered the floor.

"...she will also need a thick cloak that will travel well in a pack or saddlebag without taking up too much room."

I raised my brow at what Madame LeDore was saying, wishing I'd paid more attention to the conversation.

"I do enjoy the challenges you present to me. I should be able to have everything ready and made to perfectly fit Lady Stokton come morning tomorrow. Let me just get some measurements."

The man stepped forward and wrapped the thin tape around my neck, chest, waist, arms, and legs. He barked out numbers and beckoned for someone. A young girl, no more than eight, stepped forward and held out a small piece of parchment where she had been marking down my measurements. She was dressed in basic slave garb and rubbed her arms against the chill in the room as the man looked over her work.

"I said her inseam was twenty-eight, not twenty-seven. Other than that, it looks correct. You may go and grab some lunch."

The girl's face lit up and she scampered off, not saying a word.

"You're far too kind to her. If you're not careful, she may start to think she has a chance at freedom," Madame LeDore commented as the girl disappeared.

The tailor sighed. "She will only have that chance if the gods grant it. For now, I will teach her skills and protect her from others."

The tailor conjured an orb of Light Aura that dwarfed all light in the room. I gasped, never having met a Light Mage as strong as he.

The man winked as he let the orb of Aura fade and looked back over the parchment in his hand.

"For all this, you're looking at twenty gold, sixteen silver."

I choked on my gasp and spent a few moments coughing while Madame LeDore finished speaking with the tailor and turned to lead me away.

I finally caught my breath once we were out on the street. "The Magistrate only sent me with twenty gold, and I spent half of that on rooms on the way here. There's no way I can afford everything you ordered."

Madame LeDore laughed. "Don't worry about that, my dear, I'm paying for it."

I tried to protest, but she held up her hand.

"I won't hear it. Part of my job as lady of Gathon is to provide for those working for the greater good of the country. Now, let's get some cocoa and we can decide on where to go next."

Madame led me a few shops down the street and my stomach growled as the smells of the cakes and pastries floated through the door, though there was no way I should be hungry after the large breakfast I had.

The bell above the door tinkled as madame and I entered the shop and a young girl, maybe a year or two younger than I, greeted us from behind a counter.

"Welcome. The mistress just pulled some cakes out of the oven and will bring them to the front as soon as they're frosted."

"Thank you, my dear," madame said as we strolled toward the case and pointed at a few different things. "We'll take two of these, three of those, two slices of cake, and some hot cocoa."

I marveled at the sweets in the case, never having seen such intricate designs on desserts. There were cakes shaped like birds and one even painted to look like the flowers in the windows of the homes we passed. The most impressive ones were the sweets that shimmered when you looked at them just right, faint golden lines on the surface making the designs come to life.

I turned and saw madame had taken a seat at one of the small tables in the corner, and I took a seat next to her.

"These are some of the best sweets in Klohaven, possibly even in all of Lunen."

"Madame LeDore, you flatter me so."

A woman placed a tray full of sweets on the table in front of us, along with two steaming mugs with a blob of cream floating on the top. I took a small sip, very aware of how hot the drink was, the sweetness surprising me.

"Have you never had hot cocoa?"

I took another sip and shook my head. "Chocolate is a rare thing to find in Altava. It's difficult to transport across the desert; it either melts or the beetles infest it."

"Well, we will have to make sure we get you another cup before you leave."

Madame LeDore must've seen the worry on my face because she reached forward and grabbed my hand.

"That's still a bit off and you won't be traveling alone."

My brows knit in confusion. "What do you mean? My traveling companions are dead and few others would want to risk their lives for a stranger."

Before I could continue, the bell above the door tinkled again, signaling more customers entering the shop. I turned to see two Mages enter, their hair secured in long plaits behind them.

"Ah, Lea and Tara, thank you for joining us."

The two Mages walked over to our table and sat down. The girl at the counter came over and dropped off another tray of sweets and hot cocoas. The Mages had their jaws set and seemed like they wanted to be anywhere other than the small cafe. I looked at Madame LeDore, hoping to get some sort of reading from her, but found nothing.

Once the girl from behind the counter left, the whole demeanor of the Mages changed. They relaxed their posture and the Mage to my left shoved a whole cake in her mouth. She was introduced as Lea and had the familiar brown hair and brown eyes of Altavians, a few freckles dotting her cheeks. The other, Tara, had blonde hair and brown eyes, something I heard was more common in the eastern part of Klohaven. Both Mages wore robes, but in a much different style than my own, the fabric soft looking and dyed green, worn tight around the arms and loose around the legs.

Lea turned to me after taking a sip of her hot cocoa. "What do you think of Gathon so far?"

"It's different from Altava. I'm not used to seeing such

diversity in clothing as well as people. Everything seems so much more lively here, the whole city feels much warmer."

"That's one thing I love about the city," Tara said. "The welcomeness we give to all who visit. We try to be as kind as we can to outsiders, making them feel like they belong."

"Exactly," Lea agreed, taking another sip of her cocoa, the cream leaving a mustache on her upper lip.

We made some more small talk, getting to know one another and sharing a few laughs about some of the more interesting visitors the city had. We stayed for quite a while and left the cafe long after finishing our sweets, deciding we wanted to talk somewhere more private and climbed back in the carriage that somehow knew to be waiting outside the shop. Mr. Bratton helped us into the back and shut the door. Madame and Lea shut the blinds and waited a few minutes after we pulled away before talking.

Tara leaned toward me. "The reason for all the secrecy is the Parans are becoming more restless and we've had reports they may have spies in the city. We don't want to risk them finding out our plans."

"That makes sense, what are the plans?"

Madame LeDore spoke next. "As mentioned before, Lea and Tara are going to be traveling with you. They are very familiar with the Klohaven forests and will be able to help you safely navigate the area so you can make it to Blackwood."

I released some of the tension in my shoulders and relaxed against the back of the seat. It was good to know I was once again going to have people with me that knew the area and would be able to get us to our destination.

I thought back to the choices made that had led us right into the bandits' grasp and shuttered at the thought. "We're not going to purposely diverge from the route, are we?"

"No, of course not." Tara started. "While there are no paths that are guaranteed to lack bandits or Parans, there are some that make it far less likely we will run into them and provide plenty of means of escape or cover depending on what the situation calls for."

"I've never fought Parans, but I know how ruthless the bandits are. Wouldn't either group have the advantage in the forest?"

"In some ways, yes," Lea answered, "but with most of the trees having lost their leaves for the winter, it will be easier to spot them than it would in the middle of the summer."

While I had my doubts about their reasons, we pulled up to the LeDore mansion before I could ask anything more.

"Would you like some help making your way in?" Lea asked

I nodded, accepting the hand she offered and leaning on her as we climbed the stairs into the mansion. Madame led us into the parlor I ate supper in the night before and Lea helped me to the sofa. There was already tea and biscuits waiting on the table for us and Mr. Bratton offered to get us tarts as well.

Once we were alone, madame and Tara moved the tea and snacks to the side tables and laid out a map so we could look at it together. I was surprised at the detail of the map, only having seen as much detail before on the diagram in Magistrate Magdra's office.

"There are three different paths that would be the best to take," madame said as she pointed to three different spots on the map. "Each one has its different challenges, but I feel the one in the middle would offer the best protection from both the bandits and Parans this time of year."

Tara shook her head. "With the rainy season ending, that path is going to be flooded. There will be no way the horses could safely navigate the mud. It would be safer if we were to take either the west path closer to the mountains or the eastern path closer to the cliffs."

"We can't take the eastern path," Lea chimed in. "The rains

created torrents and I have seen many get washed into the sea in drier seasons."

"Sounds like it's decided, then. The three of you will be taking the path closer to the mountains."

Madame accepted the tray from Mr. Bratton as he brought in the tarts and some scones.

"Mr. Bratton, please have a few of the maids work on preparing for the girls' journey tomorrow," madame said before turning to us. "Lady Emolin will be getting clothes and gear she needs for this journey in the morning, so you girls will have the rest of the day to pack any last things you may need." Madame passed around the tray of scones. "I recommend trying to make it to Ranluna before nightfall so you don't have to camp for the night and then you will only be a day's ride to the next village," madame said, pointing to a city on the map.

"Many of the farmers will be out in their fields harvesting in the day, but the inn will be quite crowded in the evening with all the men getting beer and singing songs," Tara pointed out.

"Yes, but the rooms should be fairly empty and, if you let the owner know I was the one who sent you, they will most likely have one of their girls bring your food up to your rooms so you wouldn't have to fight for a table."

"Alright, then from there it will be another two days ride to Blackwood." Lea turned to me. "Is Grandmaster Sphera expecting you?"

I tried to remember if the Magistrate mentioned anything about that, but nothing came to mind.

"I'm honestly not sure. I only found out about this journey the day before I left, so I don't know of any plans he may have had in place prior."

"Then we will have to plan time to go through the checkpoints in the city."

"Checkpoints?" I asked, confused.

Tara nodded. "Grandmaster Sphera is well known for the

amount of security she has in the city. There has never been a raid that made it past the walls, and even if they did, there would be several more spots they could be stopped before getting anywhere near the center of the city."

I tried to picture what the city must look like with all their security and guards. There had to be several sections of the city that were walled off, how else would the guard be able to prevent people from getting farther in.

Before I was able to ask any more questions, Mr. Bratton entered the room again and announced it was time for dinner. The four of us stood and followed Mr. Bratton to the dining room, Lea helping me along the way.

There was another enormous meal spread before us, and I found myself no longer hungry. I sat at the table, staring at all the food in front of me, and took only a small helping of vegetables to be polite. Madame and the other Mage's held a lively conversation, including me now and then, but let me be in my head for most of the evening.

I was already halfway through my journey and I still didn't understand how I was going to save the Parans, or at least make it so Hajana wouldn't hate me for what I did. I wondered what she had been doing since I left and my guilt gnawed at me for not trying to say goodbye, the pain on her face as I left haunting my dreams.

There was a reason Fonir continued to visit me even after leaving Altava, I just needed to figure out what he was trying to say. The priests said time and time again the gods would lead us down the right path, but they never said how puzzling the path or the gods would be.

The servants served dessert, and I had a small piece of cake before excusing myself to my room. There were many things I needed to figure out, and I wanted to be alone to do so.

CHAPTER TWENTY
EMOLIN

The sun was well past rising when a maid came to wake me, and it surprised me I'd slept so late.

"Madame LeDore wanted to make sure you had ample rest before you leave today," the maid explained when I asked her.

She helped me dress in a pair of robes I was unfamiliar with, the material much softer but less flexible than the ones I usually wore and the fit being much tighter around my arms while looser in the legs. I had seen the difference in the robes on Tara and Lea, but I they amazed me with how much freedom I had considering how stiff the fabric was, and thoroughly intrigued by the hood attached to the back instead of having a separate headscarf to protect my skin from the sun.

I walked over to the mirror, enjoying the freedom of being able to walk on my own without pain since I first injured my ankle, and stared at my reflection. It amazed me how the fabric made the shadows on the greens merge like the leaves and branches of a tree. As much as I tried to, I couldn't ignore the scars that spread across my hands and neck. They'd faded more since I first saw them, but they were still there, a permanent reminder of the things that happened.

I grabbed the brush from the vanity and worked out the tangles from tossing and turning for most of the night before working my hair into a single plait down my back like Lea and Tara styled their hair, starting to like the distinct red and black streaks the Lightning Aura gave me. I strapped my sword to my waist and took one final look at myself. A different girl from the one that left Altava over a week before looked back at me, different in more than just looks. She held herself differently, a sureness to her gaze. I grabbed my pack and followed the maid down to the dining room to meet with everyone else.

Madame LeDore, Lea, and Tara were already enjoying their meal when I joined them, and I took a seat next to Lea to tuck in. The meal was smaller than the others, but there was still far more food than even I had at home, and it took me a moment to decide what to eat. After a quick breakfast of eggs, potatoes, and some fruit scones, Madame LeDore led us back into the parlor to discuss the final details of our journey.

"Even though the path closest to the mountains is the safest one in regards to the weather, you will be traveling closest to Paran territory and will need to keep a vigilant watch for them."

"How close will we be?" I asked, my stomach churning. "The Magistrate never said we would be near the Parans."

Madame LeDore turned to me, brows furrowing. "That is something everyone who travels in the southern part of the Klohaven forest should know. I'm surprised he didn't warn you. The Parans are known to hunt in that part of the forest, and it is advised that only those with knowledge of the area should pass through on the path closest to the mountains.

"Lea and Tara have experience with the Parans, so as long as you do what they say and follow their lead, you should have no issues if you happen to have to deal with them."

Madame and Tara discussed a few little details, such as what sort of food we would be able to hunt for reliably, but I tuned them out. Instead, I focused on my breathing, working to calm myself down so I could think clearly. Lady Hyll made some valid points about Fonir; he wouldn't keep visiting me if there was no hope in changing the future. *Would he?* No, I couldn't think like that. *There has to be a way to prevent the—*

"What do you think, Emolin?" Tara asked, pulling me out of my thoughts.

"About what?"

"Do you feel we are prepared enough for the journey?"

"I honestly don't feel prepared at all. I was thrown into this journey with less than a day's notice. I had to leave everything I've known behind, and I wasn't able to save my traveling companions from the bandits. If anything, I feel less prepared now than when I left Altava."

Lea took a seat next to me, draping her arm around my shoulders. "You have been through a lot and witnessed some terrible things. Once everything is over, you'll be able to relax, maybe even travel some."

I gave Lea a small smile, swallowing the bile rising in my throat. *Once this is all over, the only thing I have to look forward to is marrying the Magistrate.*

Mr. Bratton entered the room before we could continue our conversation, followed by the tailor from the day before and the slave girl.

"I come bearing great gifts of fashion," the tailor said, spreading his arms wide and giving a theatrical bow.

The girl stepped forward holding a bundle of parcels and presented them to me. I thanked her and opened the one on the top, seeing the same material as the robes I was currently wearing.

"I have made five robes for you to travel with, each made to your exact size," the tailor explained. "Like the one you're currently wearing, the fabric of these robes is made with Alchemy, so there is a layer of protection against long-ranged magic attacks as well as grazing sword wounds and arrows."

I stared at the fabric in wonder. In Altava, fully trained Mages were given robes made with Alchemy fabric, but Mages in training still wore more mundane ones. I tried to sense the Aura within, but it all felt normal, like any other fabric I had worn. *If Aaron and Ziden were wearing these, would they have survived the attack?* I put the robes aside, deciding to examine them more later, and opened the next parcels, finding a few pairs of soft, slipper-like shoes and a thick cape.

"Those shoes offer sure footing on even the slickest of surfaces. The cloak is made of the same fabric as your robes with the added benefit of being strong enough to act as a rope if the situation requires it."

I slipped the shoes onto my feet, surprised at how well they fit. It barely felt like I was wearing anything, and I had to check to make sure they hadn't somehow fused with my foot. I stared at the cloak in wonder, partly excited about the possibilities of the cloak and also worried by the fact I might need so much protection.

"Thank you for bringing these over as early as you did. It is crucial Miss Emolin leaves as soon as possible," Madame LeDore said.

"But of course, it is the least I can do for such a loyal customer." The tailor bowed again and turned to go.

The girl approached madame and gave her a small curtsy before motioning for madame to lean down. Madame did and the girl whispered something to madame before hurrying off after the tailor. Madame turned to me, chuckling and shaking her head.

"It seems the young miss thinks you're one of the prettiest women she has ever seen but was too shy to tell you herself."

Warmth crept up my neck and cheeks and I turned away, not wanting the others to see how much I was blushing "That was very kind of her."

Tara tapped me on the shoulder and said she and Lea would

go outside to get the horses ready. I nodded, feeling my Well contract at the realization I was leaving again.

"I know saying this won't change how you feel, but you have no reason to worry," Madame said as she approached.

I nodded. "I know, but there are still so many things expected of me."

Madame pulled me into a hug, and I didn't know what to do at first, not having hugged very many people outside my mother, but I eventually wrapped my arms around her and breathed in the calm seeming to radiate off of her.

When I let go, I discovered the maid who had been helping me was holding my bag, the parcels already neatly packed away. I thanked her and slung the pack over my shoulders before giving a final nod to madame and showing myself out.

Lea and Tara were already in their saddles and Mr. Bratton was holding Sampson's reins. Sampson whinnied at the sight of me and Mr. Bratton let him go and Sampson trotted over. I stroked his nose and leaned into his neck.

"Thank you for saving me," I whispered. "I promise once this is done I will let you take a long break."

Sampson huffed and nibbled on my hood, something I hoped meant he understood.

I climbed into the saddle and looked over at my traveling companions.

"Ready?" Tara asked.

I nodded and Lea took off, Tara and I racing after her.

---

*E*ntering the Klohaven forests was like entering an entirely new country.

The world to the east of Gathon started as large fields of grass and bushes, birds, and bugs darting about in the sunshine. As we rode farther east, groupings of trees appeared more and more frequently until there was nothing but thick growths of trees surrounding us. We had to ride single file, the path carved into the wild mostly overgrown as it was, and I was glad to be in the middle so I was able to gaze at the landscape around without having to worry about getting lost.

Compared to the desert, the forest was alive with the songs of birds and bugs, the rustling of the wind blowing through the mostly barren trees, and water rushing over the rocks in the several small streams and rivers we crossed.

I hadn't noticed my hunger until Tara called for us to stop for lunch. So many things were distracting me. Because it was much cooler in the forest and the sun wasn't beating down on us, we didn't have to stop as often for water breaks. So, lunch was the first time that we stopped since entering the trees.

I dismounted and groaned as my legs stretched after having been in the saddle for so long. I sat in the grass and dug out my waterskin and a small parcel of food from my pack. We left the horses saddled but let them graze and drink from the nearby river whenever they wished. While the reason I was in the forest didn't thrill me, I had to admit it was one of the most peaceful places I'd ever been.

"You've never seen a forest, have you?" Lea asked, seeing me stare at the trees in wonder as she had the entire trip.

I shook my head. "In Altava, we have a few trees planted in the gardens of the Magistrate's estate and palm trees scattered about the desert, but other than that, I've never seen trees more than slightly taller than me."

"I can't even imagine what that must be like, always surrounded by rocks and dead plants. I hate when I have to travel to the western outskirts of Gathon."

"I have to agree the forest is much prettier than the desert is, though not being able to see far in any direction is a little unsettling," I said, taking another sip of water.

Lea nodded. "It's something you need to get used to. It's a lot easier to use your sense of smell in the forest instead of sight like you do in the desert. It's easy to hide oneself in the trees in the summer, but it's almost impossible to hide your scent."

We sat and talked a while longer, enjoying the break.

"So, Emolin," Tara started, "how did you get so lucky to get Reshilian hair?" she asked, leaning against the trunk of a tree.

"I wouldn't say I'm lucky."

"No?" Tara asked.

"My father is a merchant and spends most of his time at sea. My mother is from Reshil, and Father says when he was there, he saw her and they fell in love. My father doesn't allow Mamma to tell me about her country or family. She could only teach me Reshilian in secret, and I've lost count of the number of times Mamma has been in a fog when Father is around."

"Oh, Emolin, I'm so sorry, I didn't know…" Tara trailed off.

"It's okay, I know you didn't mean it. My father is a terrible man, and I'm glad he's at sea so Mamma isn't alone with him."

The three of us sat in silence listening to the birds before Tara stood up and brushed off her robes. "Are we ready to go?"

Lea looked over at me and I nodded.

The three of us climbed back in the saddle, much to the complaint of my legs and rear, and continued on our journey. This time Lea took the lead, with Tara in the back.

A small hare bound though the brush, scratching at the dirt when Sampson stopped, causing me to lose my balance and almost slip out of the saddle. Lea was sitting completely still, hand raised to call us to stop, nose turned toward the mountains. I turned the same way and tried to smell whatever Lea could, but caught nothing other than decaying leaves and the damp soil.

Lea turned back to me and spoke in hushed tones. "I think, whoever they were, they're gone, but just keep an eye on your surroundings."

"Who do you think they were?" I asked, still scanning the area.

"It could only be Parans or bandits. If it were someone from Gathon, they would've called out."

I nodded and urged Sampson on, not wanting to let my fear overwhelm me. I may have dealt with bandits several times and survived every encounter, but that made it worse. Any time I thought about Natalia, Aaron, Ziden, or even Galeal, my heart raced and my body tensed like I was still under attack. Even if I wasn't actively thinking about that night, the way the wind tousled my hair or the sounds of metal on metal could cause the same reaction.

If we were to come across Parans, I didn't know what I would do. I didn't want Hajana to be even more upset with me, but if I didn't attack a Paran and let them kill me, I wouldn't be able to help Hajana at all. *I just have to hope I don't come across any.*

The path seemed to narrow even more as Lea continued forward, the branches scraping against my legs and clawing at my arms and face. There seemed to be something different about that part of the forest. The air was still and the only sounds were from our horses making their way through the overgrown path. Not even the birds or bugs were making any noises.

Scanning the forest around me, there didn't seem to be anything in the shadows, but I didn't know enough about the forest to know if anyone was there out there or not.

Lea held up her hand again and stared deep into the woods to our left.

"Emolin, run!"

Sampson took off, crashing through the trees. I had no idea where I was going or who I was running from, but I knew I needed to get away. Sampson galloped on, seeming to completely disregard the tangled vines and weeds at his feet. My fear fueled him onward and the forest around us became a blur. I risked a glance behind and my heart caught in my throat. A figure in a deep green cloak was riding fast, catching up to Sampson and me.

I leaned forward in the saddle and willed Sampson to go

faster, not wanting to discover what would happen if the rider behind me was a Paran. The twists and turns through the forest became dizzying and I wasn't even sure we were on the path anymore. The only sounds I heard were my heart pounding in my ears and Sampson's hooves thundering against the ground.

I turned back to see if the person was still following me. Seeing no one, I relaxed a bit only to be swept off Sampson's back by a low hanging branch, my pack breaking my fall. The wind was knocked out of my lungs and I stared up at the trees for a moment, trying to see if anything was broken. Feeling nothing but a sore back, I sat up and looked around, trying to get my bearings. Sampson stood a dozen or so yards away, staring back at me and stamping his foot. There were no sounds other than my heavy breathing. Then a twig snapped.

I whipped my head toward the sound, seeing no one. Then, another snap behind me. I whirled my head around again, realizing I must be surrounded but unable to see them. I held my hands up in defense and tried talking myself out of whatever those surrounding me had in mind.

"My name is Emolin Stokton. I am just trying to pass through the forest peacefully. I mean you no harm, and I have coin I can pay you with."

I was met with silence, no response, or even snapping twigs. My breath came in ragged gasps and my arms burned from me holding them above my head. Sweat trickled down my neck and back, a gust of wind biting through my robes and causing my nose to run.

Sampson whinnied and I whirled toward him. The world became shrouded in darkness as a hood slipped over my head and my hands were roughly tied behind me. I struggled against the hands gripping my arms, holding me. I knew they were close and tried to kick at them, my foot meeting nothing but air. I tried to scream, but the person wrapped their hand around my throat, cutting off all sound.

"Don't put up a fight and I won't hurt you," a deep, scratchy voice said.

The man let go of my throat and I sucked in a deep breath of air, coughing and gasping as I did. I threw my body to my right, hoping to catch my captor off guard. His grip lessened and I found myself free for less than a second before my shoulder cracked against the ground.

A rope was tied around my ankles and legs and I realized I succeeded in making my situation worse. The man pulled me to my feet and hoisted me up onto the back of a horse, grunting as he did. A rope pulled at my arms and legs and I couldn't move more than an inch in any direction. The man climbed up and the horse started off, my body tossed around and the ropes were the only thing keeping me on the horse.

CHAPTER TWENTY-ONE
HAJANA

A couple of days passed and the air between the girls left in the room grew tenser. Arguments broke out and several girls had large bruises or deep scratches from fights about the smallest things, like one girl looking at someone else the wrong way. It didn't help that five of the fifteen girls in our room died from the Pox and three by their own hands. At least seven others taking on the rest of our chores perished as well.

Dalila and I spent most days talking and doing our best to stay out of arguments. I eventually shared the book with Dalila, and the two of us discussed what we thought about the slave's life and the different choices she made. Far too often, one of the girls would ask me for my opinion on different arguments, trying to get me to side with them.

"Hajana, do you think slaves should feel guilty when other slaves die?"

"Hajana, isn't it terrible that we aren't in our rooms?"

"Hajana, if slaves were given better food and living conditions, do you think Serf Pox would be as bad?"

Every time a girl asked for my opinion, I grew more and more aggravated, tired of being consistently interrupted. Dalila and I were in the middle of discussing a recent passage we read when my name was called again.

"Hajana, what—"

"Enough!"

The volume of my voice caused the room to hush.

"What is all this squabbling going to change? We're all stuck here until the healer gives us the okay to leave, and when we do, nothing is going to change. The master will still consider us expendable, and we'll be once again forced to do unmentionable things. Talking about your opinions and the things you want to change isn't going to make a difference. Only action will."

Some of the girls stared at me, mouths hanging open, others looked anywhere but at me.

"If you're so against us arguing over things we have no control over, then what are you going to do, oh high and mighty one?"

I turned to the girl, Auri, who had been a slave as long as I had. Two girls snickered, but the rest were silent, waiting to hear what I was going to say.

Dalila stood behind me and squeezed my shoulder. "Read the book to them."

I turned to grab the book on my bed and glanced out to see yet another body carried away, the sixth body in five days and the eighth I knew of. I couldn't bear to watch anymore and turned back to the girls in the room.

"This is a book given to me by a woman in the city, a woman who is a freed slave."

"Who cares?" Auri asked.

"Have you ever met a freed slave?"

"No, bu—"

"Let me read this to you, then you may say whatever you feel is pertinent. 'It was at that moment, seeing yet another girl senselessly beaten to death for not moving fast enough, that I decided I needed to do something, anything, to prevent my fate from being the same as all the others.' "

"That's great and all," Auri started, "but how does that help us here?"

I thought back to the woman in the apothecary. She had been a slave but now owned her shop and could help others. If she was a pharmacist, then she had to have learned it somewhere; it had to be a skill she knew. *Was that what helped her get free? Her knowledge of plants and herbs?* I didn't know for sure if it was true, but it gave me an idea.

"That passage is not only proof we can escape slavery but also the key. The woman who gave the book to me owns an apothecary. She has a skill people need and used them to escape."

"If I tried to make medicine for anyone, I'd probably kill them," Auri said.

"Then don't make medicine. Para has given us all special gifts, each one unique and important. It is up to us to discover those gifts and share them with the world." I turned and pointed to Layla. "Not worrying about how you would do it now, what is one thing you enjoyed doing before becoming a slave? Or maybe something others said you excelled at?"

She didn't hesitate in her response. "I loved playing the lyre."

I nodded at her and pointed to another girl at random. "How about you?"

"Pa always had me help him when livestock was giving birth. He said I could calm any animal down."

I pointed to another.

"I've delivered seven babies, the mum and child both surviving."

All the other girls went, listing the skills and talents they had. Then I turned to Auri.

"What about you?"

"I like to draw, but I'm no good at it. None of this makes any difference, though. We don't have a lyre, or livestock, or paints. And unless one of you wants to hide a pregnancy, we don't have a mother in labor either."

"We don't have any of that yet. What's important is to make sure you know what you're good at. I have a way for us to get free. A plan that could have all of us free in less than two months."

"What would that be?" Auri asked, all the girls staring at me.

"According to the woman at the apothecary, Minister Aldous doesn't have much longer to live. When he departs, the mistress will have to sell the estate and everything inside if she wants to continue her current way of living."

"That just means we'll be sold to another person and will be their slaves instead."

"And I know someone who would buy our freedom."

The silence in the room sent a shiver through my body and caused my palms to sweat as I waited for someone to speak.

"So," Layla started, "you're saying you managed to meet someone who not only has the money to buy all of our freedom but would be willing to actually free a bunch of Parans?"

"I know it sounds impossible, but it's true."

"Then why did you want to know all of our skills and talents?" Auri asked.

"Once we're free, we will have to find our way to make a living. It will be difficult, I don't want any of you to have the wrong idea, but knowing what you're good at and where you can look for jobs or apprenticeships will help with some of the stress."

"I hope you're right," Auri said, turning back to her bed.

The rest of the girls returned to their beds as well, some excitedly discussing the possibility of what might happen if I was right.

"What about you, Ra? What are you going to do? How is this going to help you?" Dalila asked.

Dalila and I went back over to our beds and sat on the floor between them.

"I'm going to write, share stories of our slavery, the treatment we face."

"Why is anyone going to hire freed slaves who can write or paint or play music? The more useful skills such as caring for livestock make sense, but what would being artistic solve?"

"Stories, music, and art are what make being alive worth it. Why do you think the masters beat us when they hear us singing or destroy any writing or drawing we may have tucked away? They want to break our spirits and know it would be impossible to do so if we have our art."

"I don't understand what you mean, but I pray to Para your idea works. For now, I am going to get some sleep. I'm rather tired."

She stood and hugged me before climbing under her covers. I crawled into my bed and dug around in my belongings until I found a small piece of charcoal I had taken from the kitchen fire. I scraped the side of the charcoal on the edge of the bed frame so it was sharp enough to write with, then turned to the back of the book where there were quite a few empty pages. I prayed the pharmacist wouldn't be too mad, and I worked on jotting down my ideas and the next steps I needed to take.

I wrote late into the night, not wanting to miss anything. I had a goal to work toward, something I could use to keep myself going when things got difficult. There was a purpose to my life I never knew before.

The next morning, I rolled over to tell Dalila what I discovered. Everyone else was still asleep, so I slid out of bed and went over to wake her.

"Dalila, I have so many..." I trailed off, Dalila's body burning up and her hair plastered to her neck and face with sweat.

"Dalila, are you okay?" I rolled her onto her back and her eyes flickered open, dark and glassy.

Her breathing was shallow and raspy, lips dry and cracked.

"Hajana, you look so well." She smiled before delving into a coughing fit, bits of blood splattering her blanket.

"Dalila, no, please, no…" I knelt by her bed and held her hand, terrified and not knowing what to do. There were no signs of the sores the Pox caused, so I was still safe to be with her, but she was close to the end.

"Don't worry about me, Ra…"

"No, please don't leave me, please. I just found you and I'm not ready to lose you again." Tears blurred my vision and I brushed them away with the back of my hand. "Here, let me get you a cool cloth and some water." I moved to stand and Dalila gripped my wrist, barely having the strength to tug me back to her.

"No, please stay with me. I don't want to be alone, not again."

"Why you? Why not me or someone else?" I choked on my tears and squeezed her hand.

"Because there's still much more you need to do, so many more lives you need to help."

"Why can't Para let you stay longer? I still need you."

"Because I've already been gone for a long time."

"No, you're not making sense. You'll be okay, you just need rest and some water—"

"Ra, look at me." The strength in Dalila's voice caught me off guard.

I looked at her and saw a flicker of something in her eyes. "I've been dead for months; the Serf Pox took me a long time ago. Para let me come back and see you, to help you figure out what you needed to do in this life to prevent others from suffering the way we have."

"But if Para brought you back, he can let you stay. I need you here, I need you to help me figure all this out and make the changes I need to."

"I will still be with you, Ra, you'll never lose me. I'll be cheering for you every step of the way and I'll be there to help you when you feel you can't keep going."

"No, I want you here, I want you to laugh and celebrate with me and travel the world once we're free. Please, don't go."

I threw my arms around Dalila and sobbed into her shoulder, not understanding what was going on. She wrapped her arms around me and held me tight.

"I love you, Ra, your parents do too. Stay strong. Save the others."

I sat there and held her for a long time, sobbing and hoping she could stay. When I let go to look at her, she was gone, her bed empty.

I sat and leaned against my bed, letting the tears roll down my cheeks. I had Dalila back for eight days after losing her over five years before, only to lose her again. *Why, Para? Why would you give her back only to take her away again?* Anger boiled in the pit of my stomach and the need to punch something grew. Not wanting to risk breaking my hand again, I balled my hands into fists and dug my nails into my palms.

Ra, get up. You have things you need to do.

My head snapped up at Dalila's voice, but I was still alone in the corner.

"Dalila?"

I have to go now, Ra. I can't do this often, but Para has permitted me to speak to you. Now, look under my bed.

As Dalila's words faded, a small warmth settled in my chest. "I love you, Dalila."

I shifted to my knees and peered under Dalila's bed. Among the dead spiders and bits of torn parchment, I found a small, leather-bound book.

I flipped it open to find it empty. A journal. It hadn't been there when a few of the girls searched the room. *It has to be from Para.*

I curled up on my bed, wiping away the last of my tears, and flipped open to a fresh page. Writing wouldn't bring Dalila back or save the slaves already lost, but it might be enough to save me and the others, regardless of how the battle the Magistrate and Master Aldous were planning went. With a new passion and drive, I worked through the day, hoping my plans would work.

CHAPTER TWENTY-TWO
EMOLIN

I lost track of the amount of time I was on the horse, the sack on my head blocking out all light and hope of discovering where we were going. At one point, the discomfort of my bonds and the exhaustion from everything caused me to black out for an unknown period. When the horse stopped, I was dumped onto the ground and the sack ripped off my head, the light from the moons casting everything in an eerie light.

"We'll stop here for the night and continue the rest of the way tomorrow," the man said, holding up a waterskin and looking at me.

My throat completely dry from breathing in all the dust, I didn't even question the safety of the water and nodded, opening my mouth so the man could give me some to drink. Once I was done, he pulled me over to a large tree and secured my bonds to the trunk, leaving just enough slack for me to lie down.

Though the moons didn't provide a lot of light, there was enough so I could look at the man before me.

From the ring in his nose, I knew he was a Paran, the ring a tradition of married men. I had never seen a male Paran over the age of sixteen, a city without any farmland not needing many male slaves. While he was certainly large, his horse's head barely reaching his shoulder, he wasn't as unkempt as the stories made Parans out to be.

His beard was long but trimmed, a few braids tied off with string scattered throughout. His hair was cut just above the ears and his clothes were similar to what many men in Gathon wore, though far more worn and patched. His expression was gruff, but held no signs of anger or aggression. Though I had no way to protect myself, I decided to ask him some questions.

"Where are you taking me?"

He looked up, seeming a bit surprised.

"Back to camp. Advisor Falcon wants to speak with you."

"Does he think speaking to me will prevent the battle?"

"No, but *she* seems to think there's something she can do. So, she sent me to collect you."

The Paran referring to Advisor Falcon with feminine pronouns surprised me, but I pressed on. "Is she going to kill me?" I was scared of the answer, but it was something I needed to know.

"Maybe, maybe not. If ye knows what's best for you, you'll listen to what she says and consider whatever she offers."

I was about to ask him another question when the Paran held up his hand. "Get some sleep." He got up and tossed a blanket on me. "I'll wake you when it's time to leave."

He said nothing more, regardless of how many more questions I asked him, his snoring eventually filling the air. I lay on my side, trying my best to get comfortable with my hands tied to the tree. I considered trying to undo my ropes and run off, but the forest was far too dark and I didn't want to get lost and starve. The curiosity of meeting Advisor Falcon was too great as well and I decided to stay, eventually drifting off.

In the morning, the man untied my legs and turned around to give me some privacy to relieve myself before giving me more water and a bit of bread. He then tied me back onto the horse and went to put the hood on. I tried to fight, moving to bite his hand, only causing him to clamp a hand around my throat until the hood slid over my head. blocking all sight and muffling almost all sounds. Deciding to feign complacency, I spent the time trying to figure out what to say to Advisor Falcon, wondering if there was a way to talk myself out of the situation.

I worried about Sampson, Lea, and Tara, wondering how they were doing and if they managed to get away. Sampson whinnied before I was caught, but it didn't sound like he was hurt. Maybe he had gotten away. Lea told me to run, so I had no idea if she or Tara were okay. They had the benefit of knowing the forest, but an ambush could mean anything. I sent a prayer to the gods, asking for the safety of the three, and tried to distract my worries by turning my attention back to why I was out there and what the figure told me. *Was this what Fonir meant? He said I had to stop waiting for others to make the change.*

I didn't want to harm anyone, especially not when I could lose my friendship with Hajana. If I wanted to make a change, I would need to speak first. *You have the chance you've been looking for, a way to change the path of the war. This is your chance. Don't let it pass you by.* I didn't know what Advisor Falcon wanted from me, but I was determined to prevent the war and this was my only chance.

After a long time riding, the man dismounted and dragged me off the horse before leading me a long way and sitting me down in a chair. The hood was tugged off my head and I blinked against the brightness of the room, taking in the table pulled off to one side and the shelves lined with books placed against the rough stone walls.

"I'm glad to see you arrived safely."

Recognizing the voice, my head shot up, and I was staring at the man with the scar, the same man Hajana told me about, the man who had been meeting with the Magistrate. Seeing him there, in what I assumed was part of the Paran camp, but knowing his father's great success in destroying Parans, none of it was making sense.

"I'm sure you're confused by all this," he said, seeming to read my thoughts. "So let me give a brief overview. My name is Geoffraie. My father, Edgar, is known as a great general, fighting against the bandits and any that dare defy the king. My father made it his life goal to rid the Lunen Kingdom of those that threaten the crown. He has killed countless innocents, bragged about how much the women screamed and begged for him to spare their children."

"Then why are you here?" My stomach sank at the realization. "Did you kill all the Parans?"

"Goodness, no. My father gave me my name, but that is the only thing I share with him, and not by choice. I don't even look like the man. The idea of crucifying people, especially children, because they have different beliefs than my own is appalling. I have and will continue to do everything in my power to right the wrongs of my father. When he discovered me using my coin to ferry Parans to safety, he gave me this." Geoffraie pointed to his scar.

"Okay, so if you're here, where are the Parans?"

"I sent as many as I could to Reshil—"

"Wait, the Paras aren't even here?" I stared at Geoffraie in shock. "If they're not here, then why even worry about the battle at all?"

"Many of them stayed, mostly men who wanted to battle for the freedom of the Parans," Geoffraie explained, motioning to a woman behind him. "This is Advisor Falcon, a woman of great military skill. When I approached her about leaving, she pointed out that if there was no battle, both the Magistrate and the Grandmaster would get very suspicious and would go into hiding."

"Why would that matter?" I asked, struggling against my bonds, my wrists chafing from the sweat.

Geoffraie looked at the Paran I traveled with, and he cut my wrists free in one swift movement. "There's a lot about your leaders you don't know. The easiest way to put it is they're involved with something far greater than this war with the Parans. It's something that goes generations deep and the king has had enough of it."

"This involves the king??"

"Not officially, but yes, in a way. What I need to know is if I can count on you to help us or not."

"Why doesn't the king put a stop to it all?" I asked, rubbing my wrists from where the ropes chaffed them.

"Politics aren't as simple as they appear, though many wished they were. Those your Magistrate is working with have many ties with those in prominent positions, with old money. If the king were to stop it himself, the entire Lunen Kingdom would be in peril."

"What do you want me to do?"

"The same thing the Magistrate wanted you to do. Go speak to the Grandmaster and get her to join the Magistrate's cause. Lead them both into our trap." Geoffraie glanced at a map on the wall, studying it.

"How do I know I can trust you? That you aren't just going to turn around and have me killed?"

"Let me ask you this. What were you told about the Parans growing up?"

I didn't understand where he was going with his question, but I went along with it. "They're heretics, selfish, and have no love for the gods or their brethren."

"And who was the one that told you they have no love for the gods? Have you ever seen any Parans aside from the ones forced into slavery in your city?"

I thought about it for a moment before answering, "No, I haven't met a Paran before and it was my teachers and father who told me."

Geoffraie nodded, pacing the room as he continued. "And who do your teachers go to with reports and ask for advice?"

"The Magistrate. And he speaks with the priests and the Sages. I'm well aware of how the hierarchy works."

Geoffraie raised his finger. "You only think you know. What do the priests preach most often above all else?"

"What does any of this have to do with the Parans and the group you say involves the Magistrate in?"

"The priests preach love," Geoffraie said, answering his question. "Yet, what I've seen in the cities is nothing but hate toward anyone who is 'lesser' than oneself."

I thought about what he said, trying to find an argument against it. The shopkeepers looked down on their employees and any slaves and servants. The rich would look down on the poor, the poor on the homeless, and the Mages on the commoners. The only place I witnessed anything else was Cragsrest where there was no slavery.

"Also, have you noticed anything odd about the bandits?"

"Many people have," I said, referring to the commander I spoke with back in Cragsrest.

"And have you ever heard of a Mage, or anyone with a Well for that matter, siding with the bandits?"

I shook my head, not knowing what Geoffraie was trying to say, but my stomach becoming queasy listening to him. I glanced up at Advisor Falcon, she not being anything like I pictured. She was tall, not nearly as tall as the Paran who captured me, but taller than Geoffraie. She was skinny, but muscular, her skin and hair shades of brown that would blend in with the trees in the forest. Her bright blue eyes stared back at me as she kept her hand on the hilt of her sword, ready to attack if I made any attempt to flee.

"I believe you have enough knowledge to understand where I'm going with all this," Geoffraie said, bringing my attention back to him. "I don't want to get into any more details now. Just know the bandits that attacked were sent after you. The deaths of Galeal, Aaron, and Ziden were planned, and there's a chance you were supposed to die there as well."

"Sent after me? Why? By who? The bandits don't work with anyone."

"They weren't bandits. The Mage should've been more than enough of a warning. From what I gathered, they were most likely hired by your Magistrate to kill you. I'm not sure why, but from the things I've heard, the Magistrate wants you dead."

The words echoed in my head, the room beginning to spin. *Why would he want me dead? Father told me the Magistrate was going to marry me, but if I were dead, what good would that do? The only person who may wish me dead is Father…*

"I'm sure this is a lot to take in—"

"If I join you, what will happen?" I asked, cutting Geoffraie off and causing Advisor Falcon to raise her brows at me.

"The battle will go as planned, at least that's what the Magistrate and Grandmaster will believe. My soldiers will come in and take the two into custody. We have a list of others who we believe were involved in this as well and we will have them arrested. Soldiers will travel to the cities throughout Klohaven and speak with the leaders, taking over cities that erupt in riots, so we can liberate as many slaves as possible."

I sat there, not knowing what to say or if I should fully believe him. Lord Mycroft was well known for his ruthlessness, and I had to hope Geoffraie was right about not being his father. My stomach growled and Geoffraie smirked. He stepped to the side and gestured to the door.

"Why don't you head to the mess hall and get something to eat. It's just out that door and to the right; I'm sure Lea and Tara are waiting for you. They can fill you in more this evening. Sampson is resting comfortably in the stables and you are welcome to see him anytime you please."

"Lea and Tara?" I felt my rage growing again as I realized it had been a trap.

"Yes. LeDore was the one who came up with the whole plan, though you falling off your horse because of a branch did help solve the problem of getting you safely away from Sampson."

Geoffraie turned his back to me to stare at a map on the wall again, signaling he was done with our conversation. I stood and turned on my heel. I showed myself out of the room, deciding the first place I would go would indeed be the mess hall, though I wasn't planning on just getting dinner.

Once I left the room, I realized I was in a large cavern, a river running through the center and people wandering about. There were many buildings along the walls made from wooden planks, a stark contrast to the stone walls. I had never seen a place like it in my life and I had to stand and stare for several moments before my stomach reminded me of how little food I'd eaten in the past day.

Though the cavern was large, it was easy to find the mess hall, the smells and sounds bouncing off the cavern walls. The Paran who captured me had followed me out of the room and pointed out the building as he headed off in the opposite direction. I wasn't sure what I was going to say when I found Lea and Tara, but I knew I wasn't going to fall for anything again.

The mess hall was filled with rows of long tables, hundreds of soldiers sitting around and eating, laughter and songs filling the air. Lea saw me first and called for me, waving me over to an open seat next to her and across from Tara.

"I'm guessing you must be starving," Lea said, passing me a bowl full of stew when I sat.

My hunger taking precedence over my anger, I dug in, quickly finishing my first bowl and digging into my second before I felt full enough to talk.

"I can't believe you two." I slammed my spoon on the table. "Here I am thinking you're nice and helping me, then you set me up to get captured! I was worried something happened to you two and Sampson while I'm starved and forced to travel hooded on horseback."

I wanted to say more, but people were staring and my anger was turning into tears threatening to spill.

"We're sorry," Tara said, leaning in. "We didn't like the plan much, but it was all we could come up with in the short amount of time we had."

"Why not take me closer to the mountains first? I wouldn't have known if we had left the path."

"Because we had to be cautious of the bandits. They are still a large threat in the forest and not something we wanted to worry about," Lea chimed in. "We are sorry."

I didn't know what to say so I picked at the crusty bread Lea gave me, not sure how to feel about anything.

"I'm assuming Geoffraie filled you in on most of the details?" Tara asked.

"If you mean talking in circles about the Magistrate, Grandmaster, and some things they're involved with, then yes, he filled me in."

"That is the most accurate description of Geoffraie's briefings I've ever heard," Lea said, a few soldiers nearby nodding.

"From what I've gathered," Tara said, "the Magistrate has more plans in mind for after the battle is over. He's craving power."

"If all he wants is power, then why is he trying to destroy the Parans? Why not try to conquer another country?"

"Who knows. Power can do strange things to a person. What you need to do is decide if you want to help or not."

"No, I've already decided I'm going to do this. What I need to do is figure out how far I'm willing to go."

CHAPTER TWENTY-THREE
EMOLIN

*L*ea and Tara brought me back to the room where I first spoke to Geoffraie, the table now in the center with the map spread across it. Advisor Falcon and a handful of men and women stared at the map and discussing different battle arrangements. When I approached the group, Geoffraie turned to address me.

"Good, you seem to understand the time constraints we're under." He motioned for me to join them. "Now, the Magistrate sent you to speak with the Grandmaster to gain her alliance in battle. That makes changing the plan in our favor easier in some aspects. My scouts have been watching the Magistrate well before you left. He hasn't sent any messengers in the past couple weeks, so the Grandmaster shouldn't suspect anything amiss. The Magistrate's distrust of the Alchemists and their speaking stones benefits us.

"Once you have an audience with the Grandmaster, the key thing is convincing her you are on her side. Let her believe the Parans are weak and that a peace treaty is the perfect ruse."

"How is that going to help? Won't she want to keep some

soldiers in reserve? Will she realize a peace treaty won't be enough to bring out the entire Paran army?" someone asked.

"I wouldn't worry too much about the Grandmaster. While she is cunning on the battlefield, her misandry blinds her and she will do anything to prove she and her soldiers are better than the Magistrate's."

I pulled out the pendant to rub my fingers over the smooth surface. The plan seemed too thin, too easy to see through.

"That plan won't work," I started, ignoring the collective gasp in the room. "If the Grandmaster wants to prove she and her soldiers are more superior to the Magistrate, wouldn't she want to make certain the bait to lure out the Parans is believable? Foolproof even?"

Geoffraie stared at my pendant for a few seconds before responding. "You may be right. Do you have any suggestions? A peace offering was the best idea we could come up with."

Thoughts of Hajana and the other slaves senselessly beaten on the streets were the first things that came to mind. While terrible, it would make the best bait.

"The freeing of slaves. The Parans want to free their brethren forced into slavery."

"She's right, Geoffraie," Advisor Falcon spoke up. "Many here have been fortunate enough to survive the pillaging of their villages and evade capture. There are countless Parans who weren't as fortunate and had unspeakable things forced upon them. I pray Para will forgive me for such a grave oversite. I would gladly turn in all my weapons and wealth I've amassed if it meant freeing the others."

Geoffraie nodded and gave me a small smile before turning back to the map. "Now that we have a concrete plan, Lea, Tara, and Emolin need to head to bed. They have a long day of travel ahead of them."

Lea and Tara led me out of the strategy room and down a long tunnel to a sizeable room full of beds.

"These rooms used to be full of Parans," Tara explained, "but since so many were able to escape to safety, we have the whole room to ourselves."

The three of us chose beds at random and Lea and Tara were asleep almost immediately. I had a rough time falling asleep, even with the poor sleep the night before. Even after finally drifting to sleep, my dreams were filled with visions of slaves being beaten, the Magistrate winning the war, and Fonir calling me a failure. I ended up with only a few hours of sleep when Lea woke me, saying the horses were already saddled and waiting. Late, again. I hurriedly got dressed and met the group outside of a tunnel I assumed led out of the mountains.

"Remember, we have little time to spare. While you can camp on the way back, you need to make it to Blackwood by nightfall. The Grandmaster must never suspect your involvement with us. Swift travels."

With all last-minute details in place, the three of us climbed into the saddle and set out, Tara in the lead with Lea and I riding side by side through the tunnel, the length of it alone taking the better part of three hours.

Once we were outside, I realized how high in the mountains were, and I could easily make out Blackwood from our vantage point.

"It will take the longest to get out of the mountains, especially since it looks like it might snow. Ready?" Tara asked.

"What do you say, boy?" I asked Sampson, patting him on the neck.

Sampson answered by taking off, Lea and Tara racing behind me.

The trail, though well hidden, was still easy enough to navigate, and Sampson and I had no trouble being in the lead for a bit, waiting for the others once the path disappeared into the trees.

Tara took up the lead again, and we walked single file through the forest, stopping now and then at a stream to let the horses rest and allow us to stretch our legs. We made a longer stop for lunch, but most stops were ten minutes or less, and we made it to the gates of Blackwood as the sun was setting.

"State your name and purpose," the guard said as we approached.

The three of us gave our names and I explained the Magistrate sent me, handing the guard the letter with the Magistrate's seal. The guard asked us a multitude of questions, such as how long we would be staying, where would be staying, if we planned on shopping, and what we would be purchasing. After answering the barrage of questions. the guard eventually let us through, letting us know we would need to check in with the guards by the next evening if we planned on staying longer than a day.

We headed to an inn for the night and sent a messenger to the Grandmaster's estate to let her know I would be calling on her the following day.

<hr>

After a quick breakfast the next morning, the three of us headed for the Grandmaster's estate, deciding to keep the horses stabled and travel through the city on foot.

The city was built like a target for archery practice, each section a smaller ring moving toward the center. Each ring had a large wall around it, protecting it from being seized. The gates were open to allow citizens to easily pass from one section to the other, but could close and block off each section should the city ever be attacked.

Most of the buildings were made from wood, painted an array of bright colors. Rows of flowers and small trees adorned the roads and created a cheery atmosphere to walk through. There were few horses and carts on the roads as we traveled, making us even more grateful for deciding to keep the horses stabled.

One thing Geoffraie said stood out as we walked through the city and I noticed most of the people on the streets and in the shops were women. The Grandmaster's misandry. The men I did see were usually servants or slaves, a rare sight in Altava.

Many of the women called out their wares, promising the finest silks or richest fragrances in the world. We stopped and looked at a few of the open shops to be polite, but the churning in my stomach didn't allow me to focus on anything other than my meeting with the Grandmaster.

As we neared the center of the city, the nerves of what I was about to do grew. I continuously had to dry my palms on my pants and wished I'd tied up my hair before leaving the inn, my neck covered in sweat and my hair sticking and pulling whenever I turned to look at anything.

Tara didn't have to tell me which house was the Grandmaster's once we arrived in the wealthy part of the city. Many of the homes were made of wood with brightly painted shutters and flowers in their windows, far larger than the ones in the other areas of the city. The Grandmaster's estate, however, was made from the same stone as the walls and was surrounded by a moat and wall. The drawbridge was closed, but a guard stood at attention by the tower on our side of the moat, turning to us as we approached.

"What business do you have with the Grandmaster?"

I explained everything I told the guard when entering the city. I also mentioned we sent a messenger the night before to inform the Grandmaster of needing an audience with her.

The guard scratched his chin as he listened. "I need to speak with the Grandmaster about this. Wait here."

He called for the drawbridge to be lowered and two other guards came to guard us while he disappeared for several long minutes.

When the guard came back, the other two stepped aside. "Grandmaster Sphera has agreed to meet with you."

The guard led us across the drawbridge, the large wooden structure starting to rise before we were fully off, causing me to slide down the last foot.

The grounds behind the walls were covered in stone, a handful of flowerbeds scattered about providing a small break from the overwhelming grays of the mansion and paths. A slave came out to greet us, his hair cropped close to his scalp and fresh wounds on his arms from a recent beating.

"Please, follow me."

The slave turned and led us into the mansion with a very noticeable limp. I had to wonder, knowing what I did about the Grandmaster, if he was beaten purely because he was male.

The mansion was much the same on the inside as on the outside. There were sparse decorations and the few there were made of the same grey stone, blending in more than anything else. The floors were bare slate, our footsteps echoing as we walked, even in our padded boots, and there were no paintings, tapestries, or rugs to dampen the sound. The boy led us into a parlor and gave a small bow.

"Grandmaster Sphera will be with you shortly, please wait here."

The boy left and I couldn't help but notice the numerous welts on his shoulders and the back of his legs. I wanted to reach out and help him, but I didn't want to risk angering the Grandmaster or cause her to suspect anything that could endanger the mission.

Lea and Tara sat down in the two armchairs around the table and I sat on the sofa. Though the furniture looked comfortable, it felt like sitting on the same stone the building was made of, the back far too straight.

The sofa and chairs were covered with a scratchy, red fabric that crinkled whenever we moved. There was a red, ornate rug in the center of the room under the table, far too small for the space. A desk sat in one corner, painted black and free of dust. A large fireplace sat across from the sofa, completely clean and unused despite the chill in the room.

The clock on the wall counted the minutes as they went by, and it was going on well past an hour before the door opened and the Grandmaster entered.

The Grandmaster wasn't what I expected, but her appearance didn't surprise me either. I heard she became the youngest Grandmaster in the history of Klohaven after her father died, but I still hadn't expected her to be as young as she was. A woman only a few years older than me in charge of half a country was almost as shocking as discovering how old the lady of Gathon was.

Grandmaster Sphera wore a uniform similar to those the guards in the city wore, navy blue pants and coat with a white shirt and black boots. Besides the basic uniform, the Grandmaster carried a hat under her arm and a cane in her hand.

"Hello, Lady Stokton, I hope the reason you're here won't to be a waste of my time."

I fought down the urge to shy away from Grandmaster Sphera, knowing it was beneficial I act unaffected by her demeanor.

I stood and gave a bow, hoping my manners would satiate some of her predications of me. "I can promise you'll want to hear what I have to say."

The Grandmaster was silent for a moment before she raised her hand. A servant came in and asked Lea and Tara to follow him to the ballroom for some refreshments. The two looked back at me and I gave a slight nod, letting them know I'd be alright. Once the door shut and the Grandmaster and I were alone, she motioned for us to sit.

"I received a message from your courier yesterday evening about your visit. You mentioned having something you would like to discuss with me that was too risky to send in a simple message?"

I focused on not letting myself worry about the story I was

about to weave, remembering I immediately had the upper hand because of my gender.

"That is correct."

"Then out with it. I don't have all day."

"Recently I had an encounter with a mysterious figure in an alley."

The Grandmaster stood, opening her mouth to most likely accuse me of wasting her time, but I held up my hand and continued.

"The Head Sage in Altava believes the figure was a god. Fonir, the God of Cleansing."

The Grandmaster sat again and folded her fingers. "Go on."

"Fonir shrouded the entire alley in darkness and I nearly drained my Well."

I took a breath, and the Grandmaster leaned forward, hands resting on her cane.

"Fonir spoke in riddles, never giving me a straight answer, eventually ending with something about making a change and purging the land before he disappeared and left me in the alley."

"And you said the Head Sage of Altava said it was Fonir that spoke with you? Did she say why?"

"She never gave me an exact answer, but she paid me a visit after I collapsed from almost a full Well drain. She called a meeting the next day with not only me, but my parents and the Magistrate to report her findings. I assume she wouldn't get the Magistrate involved unless she didn't doubt her beliefs."

"And what does all this have to do with me? It sounds like you're just here to brag about a blessing from the gods."

I took a steadying breath. "Once the Magistrate heard what the Head Sage said, he excused himself and rushed off to what I later learned was a meeting with Minister Aldous, Lord Geoffraie Mycroft, and several other high-ranking officers and officials."

The Grandmaster said nothing, so I pressed on.

"The Magistrate came up with a plan about how to defeat the

Parans once and for all. He believes if his army and yours strike together, with my focus being on Advisor Falcon, the land could be freed from Parans before winter."

The Grandmaster leaned back in her chair, laced her fingers, and held them up to her chin. She stared at me for a few moments and I struggled not to let my discomfort show.

"You're saying Magistrate Straven is calling for the help of Alchemists because you met with a god?"

I nodded, not sure what she was getting at but hoping my explanation was enough for her.

"Ha!"

I jumped at the Grandmaster's sudden outburst.

"Leave it to a man to not trust a female blessed by the gods with completing the ancient prophesy on her own. I bet if you were a man, he would have no issue sending you out with just a handful of Mages. Maybe not, though, if he doesn't have faith in his armies."

I sat there in shock, not how to respond to the Grandmaster. From the stories I'd heard, I knew it was going to be easy for a female to convince her, but I still assumed it would take a lot of persuading to get the Grandmaster to agree to join efforts. However, it sounded like she was eager to prove the Magistrate wrong.

"Those Parans are weak," she continued. "Their numbers are dwindling, and I have it on good authority they recently suffered a drop in numbers after a wave of sickness swept through their camp. I can't, on good conscience, let that spindle of a man, Straven, screw up this chance because of his lack of faith in his troops."

The Grandmaster's comment caught me off guard, and I struggled to keep my composure. The idea of anyone thinking the Magistrate a 'spindle of a man,' or at least admitting their thoughts out loud, would be unheard of anywhere near Altava.

Being on the other side of the country, it made sense such opinions could be voiced without repercussions.

Realizing the Grandmaster was staring at me and waiting for a response, I cleared my throat. "Does that mean you'll join us?"

"Aye, we will."

I was about to thank her when the Grandmaster held up her hand. *I thought it was too easy.*

"On one condition."

"What would that be?" I tried not to let my voice tremble and placed my palms flat on my legs to wick away the sweat.

"I sense your strength and talent. It is wasted on the limitations of being a Mage. After the battle, come live here in Blackwood and let me train you in the art of Alchemy."

I was taken aback by the request and I wasn't sure how to respond. "My father has already given my hand to the Magistrate."

"What! That's preposterous! No man should ever get to say who a woman does or doesn't marry. I will get you out of your arrangement, so there's no need to worry about that."

I wasn't sure what I could do other than say yes. I needed to have Grandmaster Sphera agree to help, but the idea of having to live in Blackwood if the Parans' plans failed, however slim that chance was, unnerved me. *Just say what will make her happy.*

"I am flattered you would like to mentor me and help me out of my predicament with the Magistrate. I have always wanted to learn the art of Alchemy. I would be honored to come to live here."

My answer seemed to satisfy the Grandmaster, and she didn't seem to mind the fact I never actually agreed I was going to move there, only that I would be honored to do so.

"Now that that's settled, what is our plan of attack?" The Grandmaster leaned forward and I pushed on, ignoring the last of my fears about being found out.

"Madame Helena LeDore suggested we use the local inn as

our meeting place. We will meet there in a week and travel from there to the battlefield south of the mountains."

"Yes, yes, I figured as much. What is the battle plan? Where are the troops going to be stationed? How many soldiers are we going to have on the front lines and how many are we keeping as reserves?"

I chewed on my lip, hoping to seem like I was trying to remember the specifics while I focused on my breathing. *Calm down, she's already agreed to help. The hardest part is over.*

"Magistrate Magdra feels it would be best to have all soldiers stationed in the field, hiding in the trees. The Parans are at their weakest right now, so attacking them with everything we have should be able to eradicate them from our lands."

The Grandmaster frowned and leaned back in her chair again. "It sounds like the Magistrate hasn't put much thought into his plan, has he? You're a smart girl, what do you think we should do."

I curled my toes in my shoes until they cramped to keep me calm. I had gone over what I would say all night. *I can do this.*

"Follow me," the Grandmaster said before I could answer, standing and smoothing out her uniform.

She walked over to a bookcase and pulled on a book with an unassuming cover, revealing a passageway. She motioned for me to follow, then disappeared into the darkness, leaving me scrambling to catch up to her.

Grandmaster Sphera led me through the narrow passage, passing several doors and heading up two flights of grey stone stairs. There were a few lamps on the walls lit by Alchemy circles, producing a faint bluish light. I desperately wanted to know where we were going, but I feared asking and potentially angering the woman in a place where no one would find my body.

I bumped into the Grandmaster, not realizing she'd stopped at a door. She looked back at me and glared before placing her palm against the wood and lighting an Alchemy circle. The runes flashed pink, and the door clicked open.

I blinked against the sudden light and stepped into the room. The Grandmaster walked over to a table and pulled a sheet off, revealing a scale model of the country. It was like the one Magistrate Magdra had, but gave far more detail, with actual plants and trees growing out of the map and rivers and streams running at the correct speeds.

"I'm sure you've seen one of these before, but not only have the grubby hand of men not soiled it, this diagram also proves Alchemy is the superior use of one's Well, being able to more accurately depict a location with the correct flora and fauna."

I looked over at the Grandmaster and she held a small figurine made of plain wood similar to the other painted figures she already had dotting the map.

"Let's see what you would do if you were in charge of the battle."

I grabbed the figurine and looked at the others. There were many red figurines over by Altava and blue by Blackwood. A small cluster of purple figurines sat in Gathon and black ones were in the mountains denoting the Parans. There were no other unpainted figurines on the table.

Alright. She wants to see what my plan would be. I placed my marker on the table just north of Gathon. I moved the red and blue figurines to surround the clearing where the battle would take place and put one of each with me in the center.

I moved the black figurines next, placing them at the base of the mountains with one figurine as Advisor Falcon in the center facing the other markers I already placed. The purple figurines stayed in Gathon.

"We need to feed the Parans information that will get them to come down to the valley to meet us. Magistrate Magdra suggested hinting at a large caravan of supplies moving through the area, but that wouldn't nearly enough of an incentive to convince an army of hunted people to leave the safety of the mountains. Instead, a ploy of an arrangement of trading their weapons and wealth for the freedom of Paran slaves would be a more surefire way of flushing them out, something they would be cautious about but also would not want to risk missing."

Grandmaster Sphera looked at the map for a few moments, frowning and chewing on the inside of her cheek. I fought to stay calm and not let my worries show.

"I believe you're right. Those filthy Parans are smarter than we would like, but they would do anything to free their people." She moved a few of the figurines around the map. "We have estimated their forces to be in the low twenty thousand, though the numbers could be much less than that. If my army of Alchemists and Magdra's army of Mages were to surround the Parans, we should easily overwhelm them and win a swift victory."

Grandmaster Sphera used her figurine to knock over the one that stood for Advisor Falcon, the residing thump sitting heavy in the pit of my stomach. I managed to complete my task, to convince the Alchemists of the grand scheme to defeat the Parans, but would it work? Sure, Geoffraie had the upper hand of knowing the truth behind the plan, but he would still be greatly outnumbered, even if Fonir hinted at a promise of great success.

I placed my plain figurine in the center of the battlefield and turned to the Grandmaster.

She spoke before I could say anything.

"I am quite glad the universe had the knowledge to choose a woman to be the one to save our country. Imagine if a man had been chosen instead."

The Grandmaster laughed as my brows knit together.

"What do you mean?" I didn't want to sound rude, but I had no idea what she implied with her comment.

"The plan Magistrate Magdra came up with would never have

worked. Any plan conceived by a man wouldn't work. There is a reason women were the first ones to walk the land."

"But they were—"

The Grandmaster waved her hand. "The history books are all written by men and can't be trusted. Women are the only ones that can make the right decisions for the world. Men always turn to war as the answer to their problems. But women," the Grandmaster tapped her temple, "women know how to strategize."

Before I could say anything in response, the Grandmaster turned and headed for the door.

"Come, I will have my servant show you to the dining room where you can join your companions. I, unfortunately, will not be able to entertain you. My lieutenant has a grand affair planned for the evening, and now I have a reason to celebrate. Would you and your friends care to join me? You would be my guests of honor and would be able to enjoy the evening without having to worry about men trying to converse with you or get you drunk enough to lie with them."

"I thank you for the offer, but unfortunately, we will have to pass. It's a long ride to Gathon, and there are some last details I need to discuss with Madame LeDore. I greatly appreciate you agreeing to meet with me and join our cause."

"You're very welcome. The world needs more women in charge or we will all die in a fiery war. It's too bad you're unable to join in the festivities, but I commend you for putting your country ahead of fun. Now, tell me. How many nights did the guards give you?"

"I have to go speak with them by this evening."

"Nonsense, you need your rest. I will send a messenger to speak with the guards and allow you three access to the city whenever you please."

"Thank you, that gives me one less thing to worry about."

The Grandmaster and I parted ways and I followed a servant to the dining room.

The dining room was similar to the rest of the mansion, the same grey flooring and walls throughout. There was a grey rug under the long, black table in the center of the room and the Grandmaster's family crest hung on the wall above the chair at the head of the table. Other than those, the room was completely barren of any decorations. Lea and Tara sat at the table with their plates laden with food. When they saw me enter, they waited until the servant left before rushing over to me.

"Well?" Lea asked, bouncing slightly.

"She agreed to join us and will meet us in Gathon in five days."

The two of them congratulated me, careful not to say anything that would reveal the true nature of my visit. They led me over to the table and I piled my plate with food while explaining everything, including our invitation to come and go as we please from the city.

In the rare moments of quiet between questions, I tried to recall anything hinting that the Grandmaster's agreement to side with us was a ruse. It seemed the plan worked, that the Grandmaster had fallen for the idea of tricking the Parans out into the open to destroy them. I couldn't be sure, though, there was too much at stake. I had done my best to explain the plan, and now all there was to do was wait and pray for the best.

After eating, we decided we would spend the rest of the afternoon shopping and exploring the city, wanting to enjoy ourselves before making the long trek back to Gathon. In one of the crowded streets, Tara informed me we were being followed and most likely would be until sometime after we left the next day, so we wanted to act as naturally as possible.

Lea ended up purchasing a new gown in hopes of a grand celebration after winning the battle. I bought a simple hair clip, small enough I could easily carry it with me. Tara surprised me when she purchased a necklace, not seeming to be the type that wore jewelry. When I asked her about it, she blushed and explained it was for a girl she was courting back in Gathon.

Learning this new bit of information about Tara, we spent the rest of the afternoon and evening discussing Tara and her beloved, learning that Tara was considering proposing after the battle was over.

We chose to turn in early, eager to soon be out of Blackwood and away from the girl who had been following us. We weren't doing anything wrong and had no reason to worry about her, but none of us enjoyed being watched, and the sooner we got back to the mountains, the better.

CHAPTER TWENTY-FOUR
HAJANA

The next day we were finally released from quarantine. The healer was waiting to see me in the parlor and I made sure I had my books with me. I'd spent countless hours recalling memories of tortures the other slaves and myself were put through. Seven more slaves died my last day in the room, having been worked to death. I wrote about them, how they were murdered by being forced to work too hard, documenting everything.

I heard two maids passing the room say that the master bought another fifteen slaves while we were still in quarantine and two of them were already gone. My heart hurt for all the girls I wasn't able to save, but I focused on the ones I could, knowing my plan would be the start of a new life for many slaves.

I tucked the books into my dress when the maid came to get me for my checkup, not wanting anyone to see them and discover what I was doing. I was looking forward to speaking with the healer, having a lot of things I wanted to tell her. A small worry popped into my head that the healer wouldn't be the same as usual, but it was quickly proven wrong when I entered to see the healer turn and smile at me.

"Hello, Hajana. How are you feeling today?"

Not wanting to waste any time, I pulled out the books and handed them to the healer. "I have been reading this book from the pharmacist and had an idea. I'm still trying to figure out all the details, but she's the only slave I know of who has escaped slavery."

The healer skimmed my book and gave me a small smile before asking me to sit.

"This is a unique idea, and it could change a lot of lives. However, you said there are still details you're trying to work out. What are they?"

"The first is to find someone reliable enough to purchase the slaves to get them to freedom. The other thing I need to figure out is how to get people to care. A freed slave will still be seen as a slave unless the minds of people change."

The healer sat back in her chair and studied me. "Why would anyone want to care? Why would people want to change their minds? Slaves are free labor to them. Why would they want to pay slaves to heal, paint, or play music? That would only be taking away jobs from those already skilled."

The healer's words stung–they had a truth to them. I had seen the effects of slaves who had been freed, women and children living on the streets, begging for food. *See, this is why slavery is good,* the man had said. *Without us, these people would starve. We provide them food and shelter in exchange for work. We are their saviors.*

"Slavery can't be changed overnight. We need to go slow, make the change gradual, like water carving a stream. We can't free all the slaves at once, but we can stop more slaves from being sold."

"Hajana, I know where your heart is, but I don't see how this can make a difference. That being said, I'll still support you in your endeavors as much as I can."

I turned to go before remembering another question I had.

"You didn't quarantine us knowing girls would kill themselves, did you?"

The healer's face dropped. "I feared that might happen, along with the sudden increase in deaths from slaves who weren't showing symptoms. That was one of the many things I had to consider when giving the diagnosis to Mistress Aldous. If I told her some slaves were sick, they would lock away the sick girls and the healthy ones would take on the brunt of the work. If I didn't tell her, then the healthy ones could get sick too and risk more dying from the Pox." She looked up at me. "I did the best I could, the best anyone could, and prayed it would be enough."

I closed my eyes, seeing the countless bodies being carted away. "It's not your fault, you were doing what you could to keep us safe. It was the fault of those in charge, the ones that let this happen, the ones whose minds need to change."

The healer smiled. "I hope they will, I do. Now, speak with Ruta and let her know you're ready to work. I'm sure she has plenty for you to do. Make sure you give her this note," she said, scribbling something down. "This tells her you need to get more fresh air, and hopefully she'll send you out to the market more."

I took the note gratefully and tucked it away with the books. "Thank you for everything."

A tear fell as she bowed her head to me. I left without another word, hoping I make the change happen.

***

*L*ater that afternoon, Ruta sent me to the docks to deliver the mistress' order to the fishmonger for the next week's meals. I ventured to Flinders' house first, hoping Geoffraie would be there, too. I needed them to help make the change I wanted, I just had to believe I could convince them to help.

I knocked on the door, the familiar pattern providing comfort.

Flinders called out as he approached the door, his feet shuffling on the floor. He cracked the door open and peered out at me, an eyebrow rising when he realized it was me.

"Ah, you're back. I heard they quarantined you and feared the worst. Please, come in." He pulled the door open enough for me to slip inside before shutting it on any prying eyes outside.

"Please, I have little time before Ruta expects me back, but I need your help." I kept my voice level, determined not to leave until I got what I came for.

"I will do what I can."

"First, Geoffraie isn't here, is he?"

"It depends on why you need me."

I looked up to find Geoffraie walking in from the back room. My cheeks warmed at the sight of him, but forced myself to focus on my task.

"When I was in quarantine, I had a lot of time to think. I saw more slaves die from being overworked or take their lives from the guilt than die from the Pox. I knew there had to be a better life for slaves, a world without slavery entirely, but I didn't know how to get there.

"Before I was quarantined I was given a book by a freed slave. The story within the book and the woman herself gave me an idea of how to solve slavery, but I need help to put it in place."

Geoffraie sat at Flinders' table and gestured. "Please, don't keep us in suspense. What is your idea?"

"The woman survived after being freed because of her skills in medicine. She didn't just keep her head down and pray someone would save her, she took her fate into her own hands and worked for it.

"If slaves are freed without a plan, they will end up as beggars and starve. However, if the slaves are taught before being freed while those in charge are being overthrown, then there won't be a worry of what will happen to the slaves once freed. Minister Aldous doesn't have much longer with us, having let a sickness go on too long. I've heard his wife will have to sell the estate and everything with it if she wants to continue living her current lifestyle. In other words, Minister Aldous' slaves are going to be for sale."

"Hmm, I see where you're going with this," Geoffraie started. "The world needs to change, but it has to do so slowly. Minister Aldous needs to stop believing his slaves are a bunch of 'wenches who can't to tell a *beardsplitter* from a squash.'"

My cheeks flushed at his comment, but I refused to shy away from his lewdness.

"From what you were saying, it sounds like you already have some plans in place, yes?"

"I do. The girls I was quarantined with have a wide range of skills and talents. I know we can't free all the slaves at once, not without risking the lives of many, Parans or otherwise. You said you helped other Parans be freed, I was hoping you could help more? Get them to a safe place and find someone to help them hone their skills before going out in the world to start their lives anew?"

"Hajana, my dear, I'm sorry, but I don't thi—" Flinders started before Geoffraie cut him off.

"No, I think she's on to something. We have all seen or heard stories of what happens to slaves suddenly freed. If we can have a program of sorts in place, one to help the slaves rediscover their skills, we should be able to negate the worry of flooding the streets and temples with homeless freed slaves."

I unclenched my jaw and relaxed my shoulders. *Finally, I have a plan.*

"Hajana, I can help with purchasing the slaves and getting them out of Altava, but putting anything into motion will have to wait until after the battle. Emolin Stokton has been a huge help in—"

I cut him off, not bothering to apologize. "Emolin's helping you?"

"Yes, it took some time to figure out how to get her alone to speak with me, but once I did, she was more than willing to help the Parans and you. The only reason she left at all was because the Magistrate threatened to kill you if she didn't."

Tears sprang to my eyes, my heart both broke and leaped at the same time. *Emolin didn't leave me.*

"How is she helping you?" I asked, trying to bury my emotions.

"We need the Magistrate and Grandmaster to believe they still have the upper hand so Emolin is pretending to go along with their original plans. In just a few days, Magistrate Magdra and Grandmaster Sphera will be meeting just north of Gathon to eradicate the Parans, or so they think. The Paran women, children, and elders have already been relocated to a safe place. Many of the men and a large group of women stayed behind to fight with my soldiers."

"You have soldiers?"

Geoffraie leaned back and crossed his arms, a smirk on his face. "I gathered an army large enough the Klohaven Mountains are bursting with them. The Paran camp has been turned into our base and we are waiting to ambush the Magistrate. It has been discovered he is part of a radical group that has been responsible for several attacks on the king's life.

"The king can't disband the group himself, but that doesn't stop a soldier acting on his own accord. And, while the Grandmaster isn't currently part of a radical group that we're aware of, there are many other things she has done that can be tied to any number of groups."

I pondered everything Geoffraie told me, how Emolin hadn't betrayed me, and the hope of changing the lives of slaves, my own included. Slaves would still be at the mercy of their masters, for now, but soon there would be a place for them to run to, to no longer have to fear for themselves.

"Is there anything I can do to help? Anything at all? I don't just want to sit here, I want to do something too."

Geoffraie looked up at me and smiled. "There is something, though I have to warn you it could be very dangerous."

"Danger doesn't scare me. Not anymore."

I surprised myself when I realized I meant what I said. After everything my master had done to me, all the violence I witnessed, there was little left to scare me.

"I need you to sneak into Minister Aldous' office and get his journal for me. It's the size of most books and is bound in a deep red leather."

"May I ask what's in the journal and why you need it?"

"Unfortunately, I can't tell you much and I highly advise against you reading it. I want you to know you don't have to do this, though, if you don't feel comfortable. I know it's a lot to ask."

I shook my head. "No, this is something that allows me to help. I'll do it. When do you need it?"

"I'll send a soldier to retrieve you in three days, as there is still much I need to do to prepare for the battle. I will need the book before that evening. We must have it. If you agree to at least try, my soldier will help you escape."

Geoffraie's offer for a chance at my freedom was something I never thought I'd hear. I had been a slave for so long and dreamed of freedom every night. My knees threatened to buckle, but didn't let them, reminding myself I wasn't free yet. I still had to get the journal.

"I can have the book for you by six that evening. I'll wait in the alley behind the potter's shop we first met in. How will I know the soldier is one of yours?"

"If they respond 'only tonight' when you ask 'are the tiger hawks flying?' you will know they are one of mine. Now that that's settled, let's get you back to your master's so he doesn't start having the REDs searching for a runaway slave."

I thanked Flinders for his help and Geoffraie gave Lodal the note for the fishmonger before leading me out to a side street where his footman was waiting with a carriage. I accepted the man's hand as I climbed in and tried not to think about how filthy I was in comparison to the plush red seats. I sat back and watched the city pass as we headed back for my master's. Not only with the hope of freedom, but a plan to get it.

CHAPTER TWENTY-FIVE
EMOLIN

The next morning the three of us rose early and got ready to leave. Nightmares about the upcoming battle plagued me throughout the night, and I needed a little extra time to wake up. Tara and Lea gave more time to get ready, the two heading down to gather the horses. I sat on my bed and tried to make sense of the dreams, running from things I couldn't see in darkness I couldn't shake. It would make sense they would have something to do with Fonir visiting me, but I couldn't string them together.

The absence of Fonir worried me. He visited me many times before disappearing altogether. *Did I do something wrong?* Glancing out the window, I hadn't realized how much time passed and hurried to meet the others downstairs, deciding to worry about Fonir another time.

As promised, by the time I was ready to leave, Lea, Tara, and Sampson were in the courtyard waiting for me. I walked over to Sampson and stroked his nose, receiving a nicker in return. He leaned into me and placed his head on my shoulder, begging for scritches. I spent a few moments petting him before placing my pack over the saddle and noticing the saddlebags were close to bursting. I asked Tara about it and she said the Grandmaster instructed the stable to replenish our supplies. While it was a polite gesture, I didn't like being in debt to anyone. At least we wouldn't have to worry about food and water on the journey.

I climbed up into the saddle and looked at Lea and Tara. "Ready?"

They nodded, and we spurred our horses on.

Sampson wanted to run, but I held him back until we passed through the city gates, not wanting to draw more attention to us. As soon as we made it to the path into the woods, I tapped Sampson's sides with my heels and he took off.

I moved with Sampson as he raced down the trail. Dust rose behind me and Lea and Tara raced after us, calling for Sampson to slow down, but there was no stopping him. The speed helped clear my head and gave me something to focus on other than the stress of the upcoming battle. The war hadn't started yet, and there was already so much blood on my hands.

Eventually, Sampson slowed, and we stopped in a small clearing by a river. I slid out of the saddle and took a seat in the shade under a tree while Sampson drank and splashed around in the water.

"I don't think I ever realized how fast Sampson could be," Lea said when they rode up a few minutes later.

I squinted against the sun as I looked up at them. "Yea, and it helped clear my mind. Not to mention Sampson was tired of being stabled."

The two nodded in understanding and let their horses get some water while they joined me in the shade.

"So," Lea started, turning to me, "what do you want to do after the battle? Is there anyone you have waiting for you?"

Thoughts of Hajana immediately came to me. *I hope she's doing okay.* "There are some things I need to do back in Altava, people I need to see, but I don't think I'll be able to stay there, especially after the battle. There are two people there I care about, but I don't know how I could take either of them with me..." I wiped away a tear and stared at the sun glinting on the water.

Tara and Lea were quiet for a moment before Tara spoke up. "I'm sure you'll find a way. I mean, you just had a meeting with the Grandmaster and convinced her to bring her troops to the battle. If you can do that, you can do anything."

The two leaned in and embraced me. While I was still concerned about Mamma and Hajana, Lea and Tara gave me hope I could figure something out.

We rested in the clearing for another quarter-hour before deciding we should move on. We were taking a different route back to the camp, one requiring us to camp for the night, but would prevent anyone from getting suspicious if they saw us heading directly to the mountains. We packed up the few things we had taken out of our packs and climbed back into the saddles, continuing down the southern path to Gathon.

Sampson didn't take off again, instead seeming to prefer staying near his other horse friends. Lea and Tara chatted about random things, leaving room for me to chime in when I wanted, but allowing me to focus on my thoughts instead. Most of the conversation revolved around the latest fashions of the cities, Tara's beloved, who Lea fancied, and the different stores they wanted to visit in Blackwood.

I enjoyed listening to the two of them chatter on, especially when they began discussing the gossip they had gotten about the capital and the royal family. I didn't think anything of it until we passed a lone traveler on the road and he nodded at Tara.

"Alright, we're safe."

I turned and noticed a faint cloud of dust rising and heading back toward the city.

"I thought they were just another traveler or maybe someone out hunting for their family."

"No, they were sent to follow us. We can head up the trail now, though, and that's what matters. If they would've continued to follow us for much longer, we would've had to backtrack," Tara said, turning into the underbrush, seeming to travel wherever she wanted on a whim.

I tried to discern any path or markings as I followed, looking at both the ground and the trees, but not seeing anything other than the occasional bird in a tree or rodent scurrying through the underbrush. After nearly an hour of traveling without seeing a path, and making certain there was no one following us, I let my curiosity take over.

"How do you know where the trails are?"

Lea pointed to a small boulder off to the right. "There are a few rocks and fallen trees we use as reference points. We keep them to our side until they are diagonal from each other, then we follow the next marker. This allows Parans to follow a path while leaving a trail even a skilled tracker would have trouble discerning from a group of deer."

We continued in silence and I tried to watch for the different markers as we passed, amazed at the ingenuity of the Parans. There were a lot of different things they used I never would've considered.

We followed the unseen trail for a few hours, stopping now and again to water the horses and stretch our legs. I tried to pick out the individual landmarks we were following, but I always picked wrong, picking a log instead of a rock or choosing something on the wrong side of the trail to follow.

As the sun moved across the sky and we traveled higher into the mountains, the air cooled more than it ever had in Altava. The clouds rolled in and specks of white floated around me. I'd heard of the white specks before but never saw it in person.

"Is this snow?"

Tara slowed and watched the white specks float around her, nodding. "I guess it is. I'm not used to seeing flurries this early in the season. We'll need to set up camp soon. You don't want to be traveling in the snow at night."

Lea and Tara discussed the options of different places to camp while we continued, my focus coming and going as I watched the snow around me. I reached out a hand to catch the falling flakes and was eventually able to grab one and examine it before it melted. The snow was made of tiny crystals forming a beautiful and unique pattern, different from each other, but all the same. The fact that nature could make some things almost identical, like flowers, but others unique, like snowflakes, intrigued me.

Another hour passed with the sun mostly behind the trees before we made camp. I worried about the possibility of bandits, but Lea and Tara promised the bandits never ventured so far into the forest without a path to follow.

At least somewhat satisfied by the answer, we stopped at the next clearing we came across, Tara explaining that the Parans had different markings to denote the next closest river or camp. I hadn't seen anything standing out from the rest of the forest, but I wasn't surprised either.

As we unpacked our bedding and Lea made a small, controlled fire with her Aura, I realized the two of them knew a lot more about the Parans than any of Geoffraie's soldiers would.

"How do you two know so much about the ways of the Parans?"

They glanced at each other, neither seeming to want to start. I wondered if I'd overstepped my bounds and was about to apologize when Lea spoke up.

"Tara and I were both babies when our families' village was destroyed. The troops were supposed to be 'liberating the lands from the Paran filth' and made sure there was nothing left when they were done. The only reason the two of us survived was because our mothers wrapped us up and placed us in some bushes by the road, hoping to return to get us that evening.

"Instead, a farmer found us on the way home from the market. He'd heard about the Paran village being attacked earlier that day and it wasn't hard to determine we were from there. He took us to his home, and he and his wife raised us as their own, only telling us about our beginning once our Wells became apparent."

"I'm sorry, I don't know what to say…"

"Don't be," Tara cut in. "We were both babes when it happened. Do we wish we knew our parents? Of course, but madame filled in more than enough for our parents when she offered to mentor us."

"Madame took you in?"

"She did," Lea continued, "she wanted to make sure we got the best education and knew how important it is to strengthen Wells at an early age. She didn't want us to forget the kindness of the farmers either, so she made sure we visited with them regularly. After all, they're the only parents we ever knew.

"Once we were old enough to make our own choices, madame introduced us to the Parans, taking us to the camp so we could decide if we wanted to worship Para or follow The Eight Devine. She encouraged us to do a lot of things ourselves and discover what we wanted in life.

"When Geoffraie arrived and told us about his plan and how he was going to stop the senseless killing of Parans, it was an immediate decision to join him, and we've been working with him for over a year trying to figure out what could be done. It was pure luck Fonir visited you the same time Geoffraie was in Altava. It gave us the perfect event to use as the jumping point for the battle."

Thinking about Fonir and everything that happened with him, I didn't think that it was luck. It was too perfectly aligned. I didn't want to bring it up with Lea and Tara though, not understanding Fonir myself.

"I think we should head to bed. Tara, do you mind taking the first watch?" Lea asked, putting out the fire.

The three of us snuggled close together to stay warm, the

horses standing close together as well, and I fell into a surprisingly peaceful slumber.

***

The next day was much of the same, traveling through the woods until noon when we reached the opening to one of the many tunnels the Parans carved out of the mountain, the mouth hidden perfectly with Alchemist ruins.

While I was glad the journey was almost over, part of the job done, something didn't feel right. I couldn't quite place it, but there was something off about the whole thing.

"Do you guys—" I started, only to be cut off by hoofbeats racing toward us from the mouth of the tunnel.

We turned to see a group of bandits poised to attack, a familiar crackling Aura filling the air, the Lightning Mage.

"Whatever you guys do, don't let the one in the center hit you!" I yelled, dismounting Sampson and giving him a hard smack on the rear to send him toward camp, hoping he and the other horses would be enough to have someone send for help.

The three of us unsheathed our swords and stood at the ready, blocking the tunnel to the Paran camp. Tara created a shield of Life Aura, giving us protection from the first strike from the Lightning Mage.

"I won't be able to hold this for very long," Tara called, grimacing after her shield absorbed the attack.

I'd never seen an Aura shield in person, but I knew enough about it to know my attacks would slip through harmlessly. Lea hurled a ball of fire at the bandits and knocked one of them off their horse, the stench of burning flesh filling the enclosed space. I yelled at Lea and Tara to close their eyes and conjured a wall of pure, white Aura, lighting the entire tunnel and blinding everyone except me, leaving an opening so I could charge forward. The Lighting Mage was capable of terrible things, and I wouldn't let Lea or Tara die because of me.

"Emolin!" Lea called, a ball of flames soaring past into another stunned bandit.

I ignored their calls and continued running toward the Mage, his vision returning and a smile growing on his face. The other bandits continued rushing forward, riding past me toward Lea and Tara, the Mage staying behind and focusing on me.

"Ah, so you've come to meet your fate at last," the man laughed, dismounting his horse and approaching me. "I've never seen someone survive my attack before, and I wouldn't want to fight someone who almost killed me. I must've fried your brain like that girl's."

Natalia was safe in Cragsrest or back in Altava with her family. Something happening during her journey back to Altava never occurred to me. The confusion must've been clear on my face, the Lightning Mage's laugh echoing off the tunnel walls.

"Oh, I'm guessing you don't know. My boys and I found her traveling back to Altava, and we couldn't leave any survivors, boss' orders."

The Mage smiled, his teeth glistening in the light from Lea's fireballs. *Did he kill her? Did he take her from me?*

"You're lying." I tried to keep myself calm, knowing better than reacting to anything my opponent was saying.

"Why don't you let me kill you so you can find out for yourself?"

I rolled to my left as a bolt of lightning struck the ground where I'd been standing. I only had a second to recover, another bolt striking a bolder, pieces of rock flying at me. Predicting his next move, I rushed forward, sword extended. Our blades collided, sparks flying as steel met steel. There was little chance for me to beat him from far away, his long-ranged attacks being far stronger than mine. There was still a chance up close, a chance I had to take.

The Mage spun his sword out of our lock and slashed at me, his movements calculated but unrefined. I had the upper hand in swordsmanship, but I didn't want to show it yet. Instead, I played at his level, hoping to hold him off from attacking anyone until others arrived.

"You're a gutsy one. I think I may have some fun before I kill you."

He slashed again, his stance far too wide to put any power behind his attack. He had a pattern to his movements, something Sojourn warned us about countless times. *Don't rely on your Well to save you, build up your sword skills. Vary your movements so your opponent can't follow your pattern.* Now, I just needed an opening.

Aura crackled in the air, a glint in his eyes hinting at his next move. I blocked a few more strikes and jumped back as he slashed at me again.

His blade became shrouded in Lightning Aura, the bluish light illuminating the tunnel. I coated my blade in my Light Aura and noticed a small warmth on my chest where the pendant hung. The Mage let a look of surprise show on his face before hiding it again.

"I was told you were a Golden Mage. This does change things. No matter, I'll still finish you quickly."

Shouts bounced off the walls behind me and I needed to finish the Mage quickly, not wanting anyone else to get hurt. No one else had experience with the Lightning Mage. I didn't have much either, but I couldn't let that stop me.

I slashed furiously at the Mage, pushing him back farther and expanding my Aura around me to a blinding brightness. The footsteps rushing toward me stalled, the clashing of blades and cries from the fatally wounded becoming silent.

The Lightning Mage stared, mouth agape. "The Magistrate said you would be simple to dispose of."

At the mention of the Magistrate, my Well expanded to fill

every part of me. Geoffraie mentioned the Magistrate most likely sent the Lightning Mage disguised as a bandit after me, but hearing it filled my Well with warmth and energy completely new to me.

"W-what are you?" the Lightning Mage asked, stumbling back and tripping over a rock.

"Someone with a Well of vengeance."

I leaped toward him, the immense power from my Well allowing me to reach him easily. Sword raised, I thrust it into his chest before he could move. The tip of my blade easily passed through his skin and breast bone, struggling as his Well fought to protect him but eventually falling as my blade slid through and exited his back. With his Well severed, his blade stopped glowing, and the smile on his face disappeared.

"How?" he asked, blood drooling out of his mouth and dribbling onto his chest.

"It may take some time, but in the end, the stone-hearted will receive their comeuppance."

I stood as his eyes dulled and became vacant. I placed my foot on his chest pulled out my blade in one, fluid motion, his body falling back in a pool of his blood. I turned around to find a large group standing behind me, soldiers and Parans alike. I bent and used the Lightning Mage's cloak to clean my sword before sheathing it and returning to the others. Geoffraie stood in the center of the group with a smirk on his face. Lea ran up and threw her arms around me, nearly knocking me over with the sheer force of her hug.

"That was foolish and unnecessary. Don't put yourself in danger like that, the fact that it worked aside," she said as she pulled away, tears in her eyes. "Promise me you'll never do that again,"

"I won't, I promise." I smiled and squeezed her shoulder.

"Well then, Lady Stokton, I do believe things have changed with our plans after your display. We have some things to discuss before you turn in for the night. For now, I think it's best to have a healer see to you."

Geoffraie turned, calling for the wagon and healer. A woman pushed her way through the crowd and bowed to Geoffraie before addressing me.

"May I take a look at you and your Well once the wagon arrives?"

"Okay," I said, swaying on my feet as the extra energy in my Well dissipated, leaving me almost entirely drained of Aura.

The healer wrapped her arm around my waist, holding me steady as a large, open-walled wagon approached. Geoffraie and the healer helped me into the wagon and the driver started toward the Paran camp.

"Emolin, how are you feeling?" the healer asked, taking my pulse after looking me over for any obvious wounds.

"Drained. I feel like I've been using my Aura all day instead of for only a battle."

"I'm going to look at your Well now..."

The healer trailed off as her Aura enveloped me. She said something to Geoffraie, but I was too tired to pay attention and drifted off.

***

The healer woke me once we neared the camp.

"Emolin, are you feeling better?"

"I think so."

I stretched and sat up, looking at the healer for the first time. She had black hair and grey eyes similar to Hajana's. What caught my attention, though, were the tattoos of creeping vines with tiny flowers trailing down her arms, ending on the back of her hands with a golden sun, the symbol of Para.

"I'm assuming you've never seen a Paran woman, have you?" the healer asked, catching me staring at her tattoos.

"Oh, I'm sorry, please forgive me…" I trailed off, heat rising up the back of my neck.

"No, it's okay," she laughed, "I know you were merely curious and didn't mean anything by it."

"May I ask you what they mean? The tattoos?"

"Of course." She gave me a warm smile. "I'm sure you're well aware of the symbol for Para. Every Paran woman is allowed to get her hands tattooed with the golden sun as a sign of respect to our god when we turn sixteen. We're not required to, Para will love and protect us the same either way. Many choose not to, wanting to form a stronger bond with Para first. Those that get their tattoos at sixteen are often blessed with Wells.

"Every Paran woman with a Well chooses a tattoo that represents their given gift. These tattoos can take years to decide on, but are only allowed after the golden sun."

I nodded, not entirely understanding what she was saying, but not wanting to ask her to explain again either. Thankfully, before there was a chance for her to realize I was utterly confused, the wagon arrived in the main cavern of the Paran camp.

Geoffraie jumped out before the wagon stopped and strode over to the strategy building. The driver slowed to a stop at the door of the building and the healer helped me down.

"I want to see you again before you leave. Your Well is stable now, but I still have no clue what caused your loss of Aura."

"Thank you, I will make sure to visit you before I head out."

Lea and Tara rode up, dismounting and handing their horses off to a nearby stable hand. He saw me glancing his way and gave me a bow.

"Your horse arrived safely and is already resting back at the stables."

I bowed my head in thanks, glad to hear Sampson was okay. Lea and Tara led me into the building where Geoffraie, Advisor Falcon, and a few other high-ranking officers stood over a map. Geoffraie welcomed us and had us join him and the others.

There were small figurines placed around the map, denoting the location of the Parans, Mages, Alchemists, and madame. Something about the figures was off, but I wasn't sure what.

"… our forces will move in from here and here," a man said, pointing to two separate locations.

"No, that won't work," I said, staring at the map.

The room turned silent and stared at me. "When I was at Grandmaster Sphera's, she took me into a hidden room where she had a large map set up with not only the hills and mountains but the rivers and valleys.

"On this map, I could see the true number of forces the Grandmaster has at her disposal. Those numbers are far larger than what you have here, and your idea of trying to surround the troops would only get you found and killed much easier."

"Then what do you think we should do?" someone asked.

"What they least expect. Have a majority of the forces stationed within Gathon, ready to attack from the rear, while the others move in from the mountain path, expecting an offer of the liberation of the Paran slaves. We have more numbers than they believe. All we need is for them to think we're weaker than we are."

Geoffraie stared at the map. "You know, Emolin, I think you're onto something." Geoffraie looked up at one of his commanding officers. "If you and Smith take your groups along the trail today and travel through the night, you'll be well within a day's march to Gathon and will hopefully get there before Magdra or Sphera. Cassandra, your commanding officer had high praises for you. Would you take the third group of soldiers to Gathon?"

"I am honored you've selected me for such an important role," she said, bowing and crossing her arms over her chest in a salute. "I promise to do my best."

Cassandra stepped up to the table next to me to study the map. Her black hair shone purple in the light, and I had never seen someone with eyes as pale as hers. I gave her a smile, and she smiled back before we returned our attention to the matter at hand. She traced the path with her finger.

"Are there any scouts we'll have to worry about?" Casandra asked after a few moments.

"Good question," Falcon started. "We have our own scouts on patrol and they have reported enemy lookouts along the roads east and west of Gathon as well as the known routes out of the mountains."

"That means they're not guarding the city?" Cassandra asked, cutting in politely but unabashed. "Isn't that concerning?"

"Normally, yes. However, with the increased bandit activity we now know was a diversion set up by the Magistrate, it makes sense the scouts would be more worried about the known roads leading to the city instead of the nearly impassable forest.

"You will head to Madame LeDore's and camp on her grounds. She lives far enough away from the rest of the city that even numbers as large as ours should be able to hide for a few days."

Cassandra nodded and focused again on the map. We covered a few other tactical measures that would be taken, but none involved me, which I found odd after Geoffraie's comment earlier.

"As for you, Emolin," Geoffraie said, turning to me, "We need you to be the one to not only lure the Magistrate and Grandmaster into the field but also keep them preoccupied while we move in, hopefully capturing and taking the two of them to the king for a proper trial."

"Do you have any suggestions on how to keep the most powerful Alchemist and Mage in Klohaven preoccupied without them killing me after discovering I betrayed them?" I asked, mostly in a sarcastic tone, but also genuinely wanting an answer.

"I saw you take down a Lightning Mage less than two hours ago. You were able to not only hold your own against him but find and exploit his weakness without letting your fears cloud your focus. The healer may also have some theories as to what happened. Speak with her and once the two of you discover what caused it, I know you'll be fine."

I stared at the others in the room, all of whom had been there to see me defeat the Lightning Mage. *Hajana and the rest of the Parans are counting on me. If I don't do this, who knows how many will die.*

"Okay, I'll do it."

"Good. Now you three should go and get some rest. I only have battle specifics left to discuss."

Lea, Tara, and I bowed and left, heading back to the room we stayed in a few nights earlier. The three of us got ready for bed and Tara and Lea were asleep within minutes. I lay awake for far too long, worrying about the upcoming battle and the things I was expected to do.

———

*E*arly the next morning I headed over to meet with the healer. Lea and Tara gave me directions to the healer's quarters and an ashberry pastry to munch on. Following a tunnel set apart from the others, I came to a plain door. A soft voice called out for me to enter after I knocked and I entered into a sparsely decorated parlor.

"Ah, Emolin, I'm glad to see you. How are you feeling?" The healer motioned for the two of us to sit at a table with tea and cookies spread out.

"I'm feeling alright considering the lack of sleep I've gotten." I accepted the cookie and cup of tea the healer gave me.

"That's understandable considering everything you've been through and the upcoming battle. Now, while I'm sure this won't calm your worries, I believe I have discovered what gave you the surge of Aura."

I put down my cup of tea and leaned forward, both eager to

hear and concerned about what she might say. "What have you discovered?"

"I noticed the pendant you're wearing and could sense a collection of Aura still left within it. I have heard of a similar pendant in stories, but nothing has been proven. It seems the pendant will collect and store Aura for the wearer until it's needed."

I looked down at the pendant, a small trinket I fiddled with when nervous. *Has it been storing Aura this whole time?*

"How does it do that?"

"I'm not sure. As I said, everything I know about the pendant comes from stories. What all the stories agree on is that the pendant is more of a curse than a blessing."

"A curse?" I had been holding onto the smooth, yellow stone, but unclasped the chain and dropped the pendant on the table in front of us.

The healer nodded, staring at the pendant. "When the wearer of the pendant is in danger, the stone gives the wearer the Aura it has been storing, effectively acting as a second Well. Because the pendant has collected Aura from countless sources, however, the wearer's Well isn't familiar with it, poisoning their Aura."

"Well poisoning?" I asked, wiping the sweat off my hands on my pants. "Is my Well..."

The look of the healer answered my question. "When I examined your Well after you defeated the Lightning Mage, there was a small section tinged purple and more sluggish than the rest."

"Then I'll just destroy the pendant. I'm sure it won't heal the poison, but it should prevent more."

"I wish it were that simple, but nothing never is." The healer picked the pendant back up and handed it to me. "If you and this pendant get separated, or it is unable to detect your Well nearby, the poison it has caused will spread rapidly. This pendant has bonded with you, helping you, and also providing potential for great harm."

"Is there nothing I can do?" I ran my fingers over the stone, any relief I had gotten from knowing Hajana was almost safe having fled with the new news.

"There's nothing you can do here. There are healers in the king's court who know far more than I. The best thing you can do is to not use the pendant at all, head north, and skip the battle."

"What about you? And the rest of the Parans?"

"While I would be lying if I said I thought we could easily win without you here, I can't ask you to stay and risk more damage to your Well either. The choice is up to you."

Once again, when everything seemed to be making sense, something came in to wreck it all.

CHAPTER TWENTY-SIX
HAJANA

I still received a beating for being gone so long, but with Geoffraie's explanation of enjoying my company, the beating was far less than it would've been. They invited Geoffraie to stay for supper, and he ended up discussing various things all evening with my master in the study.

After treating my welts as best I could with an old rag and a bucket of water, Ruta let me have an easy evening and tasked me with dusting the pictures and vases upstairs. Knowing what I would have to do in the coming days, I was very thorough while dusting the frames near the master's study in case there was anything of interest discussed.

Listening at the door, I learned Minister Aldous was going to be out of town the following few days, meeting a potential business partner in another city, and I hoped he wouldn't be taking the journal with him. *Thank you, Para. Please, let this blessing continue.*

I didn't have much time to worry about the master or the journal over the next two days, as Ruta gave me a much larger share of chores than normal. Once I finished all my chores the day before my chance at freedom, I convinced Ruta there was something from the apothecary the healer recommended I get to prevent the Serf Pox from coming back.

When I arrived, the woman was turning out some pills and dusting off each one with a tiny brush before placing them in a jar.

"Ah, Hajana, I'm glad to see you're well. Have the pills been helping?"

I took in a deep breath of the spicy scent of ground herbs before responding. "They have more than I thought they would."

"I'm assuming that's not why you're here, though."

I pulled the book out of my pocket as I tried to collect my thoughts. "I came to return the book and also ask you a question."

"The book was for you to keep, my dear. From what I've heard, it sounds like it's done its job, even better than I hoped."

"How did you hear about it?" I took a step toward the door, fearful of what might be waiting for me.

"There's no need to fret, I should've been more clear. The healer came by and spoke to me, as did another one of Minister Aldous' slaves. I'm sorry I worried you. I promise you're safe here. Now, please, what is your question?"

"Well..." I trailed off, not sure where to start, but the words tumbling out on their own. "Was I right in asking Geoffraie to help? What if the master finds out? Will they punish the other girls? I'm leaving soon and once I do, what will happen—"

"Hajana." The woman came around the counter and took my hands in hers. "I know you want to help the others, you've already done so much, but you can't hold all this on your shoulders, not without taking care of yourself first."

"I am taking care of myself, I'm getting out of the tortu—"

"You're getting out, but that doesn't mean you're taking care of yourself. Once you're free, there will be many things you will need to do to keep yourself safe and you won't have the energy to worry about others. For now, you need to focus on keeping yourself safe so you can help when the time is right."

I wanted to say something, to prove the woman wrong, that I still had more than enough energy to help. As I stood there, however, the idea of focusing on and caring for myself instead of worrying about others was a comforting one.

"Now, let me get you another jar of pills and some salve to take with you so you won't get in trouble."

The woman turned to one of the many shelves and gave me a small pot of salve labeled *Healing Salve*. Before I could argue against her giving me such an expensive gift, she shooed me out the door.

"I'm sure you have many things you still have to take care of. I wish you a safe and swift journey and will pray for your safety."

Once on the streets, I hurried to Flinders, not wanting to leave without thanking him for all the help and care he gave me.

When I turned down Flinders' street, the door to his house was hanging ajar, a slight breeze pushing it open further. *Please, this can't be.* I threw open the door and braced myself for the worst, only to find Flinders sitting at his table, sipping tea.

"Ah, Hajana, I'm glad to see you. I have the most glorious news."

"You're okay! I saw your open door and—"

"Oh, posh, you should know better than to worry about me. I'm fine. I'm better than fine. I don't know how he's done it, but Geoffraie not only found a larger place for me to live and help those in need, he also worked with the church and made it so I no longer have to help from the shadows."

"Flinders, that's amazing. I don't know what to say."

"You needn't say anything. While I'm touched you came to

say farewell, you shouldn't waste your time on a crotchety old Mage like me. Now, off with ya, wipe away those tears and smile. Now is not a time to mourn, but to celebrate!"

There was so much I wanted to say to Flinders, things to thank him for. Instead, I rushed forward and wrapped my arms around him, sniffing back the tears.

"Thank you, Flinders, for everything."

I pulled away from him and he gave me a grand bow before presenting me with a small box. "A gift for the kindest soul I know."

Opening the box, I found a gleaming purple stone wrapped in gold wire shaped into Para's golden sun. The pendant hung from a tan, leather cord, plenty long enough for me to tuck under my dress without the worry of it being seen.

"Flinders, this is beautiful." My fingers traced the sun, my vision blurring as a sob caught in my throat. "W-would you put it on me?"

Flinders took the pendant out of the box and I turned around, moving my hair out of the way.

"Make sure no one sees this. The last thing you want is to be punished before you get the chance to leave."

"I promise, I'll be careful."

Flinders handed me back the box and, not trusting my emotions any longer, I waved a final farewell and turned to head back to the master's.

I went up to the second floor where the master's study was and listened to make sure the room was empty. While no one said slaves couldn't enter, it was an unspoken rule to never enter any room with a shut door unless you were given explicit orders to do so.

Dust rag in hand, I slipped into the room, closing the door

behind me, and rushed over to the bookshelf to look for the journal. I didn't have to worry about my master finding me, seeing as he would be gone until the following evening. I wanted to know where the journal was so I wouldn't have to spend precious time the next day looking for it. What I was afraid of was the possibility he might've taken the journal with him.

After scouring all the shelves and finding nothing, I went over to his desk and rifled through the drawers, making sure to keep everything exactly as I found it. The one thing my master was particular about was the placement of his things, and if anything was even a hair out of place, he would notice.

In one of the drawers, I found a small bottle of tonic, remembering what the woman said. I thought back to the staining I found in Master Aldous' chamber pot, the weird gait he recently developed, the foul odor from his laundry, and everything made sense. While I wouldn't wish male bowel sickness on anyone, I thanked Para for the justice he seemed to be giving him.

Finally, at the bottom of the very last drawer, I found the journal. I flipped it open to make sure I'd found the right one, though there were no other books similar to it in the room, pausing when I saw my name as I was flipping through the pages.

Name: Hajana. Age: Fifteen. Procurement: Summer. Worth:

The line with my supposed worth was too smudged to read. I was about to look for the names of other girls I knew when I realized I didn't want to know, aside from the fact I'd been told not to look. I put the journal back in the drawer exactly where I found it and went back over to the bookshelf to make sure I hadn't left smudges in the dust.

Finding nothing, I paused to listen at the door before slipping out and dusting a picture frame on the opposite side of the hall. No sooner had I started cleaning when the mistress came down the hall. She ran her finger over a frame I'd yet to dust and smacked me across the cheek when her finger came back caked in dirt.

After berating me for not doing my chores correctly, she stormed off, yelling at another girl down another hall. Finding what I needed, I finished my chores quickly, waiting for the next day.

I slipped into the loft and grabbed the few belongings I hid in the floorboards. I stashed the smallest basket I could outside earlier that morning and was able to sneak my things out to it without Ruta seeing me. The basket, big enough for a single loaf of bread, wasn't even half full when I added the final things to it. The past five years of my life fitting in such a small space.

Once I had everything ready, I grabbed a dust rag and headed back up to the master's office for the last time, making sure no one was around before opening the door. I grabbed the book from under the papers, replacing it with a random one I borrowed from the master's library.

Satisfied everything was the same, I left the room without issue and tried to keep myself calm as I went about finishing the last of my chores. The mistress didn't come to check my work. Instead, she could be heard yelling at one of the other servants about something in the front parlor.

Ruta wasn't in the kitchen when I went to leave, making my departure a little easier. I grabbed my basket and headed toward the garden. Not wanting to feel nostalgic for the house, I still turned and glanced at it one last time, locking it permanently in my memory before I slipped behind the hedges and worked my way toward the meeting place. Terrible things had happened in that house, but I was still a significant part of my life.

The streets of Altava were quiet, many families eating supper, the silence more unnerving than comforting. I wasn't sure if Para was blessing me as I made my way to freedom, or if I was walking into a trap. I was so lost in thought I didn't notice Master Aldous' carriage riding down the street toward until he called out to me.

"Ha-Jana. What are you doing out here?" His voice gruff and words slurred. He was drunk. Seeing him was bad enough. Dealing with a drunkard was something I didn't have time for.

I curtsied and kept my head bowed, hoping my basket wouldn't catch his attention. "Ruta sent me out to get some more ingredients for supper."

"Why would she do something like that? There's plenty of food in the cellar. I'm tired of that wench spending all my money!"

The master threw open the door and stumbled onto the street, tripping over his feet and barely catching himself on the frame of the carriage. I risked a glance up at the carriage driver and he gave me a small nod.

My master stumbled over and grabbed my shoulders, his breath reeking of ale and his body of sex. The mistress' anger over the past few days made far more sense.

"Why don't we head home," my master's voice broke my train of thought, his eyes filled with a hunger I'd seen in many times before, "I'm sure there's something I can punish you for."

My master grabbed my arm and pulled me toward the carriage when a horse bumped into him and knocked him off balance.

"Run, girl, run!"

The carriage driver didn't have to tell me twice. I pulled my arm out of my master's grasp and took off, my master calling after me.

I left the main road as fast as I could, knowing the shouts from Minister Aldous would call the attention of the REDs and I wouldn't be able to outrun them. I needed to use the streets to my advantage, making sure I didn't get cornered.

The shouts of REDs filled the evening and for once, I was

grateful to be a slave, the few people I passed not paying attention to me or sneering in disgust as I ran by. They'd seen countless slaves caught after running away, there being nowhere for the poor girls to go even if they escaped the city. For the first time, I had a way out, a place where I would be safe. I just had to reach it.

"There she is!"

Footsteps thundering down the alley after me gave an extra burst of speed. I was still several blocks away from where I was meeting Geoffraie's soldier, but I wouldn't let such a small distance prevent me from my freedom.

I took a sharp left down the next alley, dodging a shopkeeper carrying an armload of wrapped parcels. Before I turned the corner, the REDs crashed into the shopkeeper and some most likely stayed back to help. That left only a few REDs chasing me to avoid. I leaped over a small pile of rubbish and ran into a wench. I hastily apologized and she winked at me before I ran off again.

"Did I see anyone?" her voice echoed off the walls of the allies. "Yes, they ran off toward the docks."

I thanked Para for the woman's help and hoped Geoffraie's soldier would be there already. I only had one block left when two REDs stopped in front of me, blocking my path. I turned and ran down a side street, darting in the back of a shop and running through the store. The shopkeeper, a butcher, shouted at me and threw one of his knives, grazing my arm.

I cried out, but kept running, seeing the pottery shop and knowing my safety was just behind it.

"Don't let her get away!"

The REDs chased me down the streets, catching up quickly. They were close enough their unwashed uniforms nearly overwhelmed me as I rounded the corner, one of them grabbing my arm as the carriage came into view.

"You're in a world of trouble, missy," the RED who held me

said, pulling me down the street where a barred wagon was pulling up.

"Ah, thank you for catching my slave, gentlemen," a woman dressed in a familiar grey uniform said, strolling toward us.

"I'm sorry, m'lady, but this slave belongs to Minister Aldous. We have the papers to—"

"You mean these papers?" she said, providing a document with my master's official seal and signature. "Minister Aldous lost a bet to me and was supposed to be bringing me my slave this evening. As you can see, the slave has brought her meager belongings and must've tried to escape from him on the way."

The woman grasped my arm and yanked me toward her. Her sharp brown eyes and tight knot of blonde hair at the nape of her neck gave her a stern look and caused a shiver of fear to run down my back. I struggled and tried to pull away, hoping to add truth to the story, but also genuinely worried.

"I'm glad we could help you, then, m'lady. We will be sure to let Minister Aldous know we delivered her to you safely."

The woman thanked the men and dragged me back to her carriage, shouting the whole way and calling me a slew of things. Once we were alone, the woman let me go, and I struggled for a moment before remembering what I was supposed to ask.

"Are the tiger hawks flying?"

The woman smiled, bowing and opening the door to the carriage. "Only tonight."

I climbed into the carriage and placed my basket on the bench beside me, letting out a sigh as I sank into the plush seat.

"We're not out of this yet," the woman said, staring out the window as we approached the city gate.

"What do you mean?"

The woman didn't answer, staring intently at something just out of my view.

Instead of heading across the desert, we made a sharp turn to the right and came to a stop next to the wall. I leaned forward, the shadow of the gate covering us, staring out the window as a second carriage exactly like the one I was in raced away from the wall.

Before the second carriage got too far away, a dozen flaming arrows rained down on the wooden roof, burning in seconds. The driver leaped away and the horses broke free as the fire added to the fierce orange of the setting sun.

"What happened?"

"They were waiting for you. We got a tip that a maid saw you sneak into your master's study yesterday and let Mistress Aldous know. The mistress must've known what was in there and sent word to the REDs. Either way, we were ready."

I didn't know what to say and the woman and I rode in silence as we crossed the desert.

CHAPTER TWENTY-SEVEN
EMOLIN

After meeting with the healer, Lea, Tara, and I headed for Gathon. Our first day of travel was completely in the tunnels

"If the tunnels extend to the end of the Klohaven Range, then why did I have to sleep outside when I was kidnapped?"

"Well," Tara started after a moment, "there was a lot of talk about what we should do. There was concern for your safety in regards to the bandits, the weather, and what you would do if you discovered you were heading for the Paran Camp. Eventually, it was decided the Paran would take you the long way to disorient you, as long as it wasn't snowing, so you wouldn't be able to lead others back if you decided not to join us."

"Were there any plans for bandits, though? After discovering the bandits were sent by the Magistrate, wasn't there concern? What if they came after me and the Paran while we were in the forest?"

"While it may have seemed like it, you two weren't alone in the forest. Advisor Falcon wanted to assure your safety and had at least two dozen scouts watching the area, ready to sound the alarm if bandits were spotted."

Though I didn't agree with the idea that two dozen scouts would've been enough to stop the Lightning Mage, I didn't voice the concerns as it was likely Advisor Falcon wasn't aware of the Mage.

The second day of travel was easy, the trail heading from the mountains to Gathon easy to make out once we left the tunnels. Sampson and the other horses were tired of being underground and moved as swift as the forest would let them. I enjoyed every minute of the journey, not sure when I would have another carefree day.

The three of us laughed and gossiped as we rode, making plans of what we would do once the battle was behind us. I admitted to them my dream of becoming a scholar, and Lea suggested talking to madame to see if she could help me plan a journey to the palace to use the king's library to study. The idea of leaving Klohaven for the first time and seeing the rest of the Lunen Kingdom thrilled me, and we talked about different places for me to visit. By the time the guards met us at the gate to Gathon and escorted us to madame's, I had a list so long it would take me the better part of two years just to see it all.

"Well, you three seem to have enjoyed your journey back," madame said, laughing. "Why don't we head into the parlor where you can tell me about everything that happened and let me know what the plan for the battle is?"

We followed madame into the parlor where one of the servants brought in a large tray filled with pastries and tea.

Lea, Tara, and I talked over each other as we explained the different parts of the journey. Madame apologized for my capture and explained why it was the only way she could think of to convince me to join.

"While I didn't enjoy the tree branch helping knock me off Sampson's back, the whole capture is a rather ridiculous story, and I will look back on it as fondly as one possibly can."

Lea filled madame in on what happened while I was speaking

to the Grandmaster, and I explained everything I could remember from meeting.

When we got to the part about the battle with the Lightning Mage, madame agreed with Lea that what I did was irresponsible. She also admitted that she would have done something similar had she been in my position.

"And, once it's all over," Lea said, "Emolin wants to plan a trip to the Lunen Kingdom so she can study to be a scholar. We were hoping you could help her."

Madame smiled, a glimmer in her eye. "While I can help with that, I think there is something better I can do. However, we'll discuss that more after the battle."

The three of us tried to convince madame to explain, but she was firm on her and wouldn't give in no matter our tactic. We gave up after dessert and spent the rest of the evening reading and playing cards with the servants, distracting me from the battle looming overhead.

The next morning I had to force myself to get out of bed and get dressed. I didn't allow myself to think about what was rushing toward me as the time ticked on. Instead, I thought about the meal I would have for supper that night, taking a well-deserved bath, and all the things I could look forward to after everything was over.

I headed down to the dining room without waiting for my maid. I wanted to get moving as soon as I could to make sure I would make it to the tavern before Grandmaster Sphera and Magistrate Magdra. I wanted to understand the location and make plans for unforeseen details.

"You're up early."

Madame was already at the table, sipping a cup of tea. She was wearing the same gown as the night before, and the shadows created by the crackling fire heightened the dark circles under her eyes.

"I want to get to the tavern before the others. Once everything starts, there's no telling what might happen and I want to make sure I've come up with as many plans as I can to prevent things from going wrong."

Madame nodded. "I spent the entire night thinking over the same things. It's not a good habit to get into, you'll drive yourself insane."

I knew exactly what she meant, having spent countless hours going over the different outcomes to every scenario. It wasn't something I wanted to do, but it wasn't the time to chide myself over something that would take time to work on.

I took a seat and nibbled on some toast, my leg jittering as I watched the clock on the mantel over the fireplace. There wasn't much I could do but wait, and that was the worst part.

I couldn't sit still any longer and needed to move. I paced the room and counted the steps it took to cross the floor, thirty-seven of them. I don't know how many times I passed the clock, but eventually I decided it was time for me to go.

"I will see you later this evening. Please ask the cook to have some cookies for dessert," I said as I turned to leave.

Madame nodded and I walked out of the room to gather my things. I asked one of the maids to have Sampson saddled for me and said I would be down shortly.

I grabbed my cloak and the essentials, not wanting to weigh myself down with all my belongings. I tied my hair back in a tight plait and looked at myself in the mirror before turning to go.

Lea and Tara met me outside of their rooms, the two of them heading down for a bit of breakfast before meeting up with the troops on madame's grounds.

"You're going to do great!" Lea said, hugging me.

Tara seemed as nervous as I was, fiddling with the sleeve of her robes and chewing on her already bleeding lip. We shared a small smile before I headed downstairs and out to the courtyard where Sampson was waiting.

Sampson seemed to understand the tension of the day and shifted from foot to foot, his breath fogging in the frosty morning air.

"You ready?" I whispered in his ear as I stroked his nose.

He nuzzled my face and rested his head on my shoulder as I hugged him, trying to get myself to relax. I had gone over the plan as many times as I could, but it still didn't feel like enough. *I know what my part is, I just have to complete it.*

I stepped away from Sampson and nodded to the gathered servants as I climbed into the saddle. I refused to look back as I guided Sampson out the gate and down the mostly deserted city streets. There wasn't much I could do but pray to the gods and keep a firm head on my shoulders. I needed to keep a clear mind and I was grateful for the crisp air as I traveled down the road.

The tavern appeared near the edge of the forest, and I wondered how many other rivals met there, how many battle plans were discussed over pints of ale. I refused to let some nibbles of bread be my last meal and I secured Sampson to a post before confidently striding inside.

I asked the barmaid for a small glass of watered wine before setting my belongings down at one of the many empty tables. There was nothing much to see and I found myself staring into the fire as I sipped on the wine and waited for the others to arrive.

I had been waiting at the tavern for close to an hour before Grandmaster Sphera entered. She carried her hat under her arm and nodded at the barmaid before sitting at the table across from me.

"I'm glad to see you're okay. When I heard the snow started after you girls left, I worried about the three of you staying warm without being able to build a fire. Then, I heard of several bandit attacks on the paths back to Gathon and, while I was certain you three would be more than capable of holding your own, the bandits have been far more dangerous than usual."

I couldn't help but wonder how the Grandmaster heard about the bandit attack, but I ignored it, not wanting to dwell on something that could distract me from the battle.

"We did get caught in the snow, but it was light, and we were able to huddle together for warmth, as did our horses. We happened upon a group of bandits as well, but the three of us were more than able to fight them off."

"It does sound like you had a rough journey back. I hope you feel well enough to fight today."

I didn't want to think about it, but I didn't have a way to avoid answering the question. I took a deep breath, letting myself calm down as much as I could before answering.

"I feel as well as one can. I want this battle to be a swift one with as few casualties as possible, and I will do everything I can to make sure the battle is won."

A slight frown crossed the Grandmaster's face at my comment, but before she could say anything, Magistrate Magdra sauntered in, his armor clanking as he walked through the door.

"Ah, Emolin, I'm so glad to see you're okay. I heard about what happened to your group and couldn't help but worry about you and pray to the gods for your safety. When Natalia arrived back and said you were still alive, I came here today on faith alone that the gods would help see your journey through so we can once and for all be rid of the Paras."

Relief filled me when I heard Natalia was still alive. I had no way to confirm or deny what the Lightning Mage said, and the idea of having to wait until I could get back to Altava to know the truth had been a difficult thing to accept. I gave the Magistrate a genuine smile before turning my attention back to the fire.

There was more than enough room at the table for the Magistrate to sit with us. He, instead, pulled a chair out from another table, plopped his feet on the polished wood, stretching out as he snapped for the barmaid to come over. The Magistrate had his back to the young woman so he didn't seen her throw her towel and roll her eyes as she leaned over the counter.

"Yes? May I help you?" she asked, giving him a fake smile.

"Yes, bring me a pint of ale and a slab of meat pie."

"I'm sorry, sir, but we don't serve customers at their table when there's only one person to watch the counter. I would be more than happy to serve you if you come up to the bar. Or, you can watch the bar and I will gladly bring your food to your table."

"Hah!" the Grandmaster laughed as the Magistrate muttered under his breath and stalked over to the bar.

I felt bad for the barmaid, Magistrate Magdra standing there and berating the girl as she got him the food and drink he demanded. She didn't seem to care, however, and even gave me a smile when the Magistrate wasn't looking.

Once he finally had his food, the Magistrate sat back down and the three of us made a bit of small talk.

"Emolin, when we get back to Altava, you will have a day to find a dress for the wedding."

"There will be no wedding" the Grandmaster cut in. "After this battle, she's going to come back to Blackwood with me and learn the true reason the gods granted us Wells."

"I apologize for my future wife leading you on, but her father promised her to me."

"I'm sure I can easily persuade a man foolish enough to marry his daughter off to a man who could be her grandfather—"

"We will discuss this later," the Magistrate said, slapping his hands on his thighs and cutting the Grandmaster off. "I came here to kill some Parans, not sit here and gossip like a bunch of hens."

The Grandmaster's cane glowed and crackled with Aura, but before she could do anything, one of the Alchemists rushed in, saluting and reporting that Advisor Falcon and her forces were seen coming out of the mountains.

"It looks like you're getting your wish," the Grandmaster said as she stood and stretched.

The nerves came back and I swallowed before taking a deep breath and standing to follow the two. All I had to do was keep them preoccupied until Geoffraie and his soldiers were able to subdue them. We mounted our horses and rode off.

I gripped the saddle horn and Sampson kept pace with the Magistrate and Grandmaster's horses. *I don't want to do this. I'm tired of all this killing. I need to make them believe I'm eager to battle, though. Fool them long enough and hopefully not have to use the pendant.* I placed my hand on my chest where the gem was hidden under my robes. It still provided comfort in a way, giving me something to fidget with, but I would throw it in the ocean at my first chance if there wasn't the risk of it killing me.

When we approached the clearing, the first few Parans were entering, being led by Advisor Falcon. Her armor was dull compared to the Magistrate's, but she carried herself in a way that made her look like a far better soldier. I had to look away to keep from beaming as I kept up the act. It was showtime, and this was to be my greatest performance.

The ground trembled with every step of the army behind us. There were easily twenty thousand soldiers, and the now-empty battlefield would have bodies littering the ground by the end of the day.

Advisor Falcon raised her hand to halt the advance of her army and continued forward on her own. The Grandmaster, Magistrate, and I followed suit, the three of us riding to meet her. The apprehension in the air was thick, but I didn't know how much was real and how much was masked arrogance from the army behind me.

As soon as we were within range of hearing each other, Advisor Falcon spoke first. "You are proposing a treaty between us? Then why have you brought such a large army with you?"

"I have brought my soldiers to help make sure they keep the

peace; we don't want any of the civilians in the cities trying to get involved," Magistrate Magdra started. "I don't see your wagons wielding your wealth and weapons. If you are so desperate to get your people back, why is the wagon not with you?"

"One can never be too careful around their enemy. You never know when they may try to deceive you," Advisor Falcon commented.

"You are quite right." The Magistrate reached for his sword. "Too bad you weren't careful enough."

The Magistrate roared and charged forward, not giving me or the Grandmaster a chance to respond. I glanced over at the Grandmaster, not the least bit surprised to see her glaring at Magistrate Magdra. The army behind us charged, and I was swept up in the chaos.

"You head after their leader, we'll take care of the rest," the Grandmaster said as she raced off.

I turned Sampson and pretended to head off after Advisor Falcon, dodging half-hearted swings from the Parans while staying out of the way of the soldiers racing forward. I kept my sights on the Grandmaster and the Magistrate, trying to keep pace with them.

Cries of pain and the clang of metal against metal filled the air. I focused my sights forward as Sampson cantered through the massacre, not wanting to see the countless deaths surrounding me. While I wanted to get as far as I could to the other side of the battlefield before the second wave of Parans rushed in, the Grandmaster and Magistrate were well into the fight, slashing at anyone they could, even taking down some of their soldiers.

I was on the other half of the field when trumpets blared. I turned to look over my shoulder and saw the flags of the other army squads marching toward us. The Grandmaster was still ahead of me and turned to ride at the new threat when she saw what happened. I pulled Samson to a stop and turned to follow her, not daring to let her out of my sights.

It was planned that Geoffraie and his team would only enter the battle once the Grandmaster and Magistrate were fully distracted by the new troops. It was never specified how long that would take so I still had no clue as to how much longer I had to dodge attacks and be surrounded by the cries of death.

The Grandmaster charged forward and attacked anyone who wasn't wearing a navy uniform, the blood of REDs and Parans alike marking the path of destruction the Grandmaster carved. I kept watch for the Magistrate, wanting to find him before he decided to escape. While I didn't believe he would have reason to worry about being apprehended, the last thing I wanted was for him to escape when he realized he was going to lose.

As the battle progressed, I became more aware of the Aura growing inside the pendant, the stone warming more the longer the battle progressed, but never becoming uncomfortable. I vowed not to use it if I could help it, not wanting to cause yet more damage to my Well before I could learn more. However, the safety of Hajana's people and her friendship was worth far more and I knew I would use the pendent if it was the only way to end the battle.

As more troops raced toward me, I caught sight of Lea and Tara, in the midst of their own battle. While they looked like they were handing things on their own, I didn't want to risk either of them getting hurt and directed an orb of Aura at the feet of the REDs the two were facing. The REDs were momentarily distracted by the sudden heat surrounding their feet, but I didn't stay to figure out what happened.

The Magistrate pulled his horse in front of mine, blocking my path and leaving me stuck in the center of the battlefield. He turned to look at me, fire in his eyes, as he dismounted and pointed his sword at me.

"You!"

I didn't know exactly what he was accusing me of, but I decided it must've had something to do with me attacking the

REDs. I scrambled out of the saddle and smacked Sampson on the rear. I didn't want him near if I had to use the pendant and I told him so on the way from madame's. He whinnied as he ran off, shaking his head in frustration while leaping over bodies.

I turned my attention back to the Magistrate as he stalked me amongst the chaos.

"I should've known you would turn against me," the Magistrate scoffed as he got within earshot. "There was always something about you I couldn't quite understand. Now I know why the gods chose such a weak-willed Mage as their 'hero.' The priests preach that the gods want peace, but they've never stopped to question whether or not the gods are wrong. Why have peace when you can have power?"

The sounds and fury of the battle fueled the anger stirring within me. I unsheathed my sword in one swift motion and charged forward, ducking under the soldiers' attacks and reaching Magistrate Magdra, crossing swords with him.

"You're nothing but a pathetic worm and the gods should've reconsidered their choice when it was made clear your loyalties lie with the heretics. If the gods won't take care of you, I'll do so myself."

He swung at me again, wilder than before. I met every blow and grounded my stance, not wanting to let him gain the upper hand. I knew he had experience in sword fighting. I also knew he felt his age made him the better swordsman and that he could never lose to someone younger than him. All I needed was for him to make a misstep.

Before I could make a move, I got the nagging feeling I needed to duck. Without knowing why, I stepped to the right and swung my sword, connecting with the cane of the Grandmaster. What began as a single battle of distraction was now a two-on-one fight I had a real chance to lose.

I didn't give them the chance to try and attack me again. Instead, I took off into the throng of battle. I needed to get them away from the others. I wasn't sure if I should backtrack and head toward to the mountains or try for the tavern. I didn't get a chance to choose as a blast of Aura hit the ground behind my feet and tossed me into the air.

I landed hard on my shoulder and grunted in pain. I tried to use my arm but found it limp and in excruciating pain whenever I tried to move it. I scrambled for my sword that had fallen from my grasp as I fell and held it awkwardly in my left hand. I turned back to the battle and stood at the ready to face the Grandmaster and the Magistrate. I was told to keep them preoccupied, so that was what I was going to do.

"I have to commend you. I can normally see through the lies and deceit of others, but you had me completely fooled."

The Grandmaster slammed her cane on the ground and I jumped as a shockwave of Aura rushed toward me. The Magistrate followed up with a wave of Fire Aura of his own, the two of them stalking closer and neither caring if their attacks hit their own troops.

"I never lied to you. I told you the truth and nothing else. You were the one who took it to mean you were on the 'right' side of justice."

My words did nothing but feed her fury, and I had to dodge a few more attacks as her anger caused her to lash out, the Magistrate following every attack with one of his own. I knew the Grandmaster wasn't as reckless as the Magistrate and I would need to fight back. I needed to use the pendant, no matter how much I didn't want to.

The pain in my shoulder caused my head to swim, the sounds around me no longer distinct. I set my jaw and took a step forward, not wanting to let them see the fear coursing through me.

"You will be glad to die today. Your family will never have to know the traitor you turned out to be. We'll use you as a martyr to convince others to join the cause," the Magistrate said, the Aura in his hand turning an eerie green.

They rushed toward me, the Grandmaster's cane glowing, her eyes poised on me while the Magistrate grew the orb of Fire Aura in his hand. I reached out to the pendant with my Well and found a calmness I never had before. My vision was darkening from the pain in my shoulder, but I used the anguish to fuel the power within me.

I let the power grow, the pendant drawing in Aura from everywhere it could. The Aura stored in the pendant grew as I chased the Grandmaster and I noticed my mind continually trailing off to it. The Aura in the pendant called to me, begging to be released, consuming every feeling in my body and replaying it with the desire to destroy.

The world around me dimmed, the Aura from every source being drawn into the pendant, the world becoming dark as it had when Fonir appeared. I don't know if it was the rage that clouded their vision or something else, but they didn't seem to notice the sheer volume of power I was holding until they were too close to turn away.

"The gods chose me to be their messenger, to bring peace to a world where there is none. You have chosen the path of hatred and for that, you will pay."

Their expression turned from victory to pure terror as all the Aura from the pendant was directed at them in a great beam of energy.

The light blinded me as it engulfed them, the resulting boom shaking the ground and replacing my hearing with an incessant ringing. Those who were within the radius of the blast stumbled around in a daze, but other than that, they were fine.

As the light in the world returned to normal, a crater appeared and both the Magistrate and the Grandmaster lay in a heap, blood pouring out from where their eyes once were, the Magistrate missing an arm and the Grandmaster's leg bent at an awkward angle.

"Emolin," the Magistrate called out, his voice quivering. "Send for a healer, quickly now. I won't punish you for this if you get one post haste."

"You got what you wanted. Death and destruction. Enjoy your answered prayers."

I turned and walked off. The soldiers around me stared, not sure what to do, muttering to one another but no one acting.

Sampson trotted over and I swung into the saddle, finding my arm no longer in pain. I led Sampson across the battlefield, eyes following my every movement, my head held high and a fog clouding my mind.

Geoffraie rode up, calling out orders and the sounds of battle returning. I couldn't make out anything being said and whenever I tried to concentrate, there was a sharp pain behind my left eye. I made out enough to know the Magistrate and Grandmaster were contained and many of the RED generals along with those in charge of the Grandmaster's army had surrendered. Lea and Tara found me and led me away for the blood soaked battlefield and back to madame's.

CHAPTER TWENTY-EIGHT
HAJANA

After hearing the battle was a success from Geoffraie when he returned, my fears about returning to a life of slavery completely vanished. The Parans lost a good number, but nowhere near what the casualties could've been. Soldiers coming back from the battle welcomed me into their community with open arms. The Parans in the camp and helped me adjust in my first few days of freedom.

The first time I tried on a dress that wasn't my accustomed feed sack dress, I broke down sobbing, finally feeling like a person again instead of an object. The Parans made sure I had enough food to eat and gave me easy tasks to do so I could help and reduce the risk of what they called survivor's guilt.

When one of the priests came to see me, he stared at me for several moments before calling over another priest and speaking to him in hushed tones for several minutes.

"What's wrong? Has Para shunned me for the sins I was forced to do as a slave?" I asked, tears springing to my eyes as the thought of never seeing my parents again overwhelmed me.

"Oh no, child," the priest said, resting his hand on my shoulder. "You've gotten it all wrong. Para hasn't shunned you.

He's blessed you. He has opened your sights and granted you access to your Well."

I stood there for a moment, not sure what to say. I'd heard stories about people gaining Wells later in life. Para giving it to them for doing something great, but it never happened to someone normal, someone who was a slave and was barely free.

"No, that can't be possible. The mark of the slave, my tattoo, prevents one from gaining or accessing their Wells."

"I'm not sure what tattoo you're referring to, but you have no slave mark."

My hand darted up to my neck, feeling around for slightly rough texture on my skin, but finding nothing. *Is it gone?*

"Why me?" I finally asked. "Why would Para choose me? It's not like I saved an entire nation from starvation."

"You are far too humble, my child. From what Para has told us, you discovered a way to give our brothers and sisters in Altava the hope they have been missing for far too long. You created a wondrous plan. The process will be slow, but you have made a tremendous difference."

The priests had far more to say, droning on about those in the past who accessed their Wells at a much older age. However, I didn't pay much attention. Instead, focusing inward and discovering I could access my Well. I didn't know what the next steps were, but I had time for that. I had time to do whatever I chose.

I wandered through the camp with a new view on things. I still couldn't believe Para blessed me in such a way, but I promised myself I wouldn't waste my gift.

Later that afternoon, Geoffraie collected me and said we were heading to Gathon. When I asked him why, he said nothing and the two of us rode mostly in silence.

I slept for most of the first day of travel, still being quite exhausted from all the traveling and emotions over the past several days. Once out of the mountains, I gazed at the surrounding forests, wondering what the trees hid and realizing for the first time I could find out for myself without having to fear getting captured. Tears blurred my vision and Geoffraie piped up.

"Freedom is overwhelming, isn't it?"

I nodded, not trusting myself to speak.

"Remember, you fought for this and won, but there are many others still stuck as slaves or trapped by other means. While you are more than welcome to stay with the Parans and live a calm and relaxing life, I would like to invite you to come back to the Lunen Kingdom with me. I feel there is a lot of good you could do there."

I stared at him, not sure what to say. *Why is he inviting me to travel with him? What would I be able to do? Do I want to spend my first time free by having someone dictate where I should go? Does he...* "I, I would love to," was all I eventually managed to get out.

I wasn't sure what he thought I would be able to do to help, but the idea of giving others the same feeling I was having was one of the best things I could think of.

CHAPTER TWENTY-NINE
EMOLIN

The ride back to madame's was uneventful, or at least I believed it was as I didn't remember anything until I found myself sitting in front of a fireplace, wrapped in a soft blanket. I looked out the window at the last rays of sunlight streaking across the darkening sky. There was no one else in the room and I found a steaming mug of hot cocoa sitting on the table next to me. The runes on the mug shimmered in the light from the flickering flames and I wasn't sure how long the mug had been there.

I took a sip and sighed at the chocolatey goodness coating my tongue and warming me from the inside. Whenever my mind tried to drift back to the battle, I forced myself to think about something, anything else. What happened was in the past. I survived and it was time to move on.

The door opened behind me, causing me to turn and see madame walking in carrying a plate of cookies.

"I'm glad to see you're fully with us again," she said, setting down the plate of cookies and sitting in the chair next to me.

I grabbed one of the cookies and took a bite, discovering how hungry I was and devouring three more before responding.

"How long has it been? Since, you know…"

"A few days. You rode up to the gates with Lea and Tara, the guards trying to get answers from you to no avail. Once the gates were opened, you slid out of the saddle and walked in here without saying a word. You would allow us to get you water, wrap you in blankets, let my healer examine you, and change you into something less restricting, but you weren't mentally here."

I furrowed my brows as I tried to recall anything she mentioned but remembering nothing except riding off the battlefield. The door opened again and I turned to see Lea and Tara rushing toward me, each wearing a few bandages, but otherwise okay. I shrugged the blankets off and they pulled me into a hug, not seeming to fully believe I was okay.

"When I saw the Grandmaster sneaking up on you, I tried to reach her, but everything seemed to be holding me back," Tara explained. "I couldn't even call out and I thought for sure we were going to lose you. I don't know why, but you ducked right as the Grandmaster swung and caught her cane with your blade. From there we lost sight of you until you blasted all the Aura from the surrounding area away from you." They pulled me into another hug and the three of us struggled to hold back tears.

"How are things now?" I asked, pulling away.

"I can answer that," Geoffraie said, joining us. "After you took out both of the leaders in minutes and rode off like nothing happened, the battle started again, but with far less enthusiasm. many stood there staring.. Their leaders were gone in moments, their enemies victorious, and they weren't sure whether to continue attacking or retreat.

"In those moments of shock, my troops were able to capture many of the enemy commanders and sent a large number of troops back to their homes. The Grandmaster and Magistrate are currently traveling to Lunen to meet with the king."

"What doesn't that mean for you? For me?"

Madame cleared her throat and Geoffraie and I turned to look at her. "There will most likely be riots. As soon as the daze wears off, if it hasn't already, the soldiers will realize what you did, who you killed, and they will be after you."

I nodded, expecting as much. "This country may seem large, but there are not many places I could hide without endangering others." I paused. "Are the servants safe? Were those enslaved able to be freed?"

"Why don't you ask me?"

I turned to see Hajana standing in the doorway, wearing a dress, plain but made for her, her hair pulled back in elegant curls. I rushed over to her, embracing her in a hug and not wanting to let go. She quivered in my arms and I had tears streaming down my cheeks.

"I was so worried when I left that something might happen to you," I said as I pulled back, wiping away my tears.

"I will admit, I thought you were betraying me, but Geoffraie explained everything and brought me to the safety of the Paran camp nearly a week ago."

"You've been here almost a week and no one told me?"

I turned to look at Geoffraie and madame, but neither of them said anything.

"Oh, and there's something else," Hajana said, drawing my attention back to her.

My jaw dropped as Hajana held a small orb of Aura in her hand, a rainbow of colors as it hadn't settled on a single source of Aura.

"Ra, you got access to your Well? How? When?"

Ra let the orb of Aura dissipate. "According to the Paran priests, Para granted me access after Geoffraie helped me gain my freedom. Before I left, I came up with a plan to help the slaves at Master Aldous' house gain their freedom too. They're not free yet, but they will be soon."

"I've gotten many reports of riots breaking out in the cities," madame started, interrupting Ra's and my conversation. "The guards and soldiers don't know what to do. Since I govern Gathon, there isn't much to worry about here. However, that won't be the case for long. Unfortunately, you're right about not having anywhere that's safe here in Klohaven."

"I guess I'll get my wish of being able to travel across Klohaven after all."

I found myself laughing, despite feeling nothing but worry and fear. I didn't know what I was going to do, but at least the thing I was dreading most was over.

"I think the best thing to do for now is to get some rest. There is much to discuss, but it would be better to take the time to make a plan instead of trying to stumble your way through."

I nodded and yawned as exhaustion overtook me.

"I guess I'll head up to my room, then." I turned to Hajana. "Is it okay if she comes with me? There's a lot we have to catch up on."

Madame smiled. "Of course. I'll have the maids bring up an extra set of clothes."

I turned back to Lea and Tara, giving them another hug before heading out of the parlor and up the stairs to the room I worried I would never see again with the friend I worried I lost forever.

* * *

It took several days to come up with a plan. Gathon, being a city known for their generous nature and love for all, didn't change much from their normal day-to-day lives. The guards had more to do around the walls, but I was safe enough in Gathon I could stay for a while and decide what my next steps were going to be.

Hajana stayed with me for the first few days. We had plenty of time to discuss everything that happened over the past month and, for the first time since we met, we could talk without having to worry about being caught.

Eventually, Geoffraie announced it was time for him to head back to meet with the king. He gave Hajana the choice of whether to stay in Gathon, go back to the Paran camp, or go with him. Ra set out with Geoffraie; the hope being she and I would meet again in the king's palace. Saying goodbye was the hardest part, not feeling we had enough time together and wondering when we would see each other next.

I decided I would make my way to Altava, to go home and see my parents, even if only for a few minutes, before leaving the country. I needed to confront my father about my mother and, at the very least, tell my mother goodbye. After defeating the Magistrate and the Grandmaster, I knew I wanted nothing more than to help others and right whatever wrongs I could, but I needed to figure out things for myself first.

There were so many things I never had to consider until then. I was certain my father would disown me, and I would need to find work when I arrived at a place safe enough for me to stay awhile.

"I don't know if this is something you would be interested in," madame started when we were eating dinner a few nights later. "I need to head back to the king, let him know what happened, and discuss the next steps. You're already planning on trying to reach the king's palace. Would you like to come with me? You would need to dye your hair and perhaps masquerade as a man, but it would give you a place to go."

I stared at madame, dropping my fork, staining the table linen and my robes.

"Do you really mean that?"

"Yes, I believe there is a lot I could teach you and I know there's a lot you want to do in this world you would need help with."

"How would that work, though? What about my scars? Would the dye ever come out of my hair?"

"The scars on your hands and neck would be the ones we'd

have to worry about the most. It is colder in the north so you'll be able to hide the scars with gloves. The scars on your neck and face can be covered with a bit of power. As for your hair, from what I know about Reshilian hair, it's near impossible to dye for more than a few days at a time. If anything, it will be more difficult to hide your hair than anything else."

"I would love to!" I struggled to sit still and not rush over to hug madame.

"In that case, we should probably leave sooner rather than later. After dinner, go upstairs and pack your things. We'll leave first thing in the morning."

CHAPTER THIRTY
EMOLIN

When I arrived at my parent's estate a week later, I didn't know why my heart was racing as much as it was. I saw my mother in the garden when we arrived, but I was able to sneak by and reach the porch without being seen. I longed to hug Mamma, to let her know I was safe, but I needed to take care of my father first.

I pushed open the door and the servant in the hall, my maid, cried out in surprise, covering her mouth as I locked the door behind me.

"Miss Emolin, you really shouldn't be here. The town is up in arms about what you did and your father is furious. If he were to see you here—"

"Who's at the door?" Father bellowed as he walked down the stairs.

"I am."

"How dare you show your face here after everything you did! I can't believe my flesh and blood would disgrace me so highly. If you—"

"You have it all wrong, Father." I spoke calmly as I walked toward him, grateful to have him find me in the front hall so I didn't have to search the whole house to find him. "You are the one that has disgraced me."

"Preposterous!"

"Then tell me, where did Mamma come from?"

Father's expression didn't change, but a recognition flashed across his eyes.

"I've told you. She and I met and fell in love on one of many trips north to trade goods. Not that any of that matters now that you are no longer a child of mine."

"Then why doesn't Mamma talk about her life before she met you? Why have I never gotten a chance to meet my grandparents or travel with you to see where she grew up?"

"Because she doesn't want to. There have been plenty of chances for her to discuss things with you, but she never did."

"Is it because you forbade her to?" I asked, slipping into Reshilian, the confusion and anger on my father's face a joyous sight."

"When did you learn Reshilian? Why have you never spoken it before?"

"Mamma taught me when I was younger but old enough to know better than speak it around speak it around you. I have seen how fogged Mamma is when you're home, the bruising she tries to cover.

"You tried to marry me off to the Magistrate so you could get in good favor to take a second wife. Or, you helped the Magistrate organize the bandit attacks. Mamma couldn't give you the child you wanted so you tried to get rid of me instead, requiring the priests to allow you to take a second wife.

"I—"

"No, there is nothing you can say to lie your way out of this. I am taking Mamma with me. I recommend you hurry and pack now, the tax collectors in Gathon heard about the money you so conveniently forgot to declare. They didn't leave too long after me so you haven't much time." I spat in his face and made like I was turning to go.

"If you think tha—"

He didn't get to finish his sentence, his words turning into a scream as the dagger I threw landed in the side of his thigh, buried up to the hilt but missing any major veins.

I turned and walked out, heading to the gardens where Mamma sat gardening.

"Hello, Mamma," I said, wrapping her in a hug.

"Kitten, you're here! How? Does your father know?" Mamma wrapped me in a tight hug and held me for a few moments before pulling away to look at me.

"He does know, but that doesn't matter anymore. Mamma, I'm taking you away, you'll be able to go home, back to Reshil if you choose."

"What do you mean, Kitten? How can I go home?"

"There's a carriage coming. It will follow behind mine a fair bit before we are safely out of the country."

"Kitten, I don't know…"

"Please, Mamma, you can't stay here. Not in this house at least. Father is going to get in a lot trouble for not giving the king his money and the house will be taken. Go, grab your things. Your carriage is pulling up soon. I'll see you in a few days."

I kissed her on the cheek before rising and walking back to madame's carriage, turning to see Mamma's maid help her inside as a butler carried out a trunk to the awaiting carriage.

"I'm assuming it went alright?" madame asked, glancing up at me.

I turned away from the window and looked at her. "As well as it could."

She nodded and went back to the book she was reading.

I went back to looking out the window, staring at the only world I had known just a month ago and dreaming of what lay ahead.

ACKNOWLEDGMENTS

Writing this book means I have achieved one of my life goals. Though writing is a solitary endeavor, there are still many people who I need to thank for helping me along the way.

First, I want to thank my parents, Buddy and Becky Muylaert. Not only did they give me life, but they supported me in every possible way. They encouraged me to follow my dreams and didn't let me give up when things got tough.

Next, I want to thank my wonderful husband, Adam. He saw me through a majority of the writing process and dealt with the ups and downs that come with writing a book. There were times when my anxiety or impostor syndrome made me think I wouldn't be able to write this book, but he was always there with the support I needed, whether it was a hug and a glass of wine or a kick in the ass to continue writing. I also can't forget my wonderful kitties, Earl, Mr. Darcy, Misschevious, and BoBo.

I want to thank my sister, Bailey. Even though we are over 1,200 mile away, she has been my biggest cheerleader not only while writing this book, but also throughout our entire lives. I honestly don't know what I would do without her.

A big thank you to my lovely critique partners, Jana Tahtinen and Katelyn VanderMolen. You ladies rock! You saw this book when it was still in pretty rough shape and helped me develop it into the story it is today! Without your encouragement and tough love, I doubt this story would be as awesome as it is today.

I also want to thank my amazing beta readers, Lizzie Adinoff, D.W., and Sherri Turquoise. Not only did they work under a very tough deadline, but they gave me amazing encouragement and opinions on what to do to help my story be both understandable and enjoyable.

To my lovely editor, Nicole DeVincentis. She was amazing! I am so happy that I found her and I can't wait to work with her again. She seriously is a phenomenal editor. And Mandi Lynn who did my cover and chapter headers. Without her expertise my book would have a wonderfully edited story, but no cover to complete it.

Thank you to Kayla hardy for making my wonderful publishing logo and Boston Brimhall for making the beautiful maps at the beginning of the book.

My English professors at Lake Superior State University: Dr. Chad Barbour, Julie Barbour, Jilena Rose, Mary McMyne, and Janice Repka. These wonderful humans helped me hone my writing skills and learn that you should never fear speaking up for what you believe in. Teresa Yelverton and all the other librarians at LSSU as well who all gave me wonderful advice and furthered my love of reading and knowledge.

The amazing writing community on YouTube was another huge supporter. Vivien Reis' videos gave me the ambition to write again back in 2018 when I first started this book and if I hadn't found her videos I don't know where this book would be. Jenna Moreci, Bethany Atazadeh, Brooke Passmore, Kate Cavanaugh, Alexa Donne, Meg LeTore, and many others also inspired me with their words of wisdom and stories of their own publishing endeavors.

For my family and friends who all inspired me or my writing in countless ways: David and Hilary Rain; Grammy and Pappy; Grandma and Grandpa; Aunt Jackie and Uncle Bob; Mimi and Bailey; Aunt Liz; Uncle Ronnie, Aunt Kathy, Bailey Elizabeth, Ryan, and Justin; Aunt Becky, Uncle Nick, Allie, Andrew, and Annie; Aunt Beth, Uncle Jonathan, Evan, Reagan, and Sophia; Uncle Todd, Aunt Holly, Kenzie, and Isalil (Bella); Uncle Ben, Aunt Laura, Berkley and Tait; Uncle Steve and Aunt Kathy; Chris, Clarissa, and Raindrop; Nick; Samantha Rose and Levi Morrison; Dawn and Doug Rose; Mary Sonnabend; Liz VanSipe; Dani Weng; Paige Hall; Ana, Frank, and Astrid; Devonte Manning; Ashley and Michael Pung; Mickey Shope; Melissa Gawura; and Ashley Nicole.

And finally, I want to thank you, my reader, for giving me and my book a chance! While all these people above supported me along the way, you are supporting me now.

Sydney Rain is an emerging author of YA fantasy. She received her B.A. in Creative Writing from Lake Superior State University in 2017. She is an avid reader and is known to stay up until the wee hours of the morning saying "just one more chapter." She currently lives in Florida with her loving husband, Adam, and two adorable cats, Earl Grey and Mr. Darcy.

You can find her at her at
Sydneyrain.com

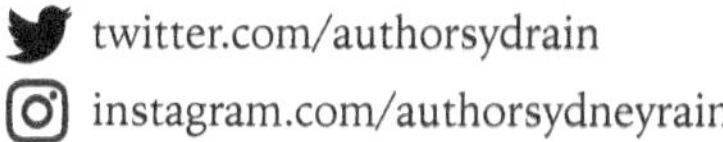

twitter.com/authorsydrain
instagram.com/authorsydneyrain

9 780578 403786